A PASSION IN ROME

A Passion

A NOVEL BY

Books by Morley Callaghan

Novels: STRANGE FUGITIVE IT'S NEVER OVER
BROKEN JOURNEY SUCH IS MY BELOVED
THEY SHALL INHERIT THE EARTH
MORE JOY IN HEAVEN THE LOVED AND THE LOST
THE MANY COLORED COAT A PASSION IN ROME

Short Stories: A NATIVE ARGOSY NOW THAT APRIL'S HERE

in Rome

MORLEY CALLAGHAN

COWARD-McCANN, Inc.   New York

For

MICHAEL and BARRY

CHAPTER 1

JUST before midnight in mid-September Sam Raymond, the photographer, came to Rome to do a picture story for the *Weekly* on the death of the Pope. He came into the airport with the other passengers from the Paris plane, headed for the baggage counter, and there stood hemmed in by a Frenchman and his wife and three Belgian priests. Sam Raymond was a solidly built man of thirty-nine. He wore a light gray jacket and dark gray slacks, and as usual he looked rather rumpled but very clean. His blue eyes kept shifting from the faces of the priests to the faces of the French couple. The two young priests were treating the old priest, who had a flushed face and feverish eyes, with great solicitude, as if they knew he had come to Rome to die. The plump, pretty wife of the healthy, stocky young Frenchman kept lifting her dress away from her chest and sighing; it was still hot in Rome. Every time she toyed with her dress she pouted, then ogled her husband, who smiled faintly, and Sam Raymond could see that they, for their part, had no intention of dying in Rome.

Nowadays Sam felt this alert awareness of everyone who came near him. It made him appear a lonely man on the watch for anything that would give him back his bearings. He couldn't get used to feeling alone. He had photographed presidents and premiers, murderers, big fires and floods, had toured the continent with a queen, won two national newspaper awards for his photographs, and could still say to himself, "I'm the best newspaper photographer there is." But the fact that he could feel this lostness here on the edge of Rome made him wonder what had happened to his life. The trouble was that he had never really thought of himself as a photographer. In the beginning he had taken the job only to give himself some security. For fourteen years he had quietly worked on the side as a painter, and no matter where he had been sent on a news assignment he had always come back eagerly to his studio. His newspaper colleagues, who knew he was the son of the great Raymond, famous for those "Men of Action" portraits that made all politicians and executives look as if they had a date with destiny, had always believed that Sam remained a photographer for so long because he had no ambition. Since Sam had resolutely kept even his oldest colleagues out of his personal life it had been long forgotten that he once called himself a painter—"first, last and always."

Only last month, sitting at a bar with Joe Swanson, a fifty-year-old photographer, Sam had made his big confession diffidently. "Look, Joe, I've done a lot of painting. It took up all my time. Now suddenly I can't seem to bring myself to pick up a brush." Then Sam had tried to laugh deprecatingly. "It's like someone came along and cut out my heart. What do you make of it?"

"What the hell, Sam," Swanson said. "Why shouldn't a man get tired of painting, or golf or a woman? They're all side lines. You're a photographer, Sam."

"Yeah, I guess that's right," Sam said, with his ironic smile, but that night he had gone to his studio and sat for a long time. He had loved the work, and now he knew it was no good. His disappointment left him desolate. But when he felt the tears in his eyes he got up angrily, went out and locked up the studio for good.

But his whole private life had been built around the painting. No matter where he had gone since on the job he had felt desperately lonely. A proud but confused man, he seemed to be waiting around, waiting for something, for anything. Last week, at home, he had been out at an airport, photographing a movie star. Now here he was in another airport in Rome. It didn't make any difference. He still had the feeling he was reaching out, looking around, yet not sure what he was expecting to find or where he would find it. He had so little interest in this Roman assignment that he hadn't taken the trouble to buy an Italian-English dictionary, or even to inquire about the rate of exchange.

From the baggage counter now he received his two bags. He always carried, himself, the small oblong brown leather one that contained his cameras, the Leica and the Miranda, and his lenses and film. While watching the other passengers so he could follow along without asking questions, he suddenly remembered he had no Italian money. Sam went back to the desk and had the clerk give him some lire notes for a twenty-dollar American bill. He didn't bother counting the bills. What was the point? Koster would explain it all to him. Koster, the world traveler, the *Weekly*'s great London man, who had got the tip from the Vatican that the Pope was close to death, had been in Rome for the last two days. Blondell had said, "Our Koster will be waiting for you at this Garden Hotel." And anyway, the other passengers now were moving out to the bus. Following along, Sam gave the bus driver a thousand-lire note. The scrupulous care with which the bus driver counted out the change impressed him. Sitting by the bus window he was soon watching the landscape flowing by in the moonlight.

There were long strips of darkness, then black trees in a pale light, and in the flickering highway lights the faint gleam of a light in a lonely cottage, then the headlights on a brown and pink cottage close to the road. This narrow road would be the Old Appian Way, he thought, quickening a little. Roman legions had come tramping along this highroad. Suddenly he remembered how Rome had been in his own mind some years ago. Drunken old Streeter, that remarkable painter, had once talked about how sure of himself he had felt and his elation on

9]

first looking at Michelangelo's work in the Sistine Chapel. He had strongly advised Sam to make the pilgrimage too. But that had been a long time ago. Or so it seemed now.

The bus headlights, cutting through the shadows, appeared to be reaching toward the old city now, as he had been reaching for the satisfaction of some gnawing need in himself. And Sam wondered if there couldn't still be some one place in the world where a man's life might take on meaning.

CHAPTER 2

WHEN the bus came to a stop at the terminal Sam was the first one out. He was also the first one to reach the clerk at the information counter, but as he stood there running his eyes down the names of hotels on the blackboard behind the counter, no Garden Hotel was listed. Had he been given the wrong name? In that case where was Koster? He simply had to find Koster. As he stood there worrying, other passengers lined up to the right of him, asking their questions of the clerk.

"Excuse me," Sam said to the clerk. "Is there a hotel called the 'Garden'?"

"Please," said the tall grave clerk who looked like a splendid undertaker in his black suit. "You must take your place in the line."

"Oh, come on," Sam said impatiently, "I was the first one in the line."

"Here is the line. You must be polite."

"Look, I'm only asking if there is a hotel called the 'Garden.' Can't you say yes or no?"

Turning elaborately to those in the line, the clerk said, "Excuse me," inviting them to have contempt for the pushing rude North American. Picking up a book he flicked rapidly through the pages. "The Garden Roxy," he said loftily, slamming the book down.

"Thanks," Sam said curtly. Yet he still didn't know whether he had the right name of the hotel. At the baggage counter he once again recovered his bags, and lit a cigarette. Finally he went out and got into an old taxi waiting at the entrance.

"*Dove?*" said the driver over his shoulder.

"*Dove?*" Sam repeated vaguely. What did it mean, this first Italian word he had heard in Rome? "Oh, the Roxy Garden," and he leaned back saying to himself, "*Dove. Dove.*" The taxi turned onto the wide Via Veneto with its brightly lit café terraces and colored canopies over the tables, patches of light flashing by in the darkness; then turning onto a long dimly lit street by a park, they went on and on, and there was always the park and the trees. And they appeared to be leaving Rome; they were out in the country, and it seemed to be all wrong. At last they came to a business thoroughfare; Sam caught the name PARIOLI on a street sign. Then they went down a short slope into a valley with a square which was a bowl of light in the darkness. When the taxi stopped, Sam gave the driver two four-hundred-lire notes, as if he knew their value, and got some coins back without a word being exchanged. Then he was left alone, holding his bags, looking up at the new brightly lit small yellow hotel.

It was now nearly one o'clock. He went in. At the desk was a clerk as dark and smooth and handsome and self-assured as the air-line clerk who had pitied Sam for his lack of politeness. At the far end of the lobby a little old man was scrubbing the floor.

"Good evening," Sam said. "Do you speak English?"

"Of course I do," said the clerk with a faint smile.

"The name is Sam Raymond. I believe you have a room for me."

"You have a reservation?"

"Mr. Koster made it. He's staying here."

After looking at the list of reservations the clerk shook his head. "We have no reservation. When was the reservation made?"

"I just told you. Mr. Koster made it."

"No one made a reservation. It is not here."

"Oh, I begin to understand. No doubt Mr. Koster has a double room and he expects me to stay with him."

"It is possible. What's the name again? Koster?"

"Koster."

"Ah, yes," said the clerk turning back the page of the registration book. "Here it is. Of course. Koster. I remember him. He left here yesterday."

"Checked out?"

"It is true."

"Impossible. Where did he go?"

"It does not say. No, there is nothing."

"But he must have left an address."

"No address is left here. I see nothing. No, I find nothing." And then, as if offended by Sam's incredulous expression, he added coldly, "It is a fact, I assure you."

"All right. I'll take a room."

"Impossible," said the clerk. He explained that it was still the season for tourists. It had been difficult to get a room this last week in Rome without having made a reservation. Everyone was coming back to Rome, with the cooler weather at hand.

"All right. Send me to another hotel."

"At this hour? What hotel? The ones I would know are filled up."

"I see," Sam said uneasily. What was going wrong? What was happening to him here in Rome? No, it wasn't even Rome, or was it? he wondered. First the wrong hotel name. Then no cable about him had come either. And Koster gone, leaving no address. Sam was troubled. He seemed to lose all his customary assurance. He grew confused. Picking up his bags he walked out, as he would have done at home, thinking, Get a taxi. Go somewhere else. There's always somewhere else. But in his confusion he was only really asking himself, "What is going on?"

Around the lighted little square in the valley rose the walls of modern apartment buildings checkered with lights. A street curved steeply up one hill in the darkness, and on the other side of the square was the street leading up the little slope to the business thoroughfare, where he had seen the street sign, PARIOLI. He headed for this street, but when he got beyond the lighted square he paused and looked back uneasily.

Once out of that big patch of light he would leave behind his world of English-speaking hotel clerks. No one would understand a word he said. He would be really alone. But down at that main corner he would get a taxi, he was sure. In his mind now was a picture of the crowded terraces with the colored canopies. Sam began to walk briskly, following the street out of the valley, up the easy slope; a five-minute walk to the corner, where he stood looking across the street at a heavy angular modern church. It didn't fit into his picture of Rome. It was solid and heavy and seemed to belong to the builders of the apartment houses. But nothing he had seen so far bore any resemblance to his picture of Rome. For fifteen minutes he stood on the corner without seeing a taxi. No one came along the street. Sometimes he would turn and look back at the lighted square in the valley, as if it had become the one familiar place in the entire world. From high up in the apartments came the sound of laughter. It seemed to him he wasn't in Rome at all; he was in some new concrete city, a rich city on the slope of a great hill. In the dim light he could see vines hanging from the balcony rails. If he could only see an old Renaissance church or house, he thought. Or some ancient monument or pillar of some old temple; or if he could get down to St. Peter's Square, anything that belonged to the Rome of his imagination! *Chug, chug, chug,* he heard. A motorcycle. No. Coming along the wide street, but on the other side, was a policeman on a scooter. Sam raised his hand. The scooter passed by swiftly. Anyway, it looked absurd to him, a toy scooter and a toy cop, like something coming into a dream, and Sam went back down the hill.

[14

At the deserted square he stood staring intently at the hotel entrance. It was still brightly lit and inviting. It was the place his home office had as his address. It seemed to belong to him and he was reluctant to leave again, but his bags began to feel very heavy.

Down that curving side street on the hill on the other side of the square came a taxi, and he thought it was going to come into the light and he hurried out to get in the way, but the taxi went right by the square; it went on down to the boulevard where he had been, then turned and was gone. Yet that street over there might be the one the taxis used in this rich neighborhood. People would be coming home; the taxis returning down the hill might be empty; and he crossed over hopefully. When he came to this street he looked up at the sign. VIA ARCHIMEDE. Archimedes. A name he knew. An old name out of his own life. Archimedes. Archimedes' Principle. He had learned it at high school, and he sighed with relief as if the name promised him a foothold in the neighborhood.

Gripping the bag more firmly, he began to walk up this dimly lit narrow street that was like a winding gulch between massive concrete cliffs, the hill getting steeper. And no car came along, and he wondered anxiously where he was going. He walked alongside stone walls fronting some of the apartment buildings. With faint music coming from open windows high up in the apartments, he would stop and look up, but the stone fence at the street level seemed to wall him in. Only the stars in the sky looked familiar. Then he became aware of the sound of his footfalls on the quiet street. It was a lonely sound. It got on his nerves. He had to stop and put down his heavy bag. For twenty-four hours he hadn't slept. On the plane over the Atlantic last night he had been dozing till he heard low voices. The man who had been in the seat beside him, Mr. Morrison, on his way to Lebanon, had got up and was having a beer with the steward. Mr. Morrison, seeing him raise his head, had asked him to have a drink with him; and afterward Sam had remained wide awake, thinking of his father

15]

and mother, and watching the red dawn light breaking through the last blue streaks of night over the coast of Scotland, while Mr. Morrison snored.

This long, dark deserted silent street suddenly began to fit into that strange sense of isolation he had been feeling at home. On this street he felt like a ghost. Then the life in him asserted itself and he became acutely aware of a pain in his right foot at the toe. The ache in his arms from the weight of the heavy bag was magnified, and he heard the beating of his own heart. A heavy shadow fell across the street and he looked around quickly. Some lights in an apartment had gone out. Down the street in a big apartment house other lights went out. A cooler night breeze came from the hills, and he mopped his head. I could drop dead here and it wouldn't mean anything to anybody, he thought. Sooner or later word would get around back home that Sam Raymond had dropped dead in Rome. And those pictures left in the locked-up studio? Well, the Latvian cleaning woman would give them to some secondhand dealer who would stick them in his window among the legs of battered chairs and tables, marked: WAS FIFTEEN DOLLARS, NOW TEN. And who would care?

Suddenly he picked up his photographic kit, as if he wanted to be found holding an object that would tell people something about him. He looked uphill, then downhill, knowing it didn't matter which way he went. Suddenly he grew disgusted with himself. He was an old-timer. He had been everywhere. A man with any common sense would get off that quiet street, get down to that main Parioli street corner where, sooner or later, he would meet someone. Grabbing the heavy bags, trudging slowly back down the hill, Sam tried to give himself some company by thinking of people back home. Blondell. Joe Swanson. The impish little stenographer he had slept with last summer. All the familiar faces. Would anyone be wondering where he was at this hour? he asked himself. No. No one was that close to him. All the way down the hill Sam kept wondering how he had come this far in life without one close friend.

At the corner in the brighter light he put down his bags and mopped his sweating forehead. No man was ever lost or without a place to sleep while he had plenty of money in his wallet, he thought. Someone would always turn up to speak the language of the man with money.

Then he thought he saw someone at the apartment entrance down the street. Sam quickened. He couldn't be sure. Moving out to the curb, he looked toward the lighted square in the shadowed valley, and against this background light he saw a figure moving just a little. Someone was standing at an apartment entrance. He sauntered about ten paces in that direction and stopped. A girl, standing in the shadowed entrance, seemed to be waiting for someone.

Shifting the heavier bag from one hand to the other so it would feel lighter, he took a few hesitant steps toward her; but while he was still some paces off she came walking directly out to the road and into the light. She had on a lime-green dress. Crossing to the other side of the street she turned, going toward the corner, and she hadn't looked over at him. She disappeared around the corner. It made him feel that he was in a dream; no one passing, no one even brushing against him. If he called out to anyone passing, "Where am I?" he would be looked at blankly, he was sure. If the girl had even glanced at him from the other side of the street he would not have felt so lost. And then to Sam's astonishment, he saw her coming back. She kept to the other side, retracing her steps, crossing back over to the apartment and her place in the doorway. But he knew now he was so conspicuous standing there on the deserted street she must have seen him.

Where did she come from? he wondered. Did she live in the expensive apartment house? Had she quarreled with someone and stepped out to get some air, or was she meeting a friend there before going in? Or maybe she was a streetwalker, a well-dressed one in an expensive neighborhood? Roman whores, he had read somewhere, were allowed on the streets if they didn't accost anyone. She could have come from the streets below Parioli to this grander neighborhood. Respectable or a whore, it didn't matter. No longer was he alone on the earth. Another human being was aware of his existence, and suddenly he was glad it was a woman.

Sauntering down the street, his eyes straight ahead, he passed the entrance, holding his breath. The girl didn't move or speak. Though she remained half-hidden in the shadow, he could feel her eyes on him. Turning suddenly, as if just noticing her, he said, "Excuse me, miss," and tried to smile. Making a helpless gesture with his head at the whole neighborhood, he held up his bags. "I'm lost. Do you speak English? Hotel? Taxi?"

He couldn't hear what she said. A few words muttered in Italian as she stepped back into the shadow; he thought she must have told him to go away. "All right," he said apologetically. "I flew in. I've crossed the Atlantic. I'm from Canada. Canada . . ."

"You Canadese?"

"That's right."

"Hotel—*palazzo?*"

"If you could only speak a little English . . ."

"What you want?" she asked, the three words coming slow, in a thick Italian accent, as she stepped half out of the shadow.

"I . . . you see . . ." he stammered, unable to take his eyes off her face. It might have been the half-light she was in, or the state of his own imagination, but the irregularity of her features seemed to have a wild beauty. Her mouth was too large, the lower lip drooping softly, her nose almost aquiline, and her eyes, almost too far apart, brown or hazel, shone and glittered as if she had been drinking. Was she drunk? he wondered. He could smell wine or brandy on her. The simple green dress and the shoes looked very expensive to him.

"The hotel down there, see," he went on, "I had a room. Room. You understand?"

"A room. Okay."

"A friend, my friend was there," he said, sounding every word separately. "My friend, newspaperman. A journalist. Understand?" She nodded. "My friend gone. Where? They know not. No address. I am a photographer, see?" and he held up his small bag.

[18

"*Palazzo*. There?" she said, pointing at the square. "No friend?"

"No."

In the street light he could see the green eye shadow, and the pale lipstick smeared at one corner of her mouth, and as her hand came out to his arm sympathetically, he saw too that the pale nail polish had been chipped off. "Where do I go?" he asked, trying desperately to keep her beside him talking the broken English that made her seem so close to him. She just stood back appraising him, and he waited on edge trying to smile, trying to say, "Don't leave me alone." When she shook her head he thought she was turning back to the apartment entrance.

"Go back. You go back," she said, pointing at the square. "Okay?"

"Back? Why?" he said, but he had cunningly started to walk, forcing her to follow a little if she wanted to answer him. "I have been there. They said no. Understand?"

"Now they say yes," and she was keeping in step with him.

"Again? Why?"

"How you say? Wrong words." Her accent was so thick he couldn't be sure he understood her, but he nodded. "Use right words," she said. "Big words."

"My name is Sam Raymond."

"Sam Raymond."

"What's yours? Your name?"

"Carla Caneli."

"I'm here. Photographer," he said, again holding up the little bag. "For the Pope's death. Pope. Die."

"The Pope. To die. Yes."

"I go to Castel Gandolfo. The Pope there."

"Castel Gandolfo." For a few steps she was silent, concentrating, frowning, yet keeping in step with him. "Alba Longa," she said softly. "Alba Longa."

"What? Alba—"

"Castel Gandolfo. Long ago they say 'Alba Longa.' "

"Oh, long ago it used to be called Alba Longa," and he

turned, astonished, but in that light he couldn't see her face. What a strange remark. Why was she giving him the old Roman name of the Pope's summer place?

To keep her with him and talking, he said, "At the hotel—palazzo . . . how do I say, 'How much'?"

"How much. *Quanto.*"

Then he said, "*Dove.* What does it mean? *Dove?*"

"*Dove?*"

"A taxi. *Dove.*"

"Ah. Where to?"

"Ah, it means 'Where to'! Thank you."

They had come to the edge of the lighted deserted square, and she stopped, pointing at the entrance, and began to talk rapidly. He couldn't understand a word and he kept shaking his head. When she paused to get her breath he said, "Slow. Speak slow, please."

Tossing her head like a great lady, and making a contemptuous gesture with her hand, she mimicked the role he was to play with the clerk. "Be boss. Push." She tapped her nose. "Down. Dirty. Servant. You, journalist. Friend. Where? Room . . ." Then suddenly she put out her hand politely. "Sam Raymond, *arrivederci.*"

"No," he said, though he was shaking hands. "Come in with me, please."

"No."

"Wait, please. You wait here, Miss Caneli. Carla Caneli. Please. We eat, drink," and he made gestures. "Please, Miss Caneli, don't leave me."

When she shook her head he knew it meant he might go into the hotel, have no luck, then be utterly isolated again. His desperate need of her seemed to quicken all his perceptions. "Look, Miss Caneli," he said very slowly, "since you find yourself left alone . . ."

"Eh?"

"You find yourself left alone, don't you?"

"You say so?"

"I need some company too. Have something to eat with me?"

And he still kept his hand on her arm. She looked at his hand and then at him, troubled that she wasn't pulling away from him. "Please," he said gently.

"Okay," she agreed hesitantly, as if something about him touched her. "Over there." And she sauntered away.

Hurrying into the hotel he saw the same night clerk at the desk, and he went over to him and slapped both palms down on the desk with complete scorn of the clerk's raised eyebrows. "I'm back. That's right," he said. "Now I want you to find out where Mr. Koster went. If you weren't speaking to him when he left, someone else was. Find out where he went." Taking an air of offended dignity, the clerk tossed his head, then turned his back, fumbling through same papers; he looked at slips, he threw his arms out angrily, muttering to himself. "I was to have a room here," Sam said. "I'm a photographer. I'm here because the Pope is dying, and it is why Mr. Koster is here."

"Mr. Koster is not here and the Pope is not dying," the clerk said sourly.

"What's that?"

"The Pope is much better. You are wrong about everything."

"I'm not wrong about one thing. It's your job to have Mr. Koster's address. I'm staying here till you find it."

"You are not polite," said the clerk, drumming his fingers on the desk. Suddenly he swung around, disappeared into some door off the lobby, and Sam thought he might be getting some big bouncer to throw him out. Pacing up and down, he wondered if the girl was waiting. From his place at the door he couldn't see across the square. Then the clerk came back, smiling and polite. "A boy talked to your Mr. Koster. Mr. Koster got sick. He drank too much. The boy got a doctor for him. But Mr. Koster is all right. But he has gone back to London."

"Oh, London. I see."

"As I say, he is convinced that the Pope is not dying."

"Thank you. Thank you very much," Sam said, and he took a five-dollar American bill from his wallet. "I know it's late, but could you get me a room in a hotel?"

21]

"It is possible," the clerk said, picking up the telephone. He had a serious conversation with someone and not once did he smile. When he hung up he called another number, and then, suddenly smiling, said, "A taxi will be here in a few minutes. The Residence Palace Hotel. Just up the hill. You'll like it, sir."

"Thanks," Sam said. "One moment," and he hurried out.

Just beyond the rim of light was the girl, talking with a well-dressed older man who had her by the arm. They were arguing. It was plain they knew each other, for Sam heard her say, "Alberto." The angry man was scolding her. Then he gripped her arm, trying to lead her away into the shadows, and she jerked her arm free. Half turning, she looked back at the lighted doorway where Sam stood. He took a step toward her, and stopped. Then she gave in and the man led her away.

The guy knows her, Sam thought. And having a place to go to now, he felt more like himself and not so much in need of her. He couldn't see how he could get further involved with an Italian girl and a man who acted as if he had a right to scold her. The girl and the man had been lost in the shadows behind the headlights of a taxi. Then Sam got his bags, and within a few minutes was entering the Palace Residence Hotel. It was a fine new hotel with a wide shining expanse of white and green vynal tile, and the clerk behind the desk might have been the brother of the one Sam had left in the other hotel— the same unsmiling elegance. He asked Sam for his passport, put it on a shelf, had him register, made no comment, showed no interest. A withered, stooped little old man in a gray apron, who had been cleaning shoes—you could smell the shoe polish on him—came and took Sam's bags and led him to a slow-moving lift, then to a room on the fourth floor. *"Grazie, grazie,"* the little man said, bowing low with a sweet gentle smile, as he made a gesture inviting Sam to inspect the room.

It was a rather small room with flowered curtains over French doors leading to a little balcony. There was a double bed with spotless inviting pillows, and in the bathroom a huge towel he could have worn as a dressing gown. As his eye caught the socket for an electric razor, on the wall by the mirror, he smiled wryly. The provincial in Rome. He had assumed his electric razor would be useless here and he hadn't brought it. Back in the bedroom he opened the French doors and stepped out in the dark onto the little balcony. It overlooked a courtyard. Across the way was a great shadowed concrete slab with squares of light at the top. And there was not a sound. Here he was on a hill at the edge of Rome, yet the city was still hidden in the night; even the night sky was hidden.

Before the girl had come along, Sam realized, suddenly troubled, what a frightening awareness of his own life had come over him. He had felt so homeless. That loneliness had made him so full of fear and self-pity, he thought, and yet it was true that he had no one close to him. No woman waited for him, either. And it was true, too, that no one at home could feel involved if he met with disaster. Nothing and no one to look back on. How did I ever get myself in this position? he wondered. How did I do this to my life? The night breeze, stronger and cooler coming past the clifflike walls, touched his face soothingly as he pondered. Things had started to go bad for him about a year ago at the time of his mother's death, he thought. At the funeral those few words with his father! The pigheaded, bitter, resentful, insulted man. Not that the actual words had been important. How could they be? They hadn't spoken to each other for years. The great Raymond's son wasn't supposed to have the right to choose his own life. He was supposed to work with his father and to follow in his footsteps. "By this time I suppose you're a great painter, eh, Sam?" his father had said with his mocking smile, the light shining on his bald head with the thick tufts of hair at the temples. Preparing to answer with a cynical jibe about the phony "Date with Destiny" portraits, Sam had suddenly seen how wrinkled was his father's face and how shriveled his body, and had been shocked and aware that a lot of time had indeed passed and that he, Sam, was getting old too. For the first time he had wondered what he had to show for all the years of painting. Then he had begun to notice that he had been starting and never finishing picture after picture. The studio was full of unfinished pictures in a dozen styles, as if the thing he had been wanting to say for years, in form and color, would always remain half-hidden in his mind and heart. He had asked himself if he was afraid of the emptiness he might see in any finished picture. It drove him to start working feverishly. When he had finished a street-corner scene, some stores slashed with bright ribbons of neon lights, he stood back and meditated, shook his head, then savagely ripped the canvas with a knife.

In the studio he had an old rocking chair by the window, and in the last days when he was finished with the picture job for the day he would come to the studio and sit in the chair, and watch the nurses passing the window on the way to the hospital nearby. Rocking back and forth he would wonder why he was so restless and discontented and unable to paint. He had tried falling back on the opinions of other people. He brought people he met casually to his studio just to watch their faces as they looked around at his pictures, hoping something he saw in a face, or some casual remark, might stir him. Last winter he submitted two canvases to the exhibition at the art gallery. When they were rejected he tried again in the spring. It was nothing new for him to be rejected, yet he had wanted to feel again all his old fiery derision and contempt, and when he couldn't he only felt more dispirited. Each night after the day's work he would come back grimly to the studio, for he seemed to have no place else to go. It had been the focus of his whole life. Then it got so that he couldn't bear to sit there in the studio and not paint, and he would go out and walk the streets or go to a movie, and wonder why he had no intimate friend he could talk to. Until now—here in Rome—he had never been aware how ruthlessly he had cut himself off from people and how small he had made his life. He had hundreds of acquaintances, people he worked with, people he lunched with, people he met at bars or on the street. Now there seemed to be no one in the world who could possibly know or care about what was going on with him.

Swaying suddenly as he stood there, he had to grip the

[24

balcony rail. He went in then and, hardly bothering to unpack his bags, got into bed. Maybe it was the soothing comfort of the bed, but now he did not feel alone. Carla Caneli. Where was she now? And he thought of her with gratitude. Falling asleep Sam muttered drowsily, "Alba Longa. Alba Longa. That was the name a long time ago."

CHAPTER 3

ROMAN sunlight streaming into the room woke him. It was past noon, nearly one, when Sam got up and filled the big bath and splashed around in it and then put on the great robe which was like a toga, and shaved with the unfamiliar safety razor. He nicked his upper lip and his right jaw and had to wait, dabbing at the little wounds; and he was still holding a facial tissue to his lip when he went outside to look around.

The hotel was at the top of a hill. But here were the night streets; one sloping down to the square in the valley, and to the left the other long street with the name that had made him feel hopeful, Via Archimede. Now drenched in sunlight, it curved down through the massive apartment houses, all the balconies like hanging gardens; and above the roofs was the bluest sky he had ever seen. He walked along to the left, passed a theatre, and came to a tiny café; just two little tables on the sidewalk. It was a milk bar, and he went in. There was a small counter on one side, and on the other a big shelf of cakes and buns. A big fat gray-haired Frenchman stood by the counter greedily eating a jar of Yogurt. "*Capuchino*," Sam said to the boy at the counter. Behind the other counter was an older gray-haired man, the owner. Holding out a handful of coins Sam pointed to a big bun, and the owner, after handing him the bun, assumed an intent and scrupulous air and took about a hundred lire from the outstretched palm. Did it touch their hearts to be trusted? Sam wondered. Were they naturally honest or were they all talented actors? The owner, with a friendly little nod, indicated the outside table in the sunlight, and Sam went out and sat down with his bun and his coffee. Everything seemed to be so clean and bright and blue in the sunlight. On one of the vine-covered balconies across the street was a clothesline with a woman's white and pink underwear, and he looked at it smiling to himself, and thought he would never have seen such a clothesline at home on the balcony of an elegant apartment house. Along the street came a plump young woman in skintight yellow slacks, carrying a basket of groceries and walking with a beautiful easy slow stride, her pelvis swaying. Her hair was almost pink, an expensive pink flower in the sunlight, and she half stopped by the theatre to speak to a young Italian. What a figure the young man cut, Sam thought. There he stood, motionless and content in his freshly laundered shirt and dark-gray suit with the short coat, a grave proud statue for the whole world to admire. In the sunlight everything suddenly appeared to be warm and bright and good to Sam, and so unlike the familiar places in his own city. The sky was so much bluer, and the light and air more pleasantly relaxing. Here in the sunlight a man could believe he had come to the place where his life could take a new turn. Suddenly he smiled to himself. He was supposed to find Koster. When he had been leaving the office, Blondell, grabbing him by the arm, had said, "If you're in difficulty, Sam, don't hesitate to hire an interpreter." Well, he was in difficulty now, he thought cynically. How was he supposed to know where Koster was or where to find him? He would go back to the hotel and ask about an interpreter.

A little way down the Via Archimede in a small apartment on the ground floor lived Signora Winters, a plump woman of forty with a round pretty face, dark auburn hair and a slow cynical smile. Signora Winters was a well-educated woman, the

27]

daughter of a Milan publisher who had left her a small income. As a fashion writer she had known princes and painters and movie men. Having gone to school in London she was able to supplement her income acting as interpreter and translator for those English and American guests at her neighborhood hotels.

After the war she had married Reggie Winters, an English journalist whom she had met in Naples when he was an officer with the British Army. After four years of marriage in London she had grown sad and discontented and had thought she was merely homesick. Since she had her own money, and had it tied up so that Reggie couldn't touch it, she had come back to Rome. Her husband saw her only when he had an excuse to come to Rome. Yet she still believed that she had loved Reggie Winters, and with him had known all that could be known of the love of a man and a woman. There had been some shyness in her, a hidden shyness no one would have suspected in so worldly a woman, and her experience with Reggie had only seemed to deepen her uneasiness. Living alone, she found she drew away from any intimacy with a man, and told herself it was because she was still faithful to her husband. Sometimes she wondered what was the matter with her. She had grown stout, of course, but even as a girl she had been high-waisted for her height. As she grew older and plumper her waistline had vanished altogether, though her legs remained shapely and slender and her face as round and pretty as ever. Bitter months of dieting hadn't altered the structure of her figure. She had had to find the one right style for her silhouette. She had discovered a little unknown dressmaker living in an attic, who had positive genius. Francesca now wore only suits, the loose coats always coming snugly to her hip line; and she wore the suits as if she had found a preferred and favorite style. When her women friends applauded her she was happy because she now liked being with women. She felt like herself again. When her affectionate gestures sometimes caused a woman to draw away from her, she would be angry and tormented because she was sure she, herself, had in her only a fire of affection. They tried to make her feel aggressive, she thought. She blamed their impression of her on the solidity of her figure, and tried to put herself in a different light by declaring often, with a voluptuous sigh, that she wished her dear husband could find an excuse to come to Rome.

That afternoon, lying down in her frilly pale-blue housecoat, taking her nap, she heard the sound of a dish splintering on the kitchen floor. "Maria," she yelled and flew into the kitchen. The little girl she called her maid, a peasant sent to her by a friend who had been visiting in Calabria, was on her knees picking up bits of crockery. Her black eyes rolling wildly, Maria rose slowly, the broken crockery rolled up in her apron; then backed away as Francesca scolded her.

"*Percha indiettreggia coses?*"

"*Ma signora, non la fa.*"

"*Ti dico che si. To lo fai abitualmente.*"

And it was true, the stupid girl had got into the habit of backing away from her; it was even worse if the stupid girl couldn't understand. She was making her appear dominating and like a man with women. Her hand out placatingly, she began gently, "*Maria . . .*" then the telephone rang. It was the desk clerk at the Palace Residence. He had an American at the hotel, he said, a photographer named Sam Raymond who had come to Rome under the impression that the Pope was at death's door, as if we weren't all at death's door. How silly all these newspapermen were, she said cheerfully. The Pope had a year or two left; hiccups never killed anyone. Send the photographer right down, she said, and humming to herself she began to put on her blue suit.

Just the same, what a relief it had been that the Pope hadn't died, she said to herself soberly as she sat at her mirror. If the Pope had died Reggie would have come with the other journalists. What if his hand touched her and stirred her? Would she burst into tears of relief? Yet supposing she learned that she couldn't bear even her husband to come near her again? It might be even more unbearable, and thinking of it made her feel nervous.

When the doorbell rang and Maria had answered, Francesca

came into the hall with her faint amused smile, her hand out. "Ah, Mr. Raymond, Francesca Winters."

"How do you do, signora?" and he smiled a little too as he took her hand. He didn't bow at all, just the easy smile as if he had met her a hundred times before, and the candor in his eyes as he sized her up baffled her. He must be rich to have such self-assurance, she thought. That gray jacket was a little too long, and his shoes—they were those heavy-soled English shoes. No one in Rome would think of wearing them. And yet he would probably smile and not care. So he must be a well-off man.

"Please sit down, Mr. Raymond," she said, leading him into her small living room with a parqueted floor, small rugs and furniture with graceful lines that she had collected piece by piece with her extra earnings from translating.

"A very nice room, signora," he said, looking around.

"Thank you, Mr. Raymond."

"And the chairs, the little tables. . . ."

"Yes?"

"Old and graceful," he began, smiling. "It's a relief after that severe utilitarian Swedish style you see around at home."

"It's out of fashion around here now," and she smiled, pleased.

"Well, we might as well get down to business," he said. "What do you charge?"

"Ten thousand lire a day," she said. "I think that's sixteen dollars."

"All right, I don't want to get up early. There's only a half day now. Let's make it eight dollars a half day."

"As you wish, Mr. Raymond. You're a photographer, I understand. Do you do fashions? Haven't I seen your work in *Vogue* and *Harper's Bazaar*?"

"I'm apt to do anything."

"I sometimes see *Life* Magazine."

"I'm a Canadian," he said. "The *Weekly*. It's a big paper. A circulation of a million."

"They must be very rich. No?"

[30

"Yes, they're rich."

"That's good, eh? Very good for you. It's nice in your work to be associated with rich people. And where would you like me to take you?"

"The Sistine Chapel."

"Ah, of course. The Pope," and then she frowned. "I see you haven't got your camera with you."

"No. Not this time," he said, smiling.

On the way out, to impress him, she pointed at the next apartment building. "The ex-king of Egypt lives in there," she said.

"Good for him," he said. And when he hardly glanced at the apartment house she decided he was one of those hard-boiled indifferent newspapermen she had encountered at the Foreign Press Club.

On the long drive by the gardens, then along the Via Veneto, she tried to make polite conversation, but something seemed to be on his mind. In old Rome the sun was shining on the chrome-yellow buildings; the old discolored walls flashed with gold; and he said suddenly, "In that neighborhood of yours are there many street girls?"

"They're all over. Didn't you see them at the airport?"

"But this one was well-dressed, expensive."

"What one?"

"A girl on the street last night."

"Didn't take you long, did it?"

"Somehow I don't think she was a street girl."

"Yet it was on the street?"

"Well-dressed, and speaking some English."

"Why not? She probably learned it from a sailor."

"No," he said, troubled. He remained lost in his own thoughts, and she wondered if he had gone home with the street girl. Then they came to the Tiber. "Wait a minute," he said. "Tell the driver to slow down." The river glinted in the sunlight, and farther up there were houseboats like colored little islands, and coming toward the bridge two racing shells skimmed along, the crews in white T-shirts. For a long time he watched the river.

" 'Golden Cynthia in Tiber's ground,' " he said softly.

"That's—that's from . . ." she began, trying to remember and looking at him with a sudden respect. Then she said, "It couldn't be 'Tiber.' You must mean Tibur."

"Oh. Maybe I do."

"Tibur is now called Tivoli."

"I didn't know," he said.

Not only was he an educated man, but he might even be a scholar, she thought, and she would have to watch her facts with him. When they were approaching the Vatican she said she assumed he knew all about St. Peter's Square, and he might like to approach the Sistine Chapel through the Vatican Museum, if he was interested in art. He was, he said dryly. In the museum corridors she would stop and point at a tapestry, offering a little helpful information, and then she noticed he was paying no attention to her. Hardly slowing down, he appeared to be absorbed in his own thoughts, a wondering, half-expectant almost hopeful expression on his face. Again she spoke to him. When he rudely ignored her she grew annoyed. A flush on her face, she came to a halt, standing there solidly, hardly concealing her exasperation. He walked on, not noticing she wasn't trailing him. He got as far as the entrance to the chapel, from which came a low hum of voices in many tongues, before he noticed she wasn't beside him, and he looked surprised. Then she caught up to him. "I don't want to break into your thoughts. But have you forgotten I'm with you?" she said with dignity. "You seem to be twenty thousand miles away."

"I'm sorry," he said apologetically, and he took her arm. "I was lost in my own thoughts. You see . . . this chapel . . . I mean, I was thinking of an old painter talking to me about it, and it all came back to me." And she thought he was going to tell her more, but then smiling self-consciously, he turned back toward the chapel: he felt he didn't know her well enough to tell her about anything that had happened to him that long ago.

[32

CHAPTER 4

IT HAD BEEN in the middle of March at the last heavy snowfall before the coming of spring, before he had locked up his studio for good. He had been on his way to Eaton's department store to buy some underwear. The snow fell in fat slow heavy gobs. The road was covered with brown slush. He had come running across the road because he had forgotten to wear his rubbers, and he entered the department store opening his overcoat and shaking off the wet snow. In this department store was a marble gallery with steps leading to the main floor. On these steps, leaning against the corner pillar, calmly smoking a pipe, was a thin old man wearing a shabby coat and a battered hat. His hair was gray, but his bushy eyebrows were sandy-red. Resting with his legs stretched out, he was utterly unembarrassed by the women who had to avoid his feet on the steps. Sam thought he recognized the old man, but he half circled around him to make sure. Yes, it was James Streeter, a painter, now on an old-age pension, whom Sam had often seen in hotel lounges drinking by himself, or talking eloquently to students who might buy him a beer. James Streeter was the only painter in the country for whom Sam had a deep respect. Most of his life Streeter had been neglected. Now when it was too late for him to enjoy fame, the galleries were collecting him, and a dealer in New York was having a showing of the Streeter canvases done over the last fifty years.

"Mr. Streeter," Sam said, sitting down beside him. "My name is Sam Raymond. I'm an old admirer." They made small talk. Then Sam asked Streeter to have a drink with him, took him down the street to a hotel lounge, got him in an eloquent blasphemous mood and then, his voice trembling, he asked the old man to come to his place. A bottle of brandy was there, he said; and in twenty minutes they were at the studio.

Streeter took off his coat and looked around, then put on his glasses. On three walls were fifteen paintings, still lifes, street scenes, portraits of girls done in different styles; as if the painter were desperately seeking a new way of painting which would give him freedom and strength. As old Streeter, who seemed to know why he had been brought there, wandered slowly around the room, Sam's heart thumped so wildly he thought he would have to sit down. Instead, he grabbed his bottle of brandy and filled the glasses with a trembling hand. The old man had gone around the room once, getting a general impression, then starting all over again, he moved around more slowly, studying a picture that caught his eye in more detail. Finally he picked up from the table a drawing of a girl's head. "Hmm. You do copy well," he said.

"Just a girl I know."

"Not bad."

"But the paintings?" What about the paintings? "I've been going on and on."

"It's a remarkable thing, now. Isn't it?" Streeter said, musing. Considering that he was supposed to be such a blunt rude man he was strangely hesitant. Again he glanced at the canvases, as if he appreciated that the most energetic years of Sam's life had gone into the work. His rheumy blue eyes became gentle. "Composition. A sense of form. The mind. The eyes in the fingers. What the hell," he said suddenly, reaching out and patting Sam's knee. "What can anybody say about these things?" and he laughed. "It's in the mind, it's in the eye first, it's in the thinking and the seeing. What then? Does it just burst out in

[34

the touch? Every touch?" At that moment Sam felt lonely. It was this loneliness that made him reach in his heart for Streeter's respect. The old man said jovially, "You and I understand these things, don't we, Sammy?"

Sammy. No one had ever called him Sammy. Yet it seemed to him that Streeter was talking as one painter to another, and then Streeter sat down, one long skinny leg thrown over the other, and smacked his lips over his brandy. Sometimes he muttered to himself, avoiding Sam's eyes. Suddenly he brightened. "I'll tell you something, Sammy. I'll tell you when I knew *I* had to go on or go crazy." Pleased with his own recollections, or perhaps satisfied that he had found a way of telling Sam something, he had an indulgent grin. "I was in Europe in the first World War. Afterward I got down to Italy. Wonderful country, wonderful people; and I spent two days in the Sistine Chapel. Ah, my boy, the magic explosion of all the senses into form. Must have read that somewhere," he said, disgusted. "Painters don't talk that way. Painters are inarticulate. Isn't that what they say? Listen though, I was in a daze in that chapel, I was so excited I didn't want to eat or sleep. I wanted to rush out and try painting the whole wall of heaven. 'Move over, Michelangelo.' Well, Sammy, that's what the great ones do to you when you have it. They make you crazy with ambition to do it yourself. That's how you know. See what I mean, my friend?" And as Sam nodded, the old man went on gleefully, "Good. We agree," and slopped up his drink. The subject couldn't be pursued any further, for as Streeter stood up, swaying, he began to sing ribald songs. Drunk as a lord, he pounded Sam's shoulder and insisted they sing together. "It's this thing we have in common," he insisted, then he passed out and Sam had to carry him out to a taxi.

Of course he had suspected that old Streeter had only been trying to let him down gently. He had been so convinced of it he hadn't bothered to go looking again for the old painter. But now, entering the chapel, a place of glory, he wanted to believe that he wasn't too old, that he hadn't come too late.

"Well, here we are," Francesca said.

The chapel was like a hall separated by a screen, iron grating between graceful pillars standing upon sculptured marble and the inlaid marble floor. Sam looked to the right at the singing gallery, then let his eyes run along the walls, divided into zones by pillars set on the walls. "The tapestries of Raphael used to be hung on those walls," she said.

"Yes, I think I read it somewhere," he said. On the walls now were the frescoes of the scenes from the life of Moses, and the life of Christ. In the upper zones were the portraits of the popes in the painted niches between the windows, and at the far end of the room the altar, and behind it, covering the whole wall, Michelangelo's "Last Judgment."

"So this is it," he said softly.

But he didn't go directly toward "The Last Judgment." His mouth open a little, he looked up at the figures in the barrel vaulting of the ceiling; awed, he stood there remote and musing. And Francesca, growing a little bored, waited for him to assure her the chapel must be one of the wonders of the world.

"If they have to have a Conclave," she said sensibly, "the chairs of the cardinals will be placed around the room, along the walls there."

"Yeah," he said, without lowering his head.

"The chairs have the canopies over them and the cardinals are in their purple vestments. They really do argue, you know. But of course, reporters and photographers aren't allowed in."

"Uhhuh."

"It's all done in here, the great discussion, and then they ballot. And the stove in which they burn the shavings to send up the smoke signals will be right over there."

"Good luck to them."

"Oh, I say," she said, her mouth twisting in annoyance, for he still hadn't even turned to her. It was as if he thought the prophets Jonas and Jeremiah, and the Sibyls had some message for him alone. Then he moved along a little, his eyes now on the "Creation of Adam," and he was as rapt and still as if he half expected the creative force in the finger of God to touch him as it was about to touch the hand of Adam. Finally he moved again, his eyes drawn to the "Sibyl of Delphi" with the blue headdress. Around the beautiful face with the wide-set eyes he began to make motions with the right hand as if he were tracing the design, and he looked so intent, she said helpfully, "It's more like sculpture than painting, isn't it? Of course Michelangelo was absolutely out of step with his time. With him, they say, well, it's mass to mass. I've heard it said that he may have linked the masses quickly with a square and compass." Then her voice trailed away. He had looked at her blankly.

"Well, I thought you might want to know," she said, following him down to the altar where he stood motionless and mute, his eyes wandering from one bold giant figure to another in "The Last Judgment." The fierce muscular athletic figures, writhing in torment in their faded bluish-greenish ivory colors, seemed to be stirring up in him a fierce protest; and he had a little scowl on his face.

"A pope's major-domo made them cover up some of the nudity," she said awkwardly.

"Yeah, there's always one of those guys around," he said, and he tried to smile, grateful to her for breaking his thoughts.

"The censors do seem to come and go. It's a pity if they're ever allowed to spoil things."

"That painter. Well, he couldn't do it like this today, Francesca."

"Like what?"

"It must have come bursting out of his mind. All at the tips of his fingers. The torment and the talent all one. Yet he probably believed with all his heart that Adam and Eve came out of the Garden of Eden six thousand years ago speaking Hebrew."

"Does it matter?"

"Not at all," he said. "That's it, it doesn't matter at all."

Then she began to feel she was in the way, for when she offered a little comment he was as withdrawn as if he had faded quietly away from her. So she wandered away.

37]

One arm folded across his chest, the elbow of the other resting in his hand, he went on staring at the powerful figures. Then a flush came on his face. Why the ache in his heart? he wondered. He had known he had no real talent when he had locked up his studio. Nothing mocking and terrible should be happening to him now. But the awful sting to his pride was there. Then he seemed to know what it was. It came from remembering the way old Streeter had talked to him. The old goat had called him "Sammy." The old bastard had been snickering to himself and mocking him with his talk about Michelangelo. Well, he had asked for it, he thought grimly. Yet he was filled with anguish. When he had known the score himself, why had he let his thoughts of Streeter lead to this chapel? What on earth had he expected? Some new conviction that at least there was still something left in the world to worship? And he was still in on it? And even if he couldn't do it himself, his faith in it would put a new glow on his life? He went to turn away, then couldn't take his eyes off the fresco. He seemed to be caught in the rhythmic movement of all those wild, tormented nude figures, so fearful and full of longing and suffering from their sense of guilt. He was held raptly though he wanted to go. Then as he came out of his trance and wrenched himself away, it struck him that for the best years of his life he had been held like this in the grip of this powerful attraction. Turning slowly, he looked at the walls and the great ceiling, a wondering bitter protest in him, a longing to break its hold on him forever. Supposing he should have been a plumber and not a painter? What did it matter? He had been just as driven in his life as the great man who had done this work. The iron will had been in him, too. What was it? How had it got in him? Where did it come from? It had got into his life. It had had him by the short hair. A ruthless, seductive, insatiable woman using up a man's life. Make something for her. Slave for her. What did it matter if your own life got distorted as these writhing figures in "The Last Judgment" were distorted? All the loneliness and heartbreak of real life didn't count. Nothing counted but the thing you made. And a man suffering, striving, reaching beyond his grasp, loving and worshiping; if he failed to make the thing that was more important than his miserable life, who cared? Let him go to hell. The thing was a ruthless tyrant. "Death to all tyrants," he whispered bitterly. Look what his obsession had done for him, look how it had emptied his life, bit by bit. There he was now cut off from his father, left with no close friends. Not interested in his job. No woman waiting in need of him. What had he to show for all this striving? Nothing but his loneliness and the knowledge that he could never paint again. He had a frantic longing to rush out of the chapel as he would have rushed out of a place where he had been imprisoned and tormented for years. . . .

CHAPTER 5

FRANCESCA came toward him, so solid, yet almost graceful in her slow-moving easy glide. "Mr. Raymond . . ." then hesitated, he looked so pale.

"Sam," he corrected her, forcing a smile.

"Sam. I've been trying to recall who Golden Cynthia was."

"Wasn't she that poet's girl friend? What's his name? Propertius."

"Oh, yes," she said apologetically. "I knew I should have remembered."

On the way out she stopped at the chapel door, thinking Sam would want to look back, or stand there musing in wonder. "Just think," she said with her little smile. "A long-standing place of beauty. Perhaps as good as the race can ever do. But when I think of what one hydrogen bomb dropped around here could also do."

"Wipe us all out, of course. The whole human race a failure. That's a consolation, eh? Come on, Francesca."

"The consolation is, I suppose," she began, taking his arm, "that if we're all wiped out the human race returns to God."

"Don't worry about us all returning to God," he said shortly. "It's not going to be that easy. The great thing is to survive."

[40

"Survive where? How? In the swamp again? What do we do?"

"We get used to it," he said grimly. "We just bloody well make the best of it."

"Oh, I say! Have I offended you?"

"Offended me? Oh, I'm sorry, Francesca," and he tried to laugh. "I must have had something else on my mind. Yes, I have to send a cable. Where's a cable office and where can we get a drink? Come on."

They went out, and in the taxi she said there was a cable office just a step away from the Foreign Press Club, on the Via della Mercedes. When he didn't answer she repeated it, and then he caught himself. "I'm sorry. I was thinking of the chapel. It's so very beautiful." But actually he had been thinking gloomily of going home. Then there flashed into his mind the blue and sunlit brightness around the milk bar where he had sat. He remembered, too, how he was touched with the expectation of some elation there in the sunlight watching the pink-haired woman in the skintight slacks, with the gay underwear on the balcony clothesline fluttering in the breeze.

Turning the corner the lurching taxi threw Francesca against him. They both smiled apologetically as if they had never seen each other before, and it made him feel they hadn't yet approached each other. Rows of tawny old buildings swept by, and they seemed to beckon to him.

"I wonder how the Pope is today?" he asked suddenly.

"Somewhat improved, they said."

"Still, he is a very old man. In his condition he could easily take a turn for the worse, couldn't he?"

"It is true he is very old. But many of the cardinals are old, and they live a long time."

"How do they do it?" he asked sourly.

"They know how to look after themselves." Then she added, half to herself, "I hope he lives to be a hundred."

"Oh."

"No. I mean— Oh, well," she said, "it's nothing."

In the cable office he sat down at one of the tables, pondering a long time, wrote his cable, wrote it again, and the third effort satisfied him. KOSTER NOT AT HOTEL. MOVED. NO ADDRESS. PLEASE CABLE ADDRESS. With luck it might take them two days to find Koster in London, and another day to get an opinion from him. In the meantime, with Francesca he could watch the Roman press for news of the Pope's condition.

The square was bright in the last of the afternoon sunlight as they came out, and a tall seminarian was passing, his soutane swinging around his long striding legs. Coming the other way was a stooped and toothless shabby old woman. Stopping the seminarian, she babbled a little, her hand out, and he fumbled in his pocket and gave her a coin. *"Grazie, grazie,"* mumbled the little old woman, bowing humbly. But when the young seminarian had gone on his way she looked at Sam and grinned and chuckled to herself crazily, and then, her face full of derisive merriment, she hobbled on her way; one of the hardy bright-eyed little old women of Rome who crouch in dark streets beside braziers, selling hot chestnuts, or who limp behind pushcarts, or who simply beg and snicker gleefully like this one. Sam followed her with his eyes.

"The Foreign Press Club is just a step along the street," Francesca said. "You can get a drink there. Come on."

From the lobby of the building they entered a corridor that led into the club, and in this corridor a large unframed canvas of a nude leaned against the wall. The club had a lounge with a high vaulted ceiling, and a wide stair led to a gallery where there were offices for the newsmen and the wire-service boys.

At that hour only four newspaper people were in the lounge. Over in the corner to the right were two of the Roman stringers for American papers, one plump and flushed with nervous eyes, the other a sad-faced gray-haired man. And at the little bar to the left a young bearded wire-service man talked to a thin serious-faced, plainly dressed girl with glasses. Their heads bobbed closer and closer together. The sense of close companionship Sam felt in the two at the bar made him feel restless. "If you don't mind my saying so, Sam," Francesca said, "I

[42

didn't know what to make of you in the chapel. You looked unhappy."

"Really," he said, protecting himself with a laugh. "It was my imagination, I guess, Frankie."

"Frankie! Oh dear."

"Don't you like me calling you Frankie?"

"It makes me feel uncomfortable. No one ever called me Frankie."

"It's a beginning. A little thing," he said, patting her hand in his need to draw someone close to him. "I said I had too much imagination. Well, it's all right to have illusions, and even to live on the illusions we have of other people. Maybe nothing much can be known about ourselves or anyone else. Just the illusion we have. But if we try to make something, a beautiful thing or a painting, it becomes an objective fact. I mean a man's illusions about his own talent may only make him ridiculous to others. Well . . . I was . . ." Then he saw the worry in her face as she tried unobtrusively to detach her hand, not pulling it away, just getting it loose slowly. In that awkward moment it was as if she had said something to him about herself and he hadn't quite heard her; but it cut him off.

"Are you married, Francesca?"

"Yes, I am."

"And you love him very much, is that it?"

"Would I have married him if I hadn't loved him?" And then almost awkwardly, "He's away in England. An English journalist. If the Pope had died he'd be here, of course."

"Ah, yes," he said, remembering that she had told him she hoped the Pope lived to be a hundred, and his eyes showed that he remembered, and she blushed. Waving her hand at the lounge, she said quickly she had been in this place many times. Last winter she had given a big party here, backed by the sales manager of an English distillery, who had, of course, paid all the bills since his product was being featured; and famous actresses who had been in Rome at the time had come, and some of the princes too.

43]

And having given herself time to recover her aplomb, she said, "What about you? Are you married?"

"No, I'm not."

"You've never been married?"

"Never."

"How odd."

"What's odd about it?"

"You strike me as a man who feels pretty sure of himself with women. I would have said you were a man who spent a lot of time with them."

"Not enough time, perhaps," he said smiling.

"Like the street girl who came along last night?" she asked pointedly.

"I tell you again I merely spoke to her."

"What hour did you say it was?"

"After midnight, and she wasn't a street girl."

"On the street at that hour speaking to strange men," she said, teasing him. "You're right, I'm sure she must have been a great princess. Still, I don't know," and she put her elbow on the bar and looked at him thoughtfully. "You have that understanding air, Sam; I'm sure you must find it very helpful with women."

"All it ever did for me," he said smiling, "was to have them understand they should marry someone else."

"Ummm. I see. But you didn't need to marry?"

"It wasn't a case of not needing to," he began, shrugging. Then the smile faded from his face in the sudden unwanted and unexpected recollection of one girl who had loved him. It stabbed at Sam painfully. It was as if Francesca knew that now at last he was vulnerable. Trying to smile again, he said awkwardly, "Oh, there's always some one girl, isn't there? Well, there was one girl, only twenty-one—it was some years ago— an art student. I remember I had a cleaning woman who used to look at her portrait and say, 'Those eyes of hers are like big blue glass alleys.' " Then Sam caught himself and picked up his glass and took a drink. Why did he feel compelled now to talk about Sue Moran? Was it because he had seen in the chapel

[44

that he had let his obsession with painting distort his life? No, the thing was that it seemed to break his heart remembering how happy and secure Sue Moran had been when she was with him.

Now he saw that Francesca, watching him, was filled with curiosity. "My life was taken up with painting," he said apologetically. "I couldn't seem to get enough time for anything else. Well . . . you know what I mean, Francesca—a girl can come along at the wrong time."

She nodded. "Men are always cheating themselves, aren't they?" A flicker of sympathy showed in her eyes. Sam grew embarrassed and turned away to light a cigarette.

"Aren't you getting hungry?" he asked, and added quickly, "I was only paying you for a half day. Please make it a full day, will you, Francesca?"

"As you wish."

"I must be getting used to you, Francesca."

"Well, you're not so bad yourself, Sam."

"Where's a good place to eat?"

"It depends on whether you want a good piece of meat. I do."

"So do I."

"Then we should go to a Florentine restaurant. Are you ready? Shall we go now?"

The Florentine restaurant was neither large nor opulent, but as soon as they entered he was charmed by the warmth and bustle and glow. The walls were slashed with red and blue triangles. "How vulgar," they would say at home, yet how it lightened his spirit. When he sat down the dining room seemed to be crowded with young Italian women in light summer dresses, or thin low-cut sweaters, whose breasts came leaping out at him.

"Such breasts on them, Frankie," he said as they sat down.

"Yes, some of the girls are lovely."

"What I can't understand is how do they manage to eat those fattening pasta dishes and have such figures?"

"They eat a lot of fruit, for one thing."

"The way they dress," he said, watching a girl going out.

45]

"The way they accentuate their behinds. I'm not used to it."

"It's simple. For the Italian girls the rear must be revealed as a feminine assertion, just as much as the front," she said.

Why did she have to sound so much like an Englishwoman? "Of course the elite here, the upper class, prefers the French style." Francesca paused.

A troubled mystified expression on his face, Sam was staring about. "The faces of these girls seem so familiar," he said. But was it any wonder? Weren't they the same Renaissance faces he had looked on that afternoon at the museum? Botticelli faces. Raphael and Perugino had used these same faces. And then suddenly the whole room appeared to Sam as Michelangelo would have painted it. There it was in the candlelight and shadow with the wide bold splashes of blue and red on the walls, and the blooming young girls with the golden skin and the solid yet warm melting flesh, and the sinister smiling whispering middle-aged men; all caught in that terrible tension and wild rhythm he had felt looking at "The Last Judgment" a few hours ago. Here they were, mocking little devils clutching at the thin sweaters of the girls, and small fiends whispering in the ears of the men, urging them on. No, it was a lie, he protested to himself. The old old lie that life was a sorrowful business, that all desire led to sorrow, and the only way to be free of the sorrow was to be free of all desire. Any fool could see that these girls, laughing and eating, were enjoying themselves. The men were having their little moments of delight too. Their mutual sin, if any, was only that they were glad they were alive.

"That girl, the one coming in," Francesca said, staring intently across the room. "Just look at her."

Plump and contented, having eaten her good piece of meat, Francesca leaned back, her eyes fixed on the bosomy young girl as if she were begging her for a glance or a smile that would bring some secret delight. "Isn't she lovely?" she sighed.

"Yes, she's very pretty, and so fair too." And then as if touched by some deep fierce yearning he felt in Francesca, he said gently, "You're really very affectionate, aren't you?"

[46

"Well, really," she said, taken aback, "you make the oddest remarks. Such a thing to say."

"A woman should be full of affection."

"Most of them are," and she was herself again with her familiar cynical smile. "It's a biological necessity, isn't it? Do you want to go?"

She presumed he would like to sit for a while at the Café de Paris. It was the fashion now, and not just for the tourists and the International Set. Even some of the princes went there. "Please lead me around by the nose," he begged, smiling. He let her select the bank notes from his hand for the waiter. She told him what to tip.

In complete charge as they went out, looking for a taxi, she took his arm. "But I'm always taking your arm," she complained as she led him across the road.

"Well, why not?"

"I'm a woman." And then as if justifying herself, "You should be taking my arm, Sam. The thing is you seem sort of helpless. I feel I have to look after you crossing a road, and you just take it for granted—like a service. I'm sure you are a rich man."

He burst out laughing. "Come on. I'll help you into the taxi."

At that hour the Via Veneto was a swirl of life and light and color with the hotel windows glowing in the darkness, and moonlight silvering the splashing fountain, and the café terraces bright as a festive island beach. At the shadowed corner by the Ambasciatori Hotel two little whores quietly took their regular places. Across the street and along a little at Doney's the patrons at the tables had a settled air as if they had been in their chairs for years. But opposite Doney's, on the other side of the street at the bustling Café de Paris, people kept coming and going and blocking the sidewalk. Here the captain of the waiters, who knew Francesca, found her a table, chattered with her in Italian, then listened grinning, as Sam asked her what she would like to drink; the same thing—the vermouth, she said. Hard liquor made her liverish. "Ah, I thought so," said the waiter, bowing. "I am never wrong after I hear the voice, sir. New York, no?"

"No, Canada," Sam said.

"Canada," he said, crestfallen. "The United States? Canada? Well, what is this difference if there is no difference in the voice?"

"It's hard to explain. It would take some time."

"I knew it wasn't an English voice. English men all sound like women."

"Not like the Italian women," Sam said, looking around. "I like the style, the careless elegance."

"Yes, a good style," he agreed profoundly. "And yet the American women, they have more . . . more . . . What is the word? They have better . . ."

"Grooming," Francesca said. "It's true. Very true," and then as she looked around her eyes lit up. "Ah," she cried. A little blond woman, accompanied by a tall young girl with long red hair, had got out of a taxi, and Francesca stood up, her arms out, her face wonderfully alive. The two girls also put out their arms. They all laughed happily. "Come here, Sam," Francesca said politely. "This is Clemente," and she introduced him to the little blond woman who was a fashionable painter. All Rome was talking about her nudes. Having no English, the painter and her handsome friend, a Norwegian model, couldn't understand a word Sam said and they giggled and he giggled and felt like a fool. Finally the little painter sauntered into the café, leaving Francesca with the young model and Sam. Watching Francesca and the girl, he wondered at the nature of the attraction such women had for each other. Their words, the touch of their hands, seemed to be born of a natural intimacy. Maybe it was a quest for an intimacy they could never achieve with a man; something without clumsiness or fear of bungling or shyness or embarrassment, all as close as if they were one. Had Francesca's husband been rough and clumsy with her? he wondered. Was that it?

Then in the light from the entrance just beyond Francesca and the young model, Sam suddenly saw the girl of last evening, Carla Caneli. He was sure it was the same girl, and he half stood up, astonished. This girl had the same wide-set eyes, and

[48

the black hair and the startling yet radiant irregularity of features. Only now she wore a yellow dress. She was with an older man in his late fifties who had on a dark-gray suit, and he looked like the man who had taken her away last night. His black hair was heavily streaked with silver, and he had a lean, gaunt, handsome face and a high-bridged nose. But in spite of his elegant superior disdainful air, he looked tired and sick. Then they were gone from the patch of light, moving into the café.

CHAPTER 6

"FRANCESCA," Sam said excitedly. The young model was leaving anyway, so she turned to him. Grabbing her hand, he drew her down beside him. "That girl," he whispered, pointing at her as Carla Caneli disappeared into the café. "I know her."

"Which one?" she said, standing up.

"In the yellow dress. The one I met last night up your way."

"That girl?" Francesca had picked her out.

"It's a fact. An Italian."

"That girl certainly lives up my way. But she's an American."

"No, an Italian. She speaks English with a heavy accent."

"Sam, that's Anna Connel. I know her. She was born in the United States. Why, she used to be in television. A singer. Don't you remember?"

"I haven't watched television much," Sam muttered, bewildered. Anna Connel? Of all those determined canaries, which one had she been? The name was only vaguely familiar. All those singers were so much alike. No, he couldn't remember her. "You say that girl's really Anna Connel?" he asked.

"It's not her real name, of course."

"There's something wrong, Francesca. This girl spoke to me in broken English and Italian. Why would she do it?"

[50

"Because she's crazy and she's alcoholic," Francesca said calmly. "Alberto's had a terrible time with her. He should put her away and have her looked after."

"Who's Alberto?"

"Alberto Ruberto. A very nice man, too."

"I can't believe it," Sam said. The girl he had met, even if she had been a little drunk, had seemed to belong so authentically to this city. No, she couldn't have been American. Then he remembered the glazed excitement in her eyes. Yet how had she known how he felt, how had she known just what to say to him? "This Anna Connel. What happened to her? Tell me," he said, as if they were talking about any girl. "And who's this Alberto?"

"I think Alberto's a kind of a saint to put up with her," Francesca said. Her casual indifference, as if she were going over an old story everyone knew, made her sound very convincing. Didn't Sam remember how Anna Connel had lost her show in New York? Francesca leaned close, whispering intimately with great relish, for Sam was hanging on every word. For the first time that day Francesca felt that she was earning her money, and Sam would see that she had the gossip of Rome at her fingertips. As Sam must know, she continued, Anna Connel had had some real success singing in night clubs and in, what do you call them? guest appearances, on television. Then she had been given her own show. Possibly it was because of her guitar. A novelty. "Something a little different," as Alberto had said. "But being as hard as—what was that American slang expression?—hard as . . ."

"Hard as nails. Go on."

Being as hard as nails, Anna had got to the top with that little bit of difference. The rest of it? Well, she didn't understand the rest of it very well, Francesca said. After three or four shows the thing was called off. The backers—what do you call them?— the sponsors were dissatisfied. The thing was that Anna, hearing the show was being dropped, had a terrible tantrum and collapsed and wouldn't go on at all. Of course, that was the end of her. Now she had dear Alberto. Surely Sam had seen Alberto's picture, *The Prisoner*?

51]

"No," he said.

"It won a prize at the Venice Festival. Still, he's very bitter about it."

"It made no money?"

"It certainly did make money. In the art houses all over the world it has made a lot of money, only Alberto didn't get it. He sold the picture to some people outright for a hundred thousand. They sold it to a distributor, and have a share in the profits. Alberto, poor man, is cheated."

Sam Raymond nodded. It gave him some pleasure to see that Francesca talked with so much more confidence about her friend Alberto than she did about the girl.

Alberto's cousins, Francesca went on, owned the finest beauty salon in Rome with a very elite clientele, and they had persuaded him to invest his money from the picture with them. Now he sat here in Rome wasting his life, letting this crazy girl torment and ruin him.

"So that was the girl," Sam said softly, and he could still see himself coming out of the Garden Roxy, the girl fading out of the circle of light, this tall man with the heavy shoulders holding her arm firmly.

"How does she ruin him?" he asked.

"Now, Sam—after she picked you up, you say—"

"I said *I* spoke to *her*."

"Oh, Sam! That girl is deep in the gutter."

"Look, Francesca," he said eagerly, "could we go in and speak to them?"

"Sam, I don't think she likes me."

"No? Why not?"

"Oh, I suppose I was too sympathetic or something. I tried to comfort her. Well, as you say, I'm an affectionate woman."

"Come on, Francesca."

"Well, all right," she said reluctantly. "Anyway, if I had seen Alberto I suppose I would have spoken to him. Come on."

They had to push their way through those who were standing at the downstairs bar, but upstairs it was not so crowded. At the bar at the back of the room, the amiable bold-eyed girl with the square shoulders in the gray sweater, who sat there all night rolling dice for drinks, was being called over to the little dicing table by a young Swede who wanted to try his luck with her. Standing at the corner of the bar, Sam and Francesca looked around them. Then they saw the girl and Signor Alberto sitting by themselves at a table near the window, the Signor talking earnestly, the girl looking bored and restless. They were a splendid pair for Alberto had an air of intelligence and dignity.

"I'll tell Alberto you loved his picture," Francesca said calmly. *"The Prisoner,* don't forget. *The Prisoner.* A love story set in a Brazilian village. Simple and primitive and all that. Primitive emotions. Passion. Beautiful photography. Alberto really is good, you know. And I'll tell him you're an important photographer, as you are." With a knowing smile she left him.

As he watched her gliding so evenly through the tables he felt nervous and yet expectant. They were all shaking hands, Francesca chatting away, telling her lies about him. It only took a minute, and then she beckoned to him and he went toward them slowly, his eyes on the girl. She had on the same green eye shadow he remembered, and the same pale lipstick, but now it was not smudged on her warm soft wide mouth. Her stillness as she watched him coming toward her touched all the gratitude he had felt last night, and he waited for some sign of embarrassment in her. Francesca would surely have told her his name and that he was staying at the hotel in her neighborhood. Not a flicker of recognition in her eyes, she put out her hand.

He held on to her hand a little too long, he couldn't help it. "Good evening, Mr. Raymond. You are staying up our way, I hear," she said. Not a trace of an Italian accent. She sounded like any other American girl, and it was a shock to Sam; he felt stupid. Alberto, who had great courtesy, invited Sam to sit down, and with the air of knowing it would satisfy Sam's North American sense of opulence, let him order a round of drinks. Then Sam told Alberto how much he had admired his movie. Sam laid it on eloquently. The camera, Sam said, had caught so beautifully the direct primitive emotions of the lovers. Signor

Alberto, his eyes lighting up, dropped his formal manner and began to talk about Brazil. He had a soft low voice and an excellent command of English, with just a trace of accent.

Then Carla Caneli, if that was her name, touched Sam on the arm, saying softly so she wouldn't interrupt Alberto, "You are alone in Rome."

"How do you know?"

"I can tell, and it's not a good feeling, is it? It takes a long time to get used to a place. Thousands of people around you in a big city and I guess you say little things to them like you say to a waiter, but they all seem to have their eyes on you, don't they? They can pick you out."

"You know how I feel."

"I think so."

Just sitting beside her suddenly seemed to envelop him with her presence. He was acutely aware of the nearness of her body. It was as though she had touched his loins. He waited for some faint movement from her.

Leaning close to him again she said in a soft tone, "Some people get used to a place quickly. Some never find such a place. The real place is the place where you don't feel alone. But you know, don't you?"

"I know," he whispered. When she smiled he felt suddenly that he had comforted her. It moved him. She was lonely, terribly lonely, he thought. She seemed to be crying out to him. She had looked at him and somehow felt compelled to reach out to him. Maybe, he hoped—he couldn't be sure—maybe she remembered that he had reached out to her last night. He felt on edge. What a beautiful face, he thought, watching her furtively out of the corner of his eye. The face was unhappy and a little tormented now, but its strange satisfying irregularity gave such variety and sudden flashes of life to her swiftly changing expressions. All afternoon Michelangelo had been in Sam's mind. And just as before he had imagined the painter dealing with the faces in the Florentine restaurant, he now had him dealing with this girl's face. Right into a corner of "The Last Judgment" she would go, Sam thought, the fingers of demons

[54

clutching at her naked body. It made him feel angry. Supposing Michelangelo had been the one wandering in the streets of Rome last night and had met her in the shadow at the corner of a building as he, himself, had done? What would the talent-driven master have made of her? No time for her? Would the great man have taken one glance at her, shaken his head and hurried on? They say he wasn't much interested in women. But the time would come when the giant would search around in his mind for a haunted face and a voluptuous body to put on a damnation fresco; then he would remember the face of the girl on the street. With his tremendous talent he would make her live as long as painting lived. But live as what? God-damn it, live as what? Naturally he would do what he wanted with her. The great talents always did what they wanted with their material. Use it. Something for form and color. A very, very great talent. Who would give a damn about what a girl named Carla Caneli was really like? Supposing she cried out, "That's not me. I don't feel like that"? Who cares? She would die. The work would live on. The work was different, anyway. Again Sam seemed to be caught up in that wild rhythm he had felt in the chapel. He struggled with some strange longing in him he didn't understand himself. Under her mask of discontent and her dreamy vagueness he thought he saw in Carla loneliness and longing. It was the spark of her spirit, he told himself fervently. No painter could ever get it in a glance unless he had some deep feeling for her. Not even Michelangelo. How could the painter bring it out in her if he wasn't able to be there watching it grow in her life? Only a man in love could achieve this masterpiece.

Sitting there in his trance, aware only of the girl beside him, he did not hear Francesca speak to him. "Sam," she repeated. Embarrassed, he said, "Excuse me, I was thinking of home," and he told himself desperately he would be allowed to stay there only if he held Signor Alberto's interest.

Shamming the greatest animation, he tried to show Alberto that they shared a common temperament. He felt at home in Rome, Sam said, because he had long admired the novels of

Moravia. Yes, indeed, said Alberto, Moravia could often be seen walking through the streets of old Rome. And then, to show his own cosmopolitan tastes, Alberto smiling brightly, mentioned Faulkner. Sam, with his own countering bright smile, gave him Silone. After a pause and sudden bright smile, Alberto countered with Saroyan and Steinbeck, as they nodded approvingly at each other. "Perhaps I should know some dramatist from your own country. Who is the man in Canada?"

"Shakespeare," Sam said gravely.

"Shakespeare? You are joking."

"You do not joke about Shakespeare in my country."

"Oh, I understand," Alberto said, and he laughed warmly and reached out and patted Sam approvingly on the shoulder. Playing the role of a man of international tastes, Sam was still alertly aware of the girl in her stillness beside him; he could feel his heart thumping against his ribs. Then he heard a little scraping sound of her foot on the carpet. Glancing down, he saw that she was rubbing her toe in a little circle, doing it over and over again, as if she didn't know she was doing it. It worried him.

"I had three Dalmatian dogs in Brazil," she said suddenly, with a bright smile. "You know, those dogs with the black and white spots. I used to walk with the three of them on the one leash."

"You must have looked lovely," Sam said.

"Alberto, what happened to the three dogs?" Carla asked, plaintively.

"I sold them, Anna. Don't you remember?" and he patted her hand. "Ah, Mr. Raymond, with those dogs on the leash she had real elegance. You should have seen her."

Turning to Francesca, Alberto said, "We could have an evening for Mr. Raymond. We could have the intellectuals in for an evening. Between the two of us, Francesca, we could arrange it and have a beautiful evening," and they began to talk rapidly to each other, mentioning names; each name evoking an enthusiastic agreement. If they ever had such an evening,

[56

Sam thought, he would be expected to foot the bills for the food and the drink, of that he was certain.

Miss Connel touched him on the elbow, drawing him closer to her. "Alberto doesn't like it here in Rome."

"No?"

"He wants to be back in America."

"Well, it's understandable."

"I left there on a boat," Carla said dreamily. "Alone on the boat, and when the ship docked, what do you think? There was Alberto waiting for me. He had followed me on a plane. Imagine! I was flattered." Alberto, who had heard her, was silent, waiting, his eyes hurt, as if dreading the revelation of details of some fierce and heartbreaking quarrel. Suddenly she laughed, her eyes shifting around restlessly. "Why don't we do something? We just sit here and talk and talk. Why don't we do something?"

"What do you want to do, Anna?"

"Let's go roller-skating."

"There's no place to go roller-skating."

"There's everything in Rome," she said, laughing. "Mr. Raymond would like to go roller-skating. Wouldn't you?"

"If you want to, I'll go."

"See, Alberto. Mr. Raymond wants to go roller-skating."

"No," Alberto said, gripping her wrist firmly. "We're going home now. You understand? Now we go home, Anna." It seemed to steady her.

"Mr. Raymond knows I was only kidding," she said, apologetically. "If we're leaving, I'll powder my nose," Carla added. "Excuse me," and she got up and went downstairs.

Ten minutes passed. Carla did not return. Alberto was now staring morosely at the head of the stairs. Francesca abandoned the pretense of conversation. Suddenly Alberto spoke to her rapidly in Italian. She answered him in Italian; they talked as if Sam Raymond was not with them. Then Francesca patted Alberto's arm sympathetically, and got up and went after Miss Connel. Alone with Sam, Alberto volunteered no information, just waited morosely. When Francesca returned, shaking her head, Alberto slumped in his chair, closed his eyes and sighed. He looked like a beaten, tired-out, old man.

"Maybe she went home," Sam said to Francesca.

"Do you think so, Alberto?" she asked.

"No."

"If you're worried, Alberto, could we look around with you?" Sam asked. "Have you any idea where she might go?"

"It's no good. Just the same, you are very kind."

"It's nothing, Al."

"Al?" and he smiled wanly. "Why did she never call me 'Al'? You know her story, Sam? Was it a big story in your country, too?"

"Well, I know the story," he lied.

"A year, nearly two. Now she's worse."

"Much worse?"

"I'm at . . ." he muttered, trying to find the words and looking helplessly at Francesca.

"Your wit's end," she said.

"I'm a crazy man," he said. "I've done everything, Sam. I come back to Rome, but I don't know what Rome means to her. It was my city, not hers—I tell you. She was not born here, she's an American. Even her mother . . . North Italy, I think."

"America is full of people having these breakdowns," Sam said consolingly. "What do the doctors say?"

"Doctors?" and Alberto put both hands to his head. "Don't talk to me any more about doctors. I'm a sick man myself; I am the very sick one. Well, I know what I have to do."

"What do you have to do, Al?"

"What else is there to do?" Francesca asked.

"It's too hard on me, waiting and wondering what she might do to herself. I can't go on. Tonight. It is the end. Excuse me, I do not feel well. I think I should go home."

It was after midnight, the brighest hour at the café in the warm evening; all the chairs on the terrace now were taken,

[58

the girls in their colored dresses looked very gay. They walked along. They passed the lighted kiosk with the newspapers and the multicolored covers of all paperback books. When they were passing the street corner by the Ambasciatori Hotel, Francesca said idly to Sam, "You're friend is still there smiling at you," and he swung around, startled.

"My friend? Where?" Two little whores, who had been there earlier, had now become bolder since it was later. The one in the fawn-colored dress was short and dumpy and round-faced, and the taller, long-faced girl wore blue. A car coming into the street slowed down and the dumpy little girl started to run after it, waddling along, lurching clumsily, her high heels drumming on the pavement. The tall one in the blue dress swung her head anxiously, waiting and ready to follow her colleague, but she had caught Sam's glance and hesitated. Flashing her smile she took a hopeful step toward him, and in the moment of mutual appraisal, the brightening hard-selling smile came zooming at him. He turned away. Wheeling, maybe cursing, she chased after her friend who had got into the car; she ran hard and heavily, but the car had pulled away from the curb. It didn't slow down for her, and she was left alone on the sidewalk.

"See what you did, Francesca," Sam said, smiling.

"The exercise won't hurt her. Look, Alberto's got a taxi."

Alberto, who had the taxi waiting under the arch at the hotel entrance, was beckoning to them. On the way home they hardly spoke. Alberto and Francesca, being neighbors, got out together, and Alberto did offer to pay, although he yielded graciously when Sam said he was on his way home anyway.

"I'll meet you at the same time tomorrow, Francesca," Sam called. "All the luck in the world to you, Alberto." And waved to him.

When he got to the hotel room Sam stood still for a moment, staring at the pattern on the rug, feeling sure Carla Caneli was wandering around somewhere by herself. He began to walk up and down restlessly. The fact that she had walked out of the café and vanished stirred up in him again all that poignant and bitter regret he had felt talking to Francesca about Sue Moran. Yet he hadn't let Carla go, he told himself. It wasn't his fault, so why should he be left with that same empty feeling he had had remembering a girl he had loved once years ago? He began to dwell on every little word Carla had said to him and every gesture she had made. Then he tried to picture her as he might have seen her two years ago in America. There came into his thoughts that bright, hard, winning, fixed smile of the street girl standing by the Ambasciatori. Why was the whore's smile so strangely familiar? he wondered. Where had he seen it before? Where? Sitting down slowly he took off one shoe, then, while still bending for the other one, he thought of the familiar smile. It would come back to him soon. He took off the other shoe, then said out loud, "Of course, of course." He knew where he had seen that smile—on television faces a thousand times. It had been in his room. It had been in his life; the happy, bright, winning, false, artificial selling smile of the television huckster girls, peddling their wares.

Having placed that one hard false street face, he still groped around in the street world. Then he was sure he could place Anna Connel. No, he couldn't remember her clearly. He seemed to get a swift fugitive glimpse of a girl with a guitar, sitting on a stool as she sang songs, laughing a little and talking to the guitar, her face full of amusement, or delight, or sorrow, as if unaware that people were watching her; her song and her strumming for her own delight. It was not a big talent. The world would never miss it, he thought; and yet, it could give a man a private delight as if coming unexpectedly on something unspoiled. That was the way he remembered it, anyway. Or was he making it up, shaping it as he thought it should be? A girl carelessly and happily herself, so fresh, spontaneous and natural, she was unaware of her distinction.

Getting up slowly, he went to the desk, took a sheet of writing paper from the drawer, got a pencil from his coat pocket and sat down and began to draw. He worked slowly and intently, as if he were trying to remember his glimpse of the girl's face. Thank God he could at least draw well. Old Streeter would admit that much. The face on the sheet gradually took on an expression of secret, mysterious, almost arrogantly untroubled self-possession; a girl proudly at peace with her own nature. Though he couldn't get all this on the paper, yet what he had there made the image he had in his mind come wonderfully alive. For a long time he contemplated his drawing. "What a shame. What a goddamned shame," he said aloud.

Suddenly he began to lace up his shoes. He put on his coat and went out and walked slowly down the hill, watching the signs and the buildings so he couldn't get lost. No one was on the street, and he followed the curve, and there at the foot of the hill was the Garden Roxy Hotel, still aglow with light. He walked up and down in front of the hotel, and then he made his way slowly up the other incline to the corner on Parioli where he had waited the first night. Only now in his quickening anxiety, it seemed to him that even on that first night he had been really waiting for her. He felt such compassion for her he whispered, "It's a shame, a shame." Yet this compassion— and it was compassion—seemed to make him ache again with that compulsive sensual awareness of her he had felt in the café. He felt mixed up. Then the two separate feelings became one deeper feeling, as if once he touched her he could be anything with her and she, anything for him. If only she would come along the street again, he thought, looking both ways. This time he would hold on to her. This time he would take her back to the hotel. She would see how he felt about her and want to come, and he would walk boldly into the hotel with her and up to the room. He waited a long time. Even the cop on the scooter didn't come around. Walking slowly back and forth, he returned sometimes to the hotel in the square. The lights suddenly went out. It was dark on the square. When he made his way back to his own hotel he had to wait at the door till they let him in.

CHAPTER 7

SHE remained in the back of his mind
all next day, and he took Francesca to dinner so they could go
again to the same café afterward. But Carla Caneli and Alberto
did not appear. When he got the cable the following day telling
him to come home, Sam phoned Francesca and told her he felt
they were pushing him around and he would stay in Rome two
days more anyway, and he asked her to have dinner with him.
She couldn't have dinner with him, Francesca explained. She
was seeing friends of her own. Then she informed him that
Alberto had put Miss Connel in the custody of a woman in the
suburbs, a Signora Spagnola, who had worked for his cousin,
and whose job it would be to make sure Anna Connel didn't
have a chance to take a drink.

"My God, no," he said, angrily, and when Francesca hung
up he couldn't stop thinking of the girl sitting beside him at the
café. Not in years had he felt such concern for anyone.

All the compassion he had felt for her seemed to deepen, and
perhaps because she now seemed beyond his reach he felt the
sharp desire for her again. He knew there was nothing he could
do. He was going home. He took a taxi down to the air-line
office to inquire about a seat on the plane, and they told him he
had a good chance for a seat the following night. From then on

Sam wandered around by himself, utterly at loose ends, wishing he had some company, wishing he knew someone in Rome. Finally he took a taxi to the Press Club where he sat alone at the bar. Of the few who came in no one spoke to him. Later, to have something to do, he went back to his hotel where he ate alone in the dining room. Afterward he wandered up and down in the lobby, feeling conspicuous and more at loose ends and restless than ever. In desperation he took a taxi down to the Via Veneto and sat by himself at the Café de Paris. He felt lonely and he kept thinking of Carla Caneli. It was a mixture of compassion and lust that he felt, and Sam knew it.

He had one more day in Rome. From the time he got up in the morning he noticed that when Carla Caneli came into his thoughts she came, not as he had seen her at the café, but as he had pictured her in his drawing, with the simple lovely warmth that must have been in her at one time. It was then that he felt a puzzling sense of incompletion in himself. It was as if she were trying to come into some emptiness within him, and be as he had imagined her, and he wasn't giving her a chance. Once and for all he tried to put her out of his thoughts. To cheer himself up he arranged to have dinner that night with Francesca, so he could pay her the money he owed her. Then he told himself he loved history, he had once thought of teaching it, and here he was in Rome with an afternoon on his hands. He had heard that in the Vatican Museum they had a fine collection of realistic stone heads of the old Romans. What did they really look like? Sam wondered. Late in the afternoon he went to the museum and wandered around aimlessly. When he looked at his watch and saw that it was time to go back to the hotel and get a confirmation of his seat on the plane, he suddenly became very upset. He wanted to take one last look at Rome, and he followed along corridors and came to a balcony overlooking the Papal grounds and the hills of Rome. In the last of the sunlight the sky was as blue as the Mediterranean, but the grass looked burned and tired; not the healthy green he would have seen in his own country at this time. From here Rome wasn't a golden city; he could only see green slopes and a villa or a monument that looked like an old temple set in the soft blueness of hills. That old Papal city whose streets Michelangelo had known couldn't be seen from here. Now it would be golden in the sunlight. As he looked out over the green and gold city he tried to tell himself it was the place where something had ended for him. Here he had really got his big nose rubbed in the mud. Yet this last look at the city was making him feel homeless again. He felt empty-handed, emptyhearted and full of denial. The city on the hills seemed to be telling him he was denying himself again. Standing there he felt as lonely as he had been when he had been lost on that first night in Parioli. He thought of Carla. Just as she had appeared that night on the Parioli street, she now reappeared in his thoughts. What was she doing now? From here could he see the place where they had taken her? Staring far over the hills he grew more troubled. He stayed there, hanging on to her in his thoughts, afraid to turn and go on his way and leave her while he felt so upset and lonely. He could see himself in a room with Carla, looking after her. And in a little while he could see a beautiful thing happening under his eyes. Bit by bit, the tormented girl began to change under his understanding touch with her. Then suddenly he stopped daydreaming. Turning away from the rail he began to pace up and down, and he seemed to be weighing a plan. Time was passing but he didn't notice it. The light over the city faded and the hills were a dark-shadowed blue, and two pale lights winked far over in the shadow to the left. The longer he weighed the plan the more he got involved in it and the more it satisfied some impulsiveness in his nature that had been lying dormant so long.

A heavy shadow now fell across the balcony. It was getting late. Hurrying in and along a corridor he took a wrong turn, then another one. He saw a helmeted Swiss Guard standing like a gaily dressed toy soldier by a door at an intersecting corridor. *"Via. Via,"* he said to the guard who smiled, led him to a stair, and swung his arm, indicating that he should go to the right.

On the stair Sam turned suddenly, looking back at the guard bedecked in the Michelangelo costume. His eyes and the guard's

[64

eyes met, and the apple-cheeked, black-mustached young man was astonished that Sam was scowling at him. It was his uniform. Michelangelo was all over this place, Sam thought. Every little thing he had ever made. "Okay, Angelo," he said to himself grimly. "I came into that chapel of yours expecting a big lift. That finger of God of yours came right down and you stuck it in my eye. Maybe my canvases should all be thrown out. Or some landlady will use them to cover holes in the wall in some cheap rooming house. But maybe it's as big, even a bigger thing to do something with a life—if it moves you—as it is to do something with a hunk of clay or some tubes of paint or some bits of cloth for a uniform. I think I know what Carla should be like." And then he hurried out to the street and walked away rapidly, trusting completely to his newborn sense of direction. It was twilight, the street lights had come on when he finally came to an intersection. People were hurrying home, working girls, poorly dressed but walking with their slow proud stride. It was a wide street with car tracks and trees and old gray buildings whose lights gleamed brighter as it darkened, and across the road was a big bright café. Admitting to himself he was late, if not lost, he began to worry about Francesca not waiting for him at the Press Club. Rushing across the road he spoke to a waiter who shrugged and walked away. Then he saw a policeman a hundred feet away. "Taxi, taxi," he said, catching up to him. "*Ah,*" said the cop, pointing at Michelangelo's Dome against the darkening sky; and all the way back Sam went, his eyes on the dome, and got a taxi. When he rushed into the Press Club an hour late, mopping his head, Francesca was still there in the corner chair, waiting with majestic calm.

"I got lost. I walked the wrong way, Francesca. I'm sorry."

"I wasn't worried, Sam."

"After all, I could have run out on you owing you money."

"It never entered my head. A man like you! Oh, Sam."

"The fact is, Francesca, I'll want you with me another day," he said, consolingly, when he had got her a drink, and then, leaning back as if it were nothing to him at all, he began to express an interest in Alberto. What a nice fellow Alberto was.

65]

What a charming, cultivated, interesting man. With Alberto he had a fine natural sympathy, Sam said. Suddenly he wondered aloud if Alberto might join them for dinner. Come to think of it, was it too late to ask him now? There was no harm in asking him, Francesca said, and she went to the telephone. In five minutes she returned, smiling. Alberto, who would be delighted to join them for a farewell dinner, had suggested the Fontana. How easy she made it seem, Sam thought. Through her, everything in Rome might come easily for him. The plump, pretty woman with lire notes in her eyes was a treasure. If he had wanted to dine with a cardinal or a member of the old black nobility, he was sure she would have been able to arrange it.

"A strange man, Alberto. I find myself wondering about his life," he said.

Yes, an interesting man, Francesca agreed. A passionate man. In the Italian Navy during the war, Alberto had been foolishly brave. Wounded twice, mind you. He was related to some good families. In fact, her uncle, the Bishop, knew Alberto had decided that Italy was ruined and that only in the Americas could a man of talent make a fortune. A great talent for movies, and splendid convictions. That was Alberto. He had been of the opinion that the Italian movie makers with their neorealism were on the wrong track, creating a drab little world for Philistines. For him, there had been the dream of doing a story of timeless simplicity, of faith and poetic passion, and he had found the story he wanted. The poor man, he had taken years on the story, scrimping and scrounging and borrowing. Nothing to sustain him but his own wonderful enthusiasm and extraordinary quiet faith. A man, mind you, with those rich cousins who owned the beauty salon, and who might have helped him. All they would do for him, an artist, a man of sensibility, was offer him a job with them. "Dear Alberto," she said, glancing at her wrist watch, "he was a beautiful man, an interesting man. It upsets me to see him deteriorating physically right under my eyes. He's too generous," she said. "A man shouldn't let any woman drag him down. Well, shall we go?"

[66

When they entered the Fontana, Alberto, in a dark silk suit, was waiting by himself. Lost in thought though he was, he had an air of splendid and distinguished superiority. But he looked tired and much older than the other night. "Ah, Sam," he cried, jumping up and putting out his arms, with his bluff, warm, indulgent air. "It is an honor, indeed. You touch my heart." Beckoning to the headwaiter, who knew him, he led the way to a table, and with grace recommended the right wine. Like a guest who knew a generous host would be insulted if his desire to be opulent wasn't respected, Alberto explained, chuckling, that Sam could order veal from Lombardy, turkey from Perugia, butter from Pavia, wild fowl from Tuscany, rice from Liguria and cheese from Piemonte. In this restaurant, Alberto recommended wild fowl. It seemed to Sam that Alberto was wise to him, had guessed what was in his heart and was resisting him fiercely by trying to make him feel like a small-town hick. Sam trembled, felt helpless. Then he took a light air. The thing that was important to him, Sam said, was not where the food came from, but what part of the country the chef came from. Then he looked around. Why did there seem to be two races of Italians? he wondered nervously; the young and beautiful, and the sober solid middle-aged who had this restaurant to themselves.

After the drinks, Sam felt himself getting out of hand, but he couldn't stop; he was dazzled by his own audacity. He began to play the role of a man of means who was always on the go. In a month or two why couldn't he meet Alberto in New York? he asked. He was putting himself in a lavish light. He was telling lies and he couldn't understand why he was doing it. Why it seemed so necessary to create the impression he was rich. He had always been so truthful. And still, he couldn't bring himself to mention Anna Connel; all his common sense seemed to be holding him back. He tried to tell himself that he still could say good-by and go back to his hotel and start packing. Then he saw Alberto and Francesca exchange a wise, amused glance, as if they knew something was on his mind. Hiding his resentment, he wondered why he seemed to know Carla much

67]

better than he knew these two polite Italians who now were making him feel so clumsy. Or was it still all in his own mind?

"Al, I wanted to talk to you about Miss Connel," he said simply.

"I see," and Alberto glanced again at Francesca.

"I asked Francesca about her."

"Then you know about her," Alberto said coolly. "It is a pity, is it not?"

"I know it's not my business, Al," Sam stammered. The words wouldn't come readily. "As I told you, she was always a great favorite of mine," he lied. "A singer, someone with fame, can mean something in a man's life. With some of these personalities we establish a mysterious sympathy. I meet her here and I hear from you what has happened. It upsets me. Maybe it's because she's over here from my world. Al, I feel I know her so well."

"Excuse me," Alberto said coldly, as if he were talking to a waiter, "I don't care to talk about Anna."

"Why not, Al?"

"It is a thing that is finished. It is nobody's business."

"I should have apologized," Sam said, glancing helplessly at Francesca, reminding her she was working for him. Get to work, he said with his eyes.

"No. It is understandable that Sam should have sympathy and interest, Alberto," Francesca said coolly. "You should not be offended, Alberto." And then she broke into Italian. She and Alberto had a rapid exchange. Feeling helpless, Sam watched Alberto's face. He watched him slump back, silent and morose.

"You see, Al," Sam began, "her friends in America—"

"Friends in America! What friends?" Alberto said bitterly. "She has no friends in America. She has no friends anywhere. She doesn't want any friends in America. She hates America."

"Al, I know you are a kind man—"

"I'm sure you are a kind man, too. We are all kind men."

"Al, I have no right to ask what happened."

"It's simple, what happened," Alberto said morosely. "The night I saw you she went to pieces again when she came home.

Stinking of liquor. Just blank and still, like you drop a curtain. It's anger. No, it's helpless rage. No? She will come out of it . . . perhaps. She always does. What does it matter? It is not the thing."

"The thing? What thing, Al?"

"If it was the only thing, this blankness of alcohol, I would wait, I would suffer as I have done. I would, oh, yes. It is not the thing. It is what she is like when she is herself now. She insults me. She destroys me," and his voice trembled. "She will only be cruel and vicious and dirty again."

"It's a hard bitter view of a woman, Al. She must have hurt you indeed." Trembling himself, Sam lowered his eyes, making a little pattern with his finger on the tablecloth. How Alberto felt meant nothing to him. Like any other sick man, Alberto was concerned with himself, Sam thought, and his own heart took a slow heavy beat. Forcing a little superior smile, he refilled Francesca's glass. "May I, Al?" he said, and as he refilled Alberto's glass too, he smiled, though his head was in a whirl. "I know you are upset, Al," he said, gently. "You are not the kind of a man who would be vicious about a demoralized girl. It would go against all your natural generous instincts. It's been rough for you, I'm sure."

"I am in a bad light with you, I see. No matter." But it was intolerable to Alberto's vanity. Toying with his glass of wine, he said wearily, "Let me guess what will happen, Sam. You will go back to America and spread the whole story, no?" He actually seemed to believe that people in America could be concerned about Anna Connel. It was laughable. "So I am in this bad light. Will you say this too? Will you say I'm in no light at all about this woman? I am in the darkness and I have suffered. Say that, too, please."

"Look, Al, you don't need to tell me a man of your culture and perception would give up easily on a woman he loved."

"Thank you." Sam's words seemed to have touched the self-respect Alberto thought he had long since lost. Though he smiled, tears came to his eyes, and the moment was so painful for both of them—Francesca, the woman, did not seem to be there—that Sam longed to change the subject and yet couldn't; something seemed to be driving him on.

"If I could understand Anna, I could, well, I could go on and on. I have great natural patience," Alberto said. "What was it in her? I don't know. Maybe it was always the look of her. I have thought of this. I have thought maybe I never knew anything about her, understand?"

"You were on the hook."

"From the beginning. Yes."

"Where did you meet her, Al?"

"In New York," he said. "Why shouldn't I tell you? If you are going to talk about me when you go home, and you surely will, you should know about me, too." At first his words came easily, and then as he grew more troubled and mixed up his accent would thicken, and he would make grammatical slips. He had first seen her one night in The Village, in one of those coffee places, he said. Young men in sweaters and beards, sloppy and dirty, sipping coffee, and pale girls who looked sexless. At that time Anna had made some records and a few appearances on television. He, himself, had been spending a few months in New York trying to interest distributors in the picture he was going to make in Brazil. The sight of Anna's face! A face all wrong. Surprising and dark and unexpected. Where could it have come from? Europe? Yes. You see such faces in the old cities, sometimes in the slums; the patrician and peasant bloodlines crossed. Something done in a quick passion in a dark alley a thousand years ago. For him, the too regular was never beautiful. Well, her face, it enchanted him. Her talent? Okay. Like a street singer. They have them in Paris, Rome . . . and the guitar, a certain amount of naturalness too. Well, she had taken a fancy to him, an older man who knew how to please a woman. A man like himself with his own dreams.

There had been things about her even then that had puzzled him. On one hand a hard businesswoman, reading all the fine print in her contracts, watching the small change and grumbling bitterly about that actor—what was his name? That big star,

[70

who took a percentage of her earnings, and got her jobs on television. She tried to be a penny pincher. But then she would suddenly blow a thousand dollars on clothes, or she would loan it to some friends of her youth. Then the ruthlessness to advance herself. This he understood. A girl who had had such a very hard time as a child. A friend of a friend of some gangster had had her make a record. The jukebox business. Of this, one was ignorant. They were all pushing her, and finally the drive got into her blood. Crazy with ambition, crazy for money. But then he, Alberto, was with her. It was not necessary to have her own place on Park Avenue, and feed the sleazy old friends. What he, Alberto, said did not matter. That shrewd old actor who had such influence was pushing her, okay. They built a show around her. Few women can successfully handle a show. She was not like the big one who oozes breathless happiness and business sense. The madame of the show. The thing did not go well. Just two shows, Anna did. When she heard the show was being dropped . . . Well then, everybody knows about the tantrum, the vulgar vicious hysterical scene. She walked out on them and got drunk. Then the rest-home for three weeks.

"But why do I tell you this when you must know it already?" Alberto asked with dignity. "I tell it to you to explain that I did not mind her debacle. Why not? I wanted her for myself. I took her to Brazil with me. It is what happened there that I don't understand. The illusions, the dreams."

"Tell him about the language, Alberto," Francesca said.

"Yes, what about the language, Alberto?" Sam asked quietly.

"Maybe it was nothing. Maybe it was affection for me. I do not know. She wanted to talk all the time in Italian. Why should this be so?"

"Good Italian?"

"She had Italian from her mother. As a child in Jersey, perhaps she spoke Italian." Then he seemed to grow bewildered. In that silence Sam, waiting, felt that he was getting his own illumination of her talk with him the first night he met her, and it so stirred his imagination he was afraid to speak. The thing was, Alberto went on, Anna appeared to be content with him in

71]

Brazil while he was making the picture. As far as he knew, she hadn't another lover; all her time was taken up reading. In a way it was natural. She had always wanted to know about Italy, she had told him, and he got the books for her to read. At first it gave him pleasure to have her take an intense and determined interest in the country of her ancestors. Then one day she told him calmly she was going to Rome. Her own plan. And him? What was he to do? They had a vicious quarrel. She sailed for Italy, leaving him in such an anguished state he couldn't think or rest, and so he had followed her on the plane, arriving before she did; and like a fool, deceiving himself into thinking she appreciated his sacrifice. He could see now, looking back on it, that she had been cruel and contemptuous to him from the time he joined her in Rome. "Go back. Why don't you go back?" she would say, cruelly. She began to drink, and wandered off at night by herself. In the whole world was there anything more humiliating or more painful for a man than knowing that a woman he loved and was waiting long late hours for, was out wandering the streets, or in some alley? Then, to have her come in with the smell of wine on her and God knows what other awful smells, and to look at her and weep and plead, and want to beat her, the stupid Roman woman! That's what she called herself. A Roman woman. What did she think she was?

"Now I am a whole hospital myself," Alberto said with a grim smile. "All the pains are in me. I got, how do you say it? run down. In the rainy season it is pneumonia. In the hospital I developed pleurisy, and then I have this thing, this nervous thing you call . . ." He made a motion with his hand around his body.

"Shingles," Francesca said, and he nodded. "It is very painful. There is nothing like it. It crushes one. And I had been big, strong, healthy all my life. Look at me. Anna saw these things happening to me. 'You see, Alberto, the trouble is you don't want to be here,' she would say and laugh. 'I did not ask you to come here with me.' A bitch," he finished fiercely.

"You have been a man of passion, Alberto," Francesca said soothingly. "It is a great thing, too, these days."

[72

"I could not help myself."

"That is the thing about you, dear Alberto."

"Tell me one thing, Alberto," Sam said, trying to control his voice, "doesn't she sing at all now?"

"Not at all," he said shortly, and he brooded. "Oh, Christ," he blurted out, his voice trembling with emotion and hatred, "it was her fault I sold my picture outright. I sold it. I needed the money for her. I needed to be able to say to her, 'We can live now in comfort, I can give you things.' If it weren't for her, I could have been a rich man now. I threw it all away to follow her here."

"Al," Sam said, hesitantly, "do you mind if I see her?"

"It's all the same to me," Alberto said coldly. "Talk to Francesca."

CHAPTER 8

It RAINED the next afternoon, rained
for the first time since Sam had come to Rome. It was still raining when he drove with Francesca to the suburb where Signora
Spagnola lived. In the taxi, off by himself in his thoughts, he
knew Francesca was annoyed that he wasn't more communica-
tive, but as yet he hadn't made a definite plan. He watched the
road and the old buildings and the houses, all thinning out in
the rain.

Then they were in the new Rome of apartment houses; the
city of corner bars and juke boxes and boys in jeans. They went
beyond the suburbs to the beginning of the countryside and
passed streets reminding him of developments of new land in
his own country. There were single houses in rows and vacant
lots and new-piled earth, and rain puddles shone on the earth
as the taxi came slowly down the street. "Here it is," Francesca
said. Gathering the collar of her rain coat over her head, she
led the way up the path to the door of the new white house.
As she rapped on the door, Sam felt a touch of panic.

My God, what excuse can I give for being here? he thought.
He took Francesca's arm. "Say I'm an old friend of Miss Connel's," he directed.

"I'll know what to say," she answered, as the door was opened by a black-haired woman of forty-five with a long, straight nose, heavy breasts and stout hips. A strong muscular woman, she had lively dark eyes full of everlasting suspicion.

She hardly opened the door. *"Buon giorno, signora,"* she said, as if recognizing that Francesca was her social superior.

Francesca talked to her in an even, superior tone; and Signora Spagnola, nodding and smiling, would flick her wrist at Sam, then push back a loose strand of her black hair. It seemed to Sam that Francesca had to keep turning her nose up higher and higher. Finally, it worked. Signora Spagnola, becoming obsequious, stood back to let them in. They followed her along the hall.

"What was all that about?" Sam whispered to Francesca.

"She says it is up to her now to say whether Miss Connel can have visitors. She says you should have written to her in advance. I had to take a certain tone to her in Alberto's name. The tone you take is very important with these women."

Signora Spagnola, who had stopped suddenly, her hands on her hips, barring the way, called out, "Anna, Anna," and Sam's stomach muscles seemed to contract; if Miss Connel had come walking along the hall he would have stammered helplessly. What could he say if she looked at him blankly?

"Anna," Signora Spagnola yelled, and then muttering to herself, she made a motion to them to stay where they were, and she hurried farther along the hall. But Francesca followed, so Sam did, too. At the kitchen door the woman blocked the way, but not entirely. They could see Anna Connel kneeling on the kitchen floor beside a pail of suds. She was wearing an old torn loose blue dress, and there was a round wet spot on the floor from her scrubbing. She still held the brush. Her eyes, fixed on some spot on the floor, were blank and startled. And at first Sam thought she couldn't see them, or make out who they were. She was crouched there stiff and motionless, as if she had just heard a sudden frightening sound, and wondered where it came from. She was too scared to move the brush. Her untidy hair fell down over her eyes. On her right cheek there was a heavy red bruise.

"For God's sake, Francesca! What's the idea? What is this?" Sam said. He felt stricken. "This is outrageous."

"Anna," said Signora Spagnola sharply, but the girl's eyes didn't turn; she remained frozen.

"Anna," Francesca said gently, and she went toward her and stooped and put out her hand. But when Anna cringed, as if she couldn't bear Francesca to touch her, Francesca lost all her splendid presence.

"Francesca," Sam pleaded desperately. He had counted on Francesca's imperturbable calm, and without the language he felt helpless; then wild with outrage. Signora Spagnola, who had been watching, her arms folded, her eyes snapping with resentment, took a step toward Anna, wagging her finger. Angry contemptuous words poured out of her, as if she were berating Anna for putting her in a false and ridiculous light.

"Cut it out," Sam said angrily. The woman didn't understand him. Anna hadn't moved. It was as if it was unbearable to her to make even a little noise, or a motion that would be an admission that she was aware of being there in such a disgraceful position.

"Francesca," Sam said sharply. "Ask this woman why she has the poor girl here like this." And Francesca did speak sharply to the woman, and while they were exchanging words, Sam stepped forward and jerked the scrubbing brush from Anna's hand. He tossed it into the pail. The dirty water splashed on her hair.

"Excuse me, Carla. Excuse me," he whispered gently, and as her eyes shifted just a little to him, the blood rose on her neck and he understood her frantic humiliation.

Signora Spagnola, with a contemptuous twist of her mouth and a wave of her hand, said, *"Lavorare un po' non fa mica male. Invece è fabena al fisico. Essa non è scontenta forse, ma non importa. Passerà . . . basta."* And Sam, hearing the word 'basta' with the woman's belittling glance stinging him, thought she was calling him a bastard.

[76

"Some women need a slap on the mouth," he said grimly. "I'd like to give her one."

"She said . . ." Francesca began.

"All right. What did she say?"

"She says a little work, the exercise is good for a girl in Anna's condition. The resentment is nothing. It is all nothing."

"Nothing, hey? It's nothing that this girl is here with this jailer?"

"Non è affar suo," said the woman.

"She says it's none of your business."

"I'm making it my business," he said angrily.

"Alberto put Anna in this woman's hands so she couldn't drink at all, not one drink, and couldn't wander out . . ."

"Look at that bruise on her face! It's from a blow. This brutal woman beats her, I tell you."

Francesca talked evenly to the woman who answered now much more calmly, even smiling and shrugging; and again Sam felt hatred for her.

"Sam, she says they had it out yesterday. By the grace of Jesus and Mary, the Signora is a very strong woman, and now she has made it clear she will take no nonsense from her, even if she is a devil; and that is why Anna isn't speaking. She hasn't spoken since yesterday. It is spite, but it is a good thing she is not speaking. It means there will be no more trouble now."

"Are you going to leave her there on the floor, Francesca?"

"What can I do? She won't move, Sam."

Then he saw that Anna was peering at him through her hair as if afraid to make one little move, and suddenly he was overwhelmed with shame that they were there staring at her and talking about her. Smiling gently, he went toward her. "Hello, Carla," he said, putting out his hand. "Sam Raymond. Remember me?"

Raising her head, she hesitated, then rose slowly. "Sam, yes," she said blushing, her eyes moist as if she were going to burst into tears, and she put out her hand to him. He tried to meet her eyes, still smiling, but she turned her head away. And yet she held on to his hand. She held it tightly. It moved him. He was suddenly happy.

"Would you come with me, Carla?" She half turned. He thought she was too dazed to speak.

But she whispered, "Yes," then darted past the two women and he heard her going upstairs.

"*Ah, ha, ha,*" and Signora Spagnola threw up her hands and laughed. It was all right now. Miss Connel had only been putting on a silly show. Crazy people are cunning. Nothing to worry about. Bit by bit she would behave better. Physical exercise would help her stay sober. It was all right now. She had said 'hello' and 'good-by' to her friend. Signora Spagnola was walking them toward the door. What more did they want?

"Francesca, tell her if she lays a hand on that girl again, I'll come back here and kick her teeth out," Sam said. It gave him satisfaction, hearing Francesca scold the woman who had opened the door.

It should have been the last word. But Signora Spagnola followed them down the path in the rain. Smiling, she made a derisive eloquent gesture with her wrist. "*Arrivederci,*" she called mockingly, following them right to the taxi. When in the taxi Sam looked back and saw her in the rain, making the gesture once again.

"My God. That poor humiliated girl," Sam said bitterly.

"Why did you call her 'Carla'?"

"Just a name."

"It was frightening," Francesca said. "Crouched on the floor in a trance. I could believe she was possessed."

"Possessed?"

"Possessed by drink, anyway."

"Oh, cut it out, Francesca."

"She has been bad, Sam. The alcohol brings out the evil in her."

"Evil! Possessed! You make me sick," he said sharply. "It's lucky it isn't a few hundred years ago. The boys would be around, I suppose, to take her out and burn her."

"As for that," she said tartly, "most of the burning was done by you northern wild men. I know I shouldn't mention good and evil and any mysterious forces in the world. You Protestants have to have a practical explanation for everything."

"I'm not a Protestant."

"What are you?"

"I don't know what I am."

"Naturally you don't. And since you have no theology, you don't know what I am talking about," and she smiled with an unruffled dignity.

"Never mind me," he said irritably. "I tell you that girl is tormented and humiliated and just plain scared. That's all."

"It would be a hopeful sign if she was scared, Sam," she said, trying to mollify him. "It would mean it is not the dreadful depression. When people know fear they are still wonderfully alive. No? I agree she should be taking a cure in a decent institution."

"All I meant," he said, "is that I can see she's at the bottom of the barrel right now. There's nothing for her to do but recover, if someone will have the patience to look after her."

"Who's going to look after her? Not Alberto. You heard Alberto."

"No, not Alberto." After a long pause, he said calmly, "I think I will."

"You will? What a silly thing to say. I thought you were going home."

"I may stay around a while."

"Really?"

"Really."

"Well, my goodness!"

"The thing is," he said, "if I stay around a while I may need your help, Francesca."

"No doubt you will," she said dryly. "I'll be glad to help," and he knew she would, too—at ten thousand lire a day.

"I'm dead sure that girl will come with me and let me look after her if Alberto tells that jailer to let her go," he said doggedly. "Don't ask me how I know, I just know. Francesca, I couldn't take her to the hotel. Anyway, it's in her old neighborhood. If Alberto consents, you'll have to find a place."

"She's physically attractive, I know, Sam. But, well, in view of what she's like now, is your response to her attractiveness in good taste? Really, a man like you!"

"When you talk in English, you start thinking in English, Francesca. You sound like an Englishwoman."

"I know that is not intended as a compliment, Sam." It bothered her, and in return she tried to dig at him. "I only meant that I didn't think you were the kind of a man who'd want a girl who had gone to pieces." When he merely smiled, it annoyed her. Yet she started defending herself. "I've seen these American girls go to pieces over here. They seem to go soft in the head. All the things they have been told must never happen to them seem to have been happening here over and over, and everyone is indifferent. The Roman indifference. Or maybe it is that there seemed to be different things to be ashamed of —as women. Well, they're ridiculous. A little Mediterranean sunlight and they think they've discovered themselves as women. It's all in their silly heads. Why . . ." and then she bit her lip. "Oh, you're not even listening to me, Sam."

"I'm sorry." Only Anna Connel was in his mind; the girl as he had seen her the night he had made the drawing in the room. As the vision got brighter and brighter for him, he grew restless and nervous. It began to astonish him that he had sounded so sure of himself, talking to Francesca about what he would do with the girl. In this frame of mind I have to watch myself, he thought. Much as he might like to throw his hat over the windmill, quit his job, reject the whole life of failure back home, he had to use his head. A free-lance photographer without connections was a nobody. Later on, he could build on his connections with the *Weekly*.

Supposing Alberto said, "Sure, you can take her off my hands." What about money? How was he going to live? What about his job? He could cable the *Weekly* and suggest he stay in Rome until the Pope died, and they would surely see they wouldn't be wasting the cost of his transportation. What if the

Pope lived on another year? Not likely. He was a sick old man. Now just how would his dear managing editor look at it? Fortunately he knew Blondell like a book; he could see him reading the cable.

"Okay, okay, Sam Raymond," he would say to himself grimly. "You may be calling it just right. In a week or so the Pope may indeed die. So we just ignore you. We've told you to come home. If the thing drags on and on and finally you come home, just try and collect any salary from us." Naturally they wouldn't send him any more expense money, Sam thought, but they'd let him keep what he had—just in case. Supposing they said, "Come home or you are fired"? Not likely. They would ignore him and keep a string on him by not asking him to return his expense money. It would mean that he might soon have to start spending his own money, and keep on spending it. But what better thing had he been saving for? In the long run he would be home free.

"Where does Alberto like to lunch?" he asked suddenly.

"Well, Alfredo's in Trastevere, as much as any place. Why?"

"Talk to him. Ask him to have lunch with me, will you, Francesca?"

"I will." And then she added, "Talking about burning, you might make a good martyr. Take care Carla doesn't burn you at the stake."

As they came into the city the rain had stopped; the wet old buildings began to look a little more familiar, and a streak of blue appeared in the sky clearing behind the dome of St. Peter's.

CHAPTER 9

SETTING out at noon for Alfredo's in Trastevere, Sam misjudged the time it would take to get there and arrived twenty minutes early. While he waited he began to dread the encounter with Alberto. It could only be horribly embarrassing, maybe humiliating too. His hands felt clammy. This sign of his nervousness made him angry. He told himself grimly that Alberto, aside from the fact he was paying for the girl's upkeep, had no right to keep her confined, without her consent, in the custody of that Spagnola woman. If Alberto got nasty with him he could threaten to go to the American Consul. He stirred up all his indignation imagining the whole angry scene. Then he told himself that if Alberto did not want to get rid of Carla he would not be meeting him. Wandering away from the entrance to the restaurant, Sam stood by the fountain in the old cobblestoned square, looking at the church of Santa Maria with its low wide-angled roof, its low square bell tower and the faded fresco of the saints, and it seemed to him he had never been so far away from home. Worried, he wandered across the square, his hands locked behind him, and soon was in a cobblestoned street without sidewalks, and with rows of low stone houses, the doors open. Women with antique faces standing at the darkened doorways motionless, an arm

[82

against the doorpost as if they had been standing there for centuries, and now were wondering where he came from. On the street, kids were shouting at play; whole families seemed to live and eat on the street. He stood watching two men playing some kind of a finger game, counting flashing fingers, violence flickering in their eyes; then yelling at each other in a swirl of fierce passion. And he smelled garbage. Short-legged girls dashed by, and ahead of him, stretching across the street was a clothesline laden with washing. What a place for such a meeting with Alberto, he thought. It seemed to him that he and Alberto could have been meeting in a restaurant in the neighborhood a thousand years ago; two men disposing of a pretty woman. And these people were as indifferent now to such a meeting as they would have been then. It made him feel out of place, out of time, and not sure of himself. He hurried back to the restaurant. Alberto, waiting, shook hands with him. In spite of his embarrassment Alberto had a resolute air.

They sat in the shade in the little courtyard, most of which was splashed with Roman sunlight, and they made no attempt to get to the point at once. They hid their embarrassment by drinking too much wine and being too polite. Then Alberto, who had been toying with his green salad, said casually, "The thing is agreeable to me. I will inform Signora Spagnola. That's all. It does not have to be discussed."

"I'm glad to hear it, Alberto."

"You are a good man. You have great charity. You do me a favor."

"It is a satisfaction to me, too," Sam said. It seemed that they had disposed of Carla Caneli as agreeably and quickly as they had disposed of the smooth *pasta* dish laden with creamy *ricotta* cheese, spiked with sharp *Parmesan* and sour *mozzarella*. They smiled as if they were sharing a bluff male comradeship. If only I can get through this lunch without mentioning her again, Sam thought. Alberto ate with great relish, for a sick man. He concentrated on the salad, finishing it off, then he looked up suddenly.

"You are being a fool, you know," he said. "What is it? A

83]

whim? Generosity?" Then his mask of indifference seemed to slip a little, and he half sneered. "Have you nothing else to do with yourself?"

"Take it easy, Alberto. The girl means something special to me. I'd like to try and give her a hand. See that she's looked after. And I'm able to. And I know she's a millstone around your neck." And in spite of his embarrassment Sam regained his air of self-assurance, smiling, his blue eyes on Alberto, as if he expected an upsetting moment or two but would remain calm and patient. His manner had a bad effect on Alberto. It was as if it made Alberto feel unimportant now. He looked at the tips of his fingers, struggling against his desire to justify himself.

"You ought to know I now have no interest in the woman," he said, putting his elbows on the table and linking his hands.

"If it is so, Al, then so much the better."

"I no longer have the mixed-up feeling. You understand?"

"I think so."

"A millstone around the neck, you say," and Alberto smiled as if he were talking about someone in another country, and the slow smile suddenly made Sam apprehensive. He could see that Alberto, writhing inwardly, was hurting himself with his air of indifference; it humiliated him to want to explain himself to a stranger from out of town whom he felt entitled to look down on.

"A man like you, Sam—in your culture where you run from women—it is easy to think of them as millstones around the neck. Not me." Suddenly he seemed to become sure of himself; he was eloquent; his English was excellent. "It is too bad that you do not know me better. All my life I have been enchanted by women. If they became a load, I carried it with happiness. I would have gone anywhere in the world for one of those women who . . . well . . . how do I say it . . . ? A woman was always the longed-for, the absolute intimacy, the glow on my life. If I saw something I thought beautiful, I compared it with a woman. If I was sick with worry, I fled from the worry by thinking about women. But now . . ." He

[84

paused, he was really moved. "But now, no woman can have this importance for me."

"You've been sick. You are not yourself, Alberto."

"Ah, but I am myself now—and with the terrible urgency. You are younger. You do not know what it is to think you are going to die."

"Not yet. It'll happen, though."

"In the hospital I was alone, Sam. I said to myself, 'Alberto, nobody in Rome cares whether you live or die,'" and his eyes filled with tears. Not accustomed to men who were so dramatic about themselves, Sam lowered his eyes, drawing his hand across his face uneasily. He wanted to get away. The thing was settled. What was Alberto trying to do to him? Yet Alberto paused, waiting for him to lift his head, and Sam did. The man wouldn't take his eyes off him. Talking with such emotion about his realization that life had passed so swiftly, and now there was little time. He had felt such a sense of urgency, Alberto said. Things had got sifted out. This feeling of urgency, it had been to hurry and do the thing that was most important to him, that would give him the most satisfaction, and that should not be left undone. He would go back to America, go back to Brazil and make the second movie. Well, he had the right story. And he had Irving Stein waiting in New York to make the correct financial arrangements. Yet when he had got out of the hospital with this feeling of urgency, he still couldn't move. He had been still sitting there in Rome, rotting.

And then Alberto paused, with an odd troubled smile, as if he were by himself. With relief Sam thought he had got away from him. Alberto had his elbows on the table, his hands linked so tightly the knuckles shone whitely. "This woman, Anna," Alberto went on, half to himself. Then Sam, keeping very quiet, felt like an eavesdropper, knowing he would be hurt painfully by what he overheard. How did he ever let her do it to him? Alberto wondered aloud, with a deep sigh. He had come out of the hospital in such a hurry with his plans, then he had been unable to move. The spiritual collapse again. "Not out of lust for her," he said. "Not at all. In that way she disgusts me. A woman no longer matters to me now. I had understood that much." Yet in no time she had him beaten again. A dull and apathetic man again. With her around, his creative vitality vanished. She had taken away all his old splendid faith in himself. And the day-by-day world? It wasn't worth while. It was a wasteland. That was the terrible thing. And she knew what she did to him. She kept it up. She kept humiliating him and dragging him down and cheapening him. Why had he put up with it so long? Why couldn't he put down the cross? Well, now he could understand it. He was a Christian humanist. A man with a conscience, and he had let her, with her twisted soul, get hold of his conscience. That woman with her wandering and her drinking, he said, his voice breaking, had been goading him to leave her. And why? Well, he had known why. She knew that if he kicked her out, being the kind of man he was, it would bother his conscience and he would be unable to work freely, and he would have no faith in himself as a man; as a creator he would be castrated. Whether he went or stayed, it was the same thing, and she had her satisfaction. After musing a moment, he said uncertainly, "Yes, how did I ever let myself get in such a position?"

"There's just one thing, Alberto," Sam said.

"Yes? What thing?"

"Why should she hate to see you at your work?"

"I do not know."

"Why should you have no faith in your own life or your talent when she is around?"

"I think it is because she has none in hers," he said uneasily, as his eyes shifted away. "She's not sick at all, and she doesn't have to drink. Ah, you'll see. For everything in her life she has this disgust. It is not a spiritual thing. It is destructive of everything. It made me apathetic. Why bother with anything? Nothing around me was real while I was with her, and I was bored to death."

A little flush on his face, Sam wanted to object, to defend Carla; then it was as if he heard an anxious little voice in his heart asking, "What do you really know about this woman?"

And Sam felt himself drawing back uneasily. He was touched by chilling doubt, wondering indeed what he might be letting himself in for. The girl could well be neurotic, twisted and a crazy drunk in the bargain. Alba Longa. Alba Longa. That was the name a long time ago. Why *was* he getting mixed up in this? Here was Alberto, a likable good man. Yet why did Alberto now look so troubled? Was he unconvinced by his own explanations? That was it, of course. Sam felt a sudden secret and fierce satisfaction.

Smiling suddenly, Alberto said, "And how right I was. As soon as I got her out of the house, I started to breathe again." His eyes were now bright with excitement. "All my energy, my faith in myself, how do you say? Like a tide, a flood, flooding over me."

"What a lucky guy you are. Full of life." Then Sam bit his tongue, holding back the contemptuous words, "And your girl out there, getting beaten up by that big Spagnola woman."

"Yes, now I will be lucky again," Alberto said, nervously eager. Already he was very busy. There were so many little things he had to do before he left Rome for America. He had gone to Naples to see his old mother who was in astonishingly good health. And he wanted to go to Venice to see a Monsignor who had been kind to him in his boyhood. The only thing that was bothering him a little was his story line for the movie. Yesterday he had gone out to cinema city and had sat in the restaurant with an old friend, Angelo Francatti, but Angelo, he had seen, could give him no real assurance about the story. Angelo, who had lost his youth and fire, now spent his late afternoons with that movie crowd of peacock people at Doney's. No, he would find someone else he could feel sure of. He really would, and soon, too.

"And now you, Sam," he said with his bluff charm.

"Me? Oh, it would be no good telling it to me."

"Not that. Oh no," and he chuckled, then said superstitiously, "I mean you coming along. I regard your appearance as providential. Simply providential. It is something further to clear the way. It is a great thing that she has touched your charity. In America I might think of Anna sometime and be worried. It would hold me up. But knowing that she is with someone else . . . you," and he turned away.

There was a little square patch of sunlight in the courtyard. Suddenly a trellis threw shadows on the patch and it was like a checkerboard. As Alberto turned again, their eyes met, and just for that moment all pretense was dropped. They hated each other. Alberto smiled cynically. "But you?" he asked. "What about you?"

"What about me?"

"You must have a strange taste."

"In what?"

"In women."

"Why?"

"An alcoholic girl with crazy fancies. Oh, come on." Though he tried to laugh good-naturedly, Alberto's eyes were full of contempt. "What does Carla care who's in bed with her? No nonsense about romantic ritual. Ah, but perhaps you are lazy, Sam?" Alberto smiled indulgently. "You do not bother killing your own game. Is that it?"

"That's it," Sam said. "I'm a scavenger." Now it was his turn to feel the humiliation; and he would have made a cutting remark, but he thought of Carla crouched on the floor, then of her rising, her hand coming out to him. He thought of her with an anguish that seemed to warn him that if he lost his temper he would quickly be put beyond the reach of her hand, and he trembled and hid his anger.

Laughing, Alberto reached out and patted Sam on the shoulder consolingly, knowing he had got under his skin, and finding some relief from the wounds of his own pride in cheapening him. "No, no, Sam," he joked. "You're no hyena. Let us face it, the fact is she's still a pretty woman. No matter what goes on in her head. Maybe all she needs is a more practical man like you who goes right to the point."

"I hope so."

"Just the same," Alberto continued cruelly, "if your taste for her grows, she will ruin you."

[88

"By that time," Sam said blandly, "maybe someone who respects me, as I respect you, Alberto, will take her off my hands too."

"Yes, yes," Alberto said, suddenly upset. "It is a fact that you must have some respect for me or you would not be here talking to me. You are helping me. You have a good heart. I do not enjoy this. Let us go. I have much to do."

They came out to the square and as they walked toward the fountain, Alberto told him a taxi would come along; he himself had a friend, a painter in the neighborhood, and would visit him. A young woman, a working girl in a green dress, was crossing the square with her slow proud easy stride, and behind her was the church of Santa Maria.

"It's quite beautiful. Close to the earth," Alberto said, frowning. "I have always been glad that Rome missed the lofty Gothic period. The ancient, then the rebirth of the ancient. Interesting, isn't it? Where else has it happened?"

"Nowhere else. Is that a wedding coming out?"

"Ah, there now. There. The bride. A small wedding. Ah, the poor girl. Look over there on the street at the side."

At the wide door a little crowd was gathered around a hearse, and in the sunlight there was a flash of many colored flowers heaped on the hearse. "A funeral waiting to get in, waiting till the wedding party gets out," Alberto said. "That's the way it is with us, eh?"

"Oh, Lord," Sam said, "can't the dead wait?"

"Of course they can't," Alberto said, bitterly. "We're dropping off like flies every minute. Just the same, that poor bride is unlucky. Look at her. She hasn't seen the dead one." He put his arm on Sam's shoulder. "I'll get in touch with Signora Spagnola. *Arrivederci*," and he walked off across the square in the sunlight, stooping a little, his suit too loose, but holding his head back proudly as if he were refusing to consider himself a broken man. And Sam, watching him go and clinging to his own view of Carla, couldn't believe she had ruined Alberto, or would want to ruin anyone. A sweet secret elation began to possess him. Taking out his wallet he counted the American money and then the travelers' checks; all told, five hundred and seventy dollars. A taxi came along, a man and woman got out and went in the restaurant, and Sam took the taxi to the cable office near the press club. As he wrote the cable, saying he would stay in Rome till the Pope died, he smiled to himself, feeling full of energy.

The next thing to do was get hold of Francesca and tell her to get busy on the apartment.

CHAPTER 10

FRANCESCA had looked for a place in that neighborhood to the side of the Via Veneto, where there were office buildings and shops and where the streets were quiet at night. She had found an apartment above a stationery store, owned by a very old widow, Signora Ferraro, who lived with her daughter, Agnese. It would be the kind of place Sam needed, Francesca told him, because the old woman and her daughter, although of established respectability, understood that people could be difficult. A son, Tomaso, had been a grave disappointment. The late husband, an official in the Bank of the Holy Spirit and a staunch worker for the Christian Democratic party, had wanted the boy to be a priest. A Monsignor, a friend of the family, had taken an interest in the boy and helped him and pushed him, and Tomaso had become a seminarian. But when Tomaso had completed his education —that is to say—when he had a good enough education, he had gone to Milan and become a journalist. So the old woman had an understanding of people with a wayward streak in them.

When Sam went with Francesca to see the upstairs apartment over the stationery store, it seemed strangely familiar to him. It was like a Catholic house he might have visited with his camera back home doing a story about a prominent immigrant in the Italian Quarter. There was a living room with a worn green carpet, a sofa and furniture he might have seen at home thirty years ago. It was as if men and women of a certain respectability had the same taste all over the world, he thought. On the walls there were two horrible colored lithographs of the Virgin Mary, and on the bedroom wall a big plaster-of-Paris crucifix. But the place was very clean.

Signora Ferraro, a bright-eyed stooped old woman dressed in black, with hair that must have been dyed black, had a prim grave manner. The daughter, a plain, short-legged, placid woman of thirty-five, who looked like her mother except that she had lonely eyes, was shy and prim. She had a few words of English. Both mother and daughter were very religious. The old woman told Francesca she understood Sam's wife spoke Italian. When Francesca translated, he raised his eyebrows. Smiling a little, Francesca assured the Ferraros that Sam's wife spoke excellent Italian.

On the way out Francesca said to Sam, "Your wife, of course. My goodness, what else was I to tell them?"

"The thing is you haven't told it to Carla."

"Why do you insist on calling her 'Carla'?"

"Because it's her name," he said.

"What am I supposed to call her now?"

"Call her 'Carla.' "

"It is an elaborate game, Sam."

"Her name is Carla."

"I assume you want me to go with you to get her?"

"After lunch tomorrow. Get a taxi and pick me up at the hotel," he said.

The sun was shining and the sky was blue and cloudless when he had his coffee and bun that morning in the little milk bar near the hotel. He had become attached to his clean, neat, new little milk bar. It was the one place he had found in Rome that seemed to belong to him. Then Francesca came in the taxi and they picked up his bags at the hotel. He gave the Ferraro ad-

dress to the clerk and told him to forward any mail. When they
had taken his bags to the apartment, they drove into the suburbs, and he waited in the taxi watching the door. Twenty
minutes passed, the door remained closed, and he began to
believe that Carla had refused to come with him, and he got
out, going slowly toward the door. Then it opened. Francesca
came out carrying a bag, and two paces behind her was Carla.
When she saw him she stopped, staring at him in the sunlight.
"Hello," he called, smiling. A heavy frown on her face, Carla
came toward him. She gave him one quick trusting pleading
glance, and he took her bag and put it on the front seat beside
the driver. The three of them got into the back seat. The flush
on Carla's face, her stiffness and her silence told him how painfully humiliated she was. It was as if she couldn't bear to look
or speak to Francesca whom she knew. She moved a little closer
to him, and they were on their way.

"I told her what a nice little place we had for her," Francesca said helpfully.

"Good," Sam said. "Yes, it's all right," and he stammered
with self-consciousness because Carla hadn't turned again to
him. She showed her awareness of the indignity of her position
by leaning forward a little as if she were concentrating intently;
and he wanted to be gentle and show her respect. She didn't
speak or appear to be listening to them as they pretended to
make casual conversation. Sometimes they addressed a remark
to her, but she remained aloof.

"Well, here you are," Francesca said when they got to the
little stationery store. As he opened the taxi door and got out
and took the bag, waiting on the sidewalk, he was afraid that
Carla might not come any farther with him. Now that she was
on her own, why should she feel she had to come with him?
Why not laugh at him and Francesca, and go off alone? They
had no hold on her.

"If you'd like me to come in with you, Sam . . ." Francesca
began.

"No," he said firmly. "Just get her things from Alberto.
Have them sent here. I'll call you. Come on, Carla," and he

93]

put out his hand. She took his hand, doubtful, half-ashamed, and got out of the taxi.

"If you need me, do call me," Francesca said, and he nodded, then he took Carla's arm.

As they slowly climbed the stairs together and entered the apartment he felt a touch of panic. "It's not much of a place," he said. When she didn't answer, just looked around, he added uneasily, "At least it's a place, Carla." And then he showed her the little kitchen and the bedroom. She wouldn't comment. She wouldn't change her expression. "The bedroom is your room," he said. "I sleep on the couch out there." So far she wouldn't even look at him. "All right," he said, trying to smile. "You can have that cupboard. I'll get your bag," and he got it and put it on the bed.

Her eyes were on him. The embarrassment and shame were gone. She measured him boldly. "I was desperate to get out of that prison camp," she said, blunt and sullen. "All right. Now what's your game?"

"No game," he said, meeting her eyes. "I—I just hope you'll stay here."

"Don't count on it," Carla said grimly. She turned her back on him. When her shoulders shook he thought she was crying, but when she turned to him again there wasn't a trace of a tear. "There's nothing much in my bag," she said nervously. "That ugly old bitch sold my clothes. Six or seven dresses."

"A slap on her ugly mouth was what she needed, Carla," Sam said quickly. His instinct told him to keep on calling her Carla and wait for her to say, "Why do you call me that name?" Not a word of Italian had come from her. But if she let him call her Carla, he thought, they were bridging the gap between the first night in the street and the night in the café when she had been with Alberto.

"It's an old-fashioned bed, isn't it?" she said.

"The mattress isn't bad, Carla."

"I'm here for the night, anyway, eh? Is that it?" and again there was that suspicious hard challenging look in her eyes.

"What was the deal? Who did you make it with? Alberto?"

"There's no deal. No one stood in the way."

"Just a friend, eh?"

"You're my only friend in Rome." And he tried to smile.

"Why the smile? What's the matter?" she said suspiciously.

"The truth is, well," he said awkwardly, "I don't know you without any make-up on. I see I'll have to get you the cosmetics and all. Is there a shop around here?"

"Don't I look attractive?"

"You can't help looking attractive." Bowing elaborately he took her hand and kissed it.

"Oh, cut it out," she said. Opening her bag she took out a vanity case, walked over to the dresser, put on some lipstick, moistened her mouth with her tongue, regarded herself gravely, combed her hair, and then turned to him, worried. "Is that what you want?" she asked solemnly. "Am I more attractive now?"

"A little gayer looking, anyway," and then some vague uneasiness touched him as he wandered into the other room. What view did she have of him? he wondered. Whatever it was it allowed her little ease with him. Now she had followed him from the bedroom and was sitting opposite him. Again there was the awkward, embarrassed silence. If it went on like this they would be, bit by bit, more like strangers to each other.

"Well, say something," she said nervously. "For God's sake, say something. Do we just sit here forever and forever?"

"Maybe it's a way of getting to know each other."

"Saying nothing? Absolutely nothing?"

"It's not so bad, Carla. It's a thing you can only do with people you feel very sure of. Isn't that right?"

"I don't know. This bothers me," and again she had that look of worried concentration he might come to dread. Then she said calmly, "Why should we want to be so sure of each other?"

"I know how it is with me," he said. "I'm alone here in Rome. I'm a stranger."

"And you have to watch your step, eh?"

"That's right."

"It doesn't make any sense," she said, cynically. "If you were watching your step you wouldn't be bothering with me. You know what I think?"

"Tell me, Carla."

"I read somewhere that a man in a foreign land, a strange city, always gets to know it better through a woman of the town."

"It's probably true."

"I also read somewhere," she went on in her strange tone, "that a man coming into a strange city likes to think a woman's waiting for him somewhere. The kind of a woman he couldn't meet at home or anywhere else. Is it like that with you?" Then she smiled as if she liked the sound of her words. More sure of herself with him now, she got up and ran her fingers through his hair. He blushed, it was so unexpected. "I get it, Sam," she said. "You're nice. Don't worry. Don't you worry at all. You'll be all right with me."

A strip of sunlight from the street window, that had been falling across the rug, suddenly faded away. He lit a cigarette for her, and she drew her feet up under her on the chair. Now she was apparently content to be with him and even a little amused. She asked how he got tied up with Francesca, and he told her. "Well, I hope we're not going to have her hanging around," Carla said. "It was pretty painful having her come for me, since I've always looked down my nose at her."

But Francesca was a woman who really knew Rome, Sam said, teasing her—a real authority on fashions, although she preferred the French fashions as did the elite of Rome. "Oh, my God," Carla sneered. Her contempt seemed to bring her to life. Had he taken a look at that figure of Francesca's? Naturally a woman in that shape wanted to wear tailored suits, since the careless Italian style would murder her. Imagine Francesca in skintight slacks! Oh, sure! The little snob world went to Paris for styles. But French fashions from Rome! Imagine! What a joke. Didn't he know that for two thousand years

[96

the Italians had given Europe whatever it had of real style, and now they were doing it again with clothes?

"You don't have to sell me. I'm sold." Her flow of indignation as she leaned toward him, her legs curled up under her, delighted him. Moistening his lips and smiling, he waited for her to relax and smile, too. She sounded now like a normal indignant woman. Not moody or depressed at all. And then he thought, Now's the time to have her meet the Ferraros.

"Let's go down and I'll introduce you to the Ferraros," he said. "We've got to meet them. Might as well get it over with, Carla."

"Why should I bother with them?"

"We don't want them up here calling on us, Carla. It might be hard to get rid of them. Come on," and he took her hand, and led her down the stairs and into the shop.

Signora Ferraro, in her black dress with the high collar, was behind the counter. She received them graciously and called her daughter. They all shook hands. They eyed Carla, and said nice things, and wondered about her. Carla had to do the talking in Italian. All on edge, Sam watched the faces of mother and daughter for some sign that Carla had made a wild remark, or had taken an alien tone to them. And Carla kept her arm in his. It seemed to go well. Then the women smiled and bowed, and he knew by the pressure of Carla's arm that she was drawing him away. They went back upstairs.

"What did they say?" he asked, sighing with relief.

"What is this?" she said, turning on him, her eyes smoldering. "Come on, what is this?"

"What do you mean?"

"Am I supposed to be sick?"

"Who said you were sick?"

"Who told those clowns I'm sick? I don't think it's funny. It's ridiculous! It was you. You have a big mouth."

"How could I if I can't speak Italian?"

"Neither you can. So it was Francesca, eh? Well, she's the one who's sick, real sick. Such women disgust me."

"Carla, keep your voice down, please."

97]

"You're right, Sam, you bet," she said, changing suddenly. "If that pious pair is listening on the stairs . . ." and going to the door she swung it open. He thanked God she could see no one on the stairs. And then, half-ashamed, she smiled a little.

"Well, Carla, we're established now," he said gently. "Come on and sit down with me."

"You're always saying sit down. Why?"

"To feel at home. It's our place now, isn't it?"

"I guess so. I don't know. It . . . well, it was just on a hunch that I came," she said, going over to the window and looking out.

Her embarrassment returned and he wondered how he could make her feel at ease. Stretching himself out on the sofa he tried talking about his life back home. She showed no interest at all. He even began to talk about his painting. She continued to stand at the window, her back to him. The street lights came on and they were there in semidarkness. "Look here, Carla," he stammered desperately, "I can draw. I grant there may be people in this world with more talent, but . . . well, look, I'll show you," and he got up and turned on the light. Opening a bag he took out the drawing he had made of her in his hotel room. The piece of paper he had used was only eight-by-ten; it was just her face as he had imagined it should be, the head back proudly, smiling and bold and superbly self-possessed. "Here, look," he said, touching her arm.

"Who's that?" she said, taking the drawing.

"Look at it, Carla."

"My God, is it supposed to be me?"

"It is you."

"Yeah. Yeah."

"Carla, in the beginning," he said smiling, "ever now, and shall be."

"I've got a sense of humor too," she said solemnly. "Just the same—say, why don't you sign it for me? No, couldn't you copy it? Make it big. About two feet. Could you, Sam?"

"What would you do with it?"

"Hang it on the wall. Why not?"

[98

"Tomorrow," he promised her. Enormously pleased with himself, he felt he had already made a hopeful discovery. People he had known who had suffered from a depression or anxiety that made them reject their whole world, had lost interest in their appearance and all self-regard. But he could see that Carla was fascinated by herself. He liked it. Smiling, he got his coat, and said they would go out and eat if she were hungry.

"Yes, I'm hungry," she said.

Outside it was still hot, but bearable now because of the Roman night breeze. Rome was all hills and valleys, and the night breeze cooled it off quickly. Sam wanted to find a restaurant in the neighborhood where she would not be known, the kind of a place where Alberto would never go. "Let's look for a quiet little place," he said. She took a few steps, then stopped and looked up anxiously at their window as though to make sure exactly where the place was if she ever had to find it quickly.

CHAPTER **11**

THIS restaurant had a sign by the door, RECOMMENDED BY DUNCAN HINES. It was an inexpensive neighborhood restaurant with regular patrons. It had light-colored furniture, clean white tablecloths, a menu of limited variety and one dessert. Neighborhood businessmen ate there. Only three of the patrons looked up when Sam and Carla came in. The fat, gray-haired shoe merchant, Signor Cosentino, there with his plump homely wife, looked up because he was in a discontented restless mood. Business had not been good that day. The waiters could always tell when Signor Cosentino had had a bad day. He stared morosely at Sam and Carla because he was tired of looking at his wife, yet he hardly saw them. His thoughts were of his shoe store. The short, broad-shouldered, middle-aged man with the square jaw and the bald head, who appraised Carla calmly, was Signor Leone, a toy manufacturer from Naples. Whenever he came to town on business he ate at this restaurant. Right now he should have been on his way to Naples. The evening before his departure he always picked up a whore, but the one he had had last night, a girl in a hurry, had given him no satisfaction, so he was staying over another night. Being a grimly practical man, he wasted no time in contemplation of Carla when he saw that she was taken.

[100

The third patron, Joe Mosca, looked up, smiled in the friendliest fashion having judged from Sam's clothes that he was an American, too. Joe Mosca was a big-shouldered man of thirty-five, with a curl of his black hair low on his narrow forehead; he had a narrow long-nosed emptily handsome face full of smiling stupidity. Joe Mosca was a man of tremendous guile, who had lived in New York twenty-two years. He believed that everybody liked him for his careless reckless ways, and he believed, too, in his benefactor at home, Big Jim Giardello. For a year and six months Joe Mosca had been in Naples where Big Jim had connections, waiting for permission to go home. Joe Mosca was just about broke, and he had come to Rome to make some connections himself while he waited for the boys at home to send him money and transportation. A year ago when Big Jim, the benefactor, had been arrested and brought to trial for fixing fights and controlling fight managers, Joe, who might have been a damaging witness against him, had been given the money to go to Italy for a holiday. It was true that Big Jim had gone to prison, but Joe Mosca could not believe that his colleagues had left him stranded in Italy. Joe kept watching Carla. She began to look vaguely familiar. He wondered if he had seen her on one of those nights when he had wandered through the Café de Paris, pretending to be looking for a friend. Anyway, he had seen her around. The guy with her seemed to be a nobody. Joe waited until they had finished their dinner. Calling the waiter, he whispered to him.

A little later the waiter approached Sam's table with his tray, put down two Scotches, and made an eloquent gesture across the room at Joe Mosca, who grinned opulently and nodded with all the graciousness of Big Jim Giardello himself, as Carla picked up the glass. Before she could touch it to her lips Sam reached out quickly, jerked it out of her hand, put it down and spoke to the waiter. In some consternation the waiter returned to Joe's table, put down the two drinks, shrugged and walked away. Joe Mosca's pride was hurt. Joe had faith in himself as an attractive well-liked man. The girl and her guy didn't even look at him on their way out.

Outside, Carla protested, "It was just a drink, Sam. A gesture. The guy could see you were from The States."

"I'm not from The States. I'm from Canada."

"How can anyone tell the difference?"

"It's not the point, Carla. When you're with me you don't drink, see? And always remember this. You don't have to drink."

"I know I don't. Who said I wanted to drink?"

"Maybe a little wine when we're eating. Anyway, they tell me Roman women don't drink hard liquor. It makes them liverish."

"You're awfully smart, aren't you, Sam?"

"Come on, are you sore?"

"I'm telling you, I didn't want a drink."

"Anyway, that guy's just another slob from The States," and he laughed and took her arm.

"Well, do you want to go back to our place?" she asked hesitantly.

"All right."

As they passed under the street light and she turned to him, he saw the uncertainty in her face. "Yes, we'll go back—if you want to," she said.

In their place she sat down, looking at him with such great curiosity that he felt self-conscious. He began to walk up and down. As he groped for something to say that would entertain her before she grew embarrassed and withdrew from him in her thoughts, he took off his coat and tossed it over a chair. There were no sounds at all in the house.

"Sam," she said quietly.

"Yes, Carla."

"That first night on the street when you didn't know where you were and you spoke to me . . ."

"I remember."

"You said, 'Wait! Wait here!' "

"I remember."

"You wanted very much to be with me, didn't you?"

"That's right."

"Yeah, you've often thought about it, haven't you?"

"How do you know, Carla?"

"I can tell," she said calmly, as if it satisfied her to think that once she had got into the mind of someone he would dream of her as men had dreamt of legendary women. "And we're here, Sam." Upset, he tried to smile. Having got up, she sauntered toward the bedroom. She might be tired and want to sleep, he thought, stretching out on the sofa. A good long peaceful sleep while she was feeling secure would be the best thing for her. But, in a little while, hearing no sound from the bedroom, he began to worry and he got up and went to the door.

She was sitting on the bed, naked except for a little black brassiere and a black garter belt that held up her stockings. She had the smallest waist he had ever seen. As she looked up, her hands were on the garter fastener on her right leg. Her beautiful wide-set eyes were on him, her voluptuous mouth open a little. In one quick movement she pulled off her stockings and her black garter belt and stood up, unhooking her brassiere, which she tossed on the chair; and then she straightened up, her breasts thrust out. "Do you like me?" she asked. There was something lascivious in her eyes, a wanton confidence; and when she lay down on the bed and said, "Come on, Sam," it broke his heart. The corners of his eyes were moist; it seemed to him to be so pitiable that she felt the need of being sure of his desire for her. His head whirled and he stammered, trying not to belittle his concern for her by touching her while her heart and her thoughts were tormented.

"Don't just eat me up with your eyes, Sam."

"You're so beautiful, Carla," he said huskily, and he tore off his clothes.

As he lay with her he wanted to show her a tenderness she might never have known, show her she had an importance to him beyond any quick fierce satisfaction of desire. But the way she took him in her arms blinded him with sudden lust. He kissed her gently, stroking her breast and her flank softly, and tried to draw her into his own strange shy tenderness.

103]

She let him kiss and fondle her. Almost shyly she let him draw her over on her side, and into his arms, as if she knew he had some secret awareness of her, and she, in her new shyness, was sharing it. Then she seemed to remember how lonely he had been for her that first night, feeling cut off from all the world, and she put her arms around him and gently drew his head down to her breast, comforting and soothing him with all her warmth. He made love to her, not greedily but gently. Her black hair was spread on the pillow, her eyes were closed, her mouth twisted as if her own feeling hurt her. And she began to whisper words and phrases in Italian. *"Ah, Mamma mia,"* he heard in a broken whisper as she gripped him tightly. The bed creaked horribly.

Exhausted, he lay beside her, breathing heavily, the sweat glistening on his chest and shoulders; and she didn't move. She just lay there very still. Reaching for her hand, he held it tight in his, as he had done in the beginning with her, as he seemed to have been doing for days; so he would not feel shame, so he could tell himself, It had to be. There was no choice. It had to be like this with her, if I am ever to be able to do anything else with her, if she's ever to feel sure of anything else with me. He was looking up at the ceiling decoration carved in plaster around the light. Sadness touched him. It seemed to him that she was like some bird or sea nymph tossed up on his beach, waiting for him to heal her.

She said, "Sam . . ."

"What?"

"You have a lot of passion for me."

"It's the way you are for me, Carla."

"I think I knew I would be something like this for you," she said calmly.

Raising her head a little she looked down at him as he held her hand, and she smiled, very pleased with herself. Suddenly she detached her hand and hopped out of bed. Her full pointed breasts jiggled as she walked across the room to her bag which was on the chair. Opening it she took out a nightdress, pulled it over her head and went out into the hall and along to the bathroom. While she was gone he got dressed. As soon as she returned, he noticed the change in her. She looked on edge, as if she had done some thinking and it had led to restless discontent. In a panic he tried to smile, watching her get dressed.

"Well, I'm dressed. Let's go out," she said.

"Go out where, Carla?"

"I don't care. Anywhere your little heart desires. Anyway, we can have a drink somewhere."

"I don't want a drink and you don't need one."

"Come on, Sam. Buy me a drink?"

"No, Carla," he said, remembering the look in her eyes that first night when he had smelled liquor on her. And that night when she had been with Alberto, and then had vanished, she had been drinking too. With a stab of anguish he realized that Alberto also must have often faced her as he was doing now, saying no.

"So you won't come with me?" she asked, with an air of indifference.

"No, I won't."

"How about giving me some money then?"

"Not on your life, Carla."

"Well, to hell with you," she burst out, her eyes blazing as she headed for the door. "Get out of my way." But he gripped her wrists. He forced her over to the chair and pushed her down grimly and stood over her.

"Go on, you bastard," she cried, shaking with excitement. "Go on. Beat me."

"I'm not going to beat you. You're just not going out drinking."

"I'm to stay cooped up here? You don't own me. Who said you could tell me what to do? You're crazy. What rights have you got over me?"

"You're with me, that's all."

"I don't have to be with you. Who do you think you are?" Again she came at him, and again he had to grab her wrists. Struggling with him she shouted, "Take your hands off me, you thug."

"Carla, Carla," he pleaded. "Now listen, Carla," and as he exerted all his strength holding her, he tried to smile.

"Don't laugh at me!"

"I'm not laughing at you, Carla."

"Yes, you are, you ape," and he thought she was going to burst into tears. But as he tried to put his arms around her, soothingly, she backed away, hitting at his hands. "I know. I know," she half sobbed. "I'm a funny little Italian girl, eh? You just can't hate me, can you? Another funny, lovable little Italian. How can you or anyone else hate them when they're all so comical? They don't want to hate anybody, they don't want to fight anybody. They just want to be polite and comical," and she walked up and down, working herself up till she was nearly frantic. He was bewildered. He kept raising his hand placatingly, but she went on furiously. "You clowns come over here with your bucks to spend and you just love us, don't you? Here I am, a funny little Italian girl like me, and, oh look, there's a nun with goggles on riding around on a motor scooter, and there's another crazy little Italian singing opera on the streets. Oh, watch out though. They're all alike. They're after the bucks. Watch your buck with them." Close to real hysteria, her eyes blinded by tears, she cried, "You barbarian! Over here with your camera, waiting for the Pope to die."

"Come on now, Carla. Don't be childish."

"The Holy Father just won't oblige you, will he?" she jeered. "Isn't it just too bad? So you have to take a holiday and fool around with me." She tried to duck around him; he pushed her back.

"No you don't," he said.

"I'll bet they call you 'Sammy,' don't they?"

"No one calls me 'Sammy,' " he said, the blood rushing to his head.

"Get out of here. Go on home, Sammy," she cried. "Go home and chase fires with your silly flash bulbs. Get chased by cops in the rain. Out of my way or I'll scream. I'm in my own city. I'm a Roman," and she took an air, tossing her head imperiously. "Why, you're just dirt under my feet," and she spat.

"You're no Roman," he said, losing his temper. "You sound like any other little Brooklyn tramp, so calm down."

"You say that to me, a Roman woman!" she shrieked, and she swung around looking for something she could hit him with. The holy picture on the wall caught her eye. Snatching it off the wall, she threw it at him, and the corner of the frame grazed his temple. The glass in the frame splintered all over the floor.

"All right, go," he said, shaken. He was at his wit's end. The police might come. The Ferraros might be calling them now. "Go, if you want to," he whispered. "I can't hold you. Only for God's sake, shut up," and he turned away from her and let her rush by him. Grabbing the door handle with both hands she jerked the door open and rushed out. He heard her clattering and stumbling down the stairs and out to the street.

He tried to listen for the sound of her step on the sidewalk, but he was shaking. He had to sit down on the sofa. Putting his head back, he closed his eyes. He felt sick at heart. But he didn't know what he could have done. She had got away and would wander the streets till she got drunk somewhere. He couldn't go after her as Alberto used to do, for he didn't know her haunts.

Then he thought he heard a sound. Alert and listening he stood up. He was sure he had heard a quiet step on the stairs. It came again, it came on up slowly and quietly. Then the door was pushed open and she came in, pale and frightened, and closed the door and leaned against it.

"I—I forgot my purse," she whispered. There was nothing in her purse, he was sure, and he didn't bother getting it for her because she was leaning against the closed door, holding it closed with her body, and her head was back and she was trembling with fright. "I couldn't—I tried—" she began.

"Don't, Carla," he begged her, stricken himself, for he now knew why she hadn't gone off indignantly by herself after leaving the Spagnola woman's place, why she had chosen to come with him. She knew she couldn't bear to be alone any more. Underneath the need of someone sympathetic to her was her mixed-up fear of everything in her life; love, death, hostility, the time she lived in, everything in the world that could frighten her; and out of it now came that pitiable plea in her eyes for protection.

"Carla," he said softly, and he went to her and led her away from the door, back into the room. "It's all right, Carla," he said gently. "I'm here."

CHAPTER 12

IN THE hard morning light Sam raised
himself on his elbow on the bed and looked at her as she lay
beside him, her hand on his shoulder. A woman beside him in a
bed in Rome. Black hair fanned out on the white pillow. One
small lobeless ear free of the hair, and her mouth open a little.
It was her hand on his shoulder that moved him, and he
frowned, wondering why it should do so. But he knew why; she
was in his hands, and willingly, and bit by bit, watching himself, it would be as if he were rubbing away at all the dirty
smudges on a glass till her image shone through as he had seen
it so plainly in his mind. Her hand on his shoulder as she slept
made him feel exultant. But what would she be like when she
woke up?

He drew the tip of his finger lightly over her lip, watching
her tongue come out at the tickling, the tongue licking the lip;
then she frowned as he did it again. Her eyes, suddenly opening, shifted from the ceiling to the walls, then quickly to him as
if asking, Who was she and where was she? And then, was it
with relief? she sighed. "What time is it, Sam?"

"It must be eleven."

"Is it that late?"

"We slept the sleep of the just. Better get up, eh?"

109]

But she didn't move, and he thought she was having some daydream, and then he saw that her eyes were moist, her mouth began to tremble; then she turned on her side to him, stammering, "The way I went on last night, Sam—I'm ashamed of myself. I was disgusting. It just came out of me—like some fury or hate I had been nursing so long. That Spagnola woman, and all. It wasn't really you. It was just things—everything. It won't happen again, Sam, because . . . well, it's beneath me."

"I know it is, Carla."

"Yes, you do know, I think."

"Let's get up and go out and get something to eat."

"I wouldn't mind some coffee."

"We should buy a supply of food, Carla. You can run the house."

"All right. We'll get in some groceries."

"Let's go and get something to eat and then buy the groceries," he said, getting up.

Then he noticed the patch on the wall where the holy picture had been, and he began to worry. The old woman and her daughter had heard the crash of the glass and the yelling. One of them had come up the stairs, he was sure. Being strait-laced, respectable women, they might want to throw them out at once. "Watch you don't step on that glass," he said. Going into the kitchen he got a broom and began to sweep up the bits of broken glass. "I'm sure we'll be hearing from the old woman," he said. "We'd better think up a good story."

"What do you think will happen?"

"I think they'll throw us out."

"Oh no, Sam! My God, no!"

The worry in her eyes alarmed him, and he tried to laugh and console her. They would think up a plausible story at the café, he said. It was nothing to worry about. Leave it to him.

They found a little café in the next block, and while they were eating they worked on a story for the Ferraros. Her intense concern, as if they were preparing to defend a place she had come to with relief, moved him. It was out of the question to say they had been drinking, she agreed, or that they had

[110

been having a family quarrel. For a long time he pondered, and her eyes were on him hopefully. "What about this?" she would ask, making a wild suggestion. And then he had to smile. In spite of her worry she was talking about last night's frantic scene as if it were about someone else she pitied, not her.

"Wait a minute, I've thought of something," he said. He had known a woman who had suffered from a neuralgia of the face called *tic douloureux*, he explained. It was of such painfulness, the pain coming in short spasms, that the woman would howl. A change of climate, a change of place, would sometimes bring on these attacks. Wasn't it just what they wanted? Supposing they had just come to Rome from Paris? Yes, it sounded pretty good, she agreed gravely. Would the old woman swallow it?

"Here," he said, "you write it down in Italian. Write first of all, would Signora Ferraro please sell me some drawing paper, if she had it, and some thumbtacks. Got that? Now write this, Carla, 'We are sure you were alarmed by the cry of pain you must have heard last night . . .'" As he paused he couldn't help smiling for she had the anxious air of a schoolgirl faking a note to the teacher, all her faith in a big lie. "'I have a neuralgia of the face, an old disease,'" he went on. "'Perhaps you have heard of it. It is called *tic douloureux*. It strikes me suddenly, the change in climate. If we move from one city to another. We have been in Paris. The pain, as doctors know, is unbearable. I am ashamed that I cry out. But it rarely happens a second time in the same place. Today it is not bothering me at all. If the noise upset you, we are very sorry.'"

"No, she won't believe it, Sam," she said, dejected, as she handed him the note.

"Maybe not, Carla, but it will mystify her, and, therefore she may want to believe it. Come on," he said, and they went out and found a grocery store and bought their groceries.

Back at the stationery store he told her he would hold onto the bag, it would suggest a homey domestic atmosphere. "You go up to the flat. Leave it to me," he said, and she left him. "Here goes," he said to himself, and he entered the store. After the sunlight it was dark in there. It was as if the Romans, for

111]

centuries, had found shelter from the sunlight in their homes. The old woman was behind the glass-covered case that displayed the fountain pens.

"Good day, signora," he said, bowing and smiling shamelessly. Her thin old lips tightening, she stiffened with an air of dignity.

"Signor Raymond, qui siamo gente rispettabile. Io no tollero tipi che gridano la notte, e fanno venire polizia."

The expression on her face, an expression of outraged respectability he had often seen at home on the faces of hundreds of women, told him what she was saying. She was a respectable woman. She would not have her establishment disgraced. Trying to act as if he had received a warm greeting, he handed her the note. She had to stop talking to put on her glasses. As she raised her head, there was utter disbelief in her eyes. She started to jabber at him again. Putting his bag of groceries on the counter, he said, "Thank you. You are too kind," and he smiled as if he thought she was expressing her sympathy. Then he saw the daughter, Agnese, appear at the door and he bowed to her.

Forgetting Agnese had a little English, he said, "Your mother is expressing her sympathy. I thank her," and he pointed to the note on the counter which she picked up and read. Agnese stood there silently listening as her mother continued to berate him, and he continued to smile gratefully, repeating, "Thank you, you are too kind." While Agnese listened, she watched her mother go to a shelf and get some sheets of drawing paper, and from a drawer a box of thumbtacks, words of virtue still pouring out of her. "It's good of you to be so sympathetic," he said, clowning. Agnese could see that her mother was serving him, even as she berated him; her mother, counting on his not understanding a word she said, was managing to serve her own vast sense of respectability, too. When Agnese, looking ashamed, quickly withdrew, Sam knew the old woman needed his rent money, no matter how he behaved. Truly apologetic now, he held out a handful of coins so the old woman could take the right amount for the drawing paper and thumbtacks. She held up her hand, delaying him. She was lifting an expensive pig-skin bag at the end of the counter. He had to help her with it. "Signora Winters," she said, pointing to the bag.

"Thank you very much, signora."

As he bowed his way out with his parcels and the bag, she was still wagging her finger like a disapproving old mother. He climbed the stairs and Carla was waiting at the open door.

"How did it go?" she asked anxiously.

"All right," he said, grinning, "the Signora understands."

"I can't believe it. What did she say?"

"A thousand reproachful things."

"If she had no English, how did you understand her?"

"Ah, but I saw that she said enough to ease her conscience. That's the main thing. So what do we care? This is your bag, eh? Francesca sent it down."

The weight of the bag seemed to puzzle her. Kneeling, she opened it, lifted out a dress, then another one, made a face, then tossed them out on the floor. "What do I want with those old things?" she asked scornfully. There were trinkets, too; bits of jewelry, a torn blouse, a soiled sweater. As she touched each one of these articles she had a strange grim smile. It was as if Alberto was trying to get rid of the last remnants of her. But under the garments were ten books. These she looked at thoughtfully, without touching them. Kneeling beside her, he picked up one book, then another. Some were in Italian, most of them in English. *The Lives of the Caesars. Plutarch's Lives* and a book he had read himself, a translation of Catullus by the American, Horace Gregory. They were part of her little library of ancient Rome, and he looked at her in astonishment. What legends and wild fantasies had come to her from these books? he wondered. A girl with a wild imagination! How much of it all had she taken into her own life? Yet Alberto had told him that she had had little formal education and had only begun to read omnivorously in Brazil.

"I had no idea you were such a reader. History was my own subject at college, you know," he said. "What'll we do with these?"

"Oh, leave them in the bag," she said carelessly. "Here, give it to me," and she took the bag and tossed it in the cupboard. But the discarded dresses she left on the floor. In a little while he picked them up himself. It reminded him that the bed was still unmade.

"Now what about that drawing?" she asked. "Where's the smaller one? Here," she said, getting it from the bureau. "Listen, Sam, can you really make it that much bigger?"

"Sure I can. Hey, you forgot to make the bed."

"Oh, to hell with the bed, Sam. Who cares?"

"I do. I can't work near an unmade bed," and he started to straighten out the sheets himself, waiting for her to help him. When she didn't show the slightest interest, he scowled and slapped the mattress to attract her attention.

"What do you draw on?" she asked. "The table?"

"I need something to use as a drawing board."

"Like what?"

"Like a board."

"Nothing's that big around here," she said, looking around. "Wait, I've got it, Sam. Use this," and she took the big holy picture off the living room wall and showed him the back of it.

"That'll do," he said, and sitting down he tacked the paper on the frame.

As he worked, his eyes sometimes on his sketch, she watched him intently. Walking up and down she waited restlessly. "Can I look now?" she would say. "How about now?"

"Not yet, Carla."

It took him an hour to make the enlargement. With her beside him, her expression so different than the expression he had got in the little picture, he had great difficulty for as he worked he was aware that her vanity was involved. A good thing! A splendid thing! he thought. No one could be all fear, or all depression if the vanity was there. The really scared people he had known were the ones without any good opinion of themselves. Not her. Twisted and all in the imagination as she might be she had said, proudly, "I'm a Roman woman." The pitiable gesture of a poor proud actress? Perhaps. But the Latin

[114

poets. The stories. He would have to get under the layers of
fantasy to get at her real nature. He would do it, in fact; it
seemed to him he was already doing it, for she was waiting so
impatiently to look at his picture of her. His hand on the drawing board trembled a little.

"Well, here you are," he said finally, taking out the thumbtacks and handing her the big drawing.

"Why, gee! You're pretty good, Sam."

"It's just a sketch."

"Here. Give me the thumbtacks."

"What are you going to do with it?"

She tacked the drawing over the wall space that had been
covered by the broken holy picture, then stood back regarding
it thoughtfully.

"No, it's not me," she said finally. Half troubled, half wondering, she turned to him, and for the moment it seemed to him
they were saying something to each other and were in agreement
no matter how much this unsaid thing was worrying her. "I like
it, though, Sam." And then almost reproachfully, "Just think!
That's how I look to you, isn't it?"

"Sometimes, Carla."

"Well, it's too bad, I guess."

"No, it's you."

"It's not. But . . . well . . . just the same . . ." Suddenly
she put her arms around him. "I can't be bad for you when I
make you want to put a glow on me. Can I, Sam?" and she
came hard against him, rubbing against him sensuously, her
fingers undoing the buttons of his shirt.

"Come on, Carla," he said, trying to laugh. It was as if she
was intent on making him need her as she was now, not as he
imagined her to be, not as he saw her in the picture. A little
fearful, she had to feel he needed her warm animal lusciousness.
It seemed to him that she had been frightened at the glimpse
he had got of her in the silent moment when she had turned
from the drawing to him, and now was hiding from the glimpse
by blinding him with the desire she knew she could stir up in
him. When she felt him hardening against her, she laughed

115]

softly. "Oh, all right," she whispered indulgently, and began to pull off her dress. In spite of his sudden lust he felt humiliated. But he had to get on the bed with her.

"Yes, I think you still like me a little," she said finally.

"You're lovely, Carla."

"I give you real pleasure, don't I?"

"You make me love you."

"Just as I am, and I'm glad," she said, very pleased with herself, lying there quietly, street sounds coming through the open window.

In the room full of sunlight she would have been content to stay quietly beside him. But as his mind cleared, he went on doggedly thinking about those books in her bag. The olden days. The splendors of the ancient city that had captivated her imagination. Not Castel Gandolfo, but Alba Longa. They used to call it Alba Longa, she had said on that first night he met her. She had really told him then how it was with her and where in her imagination she liked to be.

"Tell me something, Carla," and he drew her head closer to him. "Do you know Rome very well?"

"What a silly question!"

"As well as Francesca?"

"In my opinion, your Francesca is ignorant of everything that didn't happen around here the day before yesterday. Why?"

"I've been paying Francesca ten thousand lire a day to show me around."

"Ten thousand lire? My God," she cried, sitting up, "you're a big fool. That fat burglar!"

"Not at all, Carla. Anyone would pay her as much. And I've needed her."

"Needed her for what?"

"It's like this," he lied. "I'm doing a picture story of Rome. Before I take any pictures I need to be with someone who has the feel of the streets, the places, and some strong sense of the past. Someone I can always turn to. Carla, I'm wondering about you."

"Just going around showing places to you? A guide?"

[116

"That's all. Someone with a real feeling for the past."

"The past? How can it be the past if it's all around us?" She stood up naked, facing him without embarrassment. "If that's all you want, it's easy. It's my life. It's all . . . well, it's my life. In Rome it's everyone's life. I can take you around, Sam."

"Great. Just great," he said, pleased by her childish earnestness. "Why don't we go out and walk around a bit now?"

"It's all right with me," she said, and she couldn't hide her satisfaction.

Congratulating himself on the insight that had prompted him to suggest the one thing that might allow him to share her view of herself in a world she had made her fortress, he told himself he could, bit by bit, undermine that world. Bit by bit he might draw her out of it. That afternoon, he said, they would just walk around a little, and he would listen to her and get the feel of the town. For as she herself had said, you don't get to know a strange city by way of a guide, or a tour, but only through knowing a woman of the town. She got dressed quickly.

Outside she took his arm, hesitated, then led him up to the Via Veneto, and across to the street that runs alongside the Ambasciatori Hotel. It was a little street of small boutiques. In these shops, she said idly, you could often get clothes beautifully made for a third of the price you would pay on the Via Condotti. He would have to get her a few dresses and some accessories, and the sooner the better. They could come back to this street when the shops opened after four o'clock. And then they came to the Hotel de la Ville, where it seemed to him they were at the edge of a plateau, looking down over Rome. The old part of the city looked like a garden, a soft intimate garden laid out with monuments and temples among the trees. Standing beside her he thought, How soft and restful it looks. Is this why she wants to stay here? Then for the first time he caught the smell of Rome, and he sniffed, trying to place it. It was not the smell of Detroit or Toronto or New York or Montreal. No heavy industrial smoke, no stockyards; more like the smell of old houses and people, and food, fresh or rotting. Turning to

117]

her he said, "It looks like a garden, Carla. Over the centuries so many strange bright plants have bloomed here. Maybe the soil is played out now."

"What's the difference, if we're still all here?"

"Oh, come on," he said impatiently, "the old Romans are a vanished race. After the sack of Rome they all took to the hills, or the rich ones got on a fast mule for Constantinople. The people around here now—well," and he glanced at her slyly, "they're like you, Carla, they're from out of town."

"Who are you trying to kid, Sam?"

"It's a fact."

"I'm not as ignorant as you seem to think, Sam. I know that most of the big Romans always were from out of town. Think of those poets, Catullus, Horace, Vergil—what were they? Boys from the provinces who came to the big town to make good."

"That's right, Carla," he said admiringly. The amount of reading she must have done astonished him; yet Alberto had wondered if she had finished high school. Now he would have to watch himself with her. Trying another tack he went on, "In any event, I know where all those old ambitious conning boys would be now. They'd be off to America to make a million. What a place it would be for their special talents. Money, energy, ambition. Bossing the world around. That's America too. All that vitality, all that money to grab if you can only get to the top. The one thing you can say about the old Romans is that they were all success crazy."

"Oh, shut up, Sam," she said impatiently. "You don't understand us, and you sound like Alberto. Success is everything here, sure. It's everything, but just the same, if you know what I mean, it's nothing too, because you know in your blood everything passes away anyway."

"World-weary little Carla," he teased her.

"My people do not get world-weary very easy, because they make the best of what they have. Your people—it's a sickness with them. No matter how much they have they can't bear to make the best of it."

[118

Her flow of words astonished him. Where was her brooding silence now?

"I don't believe it," he said, leading her on.

"Then go into the hotel bars or the cafés or the churches and what do you see?" she asked vehemently. "A lot of Americans trying, one way or another, to get sloshed. They come over here, pants pressers, professors and barbers, because they're a big success at home. They get the idea everything's in the open here. So what? So they laugh and get drunk and parade around with their stupid empty faces. I can't stand them. The ones rushing around with the prayer books have the same empty faces. Oh, you've seen them. No, they're not drunk. But look at their faces. They're so damned earnestly empty, even above their prayer books, and they're scared to get drunk."

"Carla, Carla, just a minute. You sound as if you were sore at me."

"Oh, I didn't think you were such a fool. Come on."

They walked around the church, and there descending before them was the great wide flight of steps, the Spanish Steps. In the springtime, she told him with pride, those steps would be heaped with flowers. And if you were below in the square and looked up at the steps banked with flowers, it looked like a beautiful hanging garden such as they must have had in Babylon. Did he know about Babylon? Well, thank heavens for that. As they went down the steps she was holding his arm tight and talking brightly. She had found someone to hang on to. Someone who would listen approvingly like a country cousin showing her great respect.

At the bottom of the steps he turned and looked up again at the old church with its two towers and the Egyptian obelisk planted before it.

"That clock in the tower," she said, frowning in the sunlight. "Look at it."

"Yes, it's stopped, or it's an hour slow, one or the other."

"It's always wrong," she said. "Every time I come this way I look and it's the wrong time, or it's stopped. Why is it always the wrong time?"

"Just for those who notice, Carla."

"Oh," and she frowned.

"Are you Catholic, Carla?"

"Certainly. What in the world do you think I am?"

"I just asked," he said. Still pondering he looked up the great flight of steps at the obelisk, the tall pointed pillar planted in front of the church. Perhaps because she was beside him, reminding him of the certitude she sought in her sexual appeal, he said idly, "So often here in Rome the obelisk is planted in front of the church dome. Is it a phallic symbol?"

"A what?"

"A phallic symbol. Male and female."

"I get it," she said and she actually blushed. "Good God. So you're one of those guys. Oh, you disgust me."

"Wait a minute."

"Oh, go away from me."

"Now look, Carla. It could have a deeply religious implication. I'm not being irreligious."

"No, you've just got a dirty mind."

"Carla . . ." Trying to mollify her, he took her arm but she jerked away, trembling with disgust. In the strong hot sunlight an elderly gray-haired stout American, standing beside his plump gray wife, a camera in his hand, turned, staring at them. Again Sam tried to take Carla's arm, and he was as apologetic as he might have been to a shy modest young virgin. Then her stern air touched his sense of humor, and he turned away from her to hide his smile. But she thought he was letting her walk away.

"Sam," she cried anxiously. That fear he hated was in her eyes. Coming a step closer she took his arm, holding on so tightly he thought she was going to rub herself against him there on the street. "I insulted you," she said.

Quickly he put his hands on her shoulders, smiled and bent to give her a playful kiss.

"Hey, don't do that on the street," she said, ducking away. "You can't kiss a girl on the street in Rome."

"No?"

"Honestly, Sam, you'll get arrested. You'll get fined."

"A big fine?"

"It's only a little fine. Just the same they arrest you."

"What a crazy custom. What a paradoxical city. Well, what do we do now?"

"Well, for one thing you could buy me some clothes."

"All right. Come on."

"The stores aren't open yet. It isn't four."

"We'll go home and I'll get some travelers' checks and we'll come back here to the American Express and cash them. Come on."

On their own street they saw Signora Ferraro, a basket on her arm, hobbling toward them. Dressed in black as usual, bent from the waist and bowed down with age as she was, she yet managed to go down a little lower with grave courtesy. "Ask her how the Pope is," Sam said. "I've got to know. Is he out of danger?"

When Carla had asked the question, the old woman's healthy brown wrinkled face came alive, and she was very explanatory.

Carla said, "She says his holiness is resting well."

"Ask her if the Pope is out of danger. I am greatly concerned."

The old woman had a hundred grave sympathetic gestures to go with her fund of information. "She says 'There can be no sudden change,'" Carla translated. "'The Pope is an old man, but today he is feeling a little stronger after a good night.'"

"Thank her," Sam said, "and tell her I'll keep in touch with her if she doesn't mind. She is better than any bulletin board."

"She says your concern is very touching. Not enough busy pleasure-seeking young men have your devout interest. She would like us to have a coffee tomorrow, Sam, if you are agreeable."

"We are agreeable," Sam said, bowing and telling the same thing to the old woman with his eyes; and then they went on their way.

The old woman, turning, watched them with satisfaction. A good man. A devout man. Concerned about the Holy Father.

121]

Agnese should be told about him. And even if the girl did not have a wedding ring on her finger it did not necessarily mean they were not married. The squeaking bed—it was the fault of the mattress. Agnese would not have noticed how often the bed made the squeaking noises if the girl had not been an American, and if it was not the common opinion that American girls were frank and blunt and like men about such matters. Her son, Tomaso, used to talk a lot about the American women, but they hadn't been the ones who had spoiled him for the priesthood.

As she watched Sam and Carla turn into her place, she hoped the girl would have a wedding ring on when they came visiting tomorrow.

CHAPTER **13**

IN ONE of the little boutiques Sam bought Carla two dresses; a plain and simply cut elegant navy-blue dress, and a yellow one cut low on the shoulders. And he also bought her a big brown leather purse. As he took out his wallet he knew she hadn't the slightest interest in what it cost him. And those eighty thousand lire—one hundred and twenty-eight dollars—might be only a beginning! When he got her out of the store he sighed with relief. But all that really mattered to him then was that she should want to feel beautiful again.

As soon as they got home she tried on the new dresses, first the blue, then the yellow one. Under the dress she had only a garter belt, and when she paraded up and down, her behind seemed to float and sway.

"Don't you wear a girdle or anything, Carla?" he asked.

"Of course I don't," she said impatiently. "No Italian girl with any kind of a good figure wants to wear a girdle." It was true, he supposed, as he watched her sit down at the mirror to work on her make-up. All the well-dressed women he had seen on the streets of Rome proudly displayed their behinds in this fashion, too.

"At home," he said, sitting down and folding his arms as he

watched her, "I had a rather small place of my own. A nice bachelor apartment in a place called the Lancaster Arms."

"Uhhu," she said, hardly listening as she studied her left eyelid.

"And then I had another place farther downtown I used as a studio."

"Uhhu."

"I'm not a man who has many close intimate friends, Carla," he said, wanting her to know all about him. "Oh, I'd drink with newspaper people. I think I was what you might call a convivial man, and yet it was when I was alone in my studio, doing my work, that I really felt alive. But I think a man needs at least one intimate friend to communicate with." Pausing, he waited for her to turn, to ask a question. She showed no interest at all in the life he had led back home, and it hurt him a little. "Well, what about you, Carla?"

"Me?" she asked, turning slowly. "What about me?"

"Did you make friends easily?"

"Umm, uhhu."

"Somehow I imagine that as you grew up you were alone a lot. How about it?"

"I guess so," she said, taking a Kleenex from her purse. When she had wiped some of the lipstick from her mouth, she stared solemnly at her image in the mirror.

"Are your people still alive?" he asked, trying to touch a part of her life Alberto hadn't discussed; so he could have something of her for himself. "You talk so well, Carla," he went on. "You seem to have read so much, you have a natural gift for words," he added, trying to flatter her vanity. "You must have been good at history at school. Where did you go to school?"

"What is this?" she asked, turning suddenly. "Don't you know all about me by this time? My name's Carla Caneli. This is my town. I sleep with you. You know something more about me every day, don't you? Would you be happier if I made up some stories about my life, told you some lies? Why are you trying to worry me?"

"I'm not trying to worry you."

[124

"Well, all right then."

The cleansing tissues she had been using had been falling on the floor, and he got up and picked up one, then another, hoping she would notice what he was doing. At home he had been a clean orderly man, and now he had to hide his annoyance. Was she just naturally sloppy about everything but her physical appearance? he wondered. Would he have to clean up after her every day, clean the kitchen, the bathroom, and get down on his knees and scrub the kitchen floor, then hang up her dresses, pick up her stockings, make the bed while she lay around? He straightened up, ready to vent his exasperation, then grew afraid. If he dwelt on the indignities he suffered he would lose all respect for her, and without the respect he might lose his view of her, too.

"What's the matter?" she asked suddenly.

"Nothing. Nothing at all," he said quietly. "Let's go out."

"Are those the only shoes you have, Sam?"

"What's the matter with them?"

"The heavy thick soles. Look at them."

"They're an expensive English shoe for walking around a lot. I like them."

"Sam, no one around here wears such heavy soles. Can't you get another pair?"

"Maybe I could," he said, surprised that she could turn from herself and notice anything about him. "I'll get an elegant pair of thin-soled Italian shoes tomorrow, Carla."

"And I don't know why you want to go on wearing that outfit," she said, making a face.

"What's the matter with it?" He had put on the gray jacket and the dark-gray slacks and the fawn-colored shirt he had worn that first night in Rome when he had encountered her on the street.

"Oh, Sam. You look like a tweedy Englishman. Can't you wear something else and look a little more as though you belonged?"

"I don't mind at all," he said, delighted with her attention. Changing his clothes, he put on his dark-blue flannel suit, and

125]

laid away the gray jacket with the feeling that he might be putting it aside for good. But it was a hopeful sign, he told himself. She no longer wanted anything about him to remind her of the circumstances of their meeting that first night in Parioli.

That day they loafed around, just getting the feel of the city. They looked at the ruins of the old Roman wall on the lower Via Veneto, then they went to the Farnese Gardens. She had some amusing scandal about the Farneses in the old days. Then they took a taxi to Trastevere. "There's a church you should see," she said. And when they stood by the fountain in the piazza looking at Santa Maria he had to keep a straight face, not letting on he had been there with Alberto. He let her tell him all about the church. Then they had dinner. All evening she was eloquent and pleased with herself. When they got home at midnight she was tired out. And in the morning when he woke up at ten the church bells were ringing.

He had never heard so many bells, and as he lay there listening, he thought of her scolding him for his remarks when he had looked up at the obelisk and the church at the top of the Spanish Steps. It was a good thing that she clung to her religion, he thought. She might like to take him to St. Peter's.

"Carla, wake up," he said shaking her. "It's ten o'clock. Aren't you going out to mass? You could take me to St. Peter's."

"Uhhu," she muttered.

"Come on, you'll be late."

"I think I'll sleep in this morning," she said drowsily, and as she snuggled against him, he wondered if she ever went to church. Why did he want her to go to church? he wondered . . . Probably because it was a place where she might get a feeling of certainty and security. It would be good for her. It was too bad he had no feeling himself for church. Not his poor mother's fault. She would have been better off if she had stuck to her Bible. As for himself, he just didn't have the temperament for it. From the time he had been at college he had achieved a certain tranquility and composure by accepting the fact that there were certain things he could never know. Then he thought of those Old Testament figures on the ceiling of the Sistine Chapel. Just figures out of a tribal folklore. Could he honestly believe it would be good for Carla to have those old prophets gripping her imagination now? Being a woman though, she would take only what she needed from church. It was too bad he wasn't a Catholic himself. Or a Protestant, or one of those amusing dogmatic atheists, or a strict orthodox Communist. What was the matter with him that they all wearied him? It was the times, he was sure. All the ideologies changing from day to day, right under his eyes, so how could a man look to any one of them for an enlargement of his freedom? It was all too wearying. Look somewhere else. But where? Just the same, he thought, pondering over it, it would be a good thing for a girl like Carla if she got up and went to church.

A half hour later he got her up to go out for breakfast so the Ferraros, hearing them hurrying down the stairs, would think they were going to a late mass. It seemed to him that if the Ferraros felt sure of them, could place them, it would help him to feel more sure of himself with Carla.

"Since we're having coffee with them this afternoon," he said, "I think I'll ask the daughter if we can pay her to come in every day to clean for us." And he waited for her to say, "Oh, no, I can do it, Sam. There's so little to do."

"Why not?" she said. "I'm not good at that kind of thing."

"This afternoon let's take an air with them. Let's be fine superior people of great dignity," he said as if he were joking.

"If you find it necessary, Sam, go ahead," she said, turning on the stair. "I am what I am. I can't help it." Her words remained with him, worrying him for hours. He didn't know how she would behave with other people.

When they walked into the Ferraro apartment, the old lady, bowing and smiling, said softly. "Ciao," and put out her hand. Her little brown face wrinkled up, her brown eyes gleamed, and with her little gestures she said all the courteous things. Agnese, smiling too, said, " 'Ello," and then more slowly, "I am happy." And they sat down and began their little coffee party. The Ferraros offered them biscuits with the coffee. Acting only as interpreter Carla, her hands folded on her lap, was utterly

127]

impersonal. She would turn to them, then turn to him, then turn again. Watching her, he felt like a spectator at a tennis game, with the ball being bounced back and forth. Signora Ferraro, bobbing her head encouragingly, asked Sam about Canada, having a special interest. Carla translated. The old woman had a nephew from North Italy, a poor boy from a lumber mill who had got tired of the seasonal unemployment, and who had migrated to Canada to work on the railway. For a year the boy had lived in the bush in a boxcar. Did many of Sam's countrymen live in boxcars in the bush? Had Sam ever lived in a boxcar? she wanted to know. Regretfully Sam explained that he had no experience with boxcars. Just the same, the old woman said, she would write to her nephew in his boxcar and tell him she had met a nice man from his adopted country. And Sam thanked her, and hoped he might meet her nephew back home, and asked her if she had any further news of the Pope.

A very great Pope, this one, the old woman explained, her black eyes sparkling. An intellectual. But very mystical too. It was said that he had had a vision. Just as thousands that day in Portugal had seen the sun dancing in the sky, he had seen the same thing later in his own garden, and she turned to Agnese for confirmation. Agnese had been sitting quietly, listening with the serenity of the unaware. Now a little flush came on her pale homely face and enchantment in her eyes. The Holy Father would die soon, she said to Carla, so she could translate for Sam, although he had a brilliant doctor, a man who did not need the assistance of those doctors offered by the great rulers of the world. Yes, the Pope could die and quickly be made a saint. No, he was indeed a saint now. Nodding approvingly and swelling with importance, the old lady whispered confidentially. There was a certain discontent among the cardinals. The Pope, in the splendor of his great intellect, had neglected them a little. There would be changes made, and Signor Raymond should understand that when the Pope died it was like the end of a regime in Rome. Jobs would be lost and new faces would become prominent.

Did Signor Raymond understand? Indeed he did, Sam said solemnly, trying to get Carla's eye. Surely she could see that these women were her Italians, too, he thought. Devout, orthodox and plain like a family she might meet in Brooklyn or Malta or Ireland. But Carla's eyes were on Agnese whose glowing face and softening eyes gave her a look of warmth and happiness. And Carla, watching in wonder, turned to Sam. "It means so much to her. It's like a flame, I guess," she said in a dreamy tone. "I knew a woman once who just liked being in church, just liked sitting alone in church. It was the one place she could go where she was happy. It was her only real happiness, I think. The best she had ever known."

"You say . . . please . . . ?" said Agnese, who had got some of the English words.

"Carla," said Sam quickly. The room was so heavily shadowed, there was so little light from the small windows, that she missed his glance. She had begun to translate her story in the same bemused tone. When she had finished there was an awkward silence. Sam saw a flush come on Agnese's neck. He could have shaken Carla for being concerned only with her own thoughts. The trouble he had expected seemed to be close at hand. The old woman was out of it. But he felt caught in the lives of the two young women. With dread he watched Agnese's eyes go to Carla's legs, then to her breasts and her throat, and just for the moment she looked distressed, as if she felt she was to be pitied, and her eyes were full of virgin malice. Then Sam coughed, and Carla, catching his eye, stood up in some ashamed awareness that she had hurt Agnese.

"Sam, it's time we were on our way. We'll be late."

And he stood up, as did Agnese with a saintly smile. Then he glanced at Carla. She suddenly looked bored and restless. Yet she went to Agnese with both hands out, talking rapidly in Italian, her face alive with warm appreciation and respect. He didn't think she was acting. He thought it had hurt her that she had carelessly belittled Agnese's secret simple happiness. The graciousness with which she communicated a sense of intimate companionship with Agnese, smiling, then laughing as they held hands, filled Sam with wonder. It was as if she couldn't bear to have had a hand in the belittlement of the happiness of any other human being. And when they got outside he said, "You were splendid. And I had thought you were getting on edge."

"Of course I was on edge. What do you think I am?" she asked impatiently. "Thank God, I'm out in the sunlight. And don't you dare have that Agnese snooping around upstairs." After they walked for twenty paces she turned on him, worried. "Why did you land me in there with you and that pair? I'd look at you and look at them—" He could see she was in a bad mood.

"We had to make that visit. Forget it," he said. They walked along silently.

At an intersection a woman with a vegetable pushcart, her two dirty-faced little children crowded under the cart, was arguing with a woman in a car who had come close to hitting one of the children. And as Carla stopped, she said nervously, "Those Ferraros. Right now they're wondering what I'm doing living with you. And I'm wondering too." He could barely hear her. The pushcart woman, her children tugging at her big apron, was shouting imprecations at the other woman in the car. "Sitting with those women I never felt so out of place," she said nervously. "I'm a fish out of water." And then growing more worried she said, "Look, you drew a picture of me. Are you an artist? Do you want to paint me, or something?"

"I don't want to paint you."

"Just suddenly, you don't look right," she said uneasily. "You must be a queer man."

Then a wild angry cry came from the pushcart mother as the other woman's car, moving slowly forward, caused one of the children to grab the leg of the cart. Some fruit fell on the pavement. The screaming woman and the crying children seemed to make Sam more aware that he was losing whatever hold he thought he had on Carla. Her worried eyes told him she was questioning even the little she had seen of him. Her eyes, and the shouts of the quarreling women in a language he did not understand, made him feel completely alone again. How isolated he was in the city, he thought. Nothing he could say or do would have any meaning in the life of this city. The two people he knew in Rome, a tired and defeated movie maker, and an Italian woman with Lesbian instincts, two queer ones, would never invite him to their homes or introduce him to their friends. Moreover, he couldn't even talk to his landlady without an interpreter . . . There was only this girl, all on edge now from not having had a drink for days, regarding him sullenly in some sudden painful awareness of the indignity of her position with him. It seemed to remind her of all the shameful indignities of her life, and perhaps made her want with all her heart to find the strength and courage to kick him out of her life. A little flush came on his face. With his lonely angry eyes he tried grimly to hold on to her while he felt her pulling so fiercely away. "Who are you anyway?" she asked suddenly. "What made you think you had the right to take me to your room?" When Sam did not answer, standing there with the angry flush, the strength he showed in his silent refusal to explain himself was the strength in him that made her feel she had to give him pleasure.

"You don't look any different than any of them I met when I was with Alberto," she continued fiercely. "You and Alberto. It's disgusting. He won't come after me and beat me now like he always does, will he? You two must have something in common. Do you cry over yourself too?" When he still wouldn't deign to answer she went on, "You think you make me feel cheap and weak. Well you don't, do you hear?" And there were tears of frantic rage in her eyes. "You only make me feel ugly. Like it's been ugly for me for so long. Like it's ugly now with the dirty feel of your right to me." And then desperately, "I can't stand to be any place where I feel ugly."

The force of her urge to flee from him frightened him. It told him she could never recover a shred of her self-respect while she felt she was deep in the gutter with him. They stared at each other, tense and wondering. Suddenly he gripped her arm, and she went to jerk away and run, and then, unable to find the courage to do it, she looked trapped and desperate. She taunted him. "Why don't you tell me to go to hell, Sam? Why don't you get yourself another girl?"

"You were to show me the old places, remember, Carla? All right, why are we standing here? Now come on." And he walked her away as if he were letting her lead him back into the past, a place where she might feel more at home with him.

CHAPTER 14

AMONG the ruins, telling him lively and intimate stories about dead old Romans, she could have him with her, yet forget her abject need of him. And he too had to have a place where he could hold on to her, and yet have her feel free to be at ease and happy and excited with him. The place where they seemed best able to meet each other was in the timeless past. Their own lives, what they really were to each other, seemed to hang suspended in another time.

It had got a little cooler. The earnest Americans, the English who acted as if Rome had long been their private museum, the French, the busy Germans, all bustled around the city with their cameras; and there were always foreign priests, confident that they could not be strangers. With Baedekers and cameras they all rushed at monuments and discovered old altar pieces. But Sam and Carla couldn't feel that they belonged with the tourists. He had to watch himself with her. He couldn't forget that the urge to flee was in her. He knew that if he ever laughed at her as she told her stories, if he ever showed scorn of her for offering herself to him as a Roman woman, he would be dragging her back into the real world and her situation with him that secretly tormented her. Yet in spite of himself, her pretenses sometimes disgusted him. A girl from Brooklyn or

Jersey, or wherever she's from, actually making herself believe she's a Roman woman. Sam would think of this and he would want to sneer. Checking himself he would ponder over the protective layers, the resources in the human personality; and then look at her again in wonder.

She didn't seem to be concerned with the dead, but with living people. She had the little intimate touches, the casual bits of information, the sense of familiarity that made the people she talked about appear to be waiting around the next corner. And gradually she began to completely beguile him.

At Nero's Golden House, or when merely walking along the stone-banked Tiber under the street lights, then into the shadows, he lost his feeling that he had been walking with her in a world of ghosts. "Listen," she would say, taking his arm; she would tell him a story about someone who had drowned in the river. It was as if she were always gossiping with relish about her neighbors. "I don't go much for Cicero, but as a lawyer, he's smooth," she would say. "What a job he did on Clodia. I wonder what Clodia thought, listening to the smooth old mouthpiece proving she was the biggest tramp in Rome?" Who was Clodia? Catullus' girl friend? Sam wondered, ashamed of his ignorance. At another time it was Julia. "Maybe you can figure out what happened to Julia," she said. "I figure it had something to do with her old man. Whatever way you look at it, Augustus was just too big a wheel for a father. The old man had everything. Imagine, a girl whose father was boss of the whole world. Well, not of her. That's a natural human reaction, I think. Julia wants to feel she's her own living flesh. Something of her own that makes her wanted. Something the big wheel couldn't run over. But heavens, Sam, she does it on streets and in alleys, with everybody who picks her up, they say. The girl puzzles me. I mean, why doesn't she give a damn?" And if they were in the Borghese Gardens, it was still the place where wild wanton Messalina had fled. And since she was so much at ease with him now, Sam waited for her to talk about herself, or at least as she saw it, and when she couldn't or wouldn't he wondered if she didn't trust her own knowledge of herself.

At Hadrian's tomb she had him standing beside her, rapt and wondering. That day there were twenty other tourists within speaking distance, middle-aged women, four solemn men with glasses, a group of young girls from a school in Switzerland. But it seemed to Sam these people came from nowhere and were going nowhere; out of time, they were just shadowy spectators, for Carla was saying to him softly and with affection, "Yes, Hadrian! Every time I think of him I say, 'What a guy.' We'll go out to his villa tomorrow, eh? He has nobility, Sam, real nobility, and don't you believe those stories about him being a homosexual. What's there to go on? The guy is fond of his boy, they say. You know the one I mean? The one who was drowned in Egypt? Hadrian in his barge, and the boy swimming out and away from him. Farther and farther away, till he drowned. What went on? I don't know and neither do you. Naturally Hadrian was heartbroken. But maybe he thought of the boy as a son. What do you say, Sam?"

"What do I say . . ." And then he saw that she looked as concerned as if she were asking his good opinion of an old close friend, and he was ready to reassure her, as if Hadrian's good reputation in town was important to him too. The group of schoolgirls from Switzerland passed by; he heard their bright young voices. Suddenly he felt angry and exasperated with himself. For days he had been letting her enchant him without wanting to break the spell or change her at all.

"What do I say?" he repeated impatiently. "I say Hadrian's in his tomb and not worrying about me. I'd like a hot dog or a plate of pork and beans."

"Oh."

"It makes me feel I'd like to be at a football game, with a Coca-Cola in one hand and a hot dog in the other. I wonder how Hadrian would do as a ball carrier? What would they call him? 'Hadrian, the galloping ghost'?"

"You fool," she whispered, then she hurried away from him. Ashamed of himself he sauntered after her, but she heard him and broke into a little trot. He had to run to catch up to her.

"Come on, Carla. I was only trying to sound like a tourist,"

135]

he lied with an awkward laugh. "Where's your sense of humor?" As he went to take her arm, she swung her bag at him savagely and hit him on the mouth. "You little showboat," he said fiercely, and he slapped her face. "You behave, you hear." A middle-aged couple who had passed them turned, hearing the slap. "Try it again and you'll get it again," Sam muttered and he gripped her arm. Pale and distraught, her eyes blazing, she pulled him along. "I told you I was trying to sound like a tourist," he lied, "and that's all there is to it." Where she was leading him he didn't know, and she didn't seem to care. Behind her silence he felt her trembling violence. Sometimes he would glance at the red mark on her face, hoping it would soon vanish. Crossing a bridge, they followed the Tiber bank. They walked in silence for an hour. When he walked her to a taxi he wondered if she would get in with him. They drove to the restaurant where they had been the first night together. They ate little, without speaking. When they got home she went into the bedroom and closed the door. Much later when he came to bed she seemed to be sound asleep, and he felt much better. All the walking had tired him and he fell asleep. A rustling sound awoke him. He didn't know what time it was. The bedroom was full of moonlight, and he could see her moving against the window. Stark naked, she went to the dresser drawer and pulled it open, hesitated, and then began to pace up and down. When she crossed by the window the moonlight silvered her naked body. She was like a panther in her tense and silent pacing. His heart began to beat so loudly he thought she would hear it. In his frightened alertness he was acutely aware that at Hadrian's tomb, making jibes about her flights of imagination, crudely belitting her, he must have jarred all her emotions. It was as if her flights into the old days had completely taken the place of alcohol for her. Shaken by the apparent loss of his understanding, she was wildly at loose ends. He might just as well have touched an exposed raw nerve. Whenever it was touched she would be as tense and fierce as she was now. In her nervous pacing she had folded her arms across her breasts. Suddenly she turned to the window. The moonlight was on her left breast and her flank. Stiff and proud, she stood there, listening to the night sounds of Rome as if remembering all those sordid nights when she had wandered on the streets. Her words about Julia, he thought. The ancient night-wandering wild slut. Suddenly she turned from the window and went to the chair where she had thrown her dress. In the shadow he could hardly see what she was doing, there was just the white gleam on her hip. Suddenly he jumped out of bed. He came leaping across the room in the dark, his big body throwing a great shadow; he flashed through the moonlight. And as she straightened up, then leaped toward the door, he grabbed her. Nothing was said. They wrestled fiercely, and as their bodies lurched into the path of moonlight she tried to bite him. Grabbing her by the hair, he jerked her mouth away from his shoulder. As she panted, clawing at him, they fell on the floor, and then suddenly, with his weight on her and his fierce tight grip on her wrists, she couldn't move. They lay in shadow beside the bed, which blocked the window light. Her whole body began to tremble under his. She sobbed a little. Suddenly her arms came around him convulsively. Her hands came to his head, pulling his mouth down to her wet warm mouth. Though his thoughts whirled wildly, he seemed to know that the slap he had given her, then his body hurling through the shadows, and their cruel fierce silent struggle in the dark somehow satisfied her imagination.

In the morning she was content and gentle with him, as if she knew they were back together again.

CHAPTER 15

SHE had begun to cost him more
money than he could afford. On the streets she wanted to be
lavish with beggars, and she always seemed to be riding with
him in taxicabs. It had become important to him, too, that
she have money in her purse so she wouldn't have to turn to
him with her hand out. She had taken it for granted, as had
Alberto and Francesca, that he was a man of means. To en-
courage her to go out by herself and do the marketing, he
showed her he was keeping as much as two hundred dollars
in lire notes in the bureau drawer under his pile of shirts, and
he urged her to go out shopping alone, but she wouldn't.
Though she might be one of those ruinously expensive women,
and he worried about having no job now, yet in his heart he
didn't care. In the bank at home he had a nest egg of seven
thousand dollars, but he had some deep secret stubborn stirring
conviction that everything he had saved, the money in his bank,
any knowledge he had picked up in England and France, whatever talent he had and had tried to develop in the years of his
obsession with his painting, was all like something he had
saved up to use in his experience with her.

Having established his credit in the office of the American
Express by the Spanish Steps, he could be seen going in there,

as he used to go into the bank at home. Living as a man of means he knew he might last six months, but back in his mind he counted on the Pope dying; sooner or later, he told himself —one month, three months, six months—the Pope would die —in spite of Signora Ferraro's daily prayers—and he would get a cable from the *Weekly* asking him to go on the job, and he would have a salary again. Carla did not ask him why he wasn't using his camera at the places where she took him. It seemed to him that she wanted to forget that he was the photographer she had met in Parioli.

They wouldn't leave the apartment till early afternoon, for they slept late, and sometimes he would have to wait an hour and a half while she sat at her mirror, satisfying herself with the perfection of her appearance.

"You look fine, Carla. Come on," he would say impatiently.

"Just a minute, Sam," and she would smooth an eyebrow, wet her lower lip and mark it again or rearrange her hair, while he waited and watched and grew more exasperated and felt belittled. Sometimes as she stared at her image in the mirror she would catch his eye on her and smile faintly. Did she expect him to share her conviction that she should not appear in public with him unless she was satisfied with the smallest detail in the picture she would make walking beside him, or was she beating and bullying him? he wondered. With a sigh, he would get up finally and begin to tidy up in the bedroom. In her presence, under the sting of her indifference, he would do the cleaning while she prettied herself. He would make the bed, hang up a dress she had thrown over a chair, pick up her stockings from the floor; then stare glumly at her dresser, spattered with powder and dirty tissues marked with lipstick and know that when they came in he would have to clean up the dresser, too. When he had tidied up the room he would sit down and watch the little movements of her shoulders as she bent back and forth at the mirror, intently scrutinizing and worrying about some shadow on her face.

"What about those dirty dishes in the sink? Are you going to go out and leave them?" he wanted to say brutally, yet he couldn't. As he waited motionless, suffering in his loss of dignity, he took it out in wild thoughts about her. Why was she so careful about washing her own body? he wondered. Why did she take the little sponge baths, then oil herself with unguents and perfumes, and remain so indifferent to the look of the rooms? Was this the Roman influence, too? In his imagination, which had been tormented by all the pictures of emaciated medieval saints he had been seeing, he seemed to see an old monkish hermit, reeking of filth himself, point at her in the mirror and say, gleefully, "See, all clean on the outside and dirty with sin on the inside," and he would stand up abruptly, damning the thousand years around him.

But then she would turn and say, "I'm ready, Sam. How do I look?"

"Lovely," he would say, then tell himself with relief and compassion, she was secretly aware of what she was doing to him. She had to push him, wait for him to turn against her; always testing in the daytime that measure of security she found when she had him in her arms at night.

It was only at night, when they had come home and were undressing, that she gave him that odd confident lewd little smile, then lay naked on the bed and drained him of all his doubts and fears. When she had him exhausted she would raise herself on her elbow and look down at him gravely. Only then would she turn out the light and go to sleep, leaving him wide awake, discontented and put off from any real knowledge of her, and no closer to that picture he had of her in his mind.

The nights were still warm. The bedcovers thrown off, he would lie awake listening to her regular breathing. A night breeze came through the wide open window. The alien silence of the Roman night began to disturb him. It wasn't like night in his own city, no heavy rumbling traffic, no low everlasting subway rumble; just a lewdly whispering city. Then he would admit to himself that the woman beside him, breathing heavily in sleep, didn't care who he was or where he came from. It humiliated him. On this bed he was no closer to her than he had been day after day, following her in her fancies around

Rome. Then he seemed to hear a voice jeering, "And you in that bed with her are just another figment of her imagination. You don't touch her at all." It could be true, he thought, under the jolt of the humiliation. On how many beds in how many places had she picked up the little tricks she used in her love-making? *Ah, Mamma mia.* The soft low moan; the custom of this country's thousands of pairs in rooms like this, clinging and grappling till the practiced little moan was heard; the cry of the dove. *Dove*—was that how you pronounced it? No, *dove*, like the diver. "Where to?" says the diver—after the soft little moan.

He had been lying with his leg against her hip, and her warm woman's smell and the touch of her flesh suddenly seemed alien. A strip of moonlight reaching the bed fell on her bare leg. Her nightdress had got drawn up to her thighs. As he rolled away from her, the bedspring squeaked. A depressing sound. *Squeak, squeak, squeak,* night after night the rhythmical long squeaking, with the Ferraros downstairs listening, as if squeaks were little cries.

Little cries, little cries, telling the Ferraros he had in no way really possessed her; she was there with him only because it was better than being alone. He might have been anyone else. What about that? As a matter of fact, aside from being there with his appetite for her, how had he changed her? They got along; she gave him all he wanted in bed. Was that why he hadn't brought her one step closer to that picture he had had of her in the hotel room; a proud, happy, self-contained girl with some secret quiet enjoyment of her independence of spirit? Was he scared she wouldn't feel compelled to offer him all her sensuality if she came to see him as anyone other than her protector? Suddenly he felt he was being cheated. She was hold-ing out on him, not caring. Yet what a woman she could be if he could only shake her loose from her delusions and fears, make her mistress of her own mind and heart, voluntarily opening her arms to him. But she didn't want it this way. In her dread of the real thing, she struggled with him day by day, slipped away from him into her dreams, used all the tricks of her

141]

body to keep him away from her heart. Now he began to feel baffled and angry. The more he pondered over it, the more it seemed to him he was not only failing her, he was failing himself as he had so often failed with form and color in his studio, trying to express a vision on a canvas.

That urge to see her and have her as he knew she should be, gnawed away at him and he sat up in bed. The faint streak of moonlight had reached the far corner of the room. He bent over her shadowed face on the pillow. How sweetly and softly and peacefully she slept, he thought. If he could only break into her dreams, catch the shape of the things that gave her sweet calmness. Full of compassion he bent and kissed her cheek, and watching her, he whispered, "You're not putting me off any more, Carla. That spark, that light will come back into your face and eyes. I know it will, because I've seen it. And when it does, it'll be like meeting you for the first time. It'll be different with us then, won't it, Carla? It'll come. Because, you see, you're not such an odd one. Supposing you can't bear to be alone. It's a common predicament. It's the same with most people. How many do you know who can bear to sit alone very long in a room? They rush out and do things that are just as silly and crazy as the things you do, only they don't even know they're scared to be alone. Millions of people share your predicament, only they don't feel it as intensely as you do, Carla. They haven't got the imagination. And what's so uncommon about hating the places where you grew up and where bad things happened to you, and wanting to get away from them? It's almost normal, Carla. A common failing. A flight into the past. Okay. But I knew scholars who gave their whole lives to a love of ancient Rome or Athens. The good old days. Poets do it, and even politicians. And as for this secret nervous fear you have of anything and everything that makes you throw yourself at people, maybe you only feel a little more intensely what's in the air for everybody. You know what Francesca said? She said, 'Think of what one bomb will do to the Sistine Chapel,' and she shuddered, mind you. Solid Francesca!" Bending again, he brushed his lips against her hair. "Poor Carla. It's not the

[142

blown-up earth you worry about. I think it must be that when you're alone you seem to be standing on the shore of a world's sea of fear. Okay. I'll get you singing again. By God, I will. I'll get you, bit by bit, so you don't mind being alone, and when you don't mind any more, you'll sing. What'll you think of me then, Carla? What'll you say when you don't need me as a crutch?"

In her sleep beside him she sighed, muttered, and he thought he had awakened her, then she turned on her side and hunched up her knees. Lying down, he put his arm around her, drew close to her and went on worrying and planning.

Next day he began, very cunningly, to play little tricks on her. Out on the streets he would ask her to get him some cigarettes, and while she was in the store he would wander away, hide himself in a doorway and watch for her to come out of the store. Hurrying out, she would hesitate, look both ways, stand very still, like a child on the street, fearful of moving away in either direction; then start to go slowly the wrong way. After five minutes, if she had stopped at a street corner, he would hurry after her and pretend to be irritated. "Why did you go that way, Carla? Why didn't you look the other way? I was back there looking in a window." And she would stammer and be close to admitting to him that she felt an uneasy dread of all things when she was alone. She was able to wander off alone, as she had done the night she had met him, only after she had been drinking. Then, stiffening, she would smile too brightly.

"It's of no importance. What's the matter?" she would say. It was as if he had set a trap and, after a quick fierce struggle, she had got away from him again. The bright anxious smile made him suffer. He wanted to put his arms around her. Oh, Carla, Carla, how it hurts me to see you like this. No one should need anyone this much. You must not have this need of some-one.

By this time they were having their coffee in the morning in the little kitchen in their own place. Sometimes he would say that he had to get some cigarettes, and run out cheerfully, leaving her there alone ten minutes—then fifteen minutes—then a half hour. Each time he would make it a little longer. But after a half hour he would imagine her saying to herself, "He may never come back," and hurry home to her.

Once he went as far as the Via Veneto, and stayed away for an hour. But he stood on the corner in a position from which he could watch their street. Sometimes he looked uneasily at his watch. Yet he stood there grimly, even though tormented by thoughts of her becoming frantic and hurrying out to get a drink. When he came back, he found her sitting at the table sipping her coffee. "Hello there," she said, casually. Yet she got up and walked around, holding one arm, then the other, then turning to him, trying to laugh.

He could never tell whether she knew he was playing these tricks on her, or was still acting from her nameless fears.

Since he still owed Francesca some money, Sam telephoned her and offered to meet her. At five, she said, she would meet him at Doney's. Then he told Carla he had to meet a newspaperman at the Foreign Press Club. He wrote down the club address on the Via della Mercedes, told her to wait an hour and a half and then take a taxi. He would be outside the club, he said. He made a joke of it. Knowing her, he said, it would take her at least that long to get dressed.

"That's fine," she said, not giving in in any way. "It's just fine." When he turned at the door, her eyes, lonely and a little desperate, were on him. He could feel her pulling away, struggling, holding on to the grand illusion that she was a legendary Roman woman with a sensual grip on him he couldn't break. "Don't be late, Sam," she said, trying to smile. "I'll be there on time, I hope." But he noticed she was clutching the paper on which he had written the address, clutching it so tightly in her left hand that the knuckles gleamed.

On the street in the late afternoon sunlight, he told himself he needn't worry; her need of his protection, her knowledge that he would be waiting, would overcome any impulse she might have, born of anxiety. The sun was so strong, it was such a change from the apartment, that he felt good.

For days now he had been absorbed in Carla, as absorbed as he used to be painting at night in his studio. Why was the Roman sky so blue? he wondered, striding along. Was it because factory chimneys weren't belching smoke all day long as they did at home? Rome had so many places that would have a special interest for him. Right now he would be within fifteen minutes of the artists' quarter. At home he had kept away from painters and their parties; now he wished he could be sure enough of Carla to walk with her along that street of ruins he had heard of, the Muro Torto, have her take him one evening to a party with the painters on the Via Marguta. Was Chirico still alive, and did he live around here? Sam wondered. That sculptor, Amerigo Tot, might be only minutes away. And that pretty little painter of nudes, Novella—what's her name? Someone at the Press Club had said she lived near the Spanish Steps. Turning onto the Via Veneto he quickened. There were the café terraces with their bright-colored canopies, and sitting in the sunlight the elegant silver-blondes, the whores, a prince or two and the middle-aged Norwegians, Germans, Americans; all looking as if some cupidity, some sin of the flesh, was in their minds or they would be at other cafés. He liked the picture they made. As he sat down at the end table on the terrace at Doney's near the hotel, he noticed a middle-aged man on the corner, standing still as a statue, beautifully posed, elegantly dressed, with iron-gray hair. Surely this one ought to be the brother of that young Italian he had seen posing in the sunlight in front of the Pariola hotel his first morning in Rome, he thought, smiling.

A wedding reception was coming out of the Excelsior Hotel, middle-class people making a fine splash. Some merchant's daughter. A rich shopkeeper. An overdressed middle-aged woman, talking to a group of other middle-aged women, had on a rich green dress and a green hat with a wide wine-colored ribbon. Monstrosity. A horror. You see, Carla, he thought, as if she were sitting there with him, this is Italian style too. Not much taste, eh? You'd see these horrors in any big city. Then he seemed to see her sniff and toss her head. "At least they're not afraid of a little color, Sam. Oh, for God's sake, don't you understand this family has been saving up for six years to put on this splash for that poor homely bowlegged daughter?" And then he saw Francesca with her fresh and pretty round face, getting out of a taxi. And with her was Alberto, gaunt and noble-looking, beautifully tailored in gray. Alberto had a big warm brotherly smile for him. Yes, he would let Sam buy him a drink.

"My dear friend," Alberto said, sitting down. "How are you? I have thought of you, oh so many times."

"Yes, how are you, Sam?" Francesca asked, looking at him closely. "I have wanted so much to have a talk. I told you to call on me, Sam."

Their good-humored indulgent curiosity offended Sam. "First things first," he said calmly. From his breast pocket he took the air-line folder which he still used for his Italian money, and solemnly, like an earnest little shopkeeper with a customer, he counted out the lire he owed Francesca. Her earnest expression as she, in turn, counted the money amused him, and he enjoyed too the way Alberto, like a great gentleman, delicately looked the other way till the sordid commercial transaction was concluded.

"Now, tell us how you are getting along, Sam," Francesca said eagerly.

"Getting along? Me? Everything's fine," he said. "How about you, Alberto? Are you feeling better?"

"Much better," Alberto said warmly. "I am concluding my affairs here. I leave soon for The States. Oh, Sam, I feel it is not accidental that we met. I told you it was providential. Yes, that's the word, providential." With a charming smile, his voice full of gratitude, he reached out and patted Sam on the shoulder. "I know it must give you pleasure to see me feeling so good. It is a great thing, eh, Sam?" It was as if he felt that Sam ought to be richly rewarded to see that he had helped a good man recover the splendor of his self-esteem.

"I did all this for this good man," Sam could say to himself.

Already he had been in touch with Irving Stein in New York,

[146

Alberto went on. The money was there. The percentages arranged. Stein wanted to go over the story with him. This time, oh, this was the thing—Alberto would have his percentage. Talking on and on with a bright nervous confidence, he didn't once ask for Carla.

The unfeeling bastard. What do I care for his plans? Sam thought. It would be a pleasure to punch the self-centered maniac right on the nose. And then he caught an expression in Alberto's eyes. The man secretly didn't believe a word of what he was saying, Sam thought. Shaken and sick, Alberto had a hunch he would never get back his health and strength, maybe never get to New York again. Had he let Carla go, as he had let his movie go? In his desperate vanity was Alberto clinging to the only passion he had left that would take nothing more out of him; the quest for the right words to convince himself he would live long enough to make another good movie?

"Whatever you do, look after yourself, Alberto," Sam said gently, feeling pity for him.

"Now, now, Sam. It is you who look a little tired," Alberto said elaborately. "Is it not so, Francesca?" and he winked at her. "Look at his eyes. See how drawn he looks. I know that look, eh, Francesca?" and he laughed knowingly. "Ah, Sam. You are a glutton."

"Yes, you do look a little pale and exhausted," Francesca said, regarding him thoughtfully.

"Just the same, you are a young man," Alberto said. "A younger man than I am. That is the whole thing."

"Just the same, you are having the Italian look very quickly, Sam," Francesca said.

"What is that look, Francesca?"

"Lassitude. The women move slowly, haven't you noticed?"

"In them it is a pleasant look."

"Is it a pleasant feeling, Sam?"

"I have not this feeling at all, Francesca."

"It is not so bad if you have it," Alberto said. "At your age it comes from making love three times a day. In your case, why not? A younger man. It is a good thing for a North American to know the Italian girls. With them love is an art, a ritual."

"I'm not with an Italian girl, Alberto."

"Haven't you discovered she thinks she is, Sam?"

"Alberto is right. It is a good thing," Francesca said judicially. "If she were an American girl she would be making love because she would think it was good for her complexion. That is the way it is with the American girls. No?"

"And the Scandinavians?" Sam asked blandly.

"With them," Alberto said profoundly, "it is all practical and straightforward. They say, 'Well, I've finished my drink. Are you coming upstairs?'" As Francesca and Alberto smiled at each other in mutual approval of their wisdom, Sam laughed awkwardly; not only because he couldn't get used to their Mediterranean frankness, but because their utter lack of concern for Carla outraged him. He could see Carla sitting in their room, clutching that piece of paper on which he had written the address; she was looking at it again and again, telling herself that while she could look at it she needn't feel she was alone.

"It has been a great pleasure. I wish I could stay an hour with you. What a pity I have an appointment," Sam said, hiding his agitation as he glanced at his watch. Calling the waiter, he again paid for the drinks while Alberto, as usual, fumbled elegantly for his wallet. "Have luck, Al," Sam said, standing up. "I must go. Make a million, eh?"

"A million? Don't be pessimistic, Sam. Believe in me, please. I'll make two million."

"*Arrivederci*," Sam said. But Francesca followed him to the curb.

"If it's a matter of spending money, buying things with Carla," she said earnestly, "you might care to have me along. I know you're a very soft touch for women, Sam, and I know Carla so well."

"Thanks, Francesca. I'll call you," he said, and as he ran for a taxi that had stopped at the curb he felt in a panic; he couldn't understand why he had left Carla by herself so long, and what crazy kind of faith in himself had led him to believe she would show up at all.

CHAPTER 16

WAITING outside the Press Club, on the narrow street, he kept glancing at his watch, tormenting himself with the wildest fancies as if he now knew definitely she would not show up. Then he saw the taxi stop fifty paces up the street and she got out, looked at a store window—checking on the street number—half turned, doubtful and confused, then came hesitantly in his direction, watching the numbers. When she suddenly saw him he thought she was going to run. "Take it easy, Carla," he whispered, and he felt happy when she did slow down. Her mouth was half open, her face as pleased as a child's. And he saw something else that gave him immense satisfaction. In her relief at getting to him, she had forgotten herself; she now was walking like an American girl, with a straight-footed stride, her neck forward a little, and she did not have, as she usually did, that slow stately proud walk of the Italian girls he had seen on the streets of Rome.

"Am I on time?" she asked, her hand coming out to his arm.

"Right on time, Carla."

"I didn't want to have to wait around." And then, worried, she asked, "Why the grin?"

"I was watching the way you walk."

"Oh? What do I walk like?"

"Like any good-looking American girl."

Her eyes did turn inward, and she did seem a little confused, but she was so relieved that he was there waiting for her she couldn't concentrate on the import of his remark.

"Well, you made it on time," he said smiling. "What's the matter? Were you afraid I'd beat you?"

"No, but I kept thinking of you."

"Thinking what?"

"Just things. Things that struck me. I mean about the way I had got used to you. Things like that."

"That's good, Carla."

"But the thing is . . ." she hesitated. "You haven't been working, Sam . . . You haven't been doing a story. You've just been waiting around, isn't that right? And I suppose they're paying you to wait."

"Waiting for what?"

"Till the Pope dies. You're always asking questions and having me read the bulletins."

"It means money for me. It's a big story. Anyway, the Pope may recover and live five years."

"No, he's a sick old man, and I mean . . ." Again she hesitated, trying to hide a strange new grim concern with the facts. "When he dies and you take all the pictures . . ." As she waited, looking up at him, he knew that she had been sitting at home, trying hard to bring herself down to earth; thinking, I'm here by myself now, and this is the way it may soon be, for in a week or a month or six months he'll have no excuse for staying here with me. Hurrying here, just as he had done, she must have tormented herself too, only she had been wondering how often he would be there to meet her.

"Me and the Pope—it's a practical question," and then he smiled reassuringly. "What's happening to us that we're getting so practical? It's good, eh? Well look, Carla. I'm on my own. If they want me to work for them, fine, they'll let me know, but I'm able to stay as long as I want. I like it here. Nobody can tell me to leave. You go with me wherever I go, Carla."

"Well," she said, and tried to shrug and smile. "I mean I was

[150

just wondering. What do you want to do now, Sam? Where do we go?"

"Wherever you say."

"There should be things you want to see," she said, taking herself seriously as a guide.

"All right," he began. Now that he had seen her hurrying down the street, absorbed in the importance of the moment of meeting, he longed to be able to keep her in their own time. "What about something contemporary, Carla? I'll be asked if I saw the square where Mussolini used to make his speeches. Which way is it?"

"In the center of town," she said, showing no enthusiasm as they walked to the square by the cable office where the taxis waited. Suddenly she picked up interest. "Wait a minute, Sam. There's an interesting sight there that might amuse you. It's a little thing but it really belongs to Rome. Well, I mean it's us. It's like us. You'll see."

When they got out of the taxi he looked around the square at the sights he had seen so often in pictures. There was the brownstone Palazzo Venezia, and there was the little balcony where Mussolini had shaken his fist to the roaring crowd; and across the piazza, looking like a huge elegant white birthday cake, was the monument to Victor Emmanuel. He waited for her to shrug and tell him it was in very bad taste. Everybody in Rome seemed to know it was the correct thing to say. "It's a funny thing about Mussolini," she said, staring at the balcony. "He had a truly Roman sense of grandeur, he really did, you know. But the trouble was that he had no taste. It was too bad, wasn't it?"

"I suppose it was."

"He still has his admirers. The ones without any taste. But never mind him. Look!"

She was pointing at the helmeted white-gloved policeman in the center of the square who was directing the traffic. "There now," she said happily. "Do you get it? Don't you get it?"

It was the busiest center in Rome, with traffic flowing into the square from five directions, yet there was only this one policeman handling these converging lanes and directing them past him without the aid of traffic lights. Sam went to speak to Carla, then he saw the expression on her face. She was amused, truly amused. It was the first time he had seen such a smile. He was afraid to speak, it was such a precious moment for him. "Watch his arms," she went on. "Wouldn't you swear there was a baton in his hand? See how proudly he stands with all that confidence, Sam. He's not just directing traffic, he's handling an orchestra. Look how he makes all those cars flow in tune. Where else in Europe would you see such a sight?"

"Nowhere else," he said softly, watching her in wonder.

"It's just a little thing, but I like it," she said, "and I thought you would, too." And when she took his arm as if she were sure of him, he was moved. Laughing, he blew a kiss to the cop.

"You know what we should do now, Sam?"

"Have something to eat."

"No, we should find a butcher store. There's one around here, I'm sure."

"A butcher store? Why a butcher store?"

"Let's buy a lot of chunks of old meat and go to the old quarry."

"The old quarry?"

"That's right, and feed the cats."

"Oh, come on, Carla," and he looked at her closely. Half-starved cats in an old quarry? Was this the Roman love of cats? Amused or not, she meant it. Well, he would let her buy the meat. Since it was after seven he would suggest they look for a restaurant. And he would keep her talking until it was dark, and she would forget all about her quarry and her cats.

"Oh, well, all right," he said, pretending indifference. It took them fifteen minutes to find a butcher shop. He waited outside while she went in and bought her bag of meat, and he noticed that already there were red streaks in the sky to the west. Then they looked for a restaurant, found one, and when he complained that they could do better, they wandered around till they found another one more to his satisfaction. It was twilight now, and he intended to make sure it would be dark when they came out. While they were eating he drew on all his knowledge of history, talking eloquently about the women in the d'Este family in Renaissance Italy, trying to fascinate her and hold her there; and he did. When they came out of the restaurant the street lights were lit and he was satisfied.

"What a shame," he said, hypocritically. "No use trying for your old quarry now. The cats will have to wait, I guess."

"The hour doesn't make any difference," she said. "It's all lit up."

"To hell with it," he said angrily. "This has gone far enough. What kind of a fool are you trying to make out of me? We stop right here."

"Now don't lose your temper, Sam," she said, and she smiled. The last time he had grown impatient, they had a terrible scene. Now she was smiling, and it interested him. "Well, come on," he said. They got into a taxi. It was a short trip. She told the driver to wait, and he got out first and there he was in the floodlit area looking up at the great high curving weathered broken wall of the Colosseum.

"It's the Colosseum," he said. "What in hell is this?" And he was let down and impatient again. "Are you determined to make a fool of me? You said something about an old quarry."

"This is the old quarry," she said gravely. "It was used as a quarry for hundreds of years, wasn't it?"

"Suppose it was? Is this your idea of a . . ." Then he laughed; he saw that he was amusing her. For the first time she had amused herself kidding him, and he felt almost embarrassed. Touched by this sudden humor, she seemed to be changing under his eyes, her enchantment with the past fading away from her under his eyes.

In the floodlights the great wall shone in a ghostly silver light, tapering off, jagged-edged, into the darkness; and above was the blanket of the Roman night. A strange feeling came over him. What was he doing here in this place with this girl and her bag of meat? he wondered. "Come on, Sam," she said. Taking his arm, she led him slowly around the wall, pointing up at mended patches. "This should give you a laugh," she said. "See that patch up there? A pope repaired it. Why? Well, I never could figure out why. Maybe he had stolen the stones, and his conscience bothered him, and he came down here and put them back." She started to giggle. "All the rich families swiped the marble from here. They just raided this quarry. What a bunch of burglars. Look at the gaps in the wall."

Still giggling, her hand on his arm, she talked about the powerful old families, the Barbarini and the Farneses, with a kind of disrespectful intimacy, as if they were old neighbors and she was beguiling him, taking him into the past as she had always been able to do; but now she was amusing. "The old rich ones sit around wondering where they can pick up some marble for their palaces. 'How are you fixed for marble?' they say. 'This is confidential, but I know where we can get it wholesale. Who'll care? What do you say if we sneak down there tonight and just kind of nibble away at it? Have you still got all those wagons?' "

Again it was like listening to someone gossiping about people she might meet on the street tomorrow, only now he laughed. "What a nut you are," he said.

"Come on," she said, "the cats are waiting," and she led him through one of the great arches.

After the floodlights on the outside it was like entering a pitch-black cave. Standing beside her, he waited for his eyes to get used to the light, and heard the rustling of her paper bag as she opened it. At first he could only see the rim and the highest row of stone seats in the starlight, then gradually as it got lighter, he could make out the descending tiers. In the shadows they were like the pock-marked face of the moon. Before him stretched the blackness of the field itself. In the ghostly gray and black stillness there was no sound now, not even the rustling of the bag. She tossed out a piece of meat. Nothing moved; not a sound. Then in the darkness he saw glowing eyes. He felt a little chill on his neck. As she kept tossing out the pieces of meat, eyes shone in the darkness to the left and right of him. A cat snarled, and he jumped. The fierce spitting scratching anger of hungry cats fighting for meat made him shiver. A dark form went leaping across the aisle, then another one in pursuit, and then came the frantic fierce spitting and crying of cats making love.

The flashing eyes in the shadows, the snarling, then the glint of moonlight on the tiers of seats, made him draw back, and his mind played tricks on him. The whole arena seemed to come alive; it seemed to be there in a reddish glow as the fierce sun was strained through the giant colored awnings on the poles around the arena; and the wild animals, the leopards, the wolves, the cheetahs and the tigers were there, circling around crazily, blind with fright, sliding frantically along the barricade, crashing into it, lashing out with their tails; and now waiting with wild glowing eyes, watching him because he was standing over the underground cells where the prisoners, doomed to be tossed out as meat, waited. The fear and the terrible anxiety of the prisoners was like a smell seeping through the ground to him, and there before him, waiting with glowing eyes, half-starved, the great cats.

Tossed out, now just the cat's meat, the world's fear in the scream of agony of the first one; then another and another, torn and swallowed in fierce gulps. But now no more frantic lonely wails; those who were left—just scared to death; just hunks of meat. He shuddered.

A cat snarled and eyes flashed, and beside him— It was only the rustle of Carla's bag, yet he felt cold. As he reached out for her arm in the darkness, he thought, "What a terrible thing to be in this place with this wildly imaginative girl who can't bear to be alone. This place still stinks from those who were frightened to death here."

"Come on, let's go," he said nervously.

"Just a minute," she said. Making a ball of the paper bag, she tossed it out in the darkness. The eyes, glaring at them, suddenly turned away. There was just the darkness. Taking his arm she walked him out to the floodlight where he looked at her anxiously. She seemed to be utterly composed and cheerful. She hadn't felt him shudder in his dream. In this old place, stinking

155]

with the memories of death and torture and fear, her imagination hadn't been troubled; her own fear hadn't been touched at all. Why? Was it because she couldn't imagine fear when she was with him? How close to him, how sure of him she must be.

Suddenly he thought of that first night in bed with her, and how he had pictured her as a bird on the beach with a broken wing waiting to be healed; and if it was healed it would fly away. Touched with anguish, he began, "Carla . . ."

"What, Sam?"

"I'm a first-class camera man. There's England, France, Canada . . ." As she looked at him in surprise he faltered painfully, made desperate by the power of the temptation: Why not take her back home with him now? Right now. She would have to come with him, if he insisted. Back home, with her in his life, he would discover strange aspects of himself that would be as surprising and delightful as his times with her now. Why should she have to sing again? What would be lost to her or to him or the world if she never sang again? Even if she did sing, her song would soon be forgotten, and she would grow older. The main thing was she felt wonderfully safe with him. Then he saw how confused she looked as she waited for him to go on. With a pang of desolation, he felt like a coward; he was showing no faith in her keeping her feeling for him. Temptation was a belittlement of himself. He felt ashamed. She might come with him, yes, to feel safe, but only because she felt compelled to. In her dependence she wasn't free to say yes or no. As yet she had no freedom in her heart. It was when she was free that he would know how she felt about him. Just wait. Just wait. I don't have to settle for anything but the real thing. It's the real thing I'll have. Grimly, almost roughly, he took her hands in his, trying to smile.

"What is this, Sam?" she asked nervously. "I don't want to go away."

"I know, Carla. Of course, I know," he said, and he tried to make a joke of it as he walked her out of the bright floodlit area by the massive old ruin and back into the shadow where the taxi waited.

CHAPTER 17

HER interest in him began to extend
to his clothes. She complained that his jackets were too loose
and too long, his trousers too full and tending to be baggy, and
that she shouldn't be expected to wander around Rome with
a man who dressed like an American salesman. This sign of her
growing concern for him, and its importance to her delighted
him, and he put himself in her hands. She took him to a
tailoring shop on the Via Condotti and helped him pick out
the cloth for two suits. He was measured and fitted, and had his
suits in a week; one of dark gray, one of blue; the jackets shorter
than those he had been wearing, the pants a little tighter. She,
herself, had added five new dresses to her wardrobe. Now they
were an elegant pair, strolling on the narrow Corso on Sunday,
or sitting at a café on the Piazza del Popolo. And little things
happening every day seemed to tell him she was becoming more
like herself with him.

One afternoon they were in a square which was used as a
market place. Earlier that day there had been a market, and
bits of vegetables, celery stalks and greens still littered the
pavement. While he listened to her explaining about this neighborhood market, he was eying the statue on the pedestal in the
middle of the square. Sauntering toward the statue, with her

trailing, he read the inscription. "Why, it's Bruno. Giordano Bruno, Carla."

"Oh," she said doubtfully.

"Is this the spot where he was burned?"

"I . . . well . . . Perhaps it is," she answered, trying to hide her ignorance with a shrug.

"Just think, Carla. From the prison cell to this spot here and the flames. How long had he been imprisoned?"

"Let me see now," and she stalled him. "I think . . . No, I forget."

"Oh," he said, secretly delighted that she didn't know.

Stepping up on the pedestal base, he waved his arm to the whole square and began to deliver a grandiloquent lecture; he told her about Bruno's view of the universe and his belief in the transmigration of souls. The resentment on her face as she listened made him want to burst out laughing. She was acting like a very knowing tourist, accustomed to being listened to, who found that another tourist had more information about a monument than she had. It was intolerable to her self-esteem.

"My, aren't you clever," she said tartly. Her annoyance delighted him. Jumping from the pedestal he put his arm around her waist, and walked her across the square. As he stopped to kick aside some celery stalks, he began to hum a popular American song of some years ago. Then he started to sing in an off-key baritone, and he pretended to get the words and the tune all wrong.

"Oh, hell. That's not right. How does it go, Carla? 'I'll be seeing you in all the old familiar . . .'"

"You don't know?"

"Like this . . . ?"

"Imagine! Something you don't know!"

"If you don't know either, it's all right."

"Maybe I do know."

"It's not your day for knowing anything, Carla."

"Don't be silly. It goes like this," she said, humming the tune.

"It's got a nice melody," he said, and he started to sing.

[158

"My God, you've no voice at all, Sam."

"Where do I go wrong?" he asked, with an air of innocence.

Having displayed her historical ignorance at the statue, it seemed to give her satisfaction now to be putting him right. "Like this," she said, and she sang softly, " 'I'll be seeing you in all the old familiar places,' " and she finished the chorus. He was careful to show neither interest nor special pleasure, nor any awareness that she had been a singer. She had made a point, shown him where he was wrong, and that was all there was to it. Not again that day did he mention her little song in the square.

But next day, and from then on, whenever they were on the street, he would link his arm in hers and start to hum and get her humming with him. He made it appear that he had discovered a simple amusing little pleasure that gave her a greater hold on him. He would squeeze her arm and look carefree and happy as they walked along, humming in tune, and he had noticed that she would glance at him with a faint smile of satisfaction.

One day he stopped her in front of a music store. A mandolin and a guitar were in the window.

"At college I used to play one of those things a little," he said, sounding wistful.

"So what?"

"I don't know," he said idly. "We sit around in our place, sometimes just looking at each other. I get kind of bored," he said. "Don't you?"

"Bored? With me, Sam?"

"Oh, Lord, no, Carla. I mean . . ."

"It's what it sounded like," she said uneasily.

"I wasn't speaking of myself," and he pretended to stammer. "I was speaking of you and me and passing an idle hour, Carla. Just something to do."

"Then buy the thing. I'll play it for you," she said, carelessly. In spite of her tone she was as upset as if she had just received an intimation that the one thing she had been sure of, his lust for her, might not be enough to keep him fascinated.

159]

He felt ashamed to be taking advantage of her old fear of her inadequacy.

"All right," he said, smiling. "Why not? Something for the home, anyway, Carla." And he went into the store and bought the guitar. When they got to their place he put it on the bedroom bureau and seemed to forget about it. He was hungry, he said, and they went out to eat.

That night they came home early, and as always they faced the awkward moments when they became like strangers who shied away from talking about anything in their own lives. In a little while he went into the bedroom, picked up the guitar, hesitated as he became aware that she was watching him intently, and knew he had made a mistake. The little conversation on the street in front of the music store, when she had wondered if he was growing tired of being with her day and night, had stuck in her mind; she was waiting for some little sign, no matter how slight, that might tell her something could easily take his attention away from her. Sitting in the chair, she drew his eyes to her by stretching out with luxurious indolence, waiting for some little move that would show she had been in his thoughts all day. She did her little ritual things; she kicked off her shoes, she rubbed her hand over her leg, she drew her dress back from her chest and flipped it as if she were hot and restless. Her hand went lazily through her hair, and a few strands fell over one eye. The other eye, free of the screen of hair, watched for the taut expression on his face as he came toward her slowly, his hand to tremble as he touched her.

What a shock it would be to her if he showed that anything else was on his mind, he thought. "Carla," he said softly. Drawing her out of the chair, he rubbed his hands lovingly and greedily down her body.

"Ah, you're a glutton, Sam," she sighed. "Oh, all right." With her indulgent air and old satisfied smile he now hated, she sauntered into the bedroom. I'm almost part of her now. It's a little different now. It gets a little different each night, he thought. He had to say something to himself to save a remnant of his self-respect. He couldn't bear it now when he lay exhausted beside her, and she raised herself and looked down at him with her knowing smile that destroyed him.

When she had thrown her wrap around her and had taken that little lazy walk along the hall to the bathroom, he got up and put on his dressing gown. He knew he had to be careful about how to handle the situation. He quickly got the guitar, sat down, trying to look as if he were amusing himself while waiting for her, and when she returned and he knew she was looking at him, he tried to give the appearance of being childishly absorbed in his task. His heart began to beat unevenly, for he made it appear that he had forgotten she was in the room as he plucked at the strings. She couldn't stand being neglected, he knew. Gradually, the fact that he showed no awareness of her presence began to bother her. Walking around the room, she would stand and watch him, frowning, for his efforts were very amateurish. "Oh, cut out that awful noise," she said, irritably. Still, when he paid no attention to her, she went into the bedroom. Waiting breathlessly, he counted on her enormous concentration on herself and her need of his attention if she felt utterly at loose ends. He heard her moving around in the bedroom. Then she came to the door, her arms folded, watching him moodily.

"What's the matter?" he asked mildly.

"Are you going to keep it up all night?"

"I think I could pick it up. I've got an ear. I can chord on it already."

"You call that chording?"

"Certainly. What's wrong with it?"

"Oh, for heaven's sake. Give it to me," she said impatiently, and she took the guitar, sat down strumming away at it, ready to say, "Now, see what you can do." Then she looked at him. In his face there was so much innocent pleasure it flattered her. The simple effortless delight she gave him without having him in her arms seemed to upset her, and for an awkward moment she looked at him with shy wonder. Her eyes were gentle, as if she wanted to go on comforting him. Watching his face, she began to strum again. In the whole

161]

world there seemed to be only the two of them there in the room. He was held rapt in this lovely moment, then she smiled, began to hum and then to sing. When she made a mistake she muttered away to the guitar, then amused, she smiled to herself and sang.

Her hair had fallen over one cheek, and she would shake it back. In her quiet absorption in her song and her strumming, she seemed to have forgotten he was there. What song was it? He didn't know. He didn't care. He was afraid to speak. He had to close his eyes to hide his tears. There she was as he had imagined her. Then he felt a leap of exultation.

Old Streeter! he thought. What would the arrogant old painter say to this? Had the old man ever gotten the satisfaction out of a finished painting that he himself got now seeing Carla, as he had dreamed of her in this quiet happy amused enjoyment of herself? Alone and not caring. Was this the way a man of great talent felt when he looked at a work and knew it to be splendid? Michelangelo! Yes, the old boy would have passed her by in the street, another one of his demon-haunted women, missing the fact that she should be sitting here like this.

"Well, what do you know?" she said suddenly, with a laugh. Tossing the guitar at the sofa, she yawned. "I'm tired," she said. "Come on to bed, Sam."

"Just as you say," he said laconically, careful that he shouldn't appear to be making a big thing of her performance. It was better that she should believe they had found a new amusing little pleasure they shared. They went to bed.

Long after he thought she had fallen asleep, he lay awake nursing a peculiar kind of lightness of spirit, a triumph. A strange sensation that was new to him. A success of the heart. He could see beyond the scene in the living room. That light in her eyes he had seen tonight, the expression of an unself-conscious, happy possession of her own soul, he would soon see in her face as she walked down the street, or if she stood alone in a crowd, or if she sat alone in a room of her own. Then he heard her stir. When he heard her catch her breath he knew she hadn't been sleeping, and he put out his hand to her head, but she turned away. His hand touched the part of the pillow where her head had been. It felt wet.

"Carla, Carla," he said anxiously. "What's the matter?"

"Nothing," she whispered. "Nothing's the matter."

"Why were you crying? What's making you unhappy?"

"I'm not unhappy," she said, catching her breath, then catching it again. "I got thinking of the day on the street when I told you everything for so long had been ugly, and it got worse with Alberto, and being here with you made it even uglier. And now—in the room in there—you made me feel beautiful."

CHAPTER 18

THEN he was in the living room next day, waiting for Carla, who was taking a bath, and he heard a step on the stair. An envelope was pushed under the door. He picked it up. A cable from home, addressed to the Palace Residence Hotel and forwarded here; he opened it with a smile. It was from his Uncle Joe, a stockbroker, his father's brother. It read: YOUR FATHER HAD SECOND HEART ATTACK. KEEPS ASKING FOR YOU. DOCTOR SAYS A WEEK AT MOST.

The paper shook in his hand. The wrench at his heart, making him feel weak, bewildered him. He hadn't felt close to his father, not for years. Injured, resentful, unforgiving; his father, who had been so disappointed in him, had always seemed to be waiting for an apology. It had been absurd. Yet now the days of his childhood were flashing before him, those fine Sunday afternoons when his father used to take his hand and walk him along the street, telling him about the world. In those days his father had seemed to him to be a great man, full of laughter, wit, energy and cunning. He had had more than a father's normal affection for his son. He had wanted to suffer and bleed for his son at school. And the joy the old man had found in planning the work they could do together! In a sense, his father had worked

[164

and built his life so his son could carry it on. It had been a kind of love, a fierce possessive love. When they broke, when he went his own way, the old man understood that his son despised his work and his talent. He returned the compliment, but he thought his son was belittling himself to humiliate him. Even if he hadn't despised the phony job his father had done with his celebrated portraits, Sam would have fled. A son had a right to want to be a painter, not an elegant photographer for the rich, and not a professor, either. He had had a right to reject his father's lifework and to become a hack himself, if it gave him some money and enabled him to paint. All the emotion from this old argument was in Sam as he held the cable in his hand and felt the wrench at his heart.

And yet, for the moment, as he looked around the room, trembling, all he could think of was that he could be home in two days if he could get a seat on the plane. He had to hurry, he had to cable, he had to pack. He turned to call Carla and tell her he would be leaving her for a week or two, unless she would come with him. Then he stopped. The cable in his hand, he listened to her moving around in the bathroom, and he felt stricken. She might come with him, he thought, in her need of someone, feeling she had no choice, but she would also feel out of time and out of place. He would be taking her back in bondage; he would, with his excuse, be yielding to the temptation that had seemed so self-belittling that night at the Colosseum. As it was now she could change so quickly, and the magic suddenness of the change would be due to her being weary of wanting to be loved—when instead she would love, be carried away and out of herself by love. Weren't the little things telling him it was already happening here? Carla, here, under the star of love. Walking slowly over to the chair, he sat down, sighed and closed his eyes, then he seemed to see his father, a white-haired old man on a hospital bed, hear him say, "Sam, Sam. Where is my son?"

"I'm here. I'm here," he whispered. "I've come back." The

165]

tears would roll down his cheeks, watching the faint smile on his father's blue lips; a little gratified smile, as if some absolution had been given to their lives now his son had come back to him. Then, his eyes on the door, watching for Carla in anguish, Sam thought desperately, How false the scene would be, in spite of the emotion. He couldn't go home to anything his father had stood for; anything they had had in their lives together had become alien. What was he supposed to say to the old man? Was he to say, "Father, forgive me. I didn't know what I was doing to you, living in the same city with you, never seeing you because you thought I insulted your life"? Or was he to confess bitterly that the years of separation had been wasted years for him? Now, too late, he knew he had been pigheaded and blind, believing he had a great talent as a painter. "I'm a failure, Dad, at what I wanted to be. The thing I thought so superior to you. You and your business with the ridiculous portraits; you believed in it, you were a success. Maybe you knew your time in our country. It didn't seem to be my time."

Then Sam shook his head angrily. No. Such an apology would be a sentimental lie. His only failure now would be if he walked out on Carla.

"What are we doing, Sam? Are we going out?" she called, coming along the hall; and she looked beautiful, and her brown eyes held him a moment; then he turned away so he wouldn't show that his heart felt so heavy.

"I think it's time I sent a cable home," he said quietly. "Get dressed."

"Is it something important, Sam?"

"Just keeping in touch, that's all."

There were no further questions, and they went down to the cable office and he sent this cable to his uncle: ALL MY LOVE TO FATHER. COULDN'T POSSIBLY MAKE IT IN TIME. TELL HIM I'M WITH HIM.

Turning away from the counter, he felt ashamed and yet grim. But when he saw Carla, who was walking up and down waiting, he shuddered, knowing he had no choice, knowing he must have secretly loved the old man, and had hurt himself all his life by denying him the right to any respect.

As the day with her wore on, he tried to tell himself his father might not be so close to death. Look at the Pope. A much older man, and all summer they had been saying he was dying. The old cling desperately to life. The older they get, the tighter the grip they take on existence. But what helped most of all to make him forget his remorse was Carla singing for him that night, again.

Now he was sure the glimpse she had given him of herself as she must have been back home some years ago meant that her crazy Italian dream had broken. At last he might begin to get to know her, and she could look at him, maybe with shyness at first; then finally come to him in the fullness of herself. Then a little thing happened. It made him wonder if she could ever be openly honest about herself. They had had dinner in that little restaurant where they had eaten the first night together. They had not noticed Joe Mosca, the American, dining alone in the far corner. Just before Sam paid his bill, Carla had gone to the ladies' room, leaving him alone at the table.

Joe Mosca, with his expansive opulent grin, came over to Sam and stood with both hands on the back of the chair on which Carla had been sitting. "I see you around, Jack, but we don't talk, do we?" he said. "I look at you and think of back home. I get homesick. You understand it? Where are you from?"

"I don't stay put. I get around."

"Traveling man?"

"Right."

"The name's Joe Mosca. Mind if I sit down?"

"Don't waste your time. I'm on my way," and looking up at him coldly, Sam disliked the amiable loose face with the empty eyes and the curling lock of black hair on the forehead. A slob, he thought, a slob who knew he was living in the right time; a face seen at home a thousand times in bars and at big parties for entertainers and in poolrooms and on television shows. A sloppy, careless, ruthless, confident man who thought he could grin and cut a throat because he was so well-liked in his own crowd. "Look, why don't you go back to your own table?" Sam said sourly.

"I don't figure you, friend," Mosca said frowning. "What's your line? A tie salesman? A biscuit salesman?" As he bent down, studying Sam, he suddenly shook with suppressed laughter; his whole body shook. Yet he wasn't drunk. No smell of liquor came from him. The deep muffled chuckle, the eyes wrinkled up in mirth, was his style; his way of saying a little difference of opinion was unimportant. Grabbing Carla's chair he spun it around to sit down. Sam jerked the chair away with his foot.

"Look, Jack," Mosca said, frowning, "don't get me wrong. I was born here in Italy. I got the time, I could show you around. Like a guide, see?"

"I don't want to see the Catacombs."

"The Catacombs? What's that? A night club?"

"The best strippers in town. Good night."

"A joker. Look, Jack," Mosca said earnestly, "I'm no two-bit punk. Back home I work for Big Jim Giardello."

"Never heard of him."

"Come on, don't kid me. A national figure. Everybody's heard of him. Fights! The numbers! Juke boxes! What are you? A schoolteacher, seeing the sights here?"

"Look, I'm busy."

"Okay, Jack. I only wanted to ask you who was the little broad with you. Haven't I seen her around? Who's the broad?"

"Beat it."

"Look, I'm Joe Mosca," and he scowled.

"And you're Giardello's boy. I said go 'way."

"What?" The overhead light glinted on the yellow-brown eyes. Almost breathless, Mosca lifted the chair a little, put it down, then leaned over the table, very worried. "How would you like it if I pushed your fat head through that wall?"

"How would you like to try it?" Sam asked quietly, meeting his eyes, not moving, not smiling, just waiting. Mosca, looking puzzled, grinned slowly. Then Sam saw Carla at the door, beckoning to him, and he got up. Paying no attention to the big fellow, he brushed by and left him gaping at Carla.

"Who's your friend?" she asked, outside.

"Just some nuisance," Sam said. "Some Italian-American nosing around. Come on."

"What did he want?"

"Friendship. Perfect friendship."

"What did he get?"

"He nearly got a punch on the nose."

"What's the use, Sam? Rich or poor, these Italian-Americans are a bore," she said contemptuously. "They're neither one thing nor the other, you know, and as a result I can't stand them. They come over here thinking they're at home, and a child could tell they're as American as apple pie. We find them all so dreary and common. We all laugh up our sleeves at them."

"We? Who's we? Oh, cut it out, Carla." Again, her attitude and tone was fantastic; the big Italian-American was exactly what she was, maybe a bit closer to Italy. Could she never be honest about herself? Sam felt hopeless. Walking beside her, he felt he was the man in the myth who had kept rolling the stone up the hill, only to have it roll back on him. Then, under the street light, he saw her surprised expression.

"What? What did you say?" she asked. Didn't she know what she had said herself? he wondered. No, he could be wrong. She could have made a little slip. The affectation of the older resident in Rome about the visitor. That was all.

"What did you say?" she repeated.

"I don't know. Nothing. The guy irritated me, that's all."

"They're all around here. Why bother with them, Sam? Well, what do we do? Where do we go?"

"Anyplace you say."

"Let me see," she said, slowing down, then she brightened. "I know where we've never been together."

"Where?"

"The Campidoglio."

"The Capitoline Hill?"

"The City Hall."

"Oh, come on, Carla. I'm not an alderman trying to feel at home."

"No, it's a great place for a man and a girl to be together, if it's night and there's no one else there. No, come on. I'll show you."

He thought she might be playing another little joke on him. Yet, surprisingly, she had sounded as if she knew she was his girl. Though he was living with her and sleeping with her had never quite been able to believe she was his girl. His heart took a little leap.

He was in the mood for some new enchantment. And as soon as they got out of the taxi and approached the wide flight of steps, his whole imagination quickened. This was the Capitol, the hill of hills of his school days. He was here with her, on the high hill of the world that had shaped their lives. Half stopping, he listened alertly. No other footstep, no other voice, no one else was there. "Now, isn't it beautiful here at night?" Carla said, taking his arm as they began to ascend the steps. "Just think, the Temple of Jupiter was here. And the Tarpeian Rock. They say the temple fell down of its own weight. Interesting, isn't it? I'm not very profound, but I'll bet you could make something out of that. A world collapsing of its own weight? What do you know about Tarpeia? Let me tell you about Tarpeia. It's the deal a woman gets. Tarpeia goes all out for the Sabines, and who is it who pushed her off the rock? The Sabines, of course. Ah, well." Dreading that he might see the dreaming brightness in her eyes, he looked at her anxiously. It wasn't there. They came to the top of the steps.

There now in the floodlight that made the sky overhead a bowl of darkness was the piazza, and across the cobblestoned way, facing them, was the gravely elegant Palazzo del Senatore, and on the sides of the square, the two flanking palaces: they were there as Michelangelo had seen them in his mind, having all the lightness of his sense of symmetrical grace. "Whoa," Sam said. Just ahead of them was Marcus Aurelius on his horse, the emperor holding in the charger so he wouldn't run them down.

[170

And it all was in a soft pinkish light framed by the night shadows.

The lightness, grace and balance of the picture suddenly seemed to lift Sam out of his own life. His exhilaration held him in a happy trance. Though Carla was telling him about someone who had been stabbed and had stumbled down those wide steps they had just ascended, he hardly heard her voice. "Come on," she said. Taking him by the arm, she led him over to the rail at the edge of the great rock. Below in the night was the level land, the Forum where stood the broken columns silvered in the moonlight, and to the left, very close to him and Carla, rising out of the darkness, the rounded dome of the church of Santa Maria. The stillness of time suspended possessed him. He was happy. As he stood there with Carla, he seemed to be touched by an eternal radiance of form that was all around him. And she was so quiet, too, her eyes on the Forum columns far below. Suddenly she turned, half-troubled.

"What's the matter, Sam?"

"I don't know. I really don't know. You see, Carla, I wanted to be a painter," he stammered. "And, well . . . there can't be another spot like this in Europe."

"Now that's an odd thing," she said.

"What's an odd thing?"

"I'd call you a talkative man, Sam. I mean you joke and tease and know many things, but I've noticed you never talk about yourself. I don't know anything about you at all, do I?"

"Don't you?" he asked, hiding his astonishment that she should so suddenly have some curiosity about his life. Her interest, after all this time, was so unexpected it made him shy. The light was on one side of her beautiful face as she waited. She was showing, for the first time, a natural sympathetic curiosity about him. "What can I say?" he said with a kind of embarrassed good humor. He told her about going to college and about his father having believed he would reject the academic life and join him in the studio. "I was a great disappointment to him," he said. "I let him down, I guess. Not so much in wanting to be a painter. He might have understood that part of it, if he had thought I had any real talent. But that I should be content to be a newspaper photographer going *bang, bang, bang,* and think I was superior to all that phony fooling around with portraits he went in for. I think he thought I was making a point. I think he thought I'd rather be nothing than be like him. He was wrong, Carla. All my life really went into painting." He had to pause to hide his emotion. "He's sick. Maybe he's dead now. And I—I know I wasted my time."

"As a painter?"

"Yes."

"How do you know you did?"

"It's a thing you come to see, yourself. If you're no good, and don't ever see it, well, it means you haven't much awareness of anything. You insult your intelligence. A man ought to have this awareness of himself, of where he stands, what he is; although I don't suppose he can ever know where he's going. It seems to me if you have this awareness, even if it takes a little anguish, you've lifted yourself, Carla. You don't quit. You try something else."

"I don't know. No! A woman can't feel that way about things, Sam. But look—this other thing you say you worked your head off at, and it's not enough, eh? Is it such an awful thing to have no talent, Sam?"

"Well, look around you, Carla."

"All this is talent, eh?" The antique square all glowed in the light, and a night bird chirped behind the shadowed dome of Santa Maria. "It does last a long time, I suppose."

"At least it lasts longer than anything else, Carla. Yes, all Rome blazes with talent."

"You sound kind of lonely, Sam."

"Me? Hell, no, Carla," and he laughed. "Just sometimes, maybe. It's a thing I have in common with Michelangelo. They say he was a lonely man."

"Well, then, count me in on it with you and your friend."

"How do you mean?"

"I used to feel all by myself, too, only it wasn't like it was with you."

[172

"How do you know it wasn't?"

"When you were young—I don't mean you're old now, Sam. You're not old—you're a very virile man, you know. But when you started out you had a choice, didn't you? You could be one thing or another. Well, I had no choice. Not me. I just had to get somewhere, get anywhere as best as I could. I really had to, Sam." Her hands folded, her arms on the rail, she looked into the darkness high over the Forum. "Maybe you hated your father, or maybe you loved him; I don't know, but you were lucky. Take me. I was never even sure who my father was. You see, my mother was a little silly. No, not silly. Poor Momma was just a bit erratic." Her head raised, her eyes were still on the darkness over that patch of light below on the broken columns, as if it held the world of her childhood. He was afraid to speak as she groped in her memories. "No, I didn't have to worry about my father. I don't think my mother worried about him, either. My, she must have been pretty, but, well, featherbrained, I guess. She could sing. She could sing opera arias, she really could." It all seemed so long ago, she went on in a slow wondering tone. She had three sisters. At least these three had the same father, not hers, but he disappeared. A new father came along. That was the thing about her poor mother. There was always a new father looking after them for a while, then he would go like the others. All this was before she was eight or nine and was put out for adoption, one of those trial adoptions, you know; or maybe she had been a ward of some children's aid society. This family, the Brozis, had taken in three children like her. Brozi, a big bald construction worker, wasn't unkind, he just didn't bother with the children. His wife was practical, not loving, but not cruel either, just sensible, and she saw that they all went to school and were clean. This was in Jersey. Mr. Brozi had a construction job, building houses. All the men on the job were Italians. The boss was called Uncle Tony, and was Mrs. Brozi's brother. Uncle Tony, a big, florid man of forty, often came to the house and sang songs and drank a lot of wine till he was stupid. The family lived out near the site of the new construction work.

173]

Then she paused for a long time, and he thought he was to hear no more about her. He wanted to say, "Go on," but was afraid she would turn to him and lose the train of her thought, the mood of quiet wonder and slow words. He held his breath, he made no sound.

"I remember this one evening," she said. She told him about it. She made it stark and simple. On this winter evening Uncle Tony, driving by in his car, saw her on the street and took her for a ride. It was twilight and he drove her out to one of the half-built houses, and then he sat her on his knee and took her drawers off and put her on the floor and raped her. For years she would remember how red his face got, then how he walked up and down, frantic because she was hurt and crying and wouldn't get up. The house had just been plastered. The smell of new plaster worried her for years. Finally Uncle Tony picked her up and shook her. He told her she would die, he would kill her if she ever told anybody what had happened, and he gave her fifty cents. Then he drove her halfway home and put her out of the car. But she was afraid to go home, afraid Uncle Tony would be there, afraid she might say something and he would kill her. It was getting dark and she wandered back toward the half-built new houses. It had started to snow. At first she had liked the feel of the snow. It came down thickly and hid everything. But she didn't know where to go. It got very cold, and she crawled into one of those big culverts they use for the main drains. The culvert shut out the whole world. It was dark and cold, but at least no one could get at her. The terrifying things could only happen if she crawled out and was alone. So she fell asleep. When she woke up it was early morning, and there was six inches of snow on the ground and she was half frozen and coughing; and they found her there and took her home.

Mrs. Brozi would have beaten her, she said, shrugging, for wandering away from home, but when she was undressing her she found blood spots on her pants, and she shrieked and tried to get her to tell who had done it. How could she say Uncle Tony? She just couldn't. His big red face with the scared, wild,

[174

fierce eyes seemed to come down on her and choke off the words. It must have been one of the older boys at school, they said. Oh, dear, what trouble it made for some of those poor kids. Was it this one? How about that one? She would shake her head, dumb, really dumb. Now don't forget, she said, the Brozis were a very respectable family. Those blood spots on her pants were spots on the family escutcheon, and they began to think if there hadn't been something bad in her, she wouldn't have been chosen. So back she went to her poor pretty mother who was getting fatter, as Italian women do, and losing her looks and waiting for one of her husbands to come back to her, as they did, they really did, you know, for she was a soft pretty sentimental woman. Well, during that grand happy time, her mother taught her to play the guitar and sing with her. It was really a bright spot in her life. But it soon passed. Again she was put out for adoption. There must have been at least three of these homes before she landed with a family in Queens. But by that time she was probably a handful for any family. And around in there her mother died, a very smart thing for the poor silly woman to do. Turning to him suddenly, she said, "You've been wanting to know a little more about me, haven't you?"

"Yes, I have."

"Want me to go on?"

"Please."

She turned, as if she thought she had heard a sound. Only Marcus Aurelius was there on his horse, an old Roman out of place in that little Renaissance square. But so was she, and so was he. Or were they? he wondered, deeply moved, as he waited for her to go on.

"The one thing you've got to admit is I've got a lot of imagination," she said. "Well, listen." This Italian family she had been with in Queens was respectable and religious. An old priest who used to come to the house gave her a first-class grounding in her religion. But as she got older she used to look across the East River at Manhattan in the clouds, and think, I'll make it there some day; I'll make it or die. At school they

175]

said she was very bright when she put her mind to it. "And I am bright," she said. "You know that, Sam. I can learn anything." At sixteen, she got a job across the river as a waitress. A waitress has to take anything from the customers and she took it, but not for too long. A big fellow named Willard Morris, a hotel detective about thirty, married her. A very common fellow, and it didn't take long to discover he was a real dummy, and she looked down on him, she supposed. He would take her to bars and hotels. About then, when she was bored, she took to playing the guitar and singing to it, just to have something for herself, you understand. It was all for herself, just for her own amusement, not trying for any effects; more like a man singing to himself in the bathroom and finding it kind of comical. Or maybe it was a way of talking to herself about her life. Who knows? But Willard, that was one of the bad things about him—his name, Willard. What could you do with a big-shouldered dumb hotel detective named Willard? He had gone off somewhere and died of cancer, they said. But anyway, Willard got his kicks out of knowing friends of the "Boss Men." In that world of his there was always some hard-nosed mug called the Boss, with "the edge," they called it. One night Willard had her take her guitar along to some night club in Jersey. The boss and his boys liked her. They had her make a record. This boss man named Joe, a thug in the juke-box business, who had his tongue hanging out for her, chased Willard and took her in hand, pushed her in the smaller clubs, got her under contract; and Haskell, the shrewd comic who owns a piece of so many entertainers, heard her record and got a piece of her, too. And soon she had some spots on television, and it looked as if she had made it. "Well, that's me," she said, and for the first time she took her hands off the rail. "History, eh! Must be the scene down there in the moonlight. Had to get my story in, too, I guess."

"Carla," he began huskily. "I think—"

"Did I sound wound up?"

"No, I think—"

"Just a minute. Alberto talked about me, didn't he?"

[176

"Yes, he did."

"I know. And for me he ruined himself. Poor man," and she laughed bitterly. "For me he sold his picture, gave up everything. Well, it's just not true, Sam."

"Carla, I don't think he quite believes it himself."

"Well, he tries damned hard," she said, scornfully. "He tries to lie to himself and pin it all on me. The fact is I didn't want him to sell out. I begged him not to. The thing was important to me because . . . well, because of the things that had happened in my own life. I left him. I knew what he was going to do."

"I believe you."

"It haunts him that he lost all his faith in himself and that I know it. He had to have me with him. Yet I don't think he could stand the sight of me. He put his life into the thing he was making, and then he lost faith in it. Now he's just another fraud. We were tearing each other to pieces."

"He's going to The States."

"So he says."

"Won't he go?"

"He should go. He's really got the American religion. No, he won't go. Alberto's through, Sam, and he knows it."

"Never mind him then. Look, Carla," he said eagerly, "you're a singer. It's your life. You should be singing."

"You see, I got a little shaky, Sam," she said apologetically. "Not the real shakes, though. I drank, you know."

"I think the trouble was you forgot what you were, Carla."

"Oh, well. No, you weren't there, Sam."

"I'm here, Carla. I'm telling you. Not enough pride in what you had yourself. That was the trouble, Carla. Trying to please other people," he said fiercely. "To hell with wanting to please. You've got to be something in yourself. Listen to me, Carla. If you've got this special thing, you've got to have the arrogance."

"Arrogance?"

"It should be in your blood, Carla," he insisted, flattering her vanity, yet believing, himself, what he said. "Look down there. Okay. Now all this here. The Renaissance. Men discovering they ought to have some **pride after all** the years of fake humility. I only mean, Carla, that you have to protect your own talent with a little arrogance. To hell with trying to please people. Look," he whispered, holding her arm tight, "you're a talented—you—you make a special picture, Carla. If people will pay you for seeing you and listening, then you're damn lucky. If they won't, to hell with them. They don't know what they're missing." His own words began to move him. "You'll start singing, and you'll see what I mean, Carla. No, you'll never let them push you around again. Never."

Suddenly he put his arm around her waist. "The thing you have, Carla, is like something a man comes on unexpectedly. It gives him the feeling he just happened to stop and listen and then look. And there it is. And he says to himself, no one should ever touch it or spoil it. Just leave it alone and be thankful. It's like this square in this light. Coming up the steps, I saw it," and he looked around. "My God, and I'm just a tourist."

"Maybe everybody in the world is, Sam," she said thoughtfully.

"What?"

"Maybe here on earth we're all just a bunch of tourists."

"You say the strangest things, Carla." Impulsively he took her in his arms and kissed her. "No, you're a singer, and you'll sing and it'll be like I say." Her head went back, the light was on her throat.

In that light he, too, looked enchanted and she saw it and whispered hypnotically, "Yes, I know what you mean," and she took his arm, walking him across the cobblestones and down the wide steps into the darkness, and he was afraid to look back at the perfect radiant square.

CHAPTER 19

THE view he had given her of herself seemed to flatter and satisfy her imagination. It was on her mind all the time. Each night she played and sang for him, not like one performing, but like one having fun in good company. Those two weeks in October were the happiest time of his life. He liked watching her go out to do the shopping, taking whatever money she needed from the bureau drawer. Even the weather had begun to delight him, fine bright days and cool nights. On the streets the girls were wearing elegant sweater coats. In the hotels in the evenings the rooms were heated. It was too cool for the derelicts who had been sleeping under the spans of the Tiber bridges. The Ferraros hadn't turned on the heat, so he bought Carla an iron-gray mohair sweater with a huge turtle neck, and she wore it in the apartment at night when she was singing.

Sometimes she would put down the guitar with a puzzled smile. "Look, Sam, if I'm going to sing in front of an audience—"

"No 'if' about it. It's what you're going to do."

"There're things I don't think you understand."

"Oh? What?"

"However you look at it, it's a performance, isn't it? Unless

I establish a relationship with the audience how can I be giving a good performance?"

"Look, Carla. Here with you singing, do I seem to be pleased?"

"I think so."

"Are you trying to sell me something? No, thank God. You're enjoying what you're doing and letting me in on it."

"Sam, I happen to know you like it, don't you see? It's different with you. I'm not giving a performance."

"Just you never mind the show business, Carla. The world is full of knowing old pros. To hell with them. What you've got is there to be discovered with delight, don't you see?"

"Sam. You don't understand. I say I'm performing."

"It's not a performance. It's you. It's what you had in the beginning. It's all you need. It's like a secret thing, Carla."

She seemed to take his word for it till the end of the week. Late Friday night, as they were coming in, Agnese Ferraro, hearing them, came into the hall when they were halfway up the stairs, and called out to them. In the hall light, Agnese looked excited and close to tears. She talked rapidly in Italian.

"What's she saying, Carla?" Sam asked.

"The Holy Father is close to death. This time it is the real thing, and she thinks we should know."

"Is she sure, Carla? Ask her is she sure."

Even there on the stair Sam noticed that Agnese, her face full of sympathy, was talking to them as if they were old friends who would share her concern. "She says there is no doubt," Carla explained. "It has been on the radio and it will be in all the newspapers. Now they are praying for a peaceful death, and she thought we should know and pray, too."

"Thank her. Tell her we share her concern," and they went on upstairs.

They didn't talk much about the dying Pope. Knowing he was troubled, Carla kept her thoughts to herself, even when they went to bed. The impending death would have been flashed to all the newspaper offices of the world, he knew, and yet he had received no cable from the *Weekly*. He felt left out of it. It was his own fault, too. In the last week he had been so absorbed in Carla he had neglected to have her watch the newspapers carefully for the details from Castel Gandolfo. For a long time he pondered over what he might do. In the morning he could cable the *Weekly*. Yet it might be too late. Another man might be on his way. He was so upset he could hardly sleep. When he woke up he was still angry at himself and he let Carla sleep on. At noontime he decided that he would pay for an oversea's telephone call to Blondell, the managing editor, after he had Carla read the newspapers. As he was going out to get them, he heard the step on the stairs; a cable was slipped under the door, and he picked it up. Then it struck him that he was getting word of the death of his father, and his hand shook. The cable read: CAN YOU MEET KOSTER AT AMBASCIATORI HOTEL AND GET ON JOB? RUSH ANSWER. BLONDELL. Leaning weakly against the door, Sam started to laugh. In his relief he couldn't stop laughing, and Carla came out of the bedroom.

"Are you crazy?" she asked. "What's going on?"

"It's the cable. I'm hired, Carla. The job is mine. And look. I'll get all my expenses. The whole business may take a month, you see, and I won't go on salary. I'll sell the picture story to them. I'll do a good job. It's only a beginning. I'll do things like this for them all over Europe."

"It's such a very big thing for you, isn't it?" Carla asked. "It's what you've been really waiting for, isn't it?"

"It means some money. Look, Carla, in all the newspapers in all countries this will be the biggest story in the world. And I'm here on it."

"It's why you're really here, isn't it?"

"It was, in the beginning."

"And here it is. Well, good."

"This guy Koster will need an interpreter," he said, not noticing her tone. "I've got an idea. Why couldn't you be the interpreter? You could get paid for it." Already he was busily drawing her into it. Already he could see her with him at Castel Gandolfo or St. Peter's, her mind now free of ghosts and monuments, meeting the newspapermen from North America who would come to the Press Club. It would be the best thing that could happen to her, if at the same time she was busy on the job with him.

"Well, that's that," she said flatly.

"What do you mean?"

"I don't get to sing, do I?"

"Sing where?"

"Well, in one of the spots around here. What was I supposed to be getting ready for all this time?"

"Sing around here?"

"What's the matter? I'm at home here."

"I'm not," he said, trying to make a joke of it. "Now, take it easy. If you're busy on the job with me, it's part of the whole thing. Leave it to me, Carla."

"What about your Francesca?" she persisted. "You run to her for everything else, don't you? Why don't you ask her to get a lead on a job for me, or should you and I look around? Or are you going to be too busy now?"

"Busy? What's that got to do with it? What's it got to do with you and me?"

"What is this?" she asked angrily. "I'm not a stupid little amateur. I don't need any coaching. I'm a well-known professional. One moment you tell me I am what I am. Just be myself, it's beautiful and so am I. And now what am I supposed to be doing? Working up a routine like a girl getting ready to sing in a church basement?"

"Take it easy, Carla," he said placatingly, for she had the sullen angry contemptuous expression in her eyes he hadn't seen since the first night there when she had thrown the holy picture at him. And he began to walk up and down, groping for the right words to soothe her.

Then he noticed that she, too, was walking, her arms folded. Nothing was said as they passed each other. He couldn't be blunt, he knew; he couldn't tell her he didn't believe she was ready to meet strangers, in an audience. It was a fact that she was herself only with him. For that reason he had kept her out of the cafés she used to know. It had been his plan to take her, one night, among the foreigners at the hotels, to have her be out with Americans at the Café de Paris, to go to the fashionable restaurants, and bit by bit, he would have her get used to herself as an American girl among Americans in Rome. But better than all this, he honestly believed, would be the experience of being with newspapermen who would come for the Pope's death.

Once more she passed him in her silent pacing, then she turned suddenly. "Well, don't worry, Sam," she said bitterly. "I've got it figured out."

"Got what figured out?"

"Well, as a matter of fact, I don't think you care if I ever sing professionally again."

"You say that to me?" he asked, shocked. "Are you that blind and stupid? What do you think I'm doing here?"

"Well, you go for me, that's all."

"That's all, eh?" But the color drained from his face. She seemed to be coolly belittling all his patience and loving concern and the rare quiet joy and elation he had felt in her progress. Outraged, he lost all patience. "So it's just that I go for you," he shouted. "Listen, you little fool." His eyes were wild. The thoughts he had had about her whirled in his head. He remembered how he had imagined Michelangelo passing her on the street. And how he himself had longed to do as much for her; no, more for her—something greater than Michelangelo could do on a canvas—transform her so she could have her own being and be free again in her life. "What I've thought about you you'll never know," he shouted. "My dreams about you . . ." Then he stammered. He remembered the first night he had sat beside her at the café, feeling she had touched his loins, wanting to get her into his room. Tormented, confused, he looked at her with her black hair above the big-necked sweater, and her big warm mouth and her wide-set eyes. My God, what a picture she makes, he thought desperately, feeling a stab of pain as if she were confronting him with the possibility of her not being there.

His anguish must have shown in his eyes, for she said scornfully, "It's the real reason why I'm here, and you know it. You just go for me. You bet your life you do."

"I don't give a damn what you think," he said fiercely. "You're going to listen to me," and he grabbed her arm. "You want to make everything dependent on a stupid singing job. I don't give a damn about a job. You'll sing because you have to. It's not just your singing. It's you. It's your whole life. It's the way you feel about the world and everything." And he gave her a violent shake, as if he were going to slap her. "I'll see you sing in public, but it'll be when you're ready to do anything else you want to at any time. It's not just your singing, it's all of you." Then his voice broke, and he shouted, "And you're not going to be stupid enough to spoil it. You hear?"

"Yeah. Yeah. That's right," she whispered, backing away, frightened a little. As he glared at her, waiting, she was silent. Then something she saw in his face seemed to tell her he was driven to say such things. The fright left her and she relaxed with a little sway of her body. Sure of herself, she smiled faintly. "You've got it bad, haven't you, Sam? All right. Look. I'm here. I'm sorry. Kiss me."

"All right, Carla," he said gruffly, worried by her secret smile. "It's all right," and he kissed her gently.

"Honestly, I get the picture, Sam," she said. "Well, I have to do some shopping. Want to come with me?" And her little practical domestic consideration convinced him and made him sigh with relief.

He told her that she should do the shopping and he would go up the Ambasciatori Hotel, find out when they expected Koster, then go down to the cable office and wait for her at the little corner café. She agreed readily, and he left her. He walked up to the hotel and asked at the desk if they had a reservation for Koster. The clerk, a middle-aged and balding man, told him they had the reservation for tomorrow night.

It was about seven in the evening, a little early for the cafés to be crowded, but already it seemed to him that word had

[184

got around that the Pope was dying. More people seemed to be on the street. Taking a taxi down to the cable office, he sent his cable telling Blondell he was back on the job. When he came out he stood looking across at the café where he was to meet Carla, then he realized she wouldn't have had time to get there, so he walked along to the Press Club to see how many foreign newspapermen were already in town. The atmosphere in the club had changed magically; it now hummed with voices —American, English, Dutch, French, Scandinavian. He couldn't get a stool at the crowded bar. He had his Scotch-and-soda at a table in the corner. Nowadays he was a secret drinker. When he was with Carla he drank only wine. Denying himself a second drink now, he went back to the corner café, and sat down and ordered a coffee.

Across the cobblestone square at the taxi stand, two drivers were having a violent argument. In the gathering darkness he could hear their voices but he couldn't see their faces. There was no end to the argument. It went on for half an hour, and he watched intently, rather than look at his watch. If he didn't look at his watch he would see Carla getting out of a taxi, he hoped; she would be there before he realized how much time had passed. Finally, he couldn't sit there quietly any longer. And he crossed toward the lighted cable office, yet he kept turning and watching the café; and soon he went back and sat down again. At last he said aloud, "It's two hours. Carla's not coming."

The shadowed faces of the old stone buildings around the piazza suddenly seemed to creep closer and closer to him until they walled in the little café and made it a prison, holding him while terrible things happened to Carla in some other place.

"Hey, taxi!" he called, hurrying across to the stand. He went home. In the hall, in the dim light, he went to run up the stairs, then stopped, listening. Carla shouldn't hear him running up the stairs. She should hear his slow and natural step moving toward her. He seemed to see her in the chair before her mirror; he could see her absorbed in the perfection of her appearance,

185]

losing all track of time. Late, always late now, carefully shading her eyelids and making that little face as she held her head on one side.

"Carla," he called, opening the apartment door. The rooms were in darkness. Turning on the light he looked in the bedroom, and then in the kitchen. The bag of groceries was on the table. She had been out and then had come home. The sight of the bag of groceries she had carried home filled him with relief.

I'm a fool, he thought. She didn't notice the time. Time means nothing to her. It's outrageous, really. Carla, you've got to cut it out. And he ran down the stairs and out, and, walked blocks, looking for a taxi, thinking of her sitting alone at the café by the cable office, waiting.

At the café he tried to ask the waiter if a girl had been there alone. But the waiter, who smiled helplessly and with great sympathy, had no English. Carla's gone, Sam thought, shivering. My God, it means she's gone. And he stared across the road at the lighted cable office.

The familiar lighted place beckoned to him, reminding him that there he might lose his feeling that Rome had become utterly alien; there he might think clearly. But when he was in the marble office, sitting at a desk in the bright hard light, he admitted to himself there was nothing to do but go home and wait and hope. He left, wearily. Back at the apartment he climbed the stairs slowly.

As long as he could sit in the kitchen, glancing sometimes at the bag of groceries on the kitchen table, he didn't have to yield to his despair. But nervous exhaustion began to overwhelm him. He dozed. Then he put his forearms on the table beside the grocery bag and he fell sound asleep. Soon he was muttering wildly in a dream in which he had painted a picture. At last, a beautiful picture. He had worked on it for years and years, showing it to no one. Year after year he had painted, altering a little, adding, changing, knowing exactly what he had in mind; and then on the street he had met old Streeter, who coaxed him to show him this picture. The old painter, after looking in wonder at the canvas, started to laugh. "There's nothing there, you madman. It's just a daub," Streeter said. While he himself was sitting down, his hands over his face weeping bitterly, he heard a noise and looked up. Old Streeter had snatched the big picture from the easel, and was running out. "Thief, thief," he shouted wildly. "Stop, thief," and he ran after him, but one of the gang of thieves tripped him and he fell.

His head had slipped off the kitchen table, and he had half lurched off the chair. Someone was knocking on the door. "All right. All right," he called, only half awake.

At the door was a small neat young man of thirty-five, with straight, smoothed-back black hair and alert nervous eyes, smiling at him. "Good evening, Signor Raymond," he said, putting out his hand with great formality. "Be at ease. I speak excellent English. The very best. I am Tomaso Ferraro. With the Pope dying, I have come from Milan for my newspaper. I would be happy to make the acquaintance of you and your wife."

"Well, come in," Sam said vaguely. "Sit down."

"My mother and sister have great respect for you," Tomaso said earnestly as he sat down. "You are absorbed, I understand, in his holiness' illness. It is too bad. You will want to be involved in everything that goes on. No?"

"I expect to be, yes," Sam said.

"There is much to know and see. It is all familiar to me."

"You are lucky."

"If I can be of any help . . ."

"I will call on you."

"And your wife?" he said, looking around. "I would like to meet your wife."

"She is out just now. I'm sorry," Sam said awkwardly. He didn't know whether he wanted Tomaso to go, or stay and distract him. Words wouldn't come to him. The window was open. He was listening for footsteps on the street. He tried to remember what Signora Ferraro had told him about this nervous-eyed, dapper little son of hers. They made conversation about Rome. It dragged. Tomaso suggested they go out and have a drink. As he declined, Sam had a hunch that Tomaso was feeling his way, nosing around, getting his hand in, possibly wondering what there was in it for him if his mother's tenants were taken up with all the ceremonies that would take place at the Vatican. "Ah, yes, I remember," Sam said. "You were a seminarian, weren't you?"

"It is true. I was a seminarian." And then, with a hopeful glint in his eye, "I have this perfect knowledge of all ecclesiastical matters."

"I'm sure you have. I understand it was a disappointment to your mother that you did not become a priest."

"Mothers always want their sons to become priests," he said, profoundly. "A nice point, eh? It is worthy of much speculation."

"I must think more about it."

"Do not misunderstand. I have no quarrel with the Church."

"What was the matter, if I may ask? Didn't the life appeal to you?"

"It would have been a career, yes," Tomaso said, smiling. "Do not think, please, that I failed in scholarship, Signor Raymond. Believe me, I have this extraordinary capacity for scholarship. I studied St. Augustine." Leaning forward a little, he took out an elegant cigarette case, offered Sam a cigarette, took one himself and then he grew thoughtful, his head on one side as if he were letting important years live again in his mind. "It is simple," he said with a graceful gesture and a little smile. "I spent years with Augustine's thought. Can you believe this? I had such a passion for understanding Augustine that I used to want to possess his whole thought. I wanted to think and feel as he did, see the whole world out of his eyes. I was an admirable scholar. And then—"

"And then?" Sam said, as Tomaso sighed.

"Then it struck me one day. What is this? I am not St. Augustine. I am Tomaso. What a discovery! What a revolt! The whole world there to look at out of my own eyes. So it was done. I am now a good journalist. Simple, no?"

"It is understandable."

"I am boring you. You look worried, signor."

"No, I was a little sleepy," Sam said nervously.

"Perhaps it is your wife you are worried about. Is she late? Do not worry," he said standing up. He had very shrewd knowing eyes, and now he was restless. He had decided, evidently, that there wasn't going to be anything for him in the association, and he was too cynical to waste any more time. "Another time we will have a drink. It was nice meeting you, Signor Raymond," he said, going toward the door. Then he smiled sympathetically.

"If you are worried about anything, Signor Raymond, try thinking of women."

"I'll do my best."

"Think of the soft parts of women, and you will be consoled," and he bowed. "A drink tomorrow perhaps?"

"Perhaps," Sam said. "Good night."

Alone, Sam stood in a trance, then he flushed, humiliated by Tomaso's sensual words. You'd think he knew what was worrying me and was mocking me, he thought. The soft parts of Carla. My God, he couldn't stop thinking of them. Then he went slowly to the bedroom cupboard, got Carla's bag and took out one of her books, the translation from Catullus, and lay down on the couch, telling himself he would stay there till midnight. Nothing to worry about until it was after midnight. It's a lot cooler out, but fortunately she's got on that sweater with the thick high collar, he thought. But what if someone had got her drinking? Yes, someone else would have to be in on it, he thought, and he put down the book, nervously. She would not sneak off by herself to drink. She had none of the cunning of an alcoholic. Torturing himself, he tried to see in his thoughts the face of the one who had taken her off. A thief. His dream then had meaning. Someone else had her. The thought of it, and his sudden fierce lust for her bewildered him. Yet again the piercing sensual yearning was mixed up with that joy he got out of anticipating her perfect freedom in serene self-containment. To possess her freely and yet know that she did not need to be possessed. In his confusion the whole line of his thinking broke down, and he closed his eyes and knew

189]

only that without the satisfaction of his dreams with her he did not want to go on, go anywhere, be anything. Whatever happened to him now his life could have no meaning. She had come to him, her hand out, offering him new life, and he had failed to snatch it; he had let her get away. No, by God, and in a rage he jumped up, threw the book in a corner and looked at his watch. It was after midnight. He hurried out. Carla, I'll get hold of you and break every bone in your body, he thought wildly, to drown out the terrible sound of his lonely footfalls on the street. He walked on the Via Veneto. He wandered through the cafés, but the faces and the sounds and the lights seemed to bring all the terrors of the alien night city against him. He looked suspiciously into the faces of many men. "Rue Gonhorrea," the Frenchmen called this street, he thought. It seemed to him the men all had appraising lewd glances. Thieves of the beautiful, glancing at him as if they had known of his bright-colored picture of Carla. As he wandered around at loose ends, watching and hoping, there came tumbling out of his imagination all the wild, passionate and debauched figures of Carla's stories, the figures she had made live with him all month in Rome. And they were as alive for him now as they had ever been in her imagination; and he hated them. A bunch of thieves, who had got hold of her mind as someone in this same place now was trying to get hold of her in the flesh.

On the street a man called, "Good evening," and Sam swung around. Tomaso Ferraro, passing with two plump girls, waved his hand grandly, with a bright smile. As Sam stood there, Tomaso, who had got ten paces ahead, suddenly turned and darted back to him, grabbed his arm, whispered excitedly. "You asked why I left the seminary. See, see," he said, pointing to the girls who were waiting, "I am a pig. It is because I am such a pig," and he darted ahead, got between the girls, took an arm of each and strolled off slowly.

"The little son of a bitch," Sam said to himself, uneasily. "Where does he come from? What's he trying to do to me? I'd better get home."

It was one-thirty when he stood at the bedroom door looking

at the empty bed. Without getting undressed he lay down in the dark. The beating of his own heart seemed to be the only sound now in the neighborhood.

A room in Rome. A man lying on the bed in the dark in a room in Rome, wondering why the smell of the house, and the bed and the silence was now so utterly alien. If only there could have been someone he could talk to who could share his kind of loneliness. There couldn't be anyone. There never could be anyone. Yet this loneliness seemed strangely familiar; the feel of failure; the feeling he was being cheated again of some splendid satisfaction, not just in sensual hunger; something flowering out of it; something just out of reach, like a splendid radiance of form only dimly glimpsed in his own mind, which he could express. He had the talent; this time it was life, not canvas. But he hadn't been able to hold on to her. What was the matter with him? Where had he failed with her? This feeling, was it the same feeling that had so often touched him when he had been painting? The sketch; throw it away. Another one; try it on canvas. Still the gnawing dissatisfaction; finally the blind anger as he tore up the canvas and went out and walked the streets, knowing there was no one who could ever understand his kind of loneliness.

"Carla," he said aloud. "You come back here. You're not lousing this up. I'll break every bone in your body." The angry words only made him frantic with desire for her. The words warred with his concern. Even with his secret lost picture of her. Near dawn he fell asleep.

When he woke up the room was filled with sunlight. It was almost noon. The sound of an enormously heavy footfall on the street, a slow *slap, slap, slap,* the step of a monster made him jump up and go to the window. A small boy, coming along solemnly, was slapping the soles of his shoes on the pavement. Sam got dressed quickly and telephoned Francesca and asked her to have lunch with him at the Fontana.

CHAPTER 20

IN HER simple dark-gray suit Francesca looked fresh, healthy and pretty. But as soon as Sam sat down with her in the restaurant he could see that she, too, was worried. In her eyes there was the light of things remembered uneasily, and he was secretly glad. It meant she would not notice his restlessness, nor be full of cynical false understanding.

"You do not look too happy, Francesca," he said, playing on her own concern, after he had let her order the lunch.

"It's nothing, Sam. I am not in a good mood, that's all."

"Is it the fact that the Pope is dying? Is it the general sadness? I feel it everywhere."

"Oh, pooh. Everybody knew the Pope was dying," she answered irritably.

"And your husband? Will he be here?"

"My husband? Why, yes. I've heard from him. In fact, he may come in today." Then their eyes met, and just for a moment, she showed a half-furtive trusting candor.

"I may be wrong," he said sympathetically. "Just say so if I am. But are you worrying about your husband—after the months of separation—being like . . . well . . . a stranger?"

"Well, of course it'll be a little uncomfortable," she said. Then the cynical woman, with a strange shyness, averted her

eyes. "Really, Sam, you do try to get to the point, don't you?"
And she might just as well have told him she dreaded her
husband exercising his connubial privileges. "Not that I
object," she said, the color mounting in her cheeks, "but if it
means nothing—if there should be a positive distaste—well,
where am I?" And Sam thought, You'll be back with those
pretty young girls you greet with such sweet animation. Well,
if he showed sympathy for her in her dilemma, she would be
willing to help him in his trouble. He went on consolingly,
"Well, you can't be sure, Francesca."

"Sure about what?" she asked sharply.

"Where any of us stands with each other. Any of us." And then
he hesitated for her eyes had narrowed, as if she were wondering
how much he had divined of her dread of the touch of a man
whom she was sure she had loved.

"I don't mind being frank," she said, blushing. "I don't know
why I tell things to you, Sam. I've got accustomed to living
alone, and I don't want my husband moving in on me. Well,
not at first, anyway. I mean I want to see. I'm so uncertain."

"Who knows? You might like it."

"You have a savage candor." Her face was scarlet, but she was
not angry. "Well, just the same, I'd appreciate it if one of your
newspaper friends needs an interpreter to get all the papal details. The fact is, well, I could give him all my time."

"Don't worry, Francesca. I have a man coming. Koster. I'll
speak to him."

"Thank you," she said gratefully.

"Just one thing, though. If you talk to this man Koster, I'd
appreciate it if you didn't mention me and Carla."

"Not a word, Sam. On my honor. How is she?"

"She got away," he whispered.

"Got away?"

"Yeah."

"How did she get away?"

"I mean," he stammered, growing pale, "she didn't come
home last night."

"Really?" she asked, brightening.

Controlling his anguish, he said, "The trouble is, Francesca, I don't know where to look for her."

"Sam," she said gently, "you're well rid of her."

"Rid of her? Who said I was rid of her? She's around here somewhere, isn't she?"

"Of course she is, Sam." A little impatiently she went on, "By this time you ought to know what she is better than I do. My goodness, Sam, from the beginning you knew very well the woman was a slut. There's an American expression . . . bum?"

"Tramp," he said, white-faced.

"Yes. A tramp."

"You don't know anything about her life, Francesca."

"You poor dear man," she said sympathetically. "I hate seeing you being childish and sentimental about Carla, if that's what you want to call her. You go on as if—well, as if you had been trying to help an innocent girl. She's tricky, Sam. Innocence with her is a long-lost cause."

"Oh, innocence be damned," he said harshly. "I haven't the slightest interest in innocence. Furthermore, you're intelligent enough, I hope, to know that the whole human race hasn't had any innocence for about twenty-five thousand years."

"Don't snap at me, Sam. If that's your point of view, it's all right with me. I agree there must be something that bothers the girl and makes her degrade herself. It goes without saying. Now, you wouldn't consider some sense of guilt?"

"No," he said wearily. "Not that burden-of-guilt nonsense. I get it in all the Sunday supplements, too. You're away off, away off. Look, Francesca, it's not guilt, it's the fear of life that has troubled the human race. No, you couldn't understand Carla."

"Maybe not," she said carefully. Then with deprecating diffidence, "If it's not just her strong sexual attraction, I don't understand this hold she has on you. What is it, Sam?"

"Of course you'd say it was just the strong sexual attraction," he said, shrugging with a disdainful smile. Then he paused, looking troubled. What if that was all it was? he wondered. No. Ah, no. On the bed with her, even in the moments of most fierce satisfaction in love-making, he had never felt touched by that mysterious quiet elation he got out of watching her play and clown and sing for him. Yes, it was something more—even if it were true that the quickening awareness flowered out of his sensual compulsion. But that look on her face as she sat in that chair! That one look he loved had seemed to lift him out of his own life. Just for the moment! Just while he watched and wondered. Now that Carla was away from him, he believed he could see what it was. The amused and perfect self-containment she showed in those moments seemed to stir him with the promise of a new kind of freedom.

Twice he went to speak, while Francesca waited, and each time he hesitated, puzzled that he should have thought of freedom. Carla ought to have been reminding him of all who had a broken spirit. Her terrible life ought to have broken her own spirit forever. No girl who had lived her life ought to have been able to sit alone at any time having that look, that smile, that invincible ever-returning freshness. In such moments she seemed to tell him of the wonderful resilience of the human spirit! The things she had endured—humiliation, brutality, despair—all drained through her spirit, all becoming, in spite of herself, summer ripeness. Out of misery and terror—the promise that the wisdom of smiling ripeness was all. Yes. In the happy glimpses she gave him of herself, he seemed to see how all the crushing experiences could be absorbed by the spirit, and refined into an awareness that the happy hunger for life was unquenchable. She gave him pride in life. An assurance that there was in him, too, the eternally unquenchable promise of spring. The real magic on earth.

"Sam—"

"Eh?" he said, flushed with emotion.

"I shouldn't ask you, I know."

"No, I'm glad you did. Look, I told you you didn't know anything about her life," he said, with an awkward smile as he tried to hide his emotion. "It ought to have made her a wreck. It was a degrading poverty-stricken life," and then he fumbled, half angry for he distrusted the expression in Francesca's eyes. "All right, Francesca. You talked the other day about atom bombs and pestilence, wondering if we'd survive. Remember?"

"I remember."

"It's comical. It's so comical. I'm telling you, the Christian, about resurrection."

"But Carla. . . ."

"Yes, Carla. All right. One girl you know. But, look. Out of the ruins of her life. That look that comes on her face. Something in her spirit survives. It's got to survive. It's the divine spark, Francesca."

"The divine spark, Sam?"

"Well," he said simply, "think me a fool, if you want to. She's just a girl, and you think she's all evil; that's your word, isn't it? But a man can grasp a truth in the dirtiest darkness. I've seen a look on her face, and to me it's a promise that no matter what happens to us, nothing we do or believe can kill off the spark."

"My goodness, Sam," she said, embarrassed.

"I know."

"What a way to look at a woman!" And then, recovering from her embarrassment, which was half pity for him, "Anyway, I don't think any woman would thank you."

"It doesn't matter. Help me find her."

"It's a big city."

"I don't give a damn how big it is."

"Poor Carla."

"Eh?"

"Look, Sam, are you sure it's Carla you're looking for?"

"What do you mean?"

"You were talking about life."

"Cut it out. It's Carla I'm looking for."

"All right, where do we look, Sam?" she asked, getting up.

"Not out in the suburbs, anyway," he said as he paid the waiter. "I know she's here in old Rome. Somewhere in my neighborhood."

"In your neighborhood?"

"Yeah, not too far away from me," and he smiled grimly.

[196

"I see," Francesca said. As she took his arm he caught the expression in her eyes, half pity, half amusement. It didn't bother him.

Wandering around the neighborhood, they walked for miles. They went to that little street of the painters, the Via Marguta; they went to the Piazza del Popolo and sat at the café and watched girls passing. Then he remembered that Carla had said no matter how often she had looked at the clock in the church tower above the Spanish Steps, the clock had always been wrong. Did it mean it had been her habit to pass that way every day? he wondered. "It's just a hunch," he said to Francesca. They went there. First they stood by Bernini's fountain. In the sunlight it was like a great bird; no, a dolphin, two heads spouting water to the sun. Standing at the top of the Via Condotti, they watched the girls in their Empire dresses, coming one by one up the street, all window-shopping at the high-fashion houses.

"That one, see that one," Francesca said. "The one in the blue dress. Isn't she lovely?"

"Yeah. Who's she?"

"A princess. I know her. She's really lovely."

"Good," he said, wishing she'd stop talking.

"Look at the stout man and the two women."

"What about them?" he asked restlessly.

"There, in front of Bulgari's."

The stout man and the middle-aged woman, his wife, and a younger woman were looking in the window of the famous jewelry store. As the man went to go in, the older woman restrained him. The three moved on a few paces and the man, laughing and expostulating, would have turned back to the store but this time the younger woman took his arm firmly.

"See. Germans," Francesca said, sniffing.

"Eh?"

"What other woman would stop a man from buying her some jewelry?"

Sam put up with her comments while he could believe that each girl they saw from a distance, coming up the street, could be Carla. "Look there," Francesca said, "the big man with his hands behind his back." A big, grave, middle-aged man came toward them. "A prince. It was in all the papers. His daughter is marrying a student who has nothing and is nobody. It's quite a scandal, Sam."

"Yeah, I guess so," and he sighed disconsolately. "We might as well go, Francesca."

"I'm sorry, Sam. It's like looking for a needle in a haystack. Is there anything more I can do?"

"I'll call you this evening after I've seen Koster," he said, putting a four-hundred-lire note into her hand. "That's for the taxi. Here's one now. Thanks, Francesca. Good-by. I'll wander over to the Press Club."

When she had gone he had a feeling similar to the one he had experienced wandering along in Parioli that first night he had come to Rome; a loss of all connection with the human race. Then he thought of his father. He took a taxi to the cable office and sent a cable to his uncle: PLEASE RUSH WORD OF MY FATHER. Feeling a little better, he walked along to the Press Club. It was crowded. Just then a newspaperman vacated a stool at the bar, and Sam moved in quickly.

The newspaperman beside him was a Frenchman of thirty-five, dark and assured, with alert intelligent gray French eyes. He had just come in from Paris, he said in English. He understood the Pope would surely die before tomorrow night. He hoped it would be tomorrow, for he knew Rome well and would like to look around the town tonight and have a little fun. "Is there a place near here where I can get some coffee and a sandwich?" he asked. "I've had nothing to eat."

"A little place, a minute away."

"Have a coffee with me."

"A pleasure," Sam said, and when they had walked down the street, and the Frenchman had gone to the counter and got his sandwich, they sat in the last of the sunlight, and Sam thought, This is the place where she was to meet me. It's better to be sitting in this place. It seemed to him he was giving Carla a second chance. Therefore, it was necessary to keep the Frenchman

[198

at this meeting place as long as possible. He would like to go from Rome to Paris, Sam said. "I have always felt indebted to the French spirit. I'm a great admirer of Albert Camus."

"Camus is all right," said the Frenchman. "But he should not have got the Nobel prize."

"No? Who should have got it?"

"You surprise me. André Malraux, of course."

"Oh, yes. He is very good, too."

"I am a friend of Malraux. If you come to Paris would you like to meet him? He is important, but I could take you to him. It would be an experience for you."

"An experience I would treasure, I assure you."

"I will arrange it for you."

As for himself, the Frenchman went on, he would be glad to be out of Rome and back in Paris in the company of such brilliant men as Malraux. The Italians were a bore. They were all actors. A man went soft in Rome, everything softened up; the Italian women were soft and uninteresting, too obvious, you know. Whatever they had to offer was thrown right at you in the sunlight. Just flesh. Now flesh was fine, but with the Frenchwomen there was light and shadow, mystery, intensity and surprise. Sam, no doubt, had learned, too, that an Italian woman in her ecstatic love moments never lost sight of the fact she was giving a performance. She had her lines to whisper. Had Sam heard them? *"Ah, Mamma mia,"* and then they whisper, *"Sei il primo chi m'ha fatto godere."* But if one heard these lines three or four times the glory wore off for one. No? He sounded brusque and confident, and very much like an American. His gray eyes were full of intelligence. But Sam had flushed; he had turned away to hide his torment; he couldn't bear to comment. He had been reminded of his own doubt of the abandonment behind Carla's own soft little cries.

"I am amused to see all these newspapermen here covering the death of a pope," the Frenchman said suddenly. "It's the biggest thing in Rome now for you, isn't it?"

"For me . . . well," Sam felt confused. The Vicar of Christ

hadn't been on his mind. "Yes, it's the biggest story," he said.

"It's not the biggest story. The biggest story in Rome and Italy is the international drug traffic."

"In that case, why don't you do it yourself?"

"And take my life in my hands? Oh, no. I have a good life. I like it. I keep it interesting."

"Then we will stick to the Pope."

"Why not? I have a big expense account."

"And the Roman nights."

"The Romans all go to bed early. They eat late, get sleepy and go to bed. The big thing here is the International Set. Take my word for it. It is worthy of your interest," he said. If one let oneself get involved with the International Set, what might happen was unpredictable and interesting. As a matter of fact, he went on, the best place to meet the International Set was in the Hotel de la Ville. Everyone came there around seven o'clock. What was Sam doing tonight? A colleague? Koster. The name was familiar. Why not show up with his colleague at the Hotel de la Ville—the upstairs bar—and they could all have a drink? the Frenchman asked, as they shook hands. And he trailed along with Sam across the cobblestone square to the taxi stand.

Why was the man clinging to him? Sam wondered in the taxi. Was the Frenchman as lonely as he was himself? Was everyone in Rome alone and looking for someone, or something? Even Carla, from the time she came to Rome, had been searching for some strange consolation. Oh, the stupid crazy dissolute scared little fool! To go into a tailspin just when he had fitted all the pieces together. Wherever she was now, was she whispering, *"Mamma mia. Sei il primo che"*— No. No. No, and he shivered and had to close his eyes.

At the Ambasciatori he asked at the desk for Koster.

Koster was in his room, the clerk said. What was the name?

"Sam Raymond. Is Mr. Koster really in his room?" he asked as if it was incredible that anyone he knew should be where he was expected to be.

"Four-four-two," the clerk said, and he watched him suspiciously as he crossed the lobby. He saw him stop to stare at himself in the mirror on the pillar.

Is it me? Sam thought. That ghost. That pale agitated worried man in the neat dark-gray suit of Italian cut. A worried slob someone had just kicked in the gut. Crack a smile, you poor fool. Have some self-respect. And when he stepped into the elevator behind the little old uniformed man, he worked the muscles of his face, loosening himself up for Koster's benefit.

CHAPTER **21**

SAM didn't know much about Koster,
but on the other hand, no one in the business knew much about
the man's personal life. Koster had some initials but never
used them. He had persuaded his editors that his dispatches
from the capitals should be signed simply "Koster." His
enemies, who didn't like his personal penetrating interpreta-
tion of world events, called him, "That Greek." Others insisted he was an Armenian and claimed, mockingly, they had
seen him in Paris in the old days with rugs on his arm, peddling
them at the cafés. In *Who's Who* he was listed as the son of a
Czarist Colonel. But there were newspapermen, claiming to
have known him for years, who insisted he was an Irish-Ameri-
can. Koster covered all the great conferences and special world
events. Before going to London for the *Weekly,* he had been in
Washington and at the United Nations. With a wise, patient,
comprehensive understanding and intimacy that infuriated
other newspapermen, he wrote of what was going on behind
the scenes on the world stage. He was at home in London, for it
was a fact that he had taken a degree from the London School
of Economics. Recently, for the *Weekly,* he had written a series
of articles on the Americanization of Europe. "The United
States is the source of a dreadful infection," he had declared.

[202

It had been a very workmanlike piece. There was nothing Koster couldn't explain in a newspaper.

"Come in," Koster called when Sam rapped on the door. Entering the room, Sam expected to be greeted by a tall, graying scholarly man. This picture of Koster had been in his mind for months. Sitting on the bed, using the phone, was a small, dark, balding man in an undershirt, one side of his face dabbed with shaving cream, a round-faced man with bright dark eyes, who waved his hand as he snarled indignantly into the telephone. "No. *Koster*. No, not *Foster*. *Koster*. Tell him Koster called. I said *Koster*. Not *Foster*. No, listen. *K. K. K,* as in *Koster*. Will you listen? K-O-S-T-E-R," and then he shouted *Koster* and a string of soft curses came from him. And then, with bitter sarcastic patience he spelled it again. "K-O-S-T-E-R. That's right, Koster. Very, very good. I tell you, you don't need the initials. Just Koster," and he put down the phone wearily, as if he had been fighting a fierce battle.

"Sam Raymond," he said. "I'm Koster."

"So I gathered."

"I was leaving a call at Geneva. What can you do if the stupid girl is deaf and can't spell?" And then he smiled with surprising freshness, as if he were ready with many helpful explanations.

"In September I nearly caught up to you at the Garden Roxy," Sam said. "What about the room you were to have for me?"

"A room? Nobody said anything to me about your coming."

"They forgot. I'm not surprised."

"I only stayed there two days," Koster said, with the same quick effortless smile. "I got the hang of it. Cleared right out. Busy in London, you know. You've been here some time?"

"Ever since."

"Good. You go for those Italian suits, eh? I'll finish shaving and I'll put on a clean shirt. There's a bottle on the bureau. Help yourself. You look as if you need a drink," and he went back to the bathroom.

Walking restlessly over to the window, Sam looked out. It

was twilight now, and it was like looking over soft bluish-green rolling landscape to a hill far beyond, on which was a villa or a temple or a church becoming slowly a part of the cool blue dusk. The beginning of another night, hiding Carla from him. No, hiding him from her if the one who was with her left her alone. Unless she started to drink she would grow uneasy, then nervous. Then, who could say what she would do trying to overcome her need to be with him? Poor Carla. He felt sick with worry.

"I heard about you," Koster called, his words muffled as if his mouth was now covered with soap, and he was laughing. "A damn good cameraman who got lost in Rome, they say. What is it with you? The Italian kick?" Now, shaving his lip, the words came through his teeth. "Take my word for it, it doesn't last. Wears awfully thin and, besides, by this time it's corny. It's for your old Aunt Mathilda. Unless you go for ruins it's just a big *pasta* palace. Another thing, it's not very stimulating intellectually. These Romans don't read anything and they don't have any theatre. And the women around here—you'll be disappointed, pal. Now Englishwomen! Don't overlook them. They seem to know they have their disadvantages, so they work hard at pleasing a man." Then he came to the door, rubbing his face with a towel. "Where are you living?"

"Eh? Oh," Sam said, turning away from the window. "Just a few blocks away. You'll find it expensive living here, Koster."

"Nuts," Koster said, grinning. "Don't fall for that stuff. You can live here more cheaply than you can in London or Paris. I hope you don't take these Italians too seriously." He was getting dressed. Now that he had his suit on, he looked like a brisk energetic clean American executive. Getting himself a drink, he sat down and outlined his plans. His sources had informed him the Holy Father wouldn't die tonight. The press-relations officer at the Vatican, who was no doctor, of course, had shown him all the bulletins. It looked as if tomorrow night would be the big one. What he was going to do was arrange to have a car take them out to Castel Gandolfo. It might be at any time—morning, afternoon or night—so they should be together or within reach of each other. His first story, he had decided, ought to be called "The Night the Pope Died." Out at Castel Gandolfo, the thing to do was to keep one's eyes open. The chances were a hundred-to-one that some Italian journalist would bribe a member of the Pope's household to signal from a window that the Pope was breathing his last. "There's a great picture for you, Raymond, if you can get it. Isn't it worth watching for? Anyway, how do you like the idea, 'The Night the Pope Died'?"

"Not bad," Sam said, trying desperately to keep his mind on what Koster was saying. "It sounds good. What do I do with the film?"

"I've made the arrangements, Sam. You give me your film and there's an air-line pilot here. He'll whip them across."

"It's nice to know that everything's looked after, Koster."

"Everything I can think of. I'll play it as big as I can. Mind you," he went on philosophically, "this isn't the biggest story in the world for me. The biggest story is going on behind the scenes at Geneva. Here you have the death of the head of a church. At Geneva, where nations are trying to deal with the control of nuclear power, we're dealing with the future of the whole human race." He smiled as if he knew he was slumming, coming to Rome to write about the Pope. "I wish I could have stayed in Geneva. You see, Sam, what's involved there is the whole question of human survival."

"You, too?"

"Me, too?"

"I mean it's what they all say," Sam stammered, confused, then with a strange smile, "Don't worry, Koster. We'll survive."

"Just like that? Automatically?"

"Just like that."

"I see," Koster said impatiently. "And why is this to be?"

"Well, we have no choice."

"No choice? Why not?"

"Don't ask me. All I know is there's a spark in us," Sam said restlessly. "No matter what we do, somehow it has to go on."

"You sound like a . . ." Then Koster started to laugh. "No, you're kidding me," he said, and then suddenly hopeful, "Maybe you're a Catholic. I certainly hope you are. Are you? I'm counting on it."

"No, I'm not Catholic."

"Damn it all. Here we are on this job, a fine pair of heathens. How I hate being confused by details I only half understand."

"Look, Koster," Sam said with an indifferent air. "What about an interpreter? I know a woman."

"No, Sam. I need someone who's a devout, pious soul."

"Just a minute, Koster. This one has a bishop for an uncle. You cannot do better than that, can you, Koster?"

"Hmmm. Sounds good. A bishop, eh?"

"A woman of forty. Perfect English. Knows everybody in Rome, too."

"What does this treasure look like, Sam?"

"A pretty face. But built like—well, you know that movie star, the singer that had such trouble with her weight because of the way she was built?"

"I don't go to the movies. Just let's say she's fat. How much does this fat woman want?"

"Sixteen dollars a day. And it's not that she's really fat. It's the build. It's not unattractive."

"What does she do for sixteen dollars? Stand on her head at high noon? No, I'll pay her by the hour."

"Or you can take her for half a day."

"Here," Koster said, pointing to the telephone. "Call the bishop's expensive niece. Get her down here. Now, let's go out and eat something. It's nearly seven. All I want is a club sandwich."

"You can get one along the street," Sam said, and he went to the telephone, called Francesca and asked her to meet them at the Café de Paris within an hour. Then he and Koster went out, and they sat on the terrace of the café. The night was still warm and pleasant, people were coming and going, and twice Sam half stood up anxiously, thinking he saw Carla.

"What's the matter with you, Sam?" Koster asked. "Do you

have to go to the bathroom, or what have you picked up around here?"

"I'm watching for Francesca," Sam lied. It gave him an excuse to keep on craning his neck. While he was there, watching so many girls come and go, he could feel hopeful. This one terrace became all of Rome because Carla had once come there with Alberto. "There's Francesca now," he said. Greeting her with relief, he introduced her to Koster, who immediately began to haggle with her about her price. While the business discussion proceeded, Sam fell into a trance.

From the great gallery of street faces he had seen in Rome, he tried to pick out the one who would be with Carla; the one who had got her drunk. It wouldn't be an American. It couldn't be Alberto, or Francesca would know. No, it would be an Italian, or a Swede or a German. Whoever it was, he couldn't keep her drunk. Sam had such faith in her need of him that he seemed to hear her calling, "Sam, Sam, where are you?" His head began to sweat, and his hand, reaching for the drink, shook. Out of the corner of his eye he could see that Koster and Francesca, having reached an agreement, were finding each other amusing. Francesca, true to her word, would not mention Carla, he knew. Yet, how could she laugh and be so amusing with Koster and not notice his own terrible restlessness? Then he remembered the Frenchman and the Hotel de la Ville. Wasn't it the kind of place where a foreigner or rich Italian would go with a girl like Carla? he asked himself as he glanced at his watch. Gradually he became convinced that Carla was at the Hotel de la Ville. It made him tense with anger. He had to close his eyes till the rage left him.

Turning to Koster he said brightly, "I've got just the thing for you. The Hotel de la Ville. This afternoon I met a newspaperman from Paris. He asked me to come around there tonight. This is the hour when it's the playground for the International Set. Everyone drinks there. Movie stars, playboys, hopped-up glamour women. What do you say we go around?"

"Did he really invite you?" asked Francesca, who had no interest in the International Set.

"Of course he did, and I said I'd show up with some friends. What about it, Koster?"

"It sounds just right for me," Koster said. "And it's all right for Francesca, too, isn't it, signora?" and he put his hand on her knee.

From the inside pocket of his coat, Sam took out that well-worn airplane-ticket folder in which, from the beginning, he had kept his big Italian lire notes. "Oh, for God's sake," Koster said in disgust. "Put that thing away. What are we supposed to be? A couple of worried tourists?" Jerking out his own wallet, he put down the note for the waiter. A flush on his face, Sam put away his ticket folder. But when the waiter brought the change and Koster tipped him, the waiter looked unhappy. Quickly, Francesca took from Koster's hand some coins, and smiled apologetically at the waiter who bowed to her gratefully. In his turn, Koster flushed. Meeting Francesca's eyes, Sam caught her faint smile, and he knew that Koster had never seen Rome or Italy until he had come there a month ago for the two days at the Garden Roxy Hotel.

"Let's go," Sam said, with a savage satisfaction.

They walked along that side street by the Ambasciatori Hotel, the street of the little boutiques where he had bought the dresses for Carla. On the narrow sidewalk there wasn't room for walking three abreast, and Sam hung back. He slowed down at the little shop, staring in the shadows at the dress displayed in the window, wondering if Carla would like it. Then he heard Koster call, "Come on, Sam," and he caught up to them.

At the hotel Sam said, "It was the upstairs bar I was to go to. I suppose we just get in the elevator and ask for the upstairs bar. Come on."

Upstairs they entered a huge carpeted, high-ceilinged double room, with gilt furniture and pinkish walls. A room big enough for an elegant and brilliant international throng. But it was as if the splendid room had been suddenly emptied on word of their arrival. The empty room, why had it been so quickly emptied? Sam wondered uneasily. No, one lone drinker sat at the bar and he was not the Frenchman. Then Sam noticed, at the far end of the room, a girl with auburn hair sitting by herself. He walked slowly toward her, the walk so long and solitary because the room was empty. All by herself she was watching television. When finally she heard his step, she looked up. She had a very pretty starlet's empty face. And he began, "Excuse me," but she looked too bored to move her lips, too unimpressed to try, and he turned away, looking back the length of the room at the distant bar where the lonely figure sat.

Francesca and Koster were also watching this man, who had his elbows on the bar and his head in his hands. Suddenly the drunk slid slowly along the bar; he would have toppled off the stool, but the bartender, leaning over, grabbed him and straightened him up. But the drunk wasn't balanced quite right on the stool. Slowly he slid, toppling toward the other side. Coming around from behind the bar, the bartender took great pains to balance the drunk on the stool, then stood back, his arms folded, regarding his engineering feat with satisfaction.

"The International Set," Koster said bitterly.

"I'm sorry," Sam said. "It must be long past the cocktail hour."

"Where's your Frenchman?"

"It's late. Maybe he's gone off somewhere with the Set."

"The whole Set? Someone must have blown the whistle. Well, I'm going to the Press Club," Koster said sourly. "Come on. Let's get out of here."

Out on the street again, with the doorman beckoning to a taxi, Sam said, "You two go along, and I'll join you later. I'm going home to write a letter. Okay? So long." As he started to walk back the way he had come, Francesca turned, watching him with pity as he had watched Alberto with pity that day in the square, in front of the church of Santa Maria in Trastevere, for he had started to walk rapidly.

CHAPTER 22

GOING up the stairs slowly he thought he detected an unfamiliar odor, and at the door he sniffed, and then his heartbeat came up high in his chest. It was a cigar. He pushed the door open. Carla was there. Still wearing her mohair sweater, she was in the big chair, and on the sofa, stretched out and smoking a cigar, was the Italian American, Joe Mosca.

"So here you are, Jack," Mosca said, swinging his feet to the floor. "I was ready to give up on you. Not Anna. She was right."

"Anna? What is this?" Sam asked.

"Hello, Sam," she said, standing up nervously.

"What is this?"

"Now take it easy, Sam."

"All last night—you didn't come home last night."

"I'm sorry. It was nothing. Just that I had to make a point for myself." Her smile wasn't a success, yet he could see that at least for some hours she hadn't been drinking.

"What's this guy doing here?" he asked harshly. "Tell him to beat it."

"Take it easy, Sam. Mr. Mosca and I want to talk to you."

"You and this guy? Don't make me laugh." Walking over

to big Mosca, he took him by the arm. "Come on, beat it," he said.

"Now you listen, Sam," she pleaded.

"Shut up, Carla. I'll talk to you later," and he swung around on Mosca. "I said 'beat it.' Go on."

"What's this 'Carla' stuff?" Mosca asked bewildered. "Who's Carla? I don't get it. Look, Jack, maybe she gives me the wrong angle on you." On his big swarthy stupidly handsome flat-eyed face was an expression of honest disappointment; as if whatever Carla had told him about Sam had been satisfactorily convincing, even though it went against all his experience. The ashes on his cigar were about to fall, and he delicately stepped over to the table, tipping the ashes on a saucer. But he took his time. He was reluctant and disappointed, and so was Carla. And the way they were waiting and watching him made Sam tremble with rage. "I do you a favor, Jack," Mosca said amiably. "I talk it over with the kid last night and we get around to talk about you . . ."

But Sam, in a sudden movement, had got between Mosca and Carla. He grabbed her wrist, he held on so tightly his arm trembled, yet she didn't try to pull away. Her eyes were on his trembling hand, and then he saw the confidence come into her eyes. He dropped her wrist quickly. "What are you doing with this big mug, Carla?"

"I met Mr. Mosca on the street yesterday. You had talked to him, so he spoke to me. Mr. Mosca knows who I am."

"And who are you?"

"I'm Anna Connel. You know that."

"Is that what you told him?"

"I just couldn't place her, Jack," Mosca said, shaking his head. "Knew I had seen her. 'Where are you from, honey? Where have I seen you?' I said."

"And you had a drink. Oh, of course you had a little drink," Sam said savagely.

"All right. I had a drink," she said.

"You and this ox," Sam whispered.

Joe Mosca, standing behind him, laughed a soft, patient, understanding, almost good-natured laugh. And as the smoke of Joe's strong cigar drifted in a little cloud over Carla's head, Sam turned from her in disgust. But the disgust seemed to drain him of all strength. He had to sit down, then watched and endured the sight of Mosca giving Carla a protective and comforting pat on the shoulder. They were chummy, he thought. They were sure of each other. He could almost see the way it had happened; the meeting on the street, the talk about Anna Connel, then the drink and another one as the big stupid illiterate nice guy went on flattering her vanity. "You were big, honey. You can still be big. This schoolteacher friend, this grocery clerk. What do you say he is? A photographer. What the hell? Does he take pictures of you?" A cheap room somewhere. Yes, he could almost smell it on her! Then the appeal Mosca's uncomplicated confidence made to her; it would seem like something she had encountered a dozen times in her tough girlhood and could handle if Mosca could help her.

"You little fool, Carla," Sam said, hating the sight of them standing together. In his eyes there was such bitter contempt that Mosca, noticing it, reddened angrily. A bit of tobacco had got on his tongue. He spat it on the floor.

"All right, Sam," Carla said fiercely, as if she could read his thoughts. "I shouldn't have come here at all."

"What's this big ape to you?"

"I could smack him," Mosca said thoughtfully. "But you tell him, honey."

"Mr. Mosca has the kind of connections I need right now, and for the time being, anyway, he's going to be my manager."

"Your manager!" Sam gasped, standing up slowly; and he showed how amazed he was. "Carla, this guy is . . ." he began. He wanted to go on and say, "My God, didn't you learn anything from what happened to you before?" But he was too shocked. This man was right out of the sleaziest part of her past, a man who would find little jobs for her, whispering always about a bigger man he knew, and if he had something to sell he would know such men; he would join with them in pushing her, as she before had been pushed and cheapened; already he would have outlined his campaign in his smooth sleazy likable knowing tough style. Turning to her contemptuously, Sam said, "Haven't you got a brain in your head? No memory?" But then, as she confronted him boldly, he saw the ruinous memory of it all in her eyes. She knew what she was doing. She knew she was facing her own past. She had made up her mind that she wanted to sing now, as she had told him, wanted to get started in any little way; felt he had put her off and was willing bravely to hurl herself at the cheapest part of her old life, thinking she had to be able to show herself she could do it; was strong enough now to use the old experience. He could only shake his head, half frightened, half astonished by the reckless rapid growth of the faith in herself he had planted in her. Her eyes remained unyielding; she thought she knew what was necessary in the break she was making.

"You were kidding me, Sam. Maybe you were kidding yourself. I told you I was ready to sing. I knew you'd keep putting me off."

"Oh, you stupid woman."

"I have to be on my own, Sam."

"With him, Carla? For God's sake, don't call it your own."

"You said a hundred times you wanted me to be on my own," she insisted. "You used to try and get me to go off on my own, don't you remember?" She waited, forcing him to think of the times when he would leave her for a few minutes on the street and hide in doorways, watching over her, protesting to himself that no human being should be so dependent on another. The memory of it was like a stab at his own hidden loneliness. "Well, it got so that you didn't notice you were kidding yourself," she went on. "Isn't that right, Sam?"

"It's humiliating," he whispered, his head whirling. "How can you bear to talk this way about you and me in front of this clown?"

"Hey now, wait, Jack," big Mosca said earnestly. "Ain't I here talking to you, Jack, and why? Ask yourself why. Out of great respect, see?" His wrinkled brow was shooting up and down as he concentrated with sincerity. "I can see something, Jack. I can see how it could be a very big thing for you to have this talented girl back on her feet, now she can stay off the juice. You get my sympathy. It's big, only you can't quite see your way clear to get her started. Right, eh? Right? All it means is that you need guidance. A little guidance, Jack. That's where I come in. I know the ropes. I cut you in, of course. Look, already I come through with the guidance. Already I'm right on the ball. Get this. There's a place on the lower Veneto. Night club. Dance hall. Spenders from all over. I'm a friend of the management. Already I give them the information on our girl. A big star. A big star, off the juice and on her way again. So they give her a spot tomorrow night. Now look, Jack," he said, leaning close. "Our girl tells me this was the biggest thing in your life. I say to her, it still is, honey. Sure it is. I'm right. Well, I'm short of funds, Jack. It should be all class. Our girl needs some new concert clothes. Nothing cheap in the way of a dress for her. I'm just about broke. I figure it would take a hundred dollars."

"From me? You want a hundred dollars—from me?" Sam whispered.

"If it means so much to you, and if you can spare it, Jack."

"You big ugly meathead," Sam cried. The rage of the whole night was in him. "Get out of here," he shouted. Leaping at Mosca, he knocked him off the chair. Grabbing him by the throat, he tried to drag him to his feet. And it happened so quickly he had Mosca up and spinning toward the door.

"Jesus, Jesus, Jesus," Mosca protested, bewildered. At the door he stiffened, rocklike, and jerked Sam's hands from his throat. Like a bull, he butted him away, stood in astonishment breathing heavily, then his face became livid. "And I'm Joe Mosca," he said, coming slowly toward Sam. He slapped him hard on the face. Sam swung at him, but Mosca, ducking, slapped him again on the mouth, and then again as he shoved him to the floor.

"Stop it," Carla cried as Sam raised his head.

He saw the raised foot, the leg swinging, and he tried to roll

[214

away. "Cut it out," Carla yelled. Sam couldn't see her; she was behind Mosca. The foot went wildly up in the air as Carla pushed Mosca off balance. "I said cut it out," she said grimly.

"He had it coming to him," Mosca said. "What was I to do?"

Wiping his hand across his mouth as he raised himself to his knees, Sam could see that Carla, standing between him and Mosca, wasn't frightened, just angry and grim, having known this kind of violence many times in her life. "It's my fault," she said bitterly. "I had it all wrong." And then she faltered, shaken by the look in his eyes as he wiped the blood from his mouth. "Oh, Sam, I'm sorry," she whispered. "Oh, Sam, Sam," and she took a step toward him, wanting to put her arms around him. Then struggling against her instinct, she shook her head desperately; she knew what it would mean. "I'm ready to sing, Sam. I'm by myself," she said fiercely. "I'm ready and I know you'll never agree I'm ready. No. Please, please don't touch me." The view of herself he had planted too firmly in her imagination was making her pull away from him wildly. "Come on, Mr. Mosca," she said stiffly, going toward the door.

"Wait a minute."

"Wait for what, Sam?"

"You think you're better off without me?"

"I'm a singer, Sam."

"All by yourself?" Sam asked bitterly.

"Isn't it what you told me a hundred times?"

"And I'm supposed to be holding you back?" he asked wildly. "You don't think I wanted you to stand alone? All right," and he laughed crazily. "Believe me, it's what I wanted. If there's a chance—even with this manager—have the biggest chance in the world. Here. If it's only a dress you need." Fumbling in his hip pocket for the wallet in which he kept the American money, he pulled it out and as he counted the bills his fingers trembled.

Mosca, watching like a startled boy, blinked his eyes stupidly. "Eighty dollars. It's all I got here," Sam muttered. One of his bruised lips was thickening. It was hard to talk. "Get yourself a dress, get gloves. Go ahead. Go to it. Good luck."

"You're a . . ." Mosca began. His surprise and wonder made him stammer. "Well, you're a white man." But she didn't hear him. A little awed, she stared at Sam, then tears came to her eyes.

"Well, why don't you drop around tomorrow night and give the lady a hand?" Mosca said awkwardly. "How about it, Jack?"

"Oh, no. He's busy with the Pope," Carla whispered. "Come on, please." But at the door she turned. The whole room seemed to hold her, and then she glanced at the money Mosca had put in her hand, and then at Sam. He had had to give it to her, she knew. He had to because of what she was to him, in spite of his humiliation. The little flicker of pride and confidence coming into her eyes made him turn away. He heard her step on the stairs, becoming one with Mosca's.

Sam listened intently until the footfalls had gone. Then he strode into the bedroom, jerked open the cupboard door and looked at all her dresses on the hangers, and at the pairs of shoes on the floor. Suddenly he grabbed at the dresses, one by one, and threw them on the bed. He tossed four pairs of shoes out on the floor. It was all he could do about them now. She could get them in the morning.

Never had he felt so tired, and when he got undressed he looked at the bed with her dresses thrown on it, and couldn't bear to touch it. His Roman bed, the bed with its squeaking springs and her lies, her little whispers he had known from the beginning were lies. Jerking the comforter from the bed, he went in to the living-room couch and lay down, drawing the comforter around him, and tried to concentrate on being with Koster at Castel Gandolfo tomorrow night.

CHAPTER 23

HE SEEMED to be ready to go to Castel Gandolfo as soon as the word came, and all day with Koster his nervous enthuisasm was admirable. His eager involvement in the story, "The Night the Pope Died," already being written —only the lead would be done at Castel Gandolfo—delighted Koster. Sam supplied colorful little mournful touches from the streets of Rome. "Wait a minute, Koster. Here's something else . . ." he would say as if he were trying to hurl all his imagination into the impending death of the Pope.

"Boy, you're on the ball," Koster would say appreciatively, for he was getting what he wanted. His story was to consist of little vignettes of Roman life, with the whisper coming along the streets and in the bars and the homes and the dance halls that the Pope was dead.

"It could be wonderful," Sam said, as if he were carried away. "But you're missing the ordinary orthodox Roman family." He told him about Mrs. Ferraro and her daughter, how they would kneel down and pray, he was sure, and how they would then go out to church; a woman and her daughter hurrying through the streets to the temple. He made it sound so vivid that Koster told him that as a cameraman he was a treasure. When Francesca came in she, too, seemed to believe he was

217]

now absorbed in the big story. It was only later on when they went down to the Vatican Press office, and Koster left them outside waiting, that she said quietly, "Any word of the lady?"

"None," he lied.

"I know you don't believe me, but I'd say you're in luck."

"Maybe so. How are you liking Koster?"

"I'm hearing a lot about conferences anyway," she said, with her perfect cynical smile. "But he fooled me last night. He told me he had a view of Rome from his hotel window. Far in the distance, he said, was a temple or a church on a hill, or something, and would I tell him what it was; and like a fool, Sam, I went there and he started crawling all over me. Imagine! My, he's blunt. He's a barbarian, of course."

"No, a well-educated man. Don't be fooled."

"Am I to be fooled by a university degree? When did a college degree ever give a man any sensitivity? The journalist who covers everything and feels nothing. I just know he hasn't any taste."

"Oh, come on, Francesca. How do you know?"

"The poor man. He wouldn't know a good picture from a bad one. Not unless he researched it. I mean, he doesn't know anything by himself. Only after a conference. 'Conference Koster.' He looks up things."

"Well, don't *you* look up. Here he is."

"All right, children, back to the hotel now," Koster said cheerfully. "I'll arrange for an automobile to pick us up at six."

At the hotel Sam told them he would go to his own place and get his photographic equipment. He agreed to meet them in time to have a drink at the café, before the car came. Outside the hotel he stood looking along the street at the terraces, a surprised expression on his face. Am I really going out to Castel Gandolfo? he wondered. As if the question were ridiculous, he walked away abruptly, crossed the street and went down to his own place and got his oblong leather bag from the cupboard and carefully examined his lenses and his cameras. Then he looked at his watch, told himself he was very tired from his lack of sleep last night, and it would be better to lie down and rest for a while and let Koster and Francesca have their drink without him. He tried to fall asleep. Everything seemed to depend on his falling sound asleep. But sometimes the muscles in his stomach would tighten from anxiety; at other times he would be suddenly alert. If Koster should come calling for him in the car, he would be trapped, he knew. Everything then depended on the timing. He waited carefully until it was ten minutes after six. He was allowing Koster the ten minutes to get disgusted, to shout at Francesca, "Where the hell does the guy live?" Again he looked at his watch, jumped up, grabbed his bag and hurried down the stairs. The street lights were lit. "My God, I'm a grown man and I'm acting like this," he groaned, but he couldn't help himself. I'm a two-faced, cheap, deceitful man, letting a colleague down. While he was accusing himself, he looked cautiously up the street, watching for the car, then he began to walk all the way around the block. On the corner there was a little dwarf, only three feet high, squatting with his cap out, begging. He had a beard. He had an old and sinister face. Sam dropped all the coins he had in his pockets in the cap. It didn't seem to be enough. He added a four-hundred-lire note. The bearded dwarf's eyes were wild. Turning the corner, Sam made his way back along the Via Veneto to the Ambasciatori, keeping on the other side of the street. It was now almost half-past six. Across the road, under the hotel arch, a private car was waiting. Then he saw Koster come hurrying out of the hotel entrance, beckoning impatiently to Francesca, who trailed him sedately, and they got into the car. When it had vanished down the street, Sam crossed the road and strode importantly into the hotel lobby, his bag swinging, making himself a conspicuous figure; and he asked at the desk for Koster. Mr. Koster had just left, said the clerk. "What?" Sam cried. "What is this?" and he dashed out of the hotel. But he stood at the entrance, looking forlornly along the street. He scowled at the doorman, making an impression on him as if he thought the man might be in the pay of Koster and watching him, then he hurried across the road. Anyone could see that he was hurrying back home, hoping Koster would be there. Anyone could see that they had missed each other and that he was frantic. Again he walked all the way around the block.

At a café, lower down on the Via Veneto, he sat down, feeling utterly exhausted, and ordered a Scotch. As his foot touched his bag, he looked down at it and frowned. It was incredible! Sam Raymond, a reliable man on a job. Sam Raymond, who had never let anyone down, had been hiding from Koster like a schoolboy. "You thickheaded fool," he muttered. "You made yourself a worm." Then he thought, Supposing she brings it off? Supposing she stands up and sings and sees she can do it and laughs and shrugs? On her way! If she did, it would be his doing. The sight of her, the picture she would make, dazzled him. Mosca was a cheap muttonheaded thief. That's what he was, a thief!

The seedy little waiter, who was bringing him another drink, drew back as Sam looked up at him wildly, wanting to shout, "Yes, I said 'thief.'" The waiter looked so startled that Sam closed his eyes and hung his head, but it didn't help him. He seemed to see himself grabbing Carla and beating her.

The expression on his face was so malevolent the waiter touched his arm in alarm. *Scusate, signore, ma mi pare che siete ammolato . . ."*

"*Che?* No. Nothing," Sam said, trying to smile as he got up. He walked away. Finally he went home and lay on the bed smoking. Not a move did he make. He lay there for two hours in utter stillness, then he got up, walked slowly up and down the room sometimes looking at his watch, and when it was ten he went out.

On his first evening with Francesca, she had given him a snooty little talk on third-rate Roman night clubs filled with foreigners. Once, in a taxi, she had pointed out a place on the lower Via Veneto, as she might have pointed at Trajan's Column, or the central office of the Communist Party. Sam had no trouble finding this place.

Entering, he did not feel as ill at ease as he had expected to. The scene was familiar; it was as if he had left Rome and was back in America. Were these places the same all over the world?

he wondered. It had the same dim light, and some B-girls, and a bar, and many tables, a floor space for dancing and a little platform for the orchestra. Even the tune the small orchestra was playing sounded familiar, only thinner and tired and stale. The faces of those at the tables—he could get only a quick nervous impression in the dim light—were the middle-aged faces of restless wanderers from many countries. The women with young pretty faces had no elegance, no air of seductive aloofness. A sudden loud laugh came from a plump woman, at a table with a stout German. The German, annoyed, spoke to her grimly. Businessmen on a holiday, trying to keep their women in hand. There would be a silence, then suddenly, noisy chatter. Then silence again, then the low hum of steady conversation which faded out as the orchestra started to play. The dancers, who got up slowly, all moved with a kind of international apathy, till one thin fair woman in a low-cut dress, her collar bone jutting out—who was dancing with a slim, mean-eyed, olive-skinned man ten years younger—suddenly planted her feet wide. Leaning back, she bumped her belly up and down obscenely to the rhythm of the music. At first her sleazy escort, with a tired smile, tried wearily to keep up with her, then couldn't be bothered, and with a shrug he walked away. Left alone on the floor, she giggled stupidly. As other dancers brushed against her, she went on giggling hysterically; then, suddenly mute and bewildered, making her way slowly to the table, she tried desperately to smile with warmth at her escort and take his hand which lay on the table. He regarded her impassively, then slapped her hand hard. Slumping in the chair in a stupor, she looked as if she wanted to cry and couldn't. And Sam, who was watching, knew he needed a drink.

"Would you like a table? Are you alone, sir?" asked the plump headwaiter in good English.

"A table. I'm alone."

"It is difficult if you are alone," said the headwaiter. "But if you would sit at the bar . . ."

"I'll be having a drink at the bar," Sam said, and he went there and sat down. At the bar, where the B-girls came and went, one was not expected to remain alone. Observing the police regulations, the girls worked only with their smiles and their eyes. Then Sam noticed that his hand, holding the glass, trembled. All the anxiety he had been feeling all day had suddenly welled up in his heart. To think of Carla being at home in a place like this, he thought. Yet, such places were part of her life. She had come out of such places, maybe even cheaper dives, all part of the shape of her mind and heart; yes, part of the wisdom of her untroubled knowing smile. Who was he kidding? Who had said it? Alberto or Francesca? "As hard as nails."

A girl had sat down beside him, a girl in a gray cloth coat. A smile on her long lean face, she waited for him to speak. I know this girl, he thought. Was she the girl who had stood at the corner near the Ambasciatori Hotel, wavering between him and the sure thing in the car that had stopped along the side street? It couldn't be her. Yet it was. That hard-selling smile. She had put on the heavy coat, needing its warmth for the cool midnight hours on street corners. If this girl's street smile hadn't been so familiar on a night that now seemed so long ago, he might not have gone back to the hotel room and drawn that picture of Carla; he would not still be here in Rome, with Koster out at Castel Gandolfo. And had the Pope really died?

The headwaiter had beckoned to him, and as he paid for his drink, he hesitated, glanced at the whore in the gray coat, took another thousand-lire note from his ticket folder, unobtrusively slipped it into her hand, and walked away. Muttering and half angry, she watched him as he disappeared with the headwaiter.

Of all the tables, Sam's was farthest from the orchestra, being back against the wall in the corner. In the dim light his eyes, shifting around, fell on Mosca at a front table with a balding florid middle-aged man; the management, no doubt. And he half rose, sick with concern for Carla. But the fierce sting to his pride restrained him. Mosca, with his big amiable grin, was puffing at a cigar. Then Sam noticed that Mosca was showing no nervousness at all. It shook him, belittled all his weeks of concern. This awful ease of Mosca's, his obvious belief that the thing was in his line, of his world, a prize he could handle having fallen into his lap, told Sam of the end of something. Everything was in its place again, Mosca seemed to say, as the little whores were in their place hovering around the bar, and as the thin, belly-bumping woman who had giggled hysterically was, too. The whole of Mosca's life, and the life lived in a thousand dives and back alleys seemed to be washing over Carla, claiming her again. It's hopeless, Sam thought desperately. Now she's really gone. Let her be the cheap thing Mosca knows he can handle, and see where it gets her. A nothing girl. And yet, in spite of his bitterness as he slumped in the chair with a grim smile, his frantic faith in all he had seen in her was struggling against the place and the time and his disgust and wounded pride. Even here, even though she was with Mosca, he wanted to see her as he had dreamed of her. Gradually he began to hope that she would be fantastically out of place here; yet not caring, just trying her wings, beautifully herself no matter where on earth she was, as he had told her she could be. His elbows on the table, his head in his hands, he waited, trembling with concern.

The full lights had come on and the orchestra leader began to make a speech which Sam didn't understand till he heard the name 'Anna Connel.' It wasn't hard to figure out he was telling the patrons Anna Connel had been a star in American television. Then the lights were dimmed into darkness and a spotlight was thrown on a single stool on the platform.

Out of the darkness, from behind the orchestra it seemed, Carla appeared wearing a low-cut white dress, carrying her guitar. With hardly a nod she sat down gravely on the stool. Loud applause came from Joe Mosca's table, and from the management, too. Other patrons applauded politely.

"Carla, I'm here," Sam whispered. "You're not alone. I'm here," and he held his breath.

Tilting her head to one side, thoughtful, half-amused by some memory, she smiled to herself, then began to sing in Italian, her voice sweet and wonderfully intimate; all by herself, unconcerned, making the picture Sam wanted her to make; and tears were in his eyes as he waited for her to give her pleased little laugh. He waited and the stillness in him was just beginning to be stirred by exultation. He forgot where he was. Then he heard the buzz of conversation at the next table. "Sh, sh," he said angrily. But as always in such places, the low conversation became general. Every night-club singer had to face it. It was the custom of the trade. Some giggled alcoholically, and someone told jokes. Carla was merely an entertainer fighting the alcohol, fighting the food, the whispering, the jokes and the laughter. If she had been a singer who belted out a song, it might have been different. "Shut up," Sam snarled viciously. Those at the next table didn't understand him. Carla had faltered. A blank expression on her face, her fingers hardly touching the guitar, her mouth open, she waited with a quick nervous smile. She tried to go on and couldn't, though concentrating desperately, puzzled, then scared stiff; and the horror of her embarrassment was there in the spotlight.

"Oh, Carla, please, please," Sam whispered, standing up, a cracked encouraging smile on his face. If she could only see him before she froze into that motionless panic he had seen in her when she knelt on the kitchen floor at the Spagnola woman's place! Now there wasn't a whisper at the tables. At last Carla, in her agony, had the undivided attention. It was awkward, even painful for everyone. There was some ridiculous applause and more laughter. A woman squealed hysterically. Sliding slowly off the stool, Carla shook her guitar at the audience. Her face contorted, her eyes blazing, she screamed something in Italian. Frantic vicious words poured out of her. Then she spat at the audience. Shaking her guitar wildly, she switched to English. "You cheap sons-of-bitches. You beat-up old bags. You cheap whores, you fingering old men. To hell with you," and as they in turn shouted at her, laughing, the spotlight was turned off. In the shadow Sam could see Carla still gesticulating, and he tried to make his way to her. In the dark he crashed into a table, knocking it over, glass splintering, and someone, cursing, grabbed his arm. In the garble of wild voices he saw a big man grab Carla by the shoulders; it was Mosca. Sam thought he could near her sobbing as she was pulled away. Angry shouts for the lights came from the patrons, and when they were turned on there was the manager on the platform with a big placating smile as he waved both hands and talked in Italian with great warm eloquence. He shrugged, he laughed. He shook his shoulders like a woman, making a joke of it. He was very good, and soon a patron laughed out loud, and good humor was restored.

In the general laughter—international laughter—there was much whispering and translating and nodding. The manager, sighing, mopped his forehead and waved his hand benevolently to the orchestra, and the dancing began again. As the patrons, with their amused smiles, brushed by him, Sam made his way out to the bar. The girl in the gray coat, to whom he had given the bill, slid from the stool and approached him timidly. The agonized protest in his eyes frightened her. When she held back, he rushed out as if he expected to encounter Mosca and Carla on the street. It was so much cooler out, and his head was so hot that he shivered. No one else had come out of the night club. "So she didn't need me, eh?" he muttered. "The poor little fool and her dumb manager. Well, let them go to it," and he began to hurry home. His own words echoing in his mind reminded him of so many lost things in his own life, not particular things nor particular moments; it was like a painful opening up of his memory. It was unbearable.

The Ferraros heard him coming in. They both came to their door. Mother and daughter had long sad faces. In her halting English, Agnese said, "Mister Raymond . . ."

"Yes."

"His Holiness is—is dead."

"The Pope is dead? Are you sure?" Then he repeated slowly, "It is true? Yes?"

"The radio," she said.

"The radio," he repeated in a trance. The women nodded at each other as if they had never seen a man look so upset. They let him go on up the stairs and into his apartment, and as he went to fling himself into a chair, his eye caught the leather bag in which he kept his equipment there on the floor, and he picked it up carefully and put it in the cupboard, and sat down trying to suppress his sense of dread, his intimation of disaster for he knew that Carla, after the hysterical screaming and foul language, would now be in a terrible depression.

Moments, then minutes, then an hour passed and when he could no longer stand the anxiety, he started to rage against her. Imagine her letting cheap night-club riffraff upset her. No guts, no pride. The little clown! Where was her arrogance. What did it matter if she remembered or forgot her song? Just laugh. One condescending arrogant smile and they'd feel like dirt and like it. He was still berating her in this way when someone knocked on the door, and he called out wearily "Yeah," thinking it would be one of the Ferraro women wanting to talk about the Pope, and then he went to the door. It was Carla in her heavy gray sweater pulled over the white dress.

"Carla," he whispered, then he couldn't get his breath.

"Can I come in, Sam?" and she waited because he couldn't take his eyes off the side of her face that was red and swollen.

"It's about time," he said harshly. "Well, don't stand there," and he grabbed her by the arm and pulled her in roughly, then closed the door. "I ought to break your neck," he said savagely. "By God, how I've been waiting to get my hands on you." Grabbing her by the shoulders he shook her roughly. Her wild startled eyes, stabbing at him painfully, only made him shake her again. "You get no sympathy from me," he said grimly. "You little fool. Don't come here begging for sympathy after you spoil everything."

"Who's asking for sympathy?" she whimpered, backing away from him. "Oh, leave me alone."

"I ought to leave you alone."

"Sam, just let me sit down. I'm so tired. Sam, please."

"Sure. Sit down," and he pushed her down on the sofa. Never had she seen him like this. He seemed to be so unlike himself it took her, for the moment, out of herself; she could only think of him; nothing in her mind now but him.

"Please, Sam. Please," she whimpered. "I'm tired. I'm out of my mind. Don't kick me out."

[226

"Yes, my God, why don't I kick you out?"

"It wasn't Mosca, Sam."

"Any big-mouthed, big-shouldered slob that can stir up the itch in you."

"I didn't itch. Damn you, I didn't itch," she cried wildly, and as he forced her to defend herself, the lost frightened beaten look went out of her eyes. "It was your fault, too. I kept seeing the thing as you sold it to me. Only, you know nothing about these things. What I know and you don't is that there's always been some guy like Mosca, and when you wouldn't make a move . . . Oh, for God's sake, Sam, you big fool. It's not Mosca. I tried the thing tonight. Don't you understand? I went out of my head. I'm half out of my head now."

"Spare me the details. I was there."

"Oh, no!"

"You bet I was," he taunted her.

"How awful," she moaned, and the fight in her vanished. "My one consolation—that you weren't there—that it couldn't have happened if you had been there. This I tried to tell myself, wanting to die." Her elbow on her knee, her head in her hand, she closed her eyes and began to cry. Her whole body shook. The tears slid down her cheeks, and each sob, coming in a tight little gasp because she tried to repress it, deepened the anguish in her twisted face.

Sam had put up with her wild and frantic moods, yet until now he had never seen her cry, and he was bewildered. "Cut it out," he said fiercely. "Do you hear? Cut it out. I'm not interested in your tears. I want to know what happened. Do you hear me?" Grabbing her wrist, he jerked her elbow off her knee so that her head, too, jerked up. "What happened there? That's what I want to know. What happened to you?"

"I don't know, Sam," she whispered.

"You were singing and you quit. Without any guts or pride, you quit."

"I just forgot the rest of the song and everything."

"You know why. Do I have to tell you?"

"My mind went blank, Sam," she pleaded. "Everything went

blank and I got scared. Scared to move out of the blank and the dark."

"Oh, sure," he said with disgust. "And you know why your mind went blank, don't you?"

"It was all the laughing and talking at the tables, the big loud murmur getting bigger."

"Well, well, well. So they weren't giving you their undivided attention," he said bitterly. "They weren't paying enough attention to Carla. No matter what's going on, nobody should neglect Carla. Little Carla'll go crazy and shout and scream if the whole world doesn't pay some attention to her. That's the story of your cheap little life. Your whole story. Any shameful disgraceful thing that gets a little attention. And take if from me, it's why you've been wasting a couple of years admiring those crazy high-born ancient Roman trollops." As the angry words of disgust poured out of him, his own eyes were wild and hard. "I'm ashamed of myself for expecting anything from you. You're ignorant. You just aren't aware of anything. Your talent is to be something rare and special. You'd think you'd be looking down your nose at the meatheads who miss it. Why should you give a damn? It should only arouse your pity and arrogance. But what do you do? You try to peddle it for peanuts to that bunch of cheap, half-drunk, tired international clowns; and go blank if they're not polite. I told you, didn't I, you were for the alert and the wise? That's the magic. That's you. Goddamn you, you hear?" he shouted and he rushed at her, his hand raised. She ducked away as if she thought he was going to slap her. Bewildered, he drew back and tried to laugh. "And what do you do? Under the pressure, what do you do? Any little tramp who thinks she's a night-club singer knows she has to fight the beer and the voices, and she knows it and she may want to scream her head off at them, but she doesn't. But you! You scream like a fishwife. In God's name, how can anyone who is so uncommon bear to be so vulgar? Oh, I know," he muttered, "your poor little mind went blank. A first on television. Little Carla, the first person in the world whose mind went blank singing a song, making a speech,

[228

preaching a sermon. All those politicians and preachers and opera singers, and the guys like me to whom it happened once when I was writing a philosophy exam at college, they don't count. Oh, grow up," he jeered. "Get wise to yourself," but then, struck by the way she was looking at him, he faltered. She was afraid to move or speak, for fear he would stop berating her; she wanted to sit there, suffering under the lash of his contempt. A dull red flush came on his face. There was wonder in her eyes, and a plea, too. She was begging him to keep pouring the words over her, waiting for more of the beating from the words, as if she knew now they came out of his faith in his view of her, and gave her back some self-respect.

"Aw, why go on with it?" he said roughly.

"No, go on, Sam."

"Damn it all, I'm tired. I'm exhausted," and he sat down wearily.

"Sam," she said, rising and coming toward him slowly and humbly. She dropped at his feet and threw her arms around his knees—the protector of her dreams. "I don't care what you say to me when you say it in that way," she whispered ardently. "It gives things back to me—holds things out to me." And then she looked around the room with its faded brown-patterned wallpaper and its garish holy pictures. "I—I started to run on the street. Like I said, I had to get here fast or go crazy and I kept seeing every familiar object in this room and I was crying out in myself again and again. Oh, Sam, what terrible thing happened that made me think I didn't need you?"

"Never mind me," he said awkwardly. "Don't start that again," and he turned away because his secret fierce exultation was mixed up with a sad awareness that something he had wanted for her had been lost again.

"I'm so tired, Sam."

"I know, and no wonder."

"Could I . . ." and she hesitated, worried. "Could I lie down? Could I go to bed here tonight?"

"Oh Carla," and her fear that he might not let her sleep there shook him. Putting his arm around her waist he led her into the bedroom.

There on the bed and on the floor were all her dresses and her shoes, and she stared at them, very pale. He tried to smile apologetically. Without saying a word they both began to pick up the dresses, hanging them in the closet again. When they had undressed she turned out the light. It puzzled him because she had always wanted the light on so she could see him delighting in her body. In the dark she seemed to feel secure, and he heard her sigh, falling asleep.

"Carla," he said, shaking her gently.

"Yeah, yeah," she muttered drowsily.

"Carla, are you awake?"

"Uhhu, Sam."

"Wake up, Carla."

"I'm awake. What's the matter?"

"I should have gone with Koster tonight to Castel Gandolfo. Koster may cable home and say I wasn't even there."

There was a little silence as they lay there in the dark. "You mean they'll drop you now, Sam?"

"I don't know. I'll have to talk to Koster."

"What'll you say?"

"Some stupid lying excuse. The thing is I'm here, and they'll bring the Pope here. I can get right to work. Well, it'll give us a chance to forget tonight."

"How do you mean?"

"You'll be coming with me," he said suddenly.

"With you, where?"

"I'll try to butter up Koster. He's nothing to me, but I have to work with him. Now, look. He's paying Francesca. I'm going to tell him you're coming along as my interpreter. Since it won't cost him anything, or cost the paper anything, it's none of his business. See what I mean?"

"Me with you, where?"

"The Vatican. The Press Club, the hotel, St. Peter's. Wherever we go, Carla."

[230

"With all those newspapermen from The States?"

"To hell with the newspapermen."

"Don't ask me, Sam."

"What am I to do? Leave you here alone all day and night?"

"No."

"Well, then?"

"But Francesca, Sam. You don't know Francesca. I think she hates me. I think she wants me to be dirt."

"Now why should she, Carla?"

"I know what I'm talking about. I had the offer of her affections. She's not sure now she is a woman, you know. At least I know what I am, and I wasn't going to let her prove anything for herself with me."

"Then she should run from you. Not you from her, Carla. I promise she'll be like a mouse." And knowing she had no choice to hang back, "I always thought you had Rome a little wrong, Carla," he said and he began to talk about Papal Rome.

A cool breeze came from the open window, and she coughed and pulled the cover around her throat. Talking on in the dark he tried to sneak into her imagination, touch her pride in Rome with stories about the Papacy. Rome without the Pope was not Rome at all. It had been Papal Rome for a thousand years, he said. A dead city was born again under the popes. After the ancient glory, Rome had become a beat-up little town with some ruins. Imagine. The Forum a cow pasture! That lovely Campidoglio she had shown him? Just a place of weeds. And the strange thing about this city, he said, was that it was the only ancient metropolis that became a world center again. Look at Athens. Babylon was covered with sand. And Luxor in Egypt? Just sand and temple columns. And who knows now where Nineveh had been? In Rome. Yes, the Caesars. But then the popes. "Lying here beside you, Carla, I have the strange feeling we're in a city that conquered time," he said softly. "It's a funny thing, but sometimes when I look at you in the other room there, singing and smiling to yourself, I have the feeling that there's some core in you that's absorbed all the good and the bad in your life, and you can look at it with a wise smile. Maybe you're right. Maybe that quality belongs to this city. What do you think?" But she didn't answer. She was asleep, with her arm tight around him. Tomorrow it would be all right, he thought, if he could only mollify Koster.

CHAPTER 24

BUT KOSTER was so witheringly sarcastic next morning in the hotel room, Sam would have punched him on the nose if he hadn't known that he had earned his contempt. With Francesca a witness to his humiliation, although not understanding it came from having to repeat his shameful lies, he said, with a flush on his face, "I'm telling you again, Koster, we missed connections. Ask the doorman, ask the clerk. Why didn't you stay in one place?" The lies made his stomach turn. He wanted to put his hands over his face.

And Koster, whirling around on him, said, "What am I supposed to be? An office boy running around the streets looking for a photographer? My God, I'm not even responsible for you. I don't care whether you get any lousy pictures or not, only don't hold me up, do you hear?" A lonely outraged man with close-cropped black hair and snapping round eyes, he went into the bathroom to get water to mix with his drink.

Then Francesca, who had remained discreetly silent with perfect Christian prudence, although hardly able to hide her impatience, whispered. "You are right to have dignity, Sam. He knows all about the mix-up. The desk clerk told him you came running in here last night. I don't think it's you

233]

who makes him furious. And believe me, there were no pictures."

"That's right. You're lucky. There were no pictures," Koster mumbled, coming out of the bathroom. "Not for newspapermen, anyway, although they say a doctor got a scandalous beauty of the Pope sucking in his last breath. Naturally, Blondell will want to know why you weren't there disguised as a doctor," and then he paused, scowling, still in the grip of some bitter recollection. "All right, I'm in a hell of a temper, and I'm sorry, Sam." The apology made Sam feel cheap and ashamed. "It was those wire men. Those busy little wire men. And first thing this morning when I went to their offices to see what was on the wires . . ." Koster explained, his eyes suddenly cruel with wounded vanity. He told how the wire men had said they were too busy to bother with him. Naturally, he had blown up. Well, wait till they came to London. Wait till one of their stupid underpaid leg men came to him, Koster, for a little co-operation. The certainty of his capacity to avenge the insult to his prestige seemed to carry him away. Brooding and muttering, he sat down, and for ten minutes they watched him. Looking up suddenly like a sweet hurt boy, he asked plaintively, "Why aren't you drinking with me, Sam?" and he was himself again. "We'll have lunch," he said, "and then I'll come back here and finish my story." A magnificently dedicated man, Sam thought remorsefully, the shame still in him. A real professional. After Geneva, Koster might feel he was slumming, having to deal with funerals and coronations, but now nothing would obstruct him. All that was on his mind now was tomorrow's funeral cortege.

At lunch Sam could see that Koster had told himself this procession was to be so unique a story by Koster that it ought to be read throughout the world. Never before, he explained to Francesca, who was accustomed now to his explanations of facts she understood far better than he did, had a pope died outside the Vatican. Nor had there ever been a funeral cortege for a pope through the streets of Rome. It could really be something worthy of all his talents. Gulping down his coffee, he said he would go back to the hotel, finish his story, file it at the cable office, then meet them at six for a drink in the Press Club. As they watched him hurrying away, his little short legs taking the quick steps, Francesca said, "I have to respect the man. For two hours this morning he had me read to him every line in the Roman press about the Pope. He has a notebook, too, full of observations about each cardinal who may be a candidate. He's a frightening monster of research. Is he not very good?"

"Yes. They say he is very good."

"It is his pride. It's something to have, you know, Sam."

"How well I know it."

"You have to respect a man, even a very limited man, if he screams at the world that he will not be slipshod and mediocre."

"What is this, Francesca? Who wants to be mediocre?"

"I thought it was a cult now—the acceptance, with a shrug, of one's mediocrity. Am I wrong?"

"Oh, those third-rate intellectuals," he said impatiently. He wanted to tell her now about Carla, but she had annoyed him. Somehow she had got under his skin, and he couldn't bear her to have an advantage over him while he talked about Carla, so he said slyly, to worry her, "How's it going with your husband? Has he moved in yet?"

"Well, I saw him early this morning," she admitted, awkwardly.

"At your place?"

"Yes."

"How did it go?"

"I regret that you weren't there with your camera," she said with dignity, "but I had to see Koster, you know."

"Ah, yes," he said, hurting her, making her as vulnerable as he was, and silencing her with his wise smile. And then he said casually, as if it had just occurred to him, "I think I'll be bringing Carla along with us from now on."

"Oh," and she looked astonished. "Good heavens, you mean she's back with you?"

"That's right. Walked in of her own accord."

"And was she drunk? Or was it after so much drinking?"

"I told you she doesn't drink now," he said quietly.

"That I would have to see, Sam."

"You'll see. But remember, Francesca, not a word to Koster about her. Just a friend of mine. Carla Caneli." Then he didn't like the way she had raised her eyebrows. "You have a certain look in your eye, Francesca. Okay. But remember this, when Koster discovers she speaks perfect Italian, he'll ask why he should be paying for an interpreter."

"You put it brutally, don't you, Sam?"

"Only because we're friends, Francesca."

"It's a fact I need the money. So count on me, Sam. Well, it's darkening up. It looks like rain. Anyway, I must go home," and she stood up, smiling faintly. "You'll walk me to a taxi, won't you?" And he did. And when he was closing the taxi door, he went to put a four-hundred-lire note in her hand for the fare, and then it was his turn to smile, knowing she would have taken it though she now was working for Koster. Waving to her, he went on his way.

But now that he was alone, doubts began to assail him. What had the awful experience of last night done to Carla? It must have marked her, crushed her spirit in some way, or she wouldn't be human. If it had happened to him, what would it have done? Shattered the last shreds of his confidence. Just a night after such a disaster, wasn't it too soon to hurl Carla among strangers? Toss her into the company of all the foreign newspapermen, many of whom would be Americans? Someone would be bound to recognize her. And Francesca, insulted by Carla's rejection of her ardent affection, and with her peculiar intensity of conviction that Carla would stoop to any other sinful indulgence if it was her whim, would be watching and waiting for Carla to make herself common. Even Francesca's guarded knowing silence would put Carla on edge. One slur, one fancied insult from a newspaperman, might scrape at last night's raw wound to Carla's twisted pride. Even a little misunderstood kidding —her humor now was so frail a thing—might stir up the panic in her. He could see her standing in a group by the bar at the Press Club, fury in her eyes as the gutter language poured out of her, then turning and running. It was so real a picture in his mind he stopped on the street, catching his breath, and looked around. On a dirty gray stone wall was a proclamation of the Pope's death. Already the proclamations were on walls all over Rome. Up the street came a young girl in a green dress, swaying her pelvis, and she didn't look at the proclamation; nor did a fat young mother, passing with three young children she tried to hang on to, but, in fairness to her as she passed the proclamation, she was busy scolding the children. He went on home.

"Carla," he called anxiously, when he had let himself in.

"Here I am, Sam," she answered, coming from the bedroom. "How did it go?" And when he saw that she showed only the anxiety of a woman who was concerned about what had happened to the man she was living with, he was moved. "What's the matter, Sam? How did it go?"

"It worked out beautifully."

"I was so worried. I had put you in such a bad light."

"It's all right now, Carla."

"Last night it all sounded so important to us."

"It still is." And then he looked at her in the suit he had bought her, and he saw that her afternoon eye shadow wasn't too heavy, and he smiled approvingly. "And you know just what to wear, don't you? Come here," and he put his arms around her and kissed her on the back of the neck, wondering why she wasn't at all worried. Then he told her they should go out and get all the newspapers and she should read them to him; they should know all there was to know about Pius XII. And when she nodded importantly, he felt more sure of her and himself and his plans. She saw herself already in some significant role. Thank God for her lively imagination, he thought.

But it had clouded up again. It began to rain a little, just a drizzle. He didn't like the streets of Rome when it was raining. So they stayed in and he made a cup of coffee. Then a shaft of sunlight came through a window. They went out and got the newspapers, and at a café she translated all the stories about the Pope's death and about his greatness as an intellectual. She read slowly and carefully, like a schoolgirl trying for a prize. Gradually the hard sunlight vanished. It became cooler. It was time to meet Koster. If she had shown a little anxiety, or excitement or nervousness, he might have felt more at ease himself. But a lump came into his throat when she merely took his arm. It was the way she held on to him, the tight grip of her hand telling him that where he was going she had to go, that his places had to be her places; and in the taxi his anxiety and concern for her made it hard for him to speak.

In the Press Club, smoke-filled, crowded now with newspapermen who were strangers to each other, each man trying self-consciously to make himself known over a drink, they stood near the door, looking for a table or at least one vacant chair; then they moved over to the crowded bar where they were soon hemmed in and made inconspicuous, for no one was able to stand back and look at Carla. A plump middle-aged red-faced reporter for the Hearst Syndicate, having drunk enough to be childish, was showing clippings of his own work to a grand middle-aged plump florid woman who had been brought out of retirement in London by a syndicate because she was supposed to have "her own sources" at the Vatican. She was treating her American colleague and his clippings with good-humored contempt, raising her eyebrows occasionally to three fair willowy young English journalists, who looked, sounded and dressed like brothers.

"Look, Carla, at the end of the bar," Sam whispered. "As I live, I swear it's her husband." A tall, stringy, balding Englishman with ridiculous long handle-bar mustaches, was talking eloquently to Francesca who listened inertly, elbows on the bar, her face impassive.

"So what?" Carla asked, without a smile.

"I'm surprised, that's all. Come on, quick." He had seen two newspapermen, Dutchmen, leaving one of the far corner tables. Two other Dutch journalists, still at the table, smiled politely, but they had no English. Leaving Carla at the table,

Sam got a rye-and-water for himself and vermouth-on-the-rocks for her. As he handed her the drink he tried to smile, telling her with his eyes it was beneath them to be concerned about her control over herself.

"Sit down, Sam," she said. "I'm not a cripple," and she took the drink, sipped it, then sipped it again with a vague absent-minded air. Her brow had wrinkled, her eyes were anxious. Then he saw that she was aware of newspapermen coming in, or hurrying down the stairs; all looked over at her, and she seemed to be waiting, solemn and tense, her tongue sometimes wetting her soft drooping lower lip, waiting for an American to recognize her. Gradually bafflement, then uneasiness showed in her face. She looked annoyed. She had grasped that they were glancing at her merely because she was a pretty woman. "I don't like it here," she said irritably. "I hate this place," and turned up her nose. Her attitude disturbed him; he felt a little dizzy; he had thought she would be praying that no one recognize her.

"Look at Francesca over there," he said hastily, trying to divert her. "If that's really her husband . . ."

"Who's interested in her husband?"

"Not the husband—the mustache. Do you think it's a wartime souvenir?"

"Which war?"

"The Crimean."

"Oh, to hell with both of them," she said, tensely.

"Sam. Hey, Sam!" It was Koster, who had come in, approached the bar, then turned. The two Dutchmen who had finished their drinks, whispered, nodded to each other and left.

"Miss Caneli, Koster," Sam said.

"A pleasure, Mr. Koster," she said, almost demurely. "Do sit down. I've heard so much about you."

"A pleasure, indeed," he said, and he had a happy, astonished smile. His display of warm affection for Sam became extraordinary as he sat down. "Old pal," he said. "I was down seeing the Vatican press officer. Nice guy. I got a briefing on the whole funeral cortege. I could write it tonight." And then

239]

with great gallantry, he turned to Carla. "Excuse me—newspaper talk, Miss Caneli. Sam and I never rest."

"Carla is coming with me tomorrow," Sam said casually. "You'll have Francesca, and we may get separated, and I'll have to know what's what. Carla is an American but Italian is her other language."

"They may have made a mistake, Sam, when they said you got lost in Rome," Koster said thoughtfully. "Do you live here, Miss Caneli?"

"She's been coming here for some years," Sam said quickly.

"What do you do, Miss Caneli?"

"Carla's been studying music, voice," Sam said.

"Uhhu. Uhhu," Koster said, thoughtful again, as if busily trying to fit an expensively dressed girl like Carla in a newspaper photographer's life. "Studying music, eh? How do you like Rome?"

"I think of it as home," she said, and her lower lip drooped helplessly. Suddenly she looked at Sam with a shy warm smile. What was she up to? He had never seen that demure expression on her face. It made him uneasy. Then he saw Francesca, who had left her husband sitting at the bar, approaching their table.

"*Ciao,*" Francesca said calmly to Carla, putting out her hand.

"*Ciao,*" Carla said indifferently, taking her hand.

"You two know each other?" Koster asked.

"Through Sam," Francesca said, sitting down.

It was as if they met every day and took each other for granted and hardly needed to bother with conversation. I don't know what's going on in either one of them, Sam thought, and he pondered over it as Koster explained that he could find no sign of mourning in Rome. It was a little disappointing. The Pope was dead, it was too bad; and who were you betting on to be the new pope? That seemed to be the general attitude. How could he write such stuff for the Catholic trade? His paper wouldn't print it.

"Why don't you just hop on a plane and go to Malta or Ireland?" Francesca said tartly. "I'm sure you won't be disappointed." Then she bit her lip, knowing she had betrayed her sense of superiority, and Koster had felt it. He looked at her thoughtfully, with a new peculiar interest.

"Not bad, Francesca," he said. "Not bad at all. What brought you out of your shell?"

"Civic pride, I suppose. I only meant that what is called Roman indifference can be badly misunderstood."

"Am I'm only writing a story and trying to understand the situation," Koster said coolly. "I have you with me to instruct me."

"Now don't be angry with me," Francesca said, with a sudden charming smile. "I know it must be very difficult for any Protestant to understand the general attitude, the atmosphere of Rome in the days between the death of one pope and the coronation of another." And then, to take Koster's eyes off her, and with a bitchy instinct, she said, sweetly, "Isn't it, Carla?"

"Yes, it is," Carla said. Sam could have slapped Francesca. As the conversation proceeded Carla seemed to withdraw into herself. Solemn and still, her big eyes shifting from Koster to Francesca, she appeared to feel neglected and alien.

"How about this for a theme, Sam?" Koster asked. "The days of the empty house?"

"Not bad," Sam said, as if he were really pondering over it.

"Why aren't you a Catholic, Sam, and a poet, too?"

"You've got what you want right here," Sam said. "Francesca's uncle is a bishop, and she herself is full of poetry. It's intuitive with you—the sympathy, isn't it, Francesca?"

"I'm not sure what Koster wants," Francesca said coolly. "Many popes have died, and you do seem to be disappointed, Koster, that everyone in Rome isn't running around crying. It is not desirable that Rome should look like a sepulcher."

"In these days," Carla said quietly, "I think they say the church is a widow."

"What's that?" Koster asked sharply.

"The church is a widow."

"I don't quite get it."

"I mean now, these days, it's the time when the widow and everyone else knows there will be a new bridegroom. And so

241]

there's excitement, as well as sorrow. I think I've heard it put that way."

"Wait a minute," Koster said slowly. "Is she right, Francesca?"

"Well, yes, I suppose she is," Francesca said grudgingly.

"Explain it to me, Miss Caneli—'the widow.' "

"It's not so strange," she said, and there was a smile in her lustrous eyes. "The Pope is the Vicar of Christ, isn't he? And Christ is to the Church as a husband is to a wife. Well, if His vicar dies, it leaves the Church a widow, doesn't it? But a widow who'll have a new bridegroom."

"I understand," Sam said, and he thanked God for that old priest in Queens who had given her a grounding in her religion.

"Yeah, I get it," Koster said. "It's beautiful." He smiled as if he had made it his own. "The days when the lady—"

"The widow," Carla said softly, her face lighting up. "The widow, waiting and wondering."

"For the step of the new master in the empty house. Of course, of course. It's beautiful. It holds the whole thing together for me. Thanks, Miss Caneli," and he patted Carla's hand appreciatively. "Only a pretty and devout woman could have such a satisfying view."

"It's a very orthodox view," said Francesca with a bored air. "It's St. Paul, you know."

"It's mine now," Koster said. "Stick around, will you, Miss Caneli? Come on. Don't be shy. Smile a little. Is she always so shy, Sam?"

"I'm not really shy," Carla said, demurely. "Really I'm not, Mr. Koster." She was a little breathless as she leaned closer, wanting, it seemed, to open her whole life. "I've lived in the world of music and art, you see. Newspapermen know what's important to the whole world. Such things only confuse me. Musicians are always afraid they'll seem isolated and stupid to newspapermen. If music is a girl's whole life she can only feel, I think that's the word, feel what the big important events are to other people. But I have this feeling that everything, everything is happening here now in Rome. You see what I mean?

[242

Do you?" and she smiled with a breathless appealing helpless-
ness, her lips parted.

"I do, Miss Caneli," Koster said earnestly.

Shaken, Sam tried to conceal his astonished embarrassment;
he thought, My God, is this what last night did to her? Is she
off again on one of her crazy fantasies? Doesn't she know she's
just telling lies? What a terrible setback, and then Francesca
caught his eye. She had been listening with blank incredulity,
but now, with a straight face she was hiding her amused satisfaction, saying to Sam with her perfect little smile, "She's been
drinking. The poor thing has been drinking." No, he thought
desperately, she's not caught up in some new illusion, and he
tried to believe she was simply telling lies, as he himself was
lying to Koster; and as Francesca, too, was pretending. It was
the Roman touch, giving Koster, the visitor, what he wanted
to find. Koster, alone, was on the level. Sam got excited himself. Torn between worry and wonder, he wanted only to help
Carla feel she was accepted for whatever she pretended to be,
and he smiled warmly. He joked. He carried Francesca along
with him, for now she was sure she could truly look down on
Carla and pity her, the shy American student!

They went out to dinner together, and there wasn't a cross
word and Carla refused a drink. They had a genteel conversation about the Pope, with Koster asking Carla many questions
because he wanted to understand a devout woman's angle.
Afterward, when they were crossing the square by the Trevi
fountain, they heard laughter and shrieking. Four half-drunken
Americans were trying to push each other into the fountain
pool. A beautiful fair girl, six feet tall, toppled in and shrieked,
"Ooooo, it's cold. It's so damn cold, help me out. I'm freezing,"
and in the moonlight her wet hair was matted on her face.

243]

CHAPTER **25**

CARLA's fey behavior troubled Sam's dreams. When he woke up in the morning and looked at her head on the pillow beside him, he thought, What if she can never come down to earth now? Safe only with me, is she always to be one thing, then another? Following her pathetic failure trying to go it alone, was the whole thing in ruins now? And he got up and stood at the window, in a trance.

There was lots of sunlight, good weather for the funeral procession. Finally he scratched his head, stretched, then pulled on his dressing gown, went along the hall to the bathroom, and came back and began to get the breakfast. Carla, in her nightdress, appeared in the kitchen doorway, scratching her flanks and yawning. "Excuse me," she said, tapping her lips.

"You slept well, Carla?"

"You bet I did. Say, Sam," she said, "I was thinking. What did you do to Francesca? Hit her on the head?"

"No, she's a practical woman. She won't make trouble."

"Sometimes I'd look at her and want to laugh. I had her knocked for a loop, didn't I?"

"You're quite a little actress, Carla."

"Well, what could I do?"

"Just be there, be yourself."

"I didn't want to be there, I told you, but I had to be with you."

"You were."

"I didn't want anything to happen that might make you feel ashamed of me."

"Why not just act normal?"

"I couldn't, Sam. I felt tongue-tied. I don't know what was the matter with me. Then I took to the role. Where the words came from I just don't know. I seemed to have a whole life of music ahead of me and I liked it," and she giggled. "I'm a real clown, eh?" she asked impishly.

"Put something around you," he said gruffly. "There's still no heat in this place."

"I'm used to it, Sam."

"Put something around you. And something on your feet."

"Oh, all right," and she went back to the bedroom.

He sighed with relief. Her performance last night had been no flight into unreality. Knowing exactly what she was doing, she had been making it easier for herself and him and Koster. Just clowning and enjoying it. Nothing to worry about at all. Sam was exultant.

Now she came hurrying back to the kitchen, in her blue silk housecoat over her nightdress, and wearing the gold-mesh slippers he had bought for her. "I'm hungry, Sam. What have you got here?" she asked. She began to move surely and confidently around the kitchen, helping him get the breakfast. It was the first time it had happened, and he was so surprised and elated, he was afraid to say anything.

"It's nearly noontime," he said when they were finishing their breakfast. "Now we'd better hurry and get dressed. One thing I know, now. Koster won't wait."

"Sam," she said hesitantly, "wouldn't it be better if I didn't go?"

"What is this? It's settled, Carla."

"After last night and my little bit of acting—and I was good, wasn't I? Hasn't it occurred to you that Francesca may have

245]

had a few things to say about me to Koster? One word can lead to another, Sam. I may blow my top."

"I told you not to worry about Francesca."

"With a woman, there comes a point where she can't keep her mouth shut."

"It means money to her, and besides, I trust her."

"That's all right. But she doesn't trust herself with me."

"Come on. Get dressed, Carla."

She put on her simple blue suit again, and then she sat down at her mirror. A little pale lipstick and only the faintest eye shadow was all she used. It took only a minute. But as usual she studied her image, smoothing an eyebrow, touching a strand of hair. Though she wanted to look demure and like a student, she had to be certain that the impression would be flawless. "Come on now, come on," he kept calling as he got dressed himself. "That's just right. Don't touch anything," giving her time to be ready to drag herself away from the mirror.

"I really look all right, Sam?" she asked, earnestly.

"If you just let it go at that," he called, taking at last from the cupboard his tweed jacket and the gray slacks, which he hadn't worn for so many weeks. He knew he wouldn't feel at home, running around with his camera, in his neat-fitting Italian silk suit. Then he put on that fawn-colored shirt with the buttoned-down collar he had also been wearing on his first night in Rome. When he had picked up the oblong leather bag containing his equipment, and stood facing her, she stared at him, frowning.

"What's the matter, Carla?"

"Now you're that photographer again."

"That's right, Carla."

"I think I must have forgotten what you looked like, Sam."

"That first night."

"On the street, yes. I remember," she said, her thoughts turning inward. It was a painful awkward moment for both of them. Then her eyes met his, although she seemed to be some distance off, regarding him gravely. "Seems a long time ago, doesn't it?" she said, quietly. He didn't know what to say. Turn-

[246

ing away, she picked up her hat which was on the bed. It was a small blue hat of angora wool, like a toque, and as she looked at herself gravely in the mirror, he understood that she accepted the memory of that first night as he would have had her do if she was all he wanted her to be. What a long way she'd come to him. If only Francesco now would leave her alone, he thought as they went out.

Ahead of them on the street were the Ferraros; the old women in her black, and Agnese in black, too, and between them, Tomaso, neat and proud, sauntering along with his hands in his pockets, slightly bored.

"Isn't it a little early for them to be lining up for the funeral?" Sam asked.

"Probably they're joining some relatives first. All Rome will watch the procession."

"Even the Communists?"

"Why not the Communists? You don't understand, Sam. It's the Papa who's dead. Rome's Papa. Political opinions have nothing to do with it. You can hate your own papa, but you'd show up at his funeral, wouldn't you?"

"Who, me? That's a funny thing to say," and he was silent, hiding the wrench at his heart. No word as yet had come from his uncle; by this time, maybe, they were burying his own father. He didn't have much to say the rest of the way to the hotel.

The door of Koster's room was open, and they could see Francesca, sitting by the window with a drink, a little vermouth, and Koster, at his dresser, was pouring himself Scotch-and-soda. "Come on in," Koster called. "We've got about half an hour, I think." Koster was in a smiling jovial charming mood. Obviously, Francesca as yet had said little about Carla. In one glance Carla seemed to understand this, and she sat down calmly beside Francesca. They exchanged a few sentences in Italian, with a kind of formal politeness. "What are you drinking, Sam? And what can I offer you, Miss Caneli?"

"I never touch anything in the daytime, not even a little wine," Carla said, and Francesca suddenly had an expectant

247]

air. While they sat around talking about a proper vantage point for viewing the procession, it seemed to Sam that Francesca, watching them and smiling, was counting on Carla finally asking for a drink. It was not malice in her now, not hate or disgust, he was sure. It was worse; her whole judgment of another woman and of herself was at stake. As it was, she had to accept what she thought of as an outrageous pretense of shyness and modesty in Carla, and be used to support it. She would rather have seen her in the gutter, quivering and begging for affection. Sam could see her growing baffled. He could hardly sit still. It seemed to him the two women were taunting each other, for Carla had smiled at Francesca, not once, but again and again. It was a condescending smile. Carla's strength was that she, in her turn, looked down on Francesca, and if they had been alone and if Francesca belittled her, Sam knew she would have turned on her and torn her to pieces.

"Are you sure you won't have a drink, Miss Caneli?" Koster asked.

"Do have a drink with us," Francesca said.

"No, thanks."

"The thing is," said Koster, enjoying his drink, "since this is to be a unique funeral procession, different than anything seen around here in a thousand years, I'll be surprised if it isn't beautifully staged."

"It can't be as colorful as the London coronation," Sam said. "Remember the coronation, Koster?"

"Indeed I do. But there you had all the military pomp. The soldiers. The precision. The whole pageantry of Empire. What can they have here as dramatically colorful?"

"Besides, this is a funeral," Francesca said. "I think . . ."

Then a big bell tolled. It tolled again. Startled by the slow heavy dull weight of the bell, they looked at each other uneasily, waiting. It was the slow heavy mournful pounding of the great bell of St. Peter's calling to all the hills and valleys of Rome, and echoing in their hearts as it echoed over all Rome.

"Come on, we're late," Koster said finally.

[248

"No. It only means the cortege has left St. John Lateran and is moving slowly across the city," Francesca said.

"It means we, too, may have to move slowly across the city," said Koster. "Come on," and they hurried out and got a taxi in front of the hotel and made good progress through the streets till they neared the Vatican neighborhood.

All the approaches were jammed with cars, just cars and people on foot streaming along the pavements, jostling each other and hurrying. Leaving the taxi they walked some blocks, then crossed under a great arch and went along a narrow cobblestoned alley to the Press Office where other journalists in little groups were waiting.

While Koster was in the Press Office, Sam stood between Carla and Francesca, trying to joke with both of them, but Francesca turned away and Carla, raising her head, looked up at the patch of blue sky, half closing her eyes and sucking her lip.

"We're in luck," Koster called cheerfully, coming out of the Press Office. His voice had sounded loud in the alley and he knew it and looked embarrassed. "We get a wonderful ringside seat," he whispered. "Where do you think? Right up on a ledge on the roof of St. Peter's."

Then a stout man with an important air came out of the office. Without a glance at the journalist, with a mere wave of his hand, as if they ought to be able to judge by his stature and his competent air that he was the one man who could be followed with confidence, he led the way. As the journalists trooped after him along the alley, the great fortress walls rising around them seemed to hurl back at them the heavy crashing echo of the bell. No one was speaking.

Sam didn't know where they were going, nor did Koster. They were led into the basilica by a side door, close to the elevator. The journalists politely stood back to allow the two women journalists and Francesca and Carla to be among the first in the elevator. Since Carla was hanging on to Sam's arm so tightly, her face pale and her eyes excited, he went with them. As the elevator rose she turned from one face to another. They were

249]

a subdued and respectful bunch of journalists, and it seemed to upset her. She looked stunned, as if asking herself, "What am I doing here rising to the roof of St. Peter's?" And Sam, touched by her wonder, went to put his arm around her protectively but the elevator had stopped. The door opened. In a moment there was a patch of blue sky ahead.

They had come out onto the roof of St. Peter's and it was like a rink, with Michelangelo's great dome sloping smoothly away into the sky like a stripped bald hill; and on each side were two smaller domes; and great shadows were thrown on the roof by the row of giant statues of the Apostles lined along the ledge, looking out over the city and St. Peter's Square below. Awed and silent, Sam and Carla stood together at the ledge, gazing down while the mournful bell clanged so close to them now and shook their nerves.

There was the huge gray square with its fountain and Caligula's obelisk, the splashing water gleaming in the sunlight. The immense colonnade, the arms of the square, opened out to the wide Avenue of the Concilliazione, which came up straight and true to the square. Crowds were lined all the way up the avenue; and jammed, enfolded in the square's arms, too, the crowds were held back by little movable wooden barricades. Turning, Sam looked out over Rome. From that high perch the city in the sunlight was all pink and gold and green, with shadows in the valleys and lighter green on the hills. A few white villas shone in the far-off hills. It had looked like this that day when he had been in the Vatican museum, he thought, when he had been thinking of Michelangelo hurrying through the night streets, stopped by a girl like Carla, and tucking the torment in her face away in his mind. And now, Sam thought, there was Carla on the ledge beside him. She had her hand up to her eyes, and the wind, blowing her skirt against her, blew strands of her black hair back as she stared intently at the fountain in the square; and a lump came in his throat.

"What's the matter, Sam?" she asked suddenly.

"Nothing. Nothing. Just that we're here. You'd better sit down, Carla."

[250

The newspapermen now squatting on the ledge made jokes, and were at ease. Koster, who had come up, sat down beside Francesca, who was supporting her weight on one hand, leaning away from Koster. Farther along, a young fellow had a typewriter set up on the rim of the ledge.

"That bell gets on my nerves," Koster said.

"What?"

"The bell. It fills the air," Koster shouted.

"I shouldn't be here at all," Sam grumbled. "I should be somewhere down there in the square. Why did we come up here?" Opening his bag he took out the Miranda; he was using a telescopic lens of German make, a beauty, and he focused on the obelisk. With this lens he could get a good picture of anything going on as far away as the entrance to the square. "Maybe I should go back to that Press Office and get on the edge of the crowd down there," he said.

"How are you going to do it?"

"Someone can show me the way."

"No one's going to show you, Sam. No one's going to bother. Why should they?" and Koster laughed. "I can write and print the most outlandish stuff and they won't even bother to contradict it. They don't have to. Why should they? They've been around too long."

"Look," cried one of the newspapermen. No one heard him with the bell clanging. He pointed far down the Via Concilliazione, where the procession was moving slowly in the sunlight, moving toward the bell-filled square. Between the great slow hammer strokes they could hear the faint faraway sound of the muffled roll of drums. As the procession came closer Sam held his breath, feeling he was all alone there, watching something no one else had seen in a thousand years. The sun, playing tricks with his eyes, made strange patches of color far down the wide avenue, and he was no longer sure he was in his own world or his own time. At the head of the procession were the Carbiniere, slowly rolling their drums, and behind them the red-uniformed noble guard with bear-skins and white doeskin breeches. The sun was making a flickering flashing blaze of light on the glass-walled hearse that carried the body of the dead Pope. The procession came on slowly to the square, as if summoned by the slow-tolling terrible bell—it came on, slow moving, twisting, a thin wavering endless line. Following the glass hearse were the great Prelates of the Church and immediate relatives; then the clergy. "I'll be damned! Bare feet," Koster said, handing Sam the glasses. With the glasses Sam could see the barefooted ones behind the clergy, the barefooted Franciscans tramping the hard pavement. And now he could see that part of the twisting line, looking like a slowly waving feather, was the white-robed Dominicans. And they were followed by the long somber black line of the priests of Rome, which seemed to flow into something light and feathery and brilliant in the sun, like a plume trailing off into the blue sky.

"That long patch of light at the end," Koster said, taking his glasses, "what is it, Francesca?"

"Just the seminarians of Rome in their white surplices," she said casually.

As the procession came into the vast square, the utter silence of the marchers and the watchers made each clang of the bell more piercing, more personal and more terrible in tone.

Deeply moved, in spite of himself, Koster turned to Carla, "What does it look like to you, Carla?"

"I don't know," she said, hesitantly. "But . . ."

"But what?"

"Yes, what, Carla?" Sam repeated, held by the wonder in her eyes and her expression of strange satisfaction.

"It's like watching a story book opening up," she began. "No, that's not it. It's like all that has happened here in Rome in the last fifteen hundred years; it's like having it all in a parade from long ago and having it all come slowly toward you. Oh, I don't know," and she was distressed. "Only it's all here, now. I don't know."

Her tone, her rapt concentration, made Sam look at her anxiously. When she smiled at him gravely he felt ashamed.

"I see what you mean," Koster said, watching the procession. "The ages creeping back to us. Now that's imagination!"

Now the cortege, filing slowly to the right of the obelisk, approached the wide sweep of steps of the church. The rolling of the drums was much louder now, the air filled with drums and the slow big crash of the bell. Now Sam was focusing his camera, but the procession, with beautiful precision, seemed to split; some went to the left and some to the right, so that a great path to the main door of the church was clear. In one hushed moment in the sunlight all the figures in the square were still and like puppets, hypnotized by the heavy beat of the bell. Sam was working rapidly with his camera. Then he saw they were going to take the Pope's body from the hearse. The angle was all wrong for him, and he began to make his way along the ledge so he could focus on the side of the glass hearse. When he had gone ten paces he heard a step behind him. Over his shoulder he saw Carla slowly following him. Her eyes were on the square. It frightened him to see her trailing him along the ledge, though not even watching him. From the position where he was now he could see in the glass hearse the body of Pius XII, all in red. He got a good shot of the hearse and the body. He took two more shots. Now they were lifting the body from the hearse, and again he clicked his camera. The silence of the multitude, under the tolling of the bell, made the square a place of desolation. A little chill went up his spine. Out of the corner of his eye he saw Carla, all alone on the ledge, coming closer to him, still not even looking at him. He motioned her back nervously, though knowing his signal meant nothing to her. Down there in the square now it was a beautiful picture, and he didn't want to be distracted. The light was good.

At the hearse, men in red damask and white stockings and white gloves, the Pope's chairmen, called the Sediarim, who used to carry him in his happy triumphs in public appearances in Rome, were lifting the light platform on which was the red-garbed frail body. Watching through his lens, Sam moved a little farther along for another shot, for all those in the procession were now on their knees, and many in the multitude, pressed against the wooden barriers, had also fallen on their knees, their heads bowed in prayer in the unbearable silence, between the strokes of the bell. Lowering his camera, Sam rubbed his fingers across his forehead, shuddering, for he seemed to be looking down into a great columned arena of death. Then he jerked his head back, blinked in the good strong sunlight, and raised his camera again.

The Sediarim, who had lifted the Pope, were carrying him toward the wide church steps and the yawning darkness of the open church door. It was a perfect picture. The little platform had tilted as they mounted the steps, and the dead Pope's head came into the light. In that most painful mourning moment, all of a sudden, there came a wild peel of little bells, the light and joyous chiming so startling, so happy, that Sam almost dropped his camera. Shaken and bewildered, he stood in a trance. The light exultant joyous chiming of wild happy bells filled the square. After the dull heavy mournful clanging of the one big master bell, the light gay chiming bells came too quickly, the relief was too swift, the light wild music pierced the heart. *Gloria, Gloria,* sang the bells, and the lightness and happiness of new life seemed to be flowing around Sam, dancing around him, high up there in the sunlight.

In the last of the Roman sunlight the Pope was borne up the steps and into the church door to the *Gloria* of the bells.

Then he heard a foot scraping on the ledge, and he half turned. Though her eyes and all her attention was focused raptly on the great open door, with the light bells chiming out in a joyous tumult around her, nevertheless she came edging sideways toward him. In the strong sunlight her face was golden, her lips parted. The light glinted on the black hair of the widow of the muttonheaded hotel detective, the girl raped as a child. Her whole face now glowed with life and exultant wonder in the beautiful hushed stillness of her spirit. Yet mechanically, in spite of herself, without even looking, she came edging along because she had to be beside him. It tore at his heart.

Was she so much in love with him that she felt a gulf of separation if she was in sight of him, yet beyond his touch? Or had she been made so unsure of herself that she blindly headed for him now even when happy?

CHAPTER 26

WHEN the rites were over and they were all having a drink at the café on the corner near the square, Sam told himself that Carla had known she needed him beside her, even before the Mosca business. What was worrying him then, he wondered? That picture of her on the roof? A woman in love, they would say? Though she had never said she loved him, something seemed to have been settled in her mind; a struggle between them was over. But did she have real love for him? If not, it could mean that more then ever, her life was not her own. No matter how carried away or stirred to wonder, she would always cautiously creep back to him. It wasn't even necessary for her to look at him, he thought. Just that she have him around. No longer need he wonder what she would think of him if she felt free to draw back. Then, he thought doggedly, What about this morning when he had put on the jacket? But even then, with the jacket, he went on tormenting himself; it might have been only a little shock to her, reminding her that he had once been apart from her, stranger, someone now she had had to wonder about. Someone out of another time. Yet there beside him now, sipping her coffee and exchanging eager impressions of the cortege with

Koster, she still had the glow he had seen on her face in the sunlight slanting over an apostle's shoulder.

"What's on your mind, Sam?" she asked, noticing him regarding her intently.

"You look very pretty, that's all," he said.

When the street lights came on and the darkness in the sky lowered over the dome of St. Peter's, Koster said he was hungry and would leave it to Francesca to lead them to a restaurant. She took them to a new place she had heard of, where four waiters descended on them with elaborate enthusiasm, kissing the tips of their fingers, bowing and beaming at her.

"Why don't I try a *pizza* pie?" Sam asked.

"In Rome? A *pizza* pie?" Francesca asked, shocked.

"Why not?"

"What are you, Sam? An American peasant from the Detroit area?" Koster asked. "That ticket folder of yours for the money, and now *pizza* pie!"

"You have to go to Naples to get a good *pizza*," Carla said calmly, and the four waiters kissed their fingers gratefully. These waiters however, having served them their entree, neglected them entirely for other patrons who came crowding in. It spoiled the dinner. Taking it out on Francesca, who had lost caste with him by underestimating his intelligence, Koster asked her if she got a commission for bringing them there. Francesca merely smiled. She had been in a thoughtful mood, having been put in a wrong light and held in it by Carla, and though they hardly spoke, there was fury in Francesca. In Carla, Koster seemed to think he had found someone fresh and unspoiled.

"If I were Sam, I'd hang on to you, Miss Caneli," Koster said confidentially. "Yes, I think I understand you."

"I don't understand you," she said playfully. "Just who is Koster?"

"I'm Koster."

"But what is Koster? What is he when he comes out from under all the great events?" she asked, keeping him on her side, protecting herself by being playful.

No one was paying any attention to Sam as he listened with a fixed little smile, and sometimes smoothed back his hair nervously. Never a word to me, he thought, watching Carla. They can see she shows no real interest in me at all; and yet I couldn't slip away, I'm in the back of her mind all the time —like her keeper, not her lover. That idiot, Mosca. Her own stupid vanity. Her lack of guts. This was what the experience in the cheap night club had done to her, he thought bitterly. After the lacerating failure, a more terrible bondage to him, in which there was no freedom for him or her. As it gnawed away at him he remembered how he had said so confidently to Francesca, "Nothing we say or do or believe can kill off the spark." All right. What was the matter with him now? Was the spark in her supposed to die in the ruins of a night club; the shambles of one nervous performance under crazily destructive auspices? Did that one ruin mean the unquenchable drive in her for summer ripeness was stilled? No, it couldn't be—it was out of her hands—out of his: it was life itself in them. The stubborn grim expression came into his eyes, and he felt restless; he had to get home with her.

"This place is really just a cellar," he said in a bored tone, looking around. "It was a good try, Francesca. Nice food, bad service. What do you say if we get a little air?"

"We'll walk," Koster said. "It'll clear my head. I don't feel like working, but I have to go on back with Signora Francesca. You can fill me in on all the ecclesiastical details."

And they went out and walked to the hotel.

"See you tomorrow, Sam," Koster said. "You too, Carla."

"Good night, Mr. Koster."

"Never mind the 'mister.' Just Koster."

"All right, Koster."

"Good night, Francesca."

"Good night."

"Good night. Oh, what about the film, Koster?"

"I'll get it down to the pilot in the morning, if you bring it around. So long."

When they had got to their own place and turned on the

light, Carla flopped in the chair, kicked her shoes off and rubbed the soles of her feet. Her legs thrust straight out, her fingers linked on her belly, she smiled and sighed, "It's nice to be back, Sam. It all went well, didn't it?"

"First rate. I did a good job," he said, stretching out on the sofa. "A photographer knows when he gets the pictures, Carla. I could develop them in the bathroom with chemicals I've got here, if I had to. There's no trick to it. But they can do the job better at home, when they get the film."

"How is it you know your pictures are good without even seeing them?"

"Experience. It's all that's needed." And then he lay back and just looked at her. Why couldn't it be that he had been making himself sick, magnifying every aspect of her behavior, he wondered? Why couldn't he stop noticing things and leave her alone and give her a chance to show him she had survived any setback?

He looked tired and dispirited, and she said, "Are you all in? What's the matter, Sam?"

"I guess I'm getting old, Carla."

"The world doesn't look so good, eh?"

"Who said I was depressed?"

"The old aren't depressed," she said, laughing. "They're just old. Poor old Sam. Look at him. Sad-eyed Sam, wanting his Carla to make him feel good about the world. Entertain him a little, till there's a light in his tired old eyes. Okay," and she got her guitar. He couldn't believe it when she sat down in front of him. Strumming a little, her eyes full of amusement, she paused, rubbing her left ear slowly, teasing him, making him wait. He was intoxicated; she was touching all his faith in her. Then she sang a little Italian folk song. "How's that?" she asked, when she had finished. "Did I bring you to life?"

"My name must be Lazarus," he said softly. "That's not all, is it?"

"What would you like, old man?"

"How about that old favorite of Piaf's? 'La Vie en Rose.'"

"I'm not like Piaf, old man."

"Who said you were?"

"Some fool once said it."

"The old man's not a fool. You can't be like somebody else, and don't forget it."

"Okay."

Stretching himself out on the couch, he closed his eyes while she went on from one song to another and he pretended to be daydreaming. In a little while he furtively opened one eye. There she was, absorbed in her own song, just amusing herself, and just as he had counted on, she had that little secret smile that was just for herself, as if she were alone and knew that nothing that had ever happened to her could spoil her spirit. And again he was enchanted, and he had to sit up. How proud and untroubled she looked and how splendidly alone, and he leaned forward, his hands clasped on his knees, knowing that he wasn't there for her. A girl alone in a room in Rome, he thought, his mind filled with glimpses of antique processions, sunlight splashing on the Pope's glass hearse, and the burst of light chiming bells. What a picture it would make for Michelangelo, he thought exultantly. A great fresco. Night in Rome. The Pope lying in splendor on his candlelit bier. In the darkness of the square a moonlit, motionless crowd; some of them on their knees. And in a corner of the mural a girl alone in a room, playing and singing softly with a sublime mysterious self-containment expressed in her beautiful face.

And then came the thought that had been gnawing away at him for weeks. I still haven't seen this expression on her face in her daily life. This is Carla.

"Well, that's that," she said suddenly, and laughed.

"Well?"

"Now what do we do?"

"Go to bed, I suppose." And then casually, "I don't know where you should be singing now. I don't know this city. But the kind of place I have in mind is here—you know where—I don't, but we're both going to look around." He added, as if it had just occurred to him, "I was thinking, watching you,

[260

it must be that you have a certain feeling about life when you're singing."

"I don't think so," she said, reflecting as she got up and put the guitar on the table."

"No mood at all."

"I don't know, Sam. Maybe when I'm singing, I just don't care. Things just are. I just am, and I'm kind of glad."

"That's it," he said, nodding. "I think it's what it looks like, too. You have it, and you just don't care. It's wonderful!" And then he got up, heading for the kitchen. "I'll make us a cup of coffee," but he turned. "You know something, Carla? On the street or wherever you are, maybe it's the way you should feel."

"You're good for me, Sam."

"You don't need me at all," he said gruffly. "People need you. You don't need anybody."

"I do, if I'm ever going to look down my nose at the world."

"It's such a pretty nose. It wrinkles a little when you smile, Carla."

"Go on, get me some coffee," she said, and she lay where he had been on the sofa and stretched luxuriously.

In the morning when he woke up he put out his arm to touch her, and she wasn't there, and he sat up fearfully. Little sounds came from the kitchen. He smelled toast. He heard the sizzling of an egg touching the frying pan. She was getting him his breakfast. Incredulous, he went to get up, staring at the kitchen door, then slowly he smiled to himself, lay back on the bed, linked his hands behind his head and now he, in his turn, stretched luxuriously and felt like a master.

CHAPTER 27

WHILE the dead Pope lay in state in
the basilica, thousands of the devout began to come to Rome
from the countries of western Europe and from America. The
hotels were crowded. Business was good. Foreigners were going
to their embassies begging for a little attention which would
amount to a supplication to some hotel keeper. The weather
was as it should be, no rain and still mild. All the visitors were
preparing to head for St. Peter's Square. The newspapers told
of the arrival of cardinals from faraway countries. In the cafés
and on the street corners, and especially in the Roman press,
there was lively speculation about the Pope's successor, a juicy
scandal or two; and the doctor who had sold the ghostly picture
of the dying Pope was pilloried.

That Sunday afternoon at five, when Sam and Carla were
crossing the Via Veneto on the way to the hotel, a woman called
out, "Sam Raymond." She was a tall, blond, vivacious woman
of thirty-five, shapely, long-legged, buxom, expensively dressed;
with her skirt a little too short and a little too tight. Sam had
met her in Montreal a year ago. This woman, with a quick
bright glance at Carla, not waiting for an introduction, said
breathlessly, hardly stopping in her stride, "Sam, I've got the
whole story. I've got a contact in the Vatican. Pay no attention

to the names of all these cardinals you're going to hear for the next few days. It's in the bag."

"It's fixed?"

"It certainly is. It's in the bag. The election is only a formality now."

"Who's it going to be?"

"That Armenian Cardinal, Sam. Look, I'm at the Flora. Call me. I'll have a drink with you," and smiling brightly at Carla, and with an elegant swish of her skirt, she ran for a taxi.

"That one really seems to think she knows. Does she?" Carla asked.

"You heard her."

"She got it right from the Vatican?"

"They all do. That one always has inside information. In her life there's always a Vatican."

"The Armenian Cardinal! What about the New York Cardinal?"

"No, that story from Paris, playing him up so big, meant they were killing off his chances. I'll tell you how we can find out who's going to be pope."

"How do we find out?"

"Let's ask a taxi driver."

"You're pulling my leg," she said, and she laughed. Not often did she laugh, although so much more than before. But when she did, it fascinated him. It was a low amused laugh, as if she found rich enjoyment in the cynical and the ridiculous, as if nothing that was ever sacred—what was sacred to her?—could ever be upset by a joke. There was a kind of wisdom about life in her soft laughter.

Koster was waiting in the hotel lobby, and they went downstairs to have a drink. In this lounge there were many Americans. At the next table was a middle-aged worried man with a good-looking young woman of thirty, in a black suit, and a middle-aged man and his wife, both gray-haired. The older woman, in an alarmed voice, said to the younger American woman, "Now, don't you think of going down there, Miss Graham."

"I've already told her it's a mistake, Mabel," the man said earnestly. "It shocked me, I tell you. I was glad to get back to the hotel."

"What's the use of being here if we can't get into St. Peter's?" asked the girl. "I mean, if we don't even try. We ought to try, anyway."

"Not a chance of making it," the man said, really distressed. "If I were you, Miss Graham, I wouldn't even think of it. It's no place for a girl like you. I've never seen anything like it. I tell you, that square is a seething cauldron of people. We couldn't get near the basilica. It scared me."

"I don't understand," the girl protested. "The newspapers all say the crowds are hushed and reverential."

"The newspapers say!" the man snorted indignantly. "I think those journalists just look at the size of the crowd and go home and have a drink. I assure you there's nothing hushed and reverential about that mob."

"No, indeed," said his wife, shuddering.

"It's shocking to a good Catholic," said the man. "That mob laughs and jokes. They trample on each other. It's a huge carnival crowd. It's frightening. Hushed and reverential!" he scoffed, red-faced. "Why don't those reporters write about the shocking outlandish carnival spirit of these people?"

Koster, who had been listening with amusement, turned to Sam and Carla. "These poor English and American Catholics," he said cynically. "I guess they just don't understand a crowd waiting for a bridegroom always has a carnival spirit. The widow. Eh, Carla? The widow waiting for the new bridegroom. By the way, I got a cable, Sam. Blondell thinks I was great on the cortege stuff."

"Oh, you're so cynical," Carla said. "You too, Sam," she added, because he also was smiling. "I'm not like you. I didn't grow up in your gloomy Protestant world of undertakers. Maybe Catholics get life and death mixed up, but at least we're cheerful about death. At least, more than you people who always want to hide the corpse."

[264

"Well, as a Protestant undertaker I've got to go down there," Sam said.

"It's a fact we should, Sam," Koster agreed.

"I should get a picture of the Pope lying in state."

"They say he looks awful. They say it's an incredible embalming job. And anyway, I hear they're not letting anyone take pictures."

"Don't worry. Let me in and I'll get a picture."

"What if they see your camera?"

"Why should they see it?"

"The girl over there just said nobody can get in."

"Would Mr. Blondell expect us to get in?"

"Do we work for the *Weekly?* Okay," Koster said, "come on."

They had the taxi stop at the apartment for Sam to get his Leica. He came out wearing his light raincoat which would not attract attention, for it had been dull and gray all afternoon and now looked like rain, and the camera was in the inside pocket of the coat. A block from the square, when they left the taxi, they were caught in a surge of people from all the neighborhood streets. All the side streets were like funnels feeding people into the square, and these people, who spoke to each other in many languages, were dressed mainly in black; mostly middle-aged or old, although there were some children. The men all had a brusque air, as if they didn't intend to be pushed aside. Hurrying along, too, Sam wished he could see at least one of those elegant women he had seen in the hotels or on the Via Veneto, or one of the girls from the fashionable cafés in a bright sweater and with a golden head, or at least one of the elegant, ageless, worldly, handsome men who stood around in Doney's. He felt out of place. He squeezed Carla's arm. Suddenly they were at the square on the fringe of the crowd, enfolded in the stone arms of Bernini's great colonnade around the square, a hundred thousand huddled together, and it was getting dark. The large crowd was held back by a barricade of trucks which was at least two hundred feet from the steps to the main door of the church. All jammed together, not moving a step, they looked toward St. Peter's, there so solidly in the gray light; like the Parthenon with a dome sitting on it. And Sam's eyes went to the roof ledge, trying to pick out the one Apostle's statue that would mark the spot where Carla had stood, her face glowing. "There," he said. "Up there," turning to her, but someone had jostled her roughly. Grim-faced, she had swung her elbow, digging it into a stout man, forcing him, scowling, away from her.

Koster said, "Let's take out our press passes and hold them in our hands. Carla, you keep saying 'Excuse us. The press.'"

"Come on," Carla said, "let's try."

Pushing and twisting, they shouldered and wormed their way deep into the crowd. Carla, flanked by Sam and Koster, saying quietly, "*Stampa. Stampa,*" and Sam and Koster trying to smile politely. Deep in the crowd they stalled as Carla argued with a fat determined woman who wouldn't be budged, and they were pressed so close together they couldn't move their arms. A solidly built little woman, olive-skinned, with three front teeth missing, scowled at Sam and banged at him angrily with her purse. Around him were the resentful irritable angry olive-skinned faces; bodies leaned against him and he seemed to be enfolded in black shapeless garments; and when he tried to look down, he saw a thin boy eating a bun. A little woman, her eyes blazing, jabbed at Sam with her purse, pushing him back so she could haul a child of ten, with scared eyes, from between his legs. As the mother jabbered fiercely, Sam thought nerv-ously, It's the Roman mob just as it was two thousand years ago; dark little people he had rarely seen on the Via Veneto, the real people of Rome and he didn't know how they thought or felt, he couldn't speak their language; he knew nothing about them except that they looked at him fiercely. Then he thought, This is the place where Caligula's chariots used to race, and somewhere over there by the church had been Nero's Circus; it had always been a place of screams and passions and death. His hand tightened nervously on Carla's arm, wondering anxiously if his thoughts were hers, too, and he tried to see her face, but couldn't. "*Stampa. Stampa,*" he heard her say.

"Fold your arms across your chest like this," she whispered. "Pickpockets."

"I can't fold my arms, but in a crowd of the devout it's a nice comment."

"They're still human beings."

"That's right," Koster said. "No matter the hour, 'every man has to exercise his profession,' as St. Paul would say, 'according to his station in life.' "

Deeper in the crowd where there was laughter and joking, they came to a pocket of children who could have easily been crushed and trampled to death. Scared eyes gleamed up at Sam. If he stepped on one of these children he would start a riot, and he knew it. With Carla repeating monotonously, *"Stampa. Stampa,"* they got a little closer to the front of the crowd. But now the turning faces looked grimmer. These people, who had been waiting, edging forward five yards at a time when those ahead were let through the barrier, were closer to seeing the corpse.

It was twilight now. It had taken them an hour to move forward a hundred yards. Lights appeared in windows to the right of the church steps. The night was slowly closing over the square, and to the right the Sistine Chapel was the color of the dark-gray sky. Then they came to the barrier, a row of trucks with police on this side, a policeman every ten feet. Carla called out to one of them who turned, wonderfully disinterested. Finally this bored policemen, reaching in among the front ranks, drew her close to him. She talked rapidly. They argued, and she beckoned to Sam. Taking Koster's arm, he tried to get through to the cop and Carla. A woman of fifty, her black hair falling over one cheek, her hat knocked crazily over her ear, heaped imprecations on him, pleading with those close to her to block the way; her eyes were wild. The policeman shouted at her, then laughed; he didn't take her seriously. "He wants to see your press passes," Carla called. They handed her the passes, and he pretended to study them, but they obviously meant nothing to him. Yet he nodded gravely and spoke to Carla. "He says we can crawl under the truck and

267]

go to that office with the lighted window, just to the right there of the door," she said.

"My God."

"Come on," Carla said. Down on her knees she started to crawl under the truck, and Sam, following her, was flat on his belly. He coughed. The dust of the square was in his lungs. He smelled oil from the truck's chassis. What am I doing here flat on my face? he wondered. Then he saw Carla's ankles ahead of him as she stood up, then her hand came reaching under the truck for his, and he felt angry and ridiculous, as if he were being treated like an old man. On his feet beside her, he waited till Koster came wiggling from under the truck, then he began to dust her skirt.

"Was it hard on your knees, Sam?" she asked.

"No," he said shortly.

"You didn't scrape your hands?"

"No," he said, trying to laugh and draw back as she began to dust the front of his coat. "I'm all right. What is this?"

"As for me, I climb under trucks on my belly every day," Koster said, breathing hard. "Let's get moving. If they ever let those people through this barricade they'll trample us down." They hurried across the open space to the small lighted open door to the right of the closed main entrance, the place to which the policeman had directed them.

"If they don't want cameras in there, this is where you quit," Koster said.

"Cameras? Who's got a camera?" he asked, innocently.

Barring the way to the lighted office was a policeman to whom Carla spoke, and who nodded and pointed at the office; but they couldn't get beyond the door for a harassed middle-aged man in there was expostulating with three earnest younger men. Minutes passed as they waited. "This could go on all night," Sam said. "Let's just saunter away." And the police-man, seeing them coming from the office and thinking they must have checked in, paid no attention; and they found them-selves out in the wide steps leading to the great main door of the basilica. Now it was almost dark. While they were on the steps, and some twenty paces away from the entrance, the great door opened slowly, and they ambled lazily toward it. Out of the shadow of the door came a policeman, leading away a weeping hysterical woman, who was clutching a small bewildered child. The woman was moaning. From somewhere back of the crowd at the barricade came the wail of an ambulance siren, weirdly loud in the dusk.

"God almighty, look out," Koster cried.

There was a scuffling, pounding sound, a tearing at the ground in the dusk, and Sam, startled, looked down the square. A dark wave seemed to be rolling from the barricade. The police had let some hundreds through, and they came charging toward the great open door, pounding along, pushing and reaching in a wild thudding to get through the big open door and get close to the corpse. Carla and Koster ran toward the door, but Sam had stopped, held motionless. Maybe it was the dusk, the lowering sky, the great shadows from the church falling over the square, the huge slabs of stone rising beside him while his ears were filled with the sound of pounding feet. Then the light from the open door reached to the broken line of faces coming closer, almost upon him, and in a moment of strange panic, he froze—breathless—waiting to be engulfed, utterly alone and alien; and in him a frantic protest that he was alone. Then he sucked in his breath; he had to breathe or drown in his panic, and his head cleared and his heart pounded, and he thought of Carla kneeling mute on the floor in Signora Spagnola's kitchen.

"Carla!" he cried wildly, looking around for her.

"Here, Sam. Here," she called from the shadow at the side of the church door. "I'm here. Run!" and she hadn't taken her eyes off him. He ran to her.

"Quick! Get in," he said, shoving her into the dimly lit vestibule as the crowd came pushing and charging up the steps, jamming at the door; the leaders reaching them like a wave lapping against them and pushing them forward.

"And you standing out there!" she said. "That was something."

269]

"For the first time in my life I felt real panic," he stammered. "It was real crowd panic, and for the first time!"

"Aren't you lucky?" she said. And then puzzled by his look, "What's the matter, Sam?"

"But you, Carla, there by the door in the shadow . . . not scared at all."

"I was too busy watching you," and she was smiling up at him; and as the crowd, jamming in behind them, pushed them forward into the mass moving slowly into the church, he cried out in his heart, I'm the right man for her, I love her desperately. In that swift excited moment of his belief in the rightness of their dependence on each other, his head whirled; he lost track of his view of her as he had wanted her to be. What a fool he was, he thought, to have missed in his understanding of her what now seemed to be so plain. She was a woman. As a woman could she ever know a fullness of being, standing alone, not needing the concern and love of someone else? And hadn't she been showing him, day by day, she knew she was nothing without him?

"There's Koster," she said suddenly.

"I don't see him."

"Just ahead—to the right—inside, now."

As the line moved, they came out of the shadows, out of the dim light into a blaze of a thousand candles. Full of emotion as he was, and after the gray light of the dusk and the shadows, the sound of the charging crowd, the contrast left him breathless. A golden brilliance of light and color came streaming at him from walls and ceilings and altars. It was so sudden a satisfaction of the longing for form and color, it made him want to cry out; all the golden baroque glory of an age falling upon him in a sudden shower. Blinking his eyes, he muttered, "To run blindly out of the dark and have this hit you."

"Haven't you been in here before, Sam?"

"No."

"Really? And you've been around here weeks and weeks."

"It just didn't happen," he said apologetically.

The slow-moving crowd was edging its way up the aisle

[270

toward the dead Pope in his bier in front of his own high altar, with Bernini's four great twisted bronze columns on the white marble bases. When Sam and Carla got to the first marble base, they saw Koster pressed against it so he wouldn't impede the flow in the aisle of the mourners. They joined him and looked at the bier. It was tilted up, the head higher than the feet. All in red, the dead Pope lay there, the folded delicate hands so frail and white that they, and the other mortal remains, seemed to belong to the beautiful church marbles.

That corpse, Sam thought, deeply moved, that embalmed figure, the face such a ghastly greenish white, brought me here. And he had enquired, and counted on, the fact that a man was soon to become this corpse here. His own story with Carla, their story, the love he now felt for her, could never have happened if word had not been given out to the world that this cold, embalmed, frail figure would soon be lying there in state. Yet what did he know about him? he asked himself. An intellectual, a centralizer, they said. An aristocrat. It didn't matter. The days of the dying had been the high point of his own life.

"It's the strangest job of embalming I ever saw," Koster whispered.

"It's true. The face is not a good color."

"Maybe it's what they want. The conqueror worm, and all."

"No, there has been some critical comment, I understand."

"What does it matter?" Carla asked.

"It's a very frail intellectual face."

"An aristocratic face."

"Well, here goes," Sam said. Slipping his camera from under his coat, he focused and took his picture; he took another from a slightly different position, feeling furtive and guilty and in a hurry. Then he became aware that among all who streamed slowly by, their eyes on the corpse, no one was paying any attention to him. It upset him. What he was doing didn't seem to matter. To shake off his sense of being inconsequential, he took many more pictures. Putting his camera back under his coat, he joined Carla and Koster who were now hugging the column at the head of the bier.

"Come here. Look," Carla said. "These marble bases are very interesting. The sculptor, what was his name?"

Out in the aisle again, and carried along by the slow-moving crowd, they had circled the altar and were moving slowly back toward the door. In this aisle the mourners had become more relaxed. After all, they were satisfied and on their way home, and it was possible to stand momentarily at the side and look at a relic or a piece of sculpture, and while doing this themselves, Sam and Carla lost Koster.

It was dark out, but across the square they could still see the barricade and the big dark shadow that was the crowd behind it. When they came to the taxi stand, they saw Koster under a street light talking to a girl two inches taller than he was, a long-legged American girl in a light-gray suit.

"Hey," he called out. "Where did you two go? Meet Miss Francis."

"Hi," she said. She was very happy to meet them, she said. She certainly meant it.

Miss Francis was a blonde of thirty-five, faded, or perhaps a little washed-out and nervous-eyed, but in that light she looked very pretty. She had given up on her plan to get into the church, she said. In the dark, the whole thing frightened her. When she had heard Koster call out, "Sam," the sound of a voice in her own language had simply intoxicated her. Right now she was full of eager pleased warm good will. Could she come along with them? She was editor of a woman's page on a Missouri paper, she said, and she had been in London, Berlin, Paris. It was her luck to be there in Rome when the Pope died. Each day she had been cabling stories to her paper, but the city editor hadn't answered any of her queries, nor had he sent her any more expense money. Maybe he thought she should be using her ticket home to her woman's page.

In the taxi, Koster, sitting with his arm protectively around Miss Francis, was charmed and amused by her lonely eagerness. "You must have dinner with us. A colleague! We will look after you. We are your hosts. You are in our town," he said. And

Miss Francis thanked him. They ate in a restaurant off the Via Veneto, a place that had a tree growing through the second story. For dessert, a beautiful chestnut pudding that Miss Francis adored. Then they went to the café, where it was a little cooler than it had been other nights, but the chill in the night air as yet bothered no one.

Sitting beside Carla on the chairs by the curb facing the entrance, Sam listened to Koster explaining eloquently about a new economic union for Europe. Then he looked at Carla, and when she smiled faintly, it seemed to him she understood they should now be alone; she should hear him, look at him, gather that whether she sang or not, he was the right man for her; and she should show that, no matter what happened, he would be the one she would choose.

It was hard for Sam to stand up abruptly and suggest to Carla they leave, for Miss Francis was being so fresh, frank and friendly. Her natural affection seemed to puzzle Koster. She was drinking rum-and-coke, and to show his sympathy, Koster was having the same drink, but he became distressed. She could really belt them down, and he couldn't; he was a sipper. Her five drinks had only wiped the faded quality from her pretty eager face. She said, in astonishment, "You don't drink much, Mr. Koster," and Koster, worried yet fascinated, had to beckon the waiter. A pretty woman, her face full of affection, who couldn't get drunk. He talked to her, thickly, about Rome and the ruins. Knowing nothing about Rome himself, he offered to take her in hand starting tomorrow and show her all the antiquities, and Miss Francis, blooming in the severe tight-fitting gray suit, said, "Gee, I'm in luck. I'll love this."

"Lady, you are in luck. So are you, Koster. We won't stay and spoil your luck. See you for the funeral mass, Koster." And he and Carla left, walking slowly along the street toward the Borghese Gardens.

"She's either a widow, or she's divorced," Carla said. "Didn't you notice the ring mark on the finger of her left hand? I think she's a widow."

"Will Koster have luck with the widow?"

"In this case I don't think there'll have to be an election," she said laughing.

Humming to herself, she walked in step with him in the gardens. They walked for hours. At the Villa Borghese, it seemed to him she had a new ease with him; it was almost an indulgent attitude, and it puzzled him. Because of his own emotion, this change in her made him feel shy.

"The trouble is, Carla," he said awkwardly, "you've got used to me as a kind of boss. Someone pushing you around, someone you count on, someone always telling you what to do."

"I count on you, Sam."

"Just someone there, who's completely dependable."

"What's the matter with it?"

In her tone there was a matter-of-fact frankness, and he hid his little smile of satisfaction. Her unawareness of her love for him no longer bothered him. He had told himself that unawareness of love was one of the phases of love, the secret that was sometimes shattering when it was known. And he wondered shyly if it was the right time to bring it out in the open for her.

"Look over there," he said. There across the sleeping city, was the dome of St. Peter's, all silvered in the moonlight. At this hour the vast square would be emptied of the mob, and the dead Pope would be lying in peace on his bier.

"When I saw that Roman mob charging across the square at the church door, you know what I should have said?" he asked thoughtfully.

"No, what, Sam?"

"The words of Julian, the apostate. 'Thou has conquered, O pale Galilean.' "

"Uhhu. Well, you're not much like this Julian."

"How so?"

"I don't think you'd ever give up, would you?"

"About what?"

"About me. Mainly about my singing. I feel almost made over, Sam. The way you see things—it's the way I see things

[274

now. It must be so. I feel this little catch in my chest after you've worked with me and talked to me. It's the way I used to feel a long time ago. Just wait. I have a feeling here, now I'll sing and you'll be proud of me. Any time now, Sam. I won't say no."

"I'm pretty stubborn, I admit, but only about the things I really believe in." Then he hesitated awkwardly. "I'm not always like you find me, Carla."

"I don't know what you mean, Sam."

"People have complained that I'm too easygoing a guy," he said, fumbling and bewildered by his new shyness. "I like to take things easy, I like to take people just as they are."

"It's not true, Sam. I don't blind myself to the fact that I'd be in terrible shape right now if you had taken me as I was."

"But now—the way you are now, Carla," he said, huskily.

"Are you making a pass at me, Sam?"

"Is it what it sounds like?"

"It's what I'd call it," and she stopped, turning to him, and the moonlight was on one side of her face, and he could see that she was surprised and ready to laugh. It hurt him. "All right, Sam, go on. Let's see how you do."

"I'm serious, Carla."

"I'm listening."

"There are things ahead for you. And I'll be in another light. You'll be indifferent to so much that has worried you, and there I'll be . . . well . . ."

"Uhhu. Go on," and she giggled.

"I'm not so bad, you know."

"No, considering how they come, you're not so bad," and she tried to keep a straight face.

"I mean," he said, upset by her amusement, "I can be a damn sight more interesting. Who the hell wants to be a woman's caretaker? Our lives can open up, Carla."

Even in that light, he thought he saw laughter in her face. Frustrated, tricked by anguish, he nevertheless felt a fierce pride in her and in himself, and then he was angry that he should feel compelled to recommend himself to her.

275]

"Come on, Sam," she said, giving him a playful push. "You don't have to sell yourself to me."

"I'm not selling myself," he said irritably.

"Look, I'll bear in mind all your good points," she said, kidding him. "Don't call us—we'll call you."

"Great," he said, "let me know, eh?" and he laughed and put his arm around her waist. And on the path he waltzed her around, swinging her faster and faster and faster until she was limp, and his own head was swimming, and they had to lean against each other, the ground swaying under them till their heads cleared. Then he walked her suddenly out of the park.

When they got home and it was time to go to bed, she would have undressed quickly and hopped in as she usually did. But he sat beside her on the edge of the bed, slowly undoing the buttons at the back of her blouse, as if she were a shy virgin, then drawing off her skirt with fumbling fingers. At first she giggled, then grew grave and puzzled, understanding that he wanted her to see that no man could prize her as much as he did.

CHAPTER **28**

ON THE way to the Vatican for the funeral mass, the taxi driver, a grim-faced, serious energetic man of fifty with short dark hair and restless discontented eyes, told them that he had worked in Detroit. In his talk he showed no ingratiating Italian charm, not even to Francesca and Carla. He wanted them all to see that his American experience had rubbed off on him, he was bluntly democratic in his opinions, refusing to be polite; and Koster, with sly malice, had encouraged him.

"There's one thing you can tell me, I know," Sam, who was paying him, said when they were getting out of the taxi.

"What's that, pal?"

"Who's going to be pope?"

"It's not a sure thing, pal. Don't take any bets."

"Narrow the field a little for me, pal."

"Okay. It'll be one of the older cardinals, for my money. The older, the better. An old one to fill in for a few years. That's right from the horse's mouth. It's the politics. Why ask me, pal?"

"I thought you might have been driving some of those cardinals around."

"Listen, pal," he said, twisting his mouth disdainfully. "A

few cardinals in my cab. Maybe one of them the Pope-to-be. A very big deal, eh?" And then with bold contemptuous assurance, his speech suddenly clipped, "I have done better than that in a cab."

"Somebody really important?"

"Mussolini. I used to drive for Mussolini. There was a man, pal." And with a hurt proud contemptuous air, he snorted, "All this? Peanuts," and started his taxi and was gone.

Smiling to himself, Sam joined the others for the walk along the alley to the Press Office where the journalists had gathered again. He started for the office door with Koster, then noticed that Carla and Francesca had been left alone, and he turned. Francesca had said. "How are you feeling, Anna?" For three days now Francesca had been left out of it, nursing her resentment of Carla's coolness, made to feel she was living a lie, supporting the wild pretenses of a girl capable of any folly, who had humiliated her by once stirring in her strange possessive emotions. She felt entitled, at least, to the intimacy that could come from expressing troubled concern.

"I'm all right. And yourself?" Carla asked, shrugging.

"Very well, thank you. You're looking so much better. It's remarkable."

"Glad you think so, darling."

"I've said nothing. Absolutely nothing," and then she flushed, as if she felt Carla was enjoying making a fool of her. "Alberto did not go to the United States," she said suddenly.

"Of course not. Are you surprised?"

"With the Pope dying, he thought he should stay for the funeral."

"What an excuse. Alberto is a coward."

"Shame on you. Alberto now is desperately ill. He may be dying, too."

"And asking for me, I suppose."

"I know you have no heart. I'm not asking that you should see him."

"You're damn right you're not," and her eyes blazing, Carla took a step closer to her. "I beg your pardon for being here at

[278

St. Peter's and not in the gutter. What a fat little bitch you are."

"I'm not a cheap little street whore, anyway."

"No, you can't make up your mind what you are. Get wise to yourself."

"I didn't think a whore could be so particular."

"You'd eat anything up. You wouldn't leave a bone. Nobody can put out your kind of fire."

"What is this?" Sam asked, coming closer and drawing Carla away. He felt her trembling. But Koster had come out of the Press Office, and following him was the official they had met the other day. And as this official, with the same grand wave of the hand, led all the newspapermen along the alley, Carla darted ahead and got in step with Koster. "I heard some of that back there," Sam said bitterly to Francesca. "What are you trying to do?"

"I am a human being," Francesca said curtly, her head back, her pretty face shining with belligerent dignity. Square-shouldered, curiously massive at that moment, her low-heeled shoes coming down with an unfamiliar flat masculine determination, she sailed along grandly. "The unbelievable arrogance of that girl is intolerable, Sam. I try to establish a sympathetic relationship; on the quiet, mind you, so we can have a gentle understanding. What am I supposed to do? Go on pretending I don't even know anything about her, even when I'm face to face with her?"

"It's ignorant female malice. It's woman's stuff. It's a woman peeking through a keyhole. Where's your noble Christian charity? Here you are, going into this church, your temple, and all you want to do is make sure that girl is rattled to the point of doing something disgraceful. Well, she won't, you understand? You're going to be disappointed."

"I'm sure I am," she said blandly, as if his anger convinced her that Carla, furious and brooding, was capable at last of wild behavior, even at the funeral mass. "Don't worry about it, Sam," she said calmly. "Your Carla and I are two women. We understand each other. The words we use are nothing.

279]

Nothing at all. Neither one of us will remember them. Now really, the mass will calm her, won't it? Won't it, Sam? Don't you think so?"

"Drop it, Francesca," he said harshly, for ahead was Carla walking in step with Koster, not once looking back for him, her step quick, feminine and hurried, knowing she was under the eyes of the heavier trailing woman, preying on her with her knowledge of her, and waiting. He was sure Carla was on edge, and he was outraged and on edge himself. They had come to a turn in the alley. On one side was the great stone wall with the small windows, and on the other the glimpse of the Vatican garden; the green fading in the autumn sunlight, the grass looking coarse and tired, beat up by long months of sunlight, with none of that golden-brown and red of autumn that made this month so beautiful at home.

"Carla, wait." He caught up to her, and he had her arm as they went into the basilica by a side door. He didn't like the flash in her eyes and her silence. He was sure she was taking into the church too many bitter passionate memories of her life with Alberto in New York and Brazil, and the shameful hours of wandering here on the streets. And if it tormented her, or wounded her pride, he wondered would she turn, wait for Francesca and try and wound her? His own uncertainty, his apprehensiveness, were so upsetting he couldn't believe Carla knew he had her arm, as they were all led to a barricaded section from which point they could see the dead Pope's bier.

He was glad they were jammed in with the other journalists. Carla pressed close to him, but would not turn at his touch. He held on to her, hiding his rage at Francesca. The journalists gathered around them were speaking many languages. He tried to become aware of them and remember why he was there. It seemed to him that Carla was staring blankly at the occupied balconies, high on the pillars. The huge church was crowded, but from their place they could only see a few rows of faces of the faithful. These people, dressed in black and middle-aged, were the established and dignified citizens of Rome. No mistaking them. In their own enclosure, he caught sight of the

[280

Frenchman who had invited him to meet the International Set. But he was not within speaking distance.

"There's Miss Francis," he whispered, trying to distract Carla. Miss Francis looked very sweet and quiet. Koster was edging toward her.

A familiar voice. That grand middle-aged woman with the warm jolly face and the grand air, Miss Malone; the woman with "sources in the Vatican," whom they had listened to in the Press Club, was saying, "It's going to be a caretaker pope. A very old cardinal, who'll be a caretaker. I have it on the best authority."

"Her source at the Vatican is our taxi driver," Sam whispered to Carla, giving her arm a little tug to break her dream. And she did turn to him, half smiling.

"What did Francesca say to you?" she whispered.

"I heard what was said. It is nothing."

"I'm glad it happened," she said calmly. "It'll be easier meeting her now," and he sighed with relief. It was like the time when she had looked at him changing into his jacket, and was reminded of the night she had first met him on the street.

Now that he could work freely, he looked around, listening. Other journalists, trying to keep their voices down, were arguing with Miss Malone. Some English journalists had it figured out that the bearded Armenian Cardinal would be a wise political choice because he had been born near Stalin's birthplace; an appeal to the East and Russia, don't you know? And others contended that the dead Pope had secretly, in his last illness, made an archbishop a cardinal so he could succeed him and carry on in his centralizing tradition. "It is my opinion," said a stocky bald Englishman, "that the choice is being made right now in some cardinal's room. I know how these things are done. They get together for a little talk, and naturally they do a little canvassing and get a vote lined up. It was so when Cardinal Verdier came to Rome and Pacelli was elected. Verdier had had all the votes for Pacelli in his pocket before they ever went into the Conclave." With the exception of the opulent Miss Malone, the journalists tried to keep their voices down.

Miss Malone assumed they all wanted to hear her. In this loud hum of conversation they weighed the merits of the candidates for the hand of the widow. No one talked about the dead Pope lying there on his bier. It upset Sam. The dead Pope now seemed to belong in his life. Leaving Carla, who appeared to be listening to the others intently, he stepped back to see who might be passing in the aisle behind them. Quickly he raised his camera. A stocky, pink-faced, purple-robed, plump cardinal, massive in his robes, waddling a little as he came down the aisle, but truly imperious in the way he carried his head, was seen and perhaps recognized by a middle-aged man in striped pants and a cutaway coat. Hurrying to the cardinal, the man in the striped pants dropped on his knees as the cardinal extended his hand to be kissed. It was the perfection of the cardinal's manner which made Sam raise his Leica so eagerly. It was benign, indulgent, graceful, princely; the cardinal's head held back, a faint wise smile on his lips. No actor in Hollywood, practicing for years, could ever have captured that princely benevolence and ease. It made a beautiful picture, Sam thought with satisfaction. Then he saw in the aisle behind them a woman of forty, heavily veiled, robed in black, moving slowly up and down, trying to get closer to the dead Pope's bier. Raising her veil, she put a handkerchief to her eyes. Tears were streaming down her face, and Sam was suddenly surprised and full of emotion himself.

"Look, Carla," he said, drawing her away from his colleagues. "That woman, actually crying!" He got a good picture of the little woman in black as her trembling hand went up to her anguished face.

"Why take her picture, Sam?"

"It's the first time I've seen anyone crying about the Pope. It's his funeral, and here's a woman really crying. With the rest of us it's only, Who's going to be Pope now? The new one."

"The dead one had a good life," she said frowning. "And now . . ." Then she turned away. The little things happening in the center aisle, by the bier, were too fascinating for her, and he wondered what she had been about to say. "And now

[282

. . ." Now what? Had he ever known what she was thinking? he asked himself.

At certain places in the aisles were detachments of Swiss Guards in armor, and detachments of Noble Guards. At beautifully timed moments these little groups would abruptly move to another point, as if some hand in a high control room had pressed a button. It was time for the mass to begin, and all sounds of life from the street outside ceased. Traffic in Rome stood still and the city was silent. In a slow procession, the parish priests of Rome moved toward the altar of the confession, and the bier; then came the uniformed members of the palace household, and the throne bearers who had once carried the dead Pope through the Roman streets. Picking up the light stretcher, these throne bearers lifted the body, feeling the weight of it for the last time. Watching carefully, Sam got a shot of the plaster-white face of the corpse.

As the great prelates, in their ancient vestments, took their places around the catafalque, Carla, who had been observing every movement raptly, whispered, "The old tombs are beneath this church. I've read about them, Sam, the tombs of the old Romans. Some happy gay inscriptions, too," but she broke off, startled as he was; voices of surpassing sweetness soared, came from nowhere, and yet drew Sam's eyes to the blaze of golden light that hung in the air beneath the great dome. It was the Julien choir singing the *Miserere,* and so sweetly mournful was the singing, it made him shiver. What had been in Carla's mind? he wondered. The tombs of the old Romans? This place. This Vatican Hill, an ancient place of the dead. What was it doing to her imagination?

In the great aisle the Swiss Guards had fallen on their knees, for the corpse was being carried by. Remembering why he was there, Sam tried for a picture, but in the blaze of color and in the movements of such solemn splendor, he couldn't see it in a pattern. Suddenly he had a frantic desire to see it all in some kind of form of life and death that would sooth and satisfy him—the painter in him again. And he swung around, looking

283]

up restlessly as if seeking a lofty perch for a fuller view with the discontent, the longing to impose some glory of form on the ritual movements, gnawing away at him.

As the procession passed his roped-in group he muttered irritably, clicking his camera again and again. From here now he could only half see the purple-robed cardinals taking their special places, standing before the other altar, all intoning the *Miserere.* He got one good shot of a figure in black surplice and white miter blessing the coffin, and another one of attendants removing this figure's white miter before he chanted the *Kyrie* and sprinkled the body slowly with holy water, giving absolution.

"I can't see anything more from this angle," he whispered bitterly. He pushed into the group and tapped Koster on the shoulder. "I can't see anything."

"Try climbing a pillar, Sam."

"I would, but I'd be yanked down. I'm not in on the deal."

"Somebody has the rights?"

"Maybe the movies, maybe television."

"Shut up, Sam," Carla whispered impatiently.

"I'm trying to do my job."

"That's what you'll say to St. Peter."

"You're damn right, if I'm there to do a job."

"*Sh, sh,*" someone whispered hoarsely.

They were closing the three coffins, one of lead, one of cypress, one of oak. Each one in turn was blessed, and then the cardinals, twenty-three of them, led by a white-bearded dean of the college, all in their solemn princely peacock splendor, filed by the coffin to look for the last time at the dead Pope. Then Sam saw that Koster, always prepared, was reading from a handout from the Press Office; he could tell what was going on. Research! He could have been sitting in the hotel room. "Now they are clothing the Pope's body in a blanket of red," he whispered. "Now they're putting a white scarf over his face, now a red silk shroud." It wasn't worrying Koster that he couldn't see any of it with his own eyes. "What

[284

are they doing now?" And he read, "They're saying the *Pater Noster.*"

When the eulogy began, Sam said, "I can't understand a word. What's the use?" and he sauntered out of the group to the free aisle. His feet had begun to hurt him, and he wanted to sit down. In the long wide deserted aisle there were no chairs, and as he walked up and down, the Italian words of the eulogist echoing in the basilica, he saw the confessional boxes, different boxes marked for the different European languages of the penitents. Sam leaned against the Slovakian box. In a little while, out of curiosity, he drew the curtain, saw the little platform about six inches off the ground, hesitated, then sat down on this platform, half in the box, his legs out, and he half closed the curtain. Undoing his shoelaces, he leaned back, sighing with relief. The voice of the eulogist rose and fell, in the language he couldn't understand, and lulled by its rhythm, he began to doze.

"Sam."

"Yeah," he said, jumping up nervously. It was Carla, watching him with an amused smile.

"Sam, you're impossible. You've no feeling for religion at all. You don't believe in anything."

"My feet were aching."

"Poor Sam. No respect at all."

"Is it respect to stand there for an hour, pretending to look intelligent? It would be an act. I'm not an actor."

"Sitting there with your feet stuck out of the confessional. It looks awful," she scolded him primly. "Don't you know how to behave?"

Up the aisle was a seminarian sitting on a lone table, reading. "Look at that one. Don't tell me he's listening while he's reading."

"Do up your shoelaces, Sam. Now, come on," and they rejoined the journalists.

"What's that pounding?" he asked. "Don't you hear pounding?"

While the eulogy flowed on, there were sounds of hammering. It was incredible to Sam that workmen could be repairing some part of the church while the Pope's funeral mass went on. The Romans were a very practical people, but not so practical as to have workmen asserting with their hammers that life must go on. The pounding began to get on all their nerves. At the fringe of the group was a tall fair English seminarian, handsome and grave.

"What's that pounding, could you tell me?" Sam asked.

"Workmen."

"Workmen? Doing what?"

"Sealing up the coffins."

"Oh," and he wanted to protest; the pounding gave him a chill, as if he knew he would hear it echoing in his dreams, and when he went to speak to Carla and saw she looked untroubled, he said to himself, "It's the drama. She has a taste for drama and the theatre. This is it." Then he had a resentful impulse to turn, saunter away, and show her she had to follow him, belonged to him, forever his girl.

On the Pope's own high altar a little scaffold of rough lumber had been raised, and over this scaffold they had erected a block and tackle with many ropes. "That scaffolding there, that hammering at the coffin going on, there's something re-morseless about it. What is it I feel?" Sam whispered. And Carla did half turn, she did meet his eyes. But the hammering had ended. A little procession came toward the altar; they were wheeling the sealed coffin to the scaffolding. The little procession and what they were doing began to fascinate Sam. The figures seemed to be far away and of a time long ago.

"You said the lovely Roman tombs were deep beneath this marble floor," he whispered.

"Yes, and I think a Mithraic temple was here, too."

This indeed had long been the place of the dead. Rapt as he was, he could believe that behind the figures in the aisle, con-ducting their burial rite on this Vatican Hill, he saw the shadowy figures of others in antique processions, precursors of those he saw now, who were perhaps saying as the others had said, that man was a unique creature on earth because he was aware of the mystery of existence and death, and now was facing it; and he looked at Carla. Her head lifted, she had an expression of aloof serenity he had never seen before. It astonished him. It was not quite like that look that had given him such elation when she sang for him. Something added or something left out. What was it? he wondered. All the calmness and the quiet wisdom, but not the happy arrogance. He thought she had been carried away, lifted out of herself, lifted so far in repose by her contemplation of the mystery of existence that she was beyond him. He felt a quick stab of wondering anguish. He had never really known her, couldn't have known this girl, and it was too late. He was left there beside her watching the priests, left in his own solitude, wondering if every aspect of her he had thought he had known had been false. This was Carla. The rest had been all pretending. Yes, she could have lied about her past, he thought uneasily, made it all up; the stories about her mother, the adoptions, the childhood rape, the hotel detective. Just look at her now! These things couldn't have been part of her life. Not this girl he was watching in wonder. And there was the way she talked; her words, her imagination, her knowledge of history, her sense of the past—more like a girl from an eastern college who had got off the track, gone alcoholic and turned to singing. Indeed, she could have lied to Alberto in the beginning, and now, carried away, rapt, lifted out of the lies. . . .

"Carla," he whispered. She didn't answer. With a pang he realized she had forgotten he was there. The priests with their burial rites were saying something to her. He went to touch her arm, and draw her back to him; then couldn't bear to disturb her. He thought he was looking at her as he had described her so fervently to Francesca—her past—all the debasement and wretchedness of her destructive experience drained through her. In church, he thought he saw something divine in her.

On the altar they were twisting the ropes around the coffin, and when it was done they hoisted the coffin with a block and tackle. For a moment the coffin swung back and forth, gently swinging against all the baroque splendor of the basilica. Then as it sank slowly into the crpyt below, it seemed to Sam, stirred as he was, that he, too, understood what they were saying; even in the ruins of death they were hurling the challenge to eternity, "We *still* live."

"Well, he made it," Carla said quietly.

"Made what?"

"I think I read somewhere that he said that to be buried close to Peter was to be close to God. Isn't the tomb of St. Peter down there?"

"So they say. Yes. Well, come on. Let's go."

It was twilight in the square and Sam, his eyes still filled with the golden light, kept blinking as they walked with Koster and Francesca in the forest shadows of the colonnade. The city was humming with life again, the traffic now moving, and because the smell of death was still with them, Sam kept watching the way Carla's breast jiggled as she walked. When Francesca, quiet and depressed, said suddenly she had to meet her husband at the Press Club, Koster asked Sam if he and Carla would have dinner with him and Miss Francis.

It was a long evening. Perhaps they were tired from being on their feet so long. Koster said he was going to show some floodlit ruins to Miss Francis. No more ruins for him, Sam said. "Not tonight, anyway." When Carla yawned and smiled, he thought she, too, wanted to get home. There had remained in him an unwelcome gravity of feeling. He could still hear the dreadful hammering; the gloom of the funeral rites still depressed him.

"Excuse me," Carla said, yawning again. And suddenly he felt a fierce longing to have her in bed, to communicate in his love-making the way he had felt about her with the coffin swinging on the ropes, to have her fold him in her new summer ripeness, to contain him in her new containment. He told Koster and Miss Francis to go to their ruins. He and Carla went home.

[288

At their place they talked a little, lazy and at ease, and as he often did, he sat in the living room while she was undressing so he could walk in, the chill of the burial still in his bones, and see her lying naked and warm and waiting. When he heard the bedspring squeak, it was as sweet to him as the unexpected sound of the choir.

Entering the bedroom, he saw her lying on her side, her face away from him, and as he undressed, watching the short little hairs at the back of her neck, he trembled. He got into bed, leaving the light on so he could look at her and have more of her. "Carla," he whispered gently, waiting for her to turn confidently as she always had done. She was dozing. His hand went to her breast, caressing it, waiting for her to stir, and then to her belly, smiling to himself. Her eyes opened.

"No, not now," she said indifferently. "Let's not do it now," and she hunched herself up cozily and closed her eyes.

On one elbow he looked down at her face, uncertain of himself, a little bewildered by his own painful dejection. It was the first time she had said no to him; she had always needed the assurance of his lust for her. Her hold on him. Not now. What did it mean? Putting out his hand to her shoulder he went to shake her; she could not refuse if he insisted; then, stung by the indifference he had felt in her 'no,' he fell back, listening to the beating of his own heart. Though she lay still beside him, she seemed to be touching softly every muscle in him till he was swollen with lust for her; yet he lay there with his eyes closed, trying not to feel so alone. Then he remembered saying to himself outside the Colosseum, "It's when she feels free that I'll know what she thinks of me." No, no, no, he told himself desperately. Any woman, sleeping night after night with a man, would have her own time, and it only meant that now they were like normal people in love. Tossing and turning, listening, hoping for her to stir and touch him, he couldn't get to sleep.

Then it got so that he didn't believe she had been indifferent. It made him want to show her, make her, in spite of herself, cling to him convulsively. As he sat up slowly, he could feel

289]

the vein in his neck throbbing; and his trembling hand went to her shoulder, drawing her, insistently pulling her over on her back. She was still asleep. The stillness of her maddened him; in the dark he wanted to steal into her stillness, thrust himself into her sleep, break into and reach her in her dreams. He lifted each arm away from her, and then as he tried to move her legs she stirred, muttered a protest, held her legs together, and he pulled at them, knowing by her breathing she was awake now. Then he fell on her. He made love to her. She didn't move, just lay there inertly. When he raised himself, shaken, his head clearing, he tried to see her face. A bit of moonlight seemed to glitter on a spot on her cheek. Slowly, he touched the spot. It was wet with tears.

"Carla," he whispered, stricken, "what's the matter? What did I do?"

"I don't know."

"Carla—" Then he shivered, as if he had heard a wild cry of anguish and didn't know whether it came from his own heart or hers. "I'm so sorry. I had to. I don't know why I had to."

"Oh, what difference does it make?" she whispered.

"Forgive me, Carla."

"It made me feel like I was back with Alberto—and wandering."

"Carla. God help me. Don't say that," he begged her. Lying down beside her, he put his arm around her gently. "It was that hammering," he said. "That God-awful hammering still in my mind," and he longed to touch her with a tenderness she had never known. But he went on thinking of the way she might look at him in the morning, feeling sure she had placed him now. It frightened him.

CHAPTER 29

HE WOKE up clinging desperately to the remnants of a rapidly fading bad dream; three Roman policemen had cornered him in the room, two of them were holding him down, and one. . . . He could no longer remember. In the room filled with morning sunlight all dreams and night thoughts seemed unimportant. Yawning, he stretched, then smiled to himself and got up.

"Breakfast is ready," Carla called from the kitchen.

"Coming," he said, rubbing his hands together. Full of bluff good will he went into the kitchen, slipped his arm around her waist and swung her around. As her eyes met his she gave no sign that she had any recollection of last night's tears.

"What time did you get up?" he asked.

"About an hour ago," she said.

Over their coffee they made casual friendly conversation. Her quiet friendliness made him wonder, suddenly, why he had been so concerned about her tears last night. He started to say, "What was really the matter?" but he couldn't. Her quiet composure was slowly soothing him into an acceptance of her woman's ancient wisdom: What had happened in the tragic dark of their bed at night could not be a thing of the day. But when he was ready to go out, waiting as usual while she sat at her mirror fussing with her black and beautiful hair, he blurted out, "I was rough with you last night."

"It was nothing, Sam," she answered calmly, without turning. "It's all right."

"It isn't all right, Carla."

"I wasn't ready for you, that's all, Sam."

"You were crying to yourself."

"That was nothing, Sam."

"No, I—I made you remember things."

"It's never a clear thing like that, Sam," she said easily, touching her left cheekbone lightly with a powder puff, and then drawing back, studying the effect in the mirror. "I was half asleep. If it's too sudden like that, there's just numbness at first and it's like a tearing at the numbness, and I guess all kinds of thoughts come into a woman's head. Maybe it's like a very old first feeling. I don't know." Pondering a little, she turned, sounding like a sensible woman. "I'd be a little liar, wouldn't I, if I said it was the first time anyone ever grabbed me and made love to me?"

"But the way you took it. The tears."

"I don't know," she said slowly. Half-troubled, she looked at him thoughtfully, and at the moment of her silence, waiting uncomfortably, he was sure she was wondering if in his way of taking her last night, so brutally, it had been like something happening between them for the first time. Under the spell of that thoughtful appraising look, it seemed to him she was pulling him into her life, plunging him back deep into her childhood. "How do I know I didn't like it?" she asked, shrugging, and it shocked him.

"Carla," he said huskily, "when are you going to marry me?"

"Are you going to ask me?"

"We could get married here in Rome."

"Oh, Sam," she said lightly, "you're not even a Catholic."

"I think you're a little pagan. Are you really religious?"

"I think I am," and then with the same light air, "I remember an old priest warning the little girls about the dangers of mixed marriages. Still, it wouldn't be mixed with you. I don't think the Pope's death, a new pope, the whole show means anything to you at all."

"You don't know me very well, Carla. I think I'm as religious as you are."

"Maybe I don't sit down and think about religion, but I'm a woman, Sam. It consoles me to have saints in heaven," she said lightly. "If they want to let me down, I can scold them. If they get sore at me, okay, I can get sore at them, too. Since they seem to neglect me a lot, I get even by neglecting them. But with you now," and she looked at him gravely. "You have some kind of faith, I know. But it's very big stuff. I've heard you talking to Koster. Back you go through Egypt tracing some line of love or truth or something right up to the events at St. Peter's. Am I right?" But before he could answer she said seriously, "If you say you want me to marry you, Sam, I would. I'd feel I had to." It upset him. Then she added, "But I'd think you'd always feel I was a lame duck, Sam."

"It's the one thing I couldn't bear to feel," and he sat down, trying to smile, not knowing that the hurt in his eyes showed how much he loved her. "Come here, Carla."

She came to him quickly and sat on his knee, put her arms around him and kissed him on the neck. "I only meant that I tried to sing, and made a mess of it. You saw it. Well, it must be that some things can still panic me if you're not around," and then she laughed and rubbed her nose in his neck. "What does it matter? I don't need to sing. I knew a piano player once whose fingers went stiff every time he sat down at the piano. Well, he's the general manager of something or other now."

"I love you, Carla," and while her face was buried in his neck he went on stroking her hair gently. "I'd never rest if I thought there was anything left in your life that could make you feel like a piece of damaged goods. I love you so much, Carla, and this thing back in your mind—it makes me feel it's like someone you used to know threatening to put his dirty hand on you, a dirty old man." And then he took her head in his hands and he kissed her on the mouth. "Let's do something about that singing, Carla."

"Now be practical, Sam. Who would want me to sing around here? Am I to arrange it myself?"

"I'll arrange it."

"You? It's not your world, Sam," and she laughed. "You don't know anything about it. It's a job. An agent. A manager. What am I to do? Go around to all the places and say, 'Here I am'? If I was that hungry, I could. I just don't feel that hungry. I've got you, Sam. Anyway, what's the hurry?"

"Cut it out, Carla."

"Don't push me around," she said defiantly.

"Then stop trying to mix yourself up."

"Don't take that tone to me," and he knew she was shying away from the memory of her last humiliation. "You stand there talking to me, Sam, as if I were some little church-base-ment singer. You're the amateur, not me. You're a babe-in-the-woods here in Rome, Sam. If I want to do something about it, all right, I will, and I'll think about it; but don't keep after me."

"All right. And look, Carla," he said quietly, "think about a little place. A place where a girl drops in and sings. Just something that comes easy. That kind of thing, eh? Think about it."

"All right, I'll think about it," she said, but her smile told him she was convinced it would remain something to talk about, and that her singing, for some time, would be for his own private enjoyment.

Late that night at the Press Club they were sitting with Koster and Miss Francis, who had been looking at ruins in the floodlight and acting like dreaming lovers. Over at the bar was Francesca with her long-legged stringy husband with the handle-bar mustache.

"I think it's time Francesca introduced me to her husband. Why doesn't she?" Sam said. "Excuse me," and he sauntered toward the bar.

[294

He didn't want to meet Francesca's husband. Loafing beside the bar, he tried to catch her eye and he did, he was sure, yet it was only when he turned away, heading for the washroom, that she left the bar and caught up to him.

"Sit down a minute, Francesca," he said, and they sat at the table near the door. "Why don't you bring your husband over? I'd like to meet him."

"Might I ask why?"

"I've never met him, that's why."

"It's of no importance to you, Sam."

"I can be curious. Aren't we friends?" and he looked over at the bar at the tall, hard-drinking, blotchy-faced Englishman who sat by himself with an air of middle-aged distinction; he could have been taken for a cabinet minister, or a retired magistrate from Kenya who had known how to handle the Mau Mau; but he showed no interest in where Francesca had gone.

"That man," she blurted out suddenly. "He bores me to death."

"Your husband?" he asked, astonished.

"I've been listening to him for days, and all he talks about is the great men he meets. One after another they said this or that to him. It's awful," she said vehemently. Sam didn't know what to say to her, for in spite of her vehemence she did not look unhappy. "Talk, talk, talk," she went on disdainfully. "Talk about what he said to Philip and what Harold said to him, and what Cardinal So-and-so told him in confidence. What a bore."

"Well, after such a long separation," he said, disconcerted, "I can understand your disappointment."

"Disappointment, Sam?" and she smiled mysteriously. "No, I'm as pleased as punch."

"Yes, you do look pleased."

"Well, it does give me a certain satisfaction, Sam. I know you think I'm a rather formidable woman, but about some things I've been as confused as a schoolgirl." And then she blushed. It gave her plump pretty face a little glow. She obviously felt she had said enough, and yet, because of comments that had passed between them, and her knowledge of his view of her, she seemed to feel compelled to justify herself. "You know, Sam. I've had a problem or two. Really, I have. I'm an Italian woman who's very conservative about marriage vows." She stammered, but she was too pleased with herself not to go on. "It always worried me that I could be in love with my husband and yet want to leave him in London and come back to Rome. Now I know why I did. It wasn't that he has the Englishman's uneasiness about female flesh. The man, from the beginning, must have bored me to death, Sam. I haven't been in love. I haven't even tried it," and she was smiling brightly.

"Well, you'd better get busy and try it."

"Koster might be surprised," she said dryly, "if he reached out and made another leap at me," and she patted his hand affectionately. "But you didn't want to ask me about my husband, Sam."

"No, I want to put you to work," he said. "You're only working half a day with Koster. Five thousand lire, and you take the rest of the day for me." Then he told her calmly that Carla was ready to sing. It should be an informal, unplanned performance somewhere, he said. Nothing staged; a first-class intimate place without spotlights or an orchestra. Somehow, it should be worked in. Maybe Carla, sitting there, could be asked to sing. One of those places where Carla could try her wings, and no skin off anyone's nose. No money involved. Who in Rome knew the restaurants better than his friend, Francesca? "How about getting to work?"

"You must be good for her, Sam," she said thoughtfully, looking over at Carla who, after listening to Koster gravely, suddenly laughed out loud. In the laugh there was such a suggestion of sudden spontaneous enjoyment of the little things of life, older men had to turn and look at her. "She has the advantage of being beautiful in an odd way, and sensual, too. Well, it's the time of the Passion in Rome, Sam. You know —the Church, the death in the house, and the widow waiting. Isn't that what we said? I suppose some of the Passion has to

[296

rub off on you. I didn't think North Americans went in for Passions. From what I've read it doesn't get into your literature at all." Her eyes still on Carla, she said, "Alberto's in the hospital. I went to see him today."

"How is he?"

"Very poorly. He asked about Carla. He blames everything on her, yet he asks for her."

"He's a liar, you know, Francesca."

"Why don't you go and see him and tell him so?"

"No, thanks. Nothing would seem real."

"It's the spell she put on him."

"Still burning those witches, eh, old girl?"

"Don't call me 'old girl.'" But she had turned again and was looking at Carla. "I don't understand it myself," she said, troubled. "Just a broken-down singer. A good figure, rather remarkable eyes. No real refinement. How can such a woman remind a man like Alberto of all impossible dreams? It's not a good thing to do to men. She may end up in an alley with her throat cut. Watch out, Sam."

"You must have been a good audience for Alberto. It must be nice for him to have you around holding his hand," and he laughed. He had a big warm friendly laugh himself, and she looked surprised, for she hadn't heard such a free and hearty laugh from him since he had come to Rome. "You look around for the right place for her, eh, Francesca?"

"I'll look around for you, Sam," she said, and when he got up he thought she would rejoin her husband at the bar; instead, she stayed with him and sat down and was gracious and at ease with Carla.

He did not tell Carla of the arrangement he had made with Francesca. When Carla mentioned that Francesca seemed to have lost her malice, he told her that Francesca now felt free in her heart of her husband, and it was a good thing; Francesca knew now she was a woman and belonged to men. When he saw Francesca next day he expected her to tell him she had found the right place for Carla. No, she was taking her time, she said; and she had lots of time free from Koster, for these were the in-between days before the cardinals went into Conclave. The news was mainly about the arrival of famous cardinals. There was so little for Sam to do he wondered if he dare cable for more expense money. He went to the mass for the diplomats at which all the cardinals in Rome were present, and he took many pictures he knew couldn't be used. But at this mass Carla gave Koster a splendid idea for a story. Koster heard her say, "Look at all those cardinals. And just think. The Vicar of Christ is among them. Yes, we're looking right at him, only we don't know him. And to make it better, he doesn't even know it himself."

Koster's candidates among the cardinals came into Rome and vanished from sight. In the clear fine weather there were big crowds at the soccer games. Carla and Sam would report to Koster's hotel as if they expected to be busy with him, and Francesca would be there, translating from the Roman newspapers and the *Osservatore Romano,* and when Francesca, meeting Sam's eyes, would shake her head, he would grow exasperated and wonder if she was running up a bill on him.

Then the Sistine Chapel was opened for inspection by the press, and when Carla said she had shopping to do, Sam went off by himself. Now she only needed to know where he was, and he had the same feeling about her. It was the kind of security a man and a woman had always sought in each other, he said to himself. At the Vatican he was late meeting Koster and Francesca; he had to run after the group of newspapermen who were not entering the chapel as he had done once before, by way of the Vatican Museum; that entrance was bricked up as were the other entrances, except for the one by which the cardinals would enter the Conclave. In the chapel he stood still, full of emotion as he looked around. The purple-covered chairs with the purple canopies, on which the cardinals would sit during their deliberations, were arranged around the walls, but he was staring the length of the chapel at Michelangelo's "Last Judgment." How long ago it seemed since he had been there. He had come there that day hoping vaguely for some miracle within himself, some new lease on life. Instead, he had accepted his complete failure. Empty and dead, he had felt. Yet now he was smiling to himself. A few yards away a Monsignor was lecturing to the English-speaking newsmen, and as Sam joined the group, Francesca took his arm, whispering, "I think I've got what you want, Sam. It's in Trastevere. You'd call it an ancient cellar. A lovely restaurant with a sense of ease. Quite expensive, but nice, really nice. I'm known there. I've talked to Sacchi, the manager. He has a little English. It'll look like something that happens every night. Why don't you and Carla take me there tonight?"

"You're a treasure, Francesca," he said, and he smiled and squeezed her arm, and he seemed to kindle with expectancy. He felt wonderfully alive, and alertly aware of everything going on. With intense interest he followed the Monsignor and the group to the corner where the black stove stood. The Monsignor showed them it was full of chips and shavings that were to be burned after the cardinals had taken a ballot. If the cardinals couldn't agree, black smoke from wet chips would go up the chimney; white smoke from dry chips if there was a happy agreement and a new pope. The stove looked like an old-fashioned wood-burner, Sam thought, a stove he might have seen thirty years ago out in the country at home. He took a picture, and then, grinning, he picked a few shavings out of the stove. The other newspapermen were embarrassed.

"For luck, you know," Sam said to the Monsignor, who frowned, then smiled and led them out of the chapel to a room he called a cell. It was the kind of cell, he explained, in which each cardinal would be confined during the days of the Conclave. It would be without adequate toilet facilities, he said; the food would be plain. The pressure of this Spartan environment would force the cardinals to make up their minds quickly so they could get out into the world again, he said. "It looks like any college professor's office or room," Sam whispered to Koster. But his head was whirling; in his thoughts he was talking to Carla.

On their way home Francesca and Koster got into a savage argument over a remark of Koster's that the cardinals nowadays ought to do their signaling with rockets, and not count on that silly stove and Indian smoke signals. "You have simply no feeling for history at all, Koster," she scolded him bitterly. Back in the corner of the taxi Sam sat with his arms folded, a grim confident belligerent expression on his face.

CHAPTER 30

THE place in Trastevere, an ancient
cellar with arching bone-white stone walls, folding with pearly
softness over oaken tables, was popular with Rome lovers from
many countries. Sacchi, the manager, a rotund, smiling, shrewd
man with a family of six children, liked the appeal his place
had for rich Italians who wanted to feel at home in a place
unlike their own favorite restaurants. He was proud of his
chef and the food that was served. The only entertainment
was provided by a group of three singers, one with a violin,
one with a guitar and one with an accordian. Wearing white
shirts and red and blue sashes, they would stroll the length
of the restaurant singing the Italian songs. Sometimes they
would chat with a guest and ask him if he had a favorite song.

At nine-thirty that night Sam and Carla were at one of the
long oaken tables with Francesca, Koster and Miss Francis.
Koster was already a little drunk. He simply couldn't keep
up with his Miss Francis, who still wore the same gray suit,
and merrily drank her rum-and-cokes. In her flushed face was
a kind of unbelieving wonder that Koster was so amused and
delighted with her.

"You know something, Carla," Sam said, looking around.

"What about this place? I think it's the kind of place we should have in mind for you."

"This place? I've been here before," she said, and he knew she wasn't giving a moment's thought to singing there. She was wearing a yellow dress and carrying a white sweater coat. Her black hair was gathered loosely on the nape of her neck. "Look at old Koster," she said. "He doesn't know what's happening to him. As soon as he leaves the job and meets her I think he gets tight with her. Not meaning to, but trying to keep up with her. Look at her. As sober as a judge. I think she must have a hollow leg."

But instead Sam looked at Francesca, and under the full force of her knowing smile, he suddenly became suspicious. Why had he placed Carla in the hands of this woman who had had such a twisted feeling about her? he wondered; and he was on edge.

"I forgot something," he said, hiding his growing anxiety. "I've got something for you, Carla."

"A present?"

"Look," and he smiled as he took the chips from his pocket. "Chips from the stove in the Sistine Chapel."

"Sacred chips from the true stove," Koster said.

"Let's light them on a plate," Carla said.

"White smoke, and it's the Armenian Cardinal who makes it," Miss Francis said.

"Black, and it's an old Italian cardinal."

"Black smoke is always wrong," Sam said.

"Black smoke or white smoke, it's never a wrong signal, silly."

"We can try this thing out right here," Koster said. "Dip some in water, and leave some dry. Will the smoke be white from the dry ones?"

"The chips are down," Carla said. Having put the chips on a plate, she took a table candle and lit them. The little flame flickered and grew. A faint wisp of smoke curled up from the plate.

"Look. What color is it?" Carla said.

"Damned if I know," Koster said.

"A dirty white," Miss Francis said.

"Oh, no. I'm superstitious. I'm very superstitious."

"As white as smoke ever is," Sam said quickly, because he knew Carla was indeed superstitious, and he didn't want a curling black smoke signal to be in the back of her mind tonight.

He turned to the three jolly musicians, who had stopped at their table. The oldest one, a man of fifty-five, with a high slanting forehead and a pointed wrinkled brown face, said, "Just name the tune, lydies."

"As I live," cried Koster, "an Italian with a cockney accent!"

"Aight years I 'ad of it in Lunnen, sir," the musician said, proudly.

They all tried talking cockney to him. They begged him to sing some cockney songs, and he said he would if they would accompany him. They sang "Burlington Bertie" and "Mrs. Brown from London Town!" They sang in different keys, their voices rasping, but they all laughed happily, imagining they were hilarious. Other patrons, even those at the tables farthest away, smiled benevolently, accustomed to the antics of these strolling singers.

Having finished his last cockney song, the leader, slipping his guitar strap from his shoulder, bowed low to Carla. "Now you sing please, signora," he said with a warm gentle smile.

"Me?" she said, startled.

"You sing. I know you sing," he said, making it happen so quickly and easily she could only give him a blank look and wait—wait to grow confused, not even turning to Sam. Then Sam touched her arm, got her eye. It was such a moment of stillness between them he was afraid to speak, for he could see she knew she had been framed and that he was hurling a challenge at her.

"Oh, yes, Carla. Yes, yes, yes," Miss Francis called, clapping her hands. "Do sing. Nobody told me you sang."

And Koster chimed in tipsily, "Yeah, a pretty song from pretty Carla."

But Carla, not hearing them, couldn't take her eyes off Sam, trying to hold on to him. Or was it feeling him desperately holding on to her? Or were they both trying to break away? Then he smiled, hiding beautifully his own terrible tension, apparently just wondering with some amusement if she had the guts. A little flicker of defiance in her eyes, she turned and took the guitar from the bowing Italian. Raising her head she smiled to herself, looked down at the guitar, strummed it a little, seemed to be amused by her own thoughts, then began to sing a French street song Sam was sure he had heard in America. It didn't matter. His shoulders hunched up, his eyes hard and challenging, shifting around from table to table, he loomed up in the candlelight, tense and still; ready to feel the first approach of panic before it reached her, and somehow hurl himself fiercely against it.

At first he thought she was singing to her own little group. No, he thought, it's not for us at all. She could have been alone. Yes, others felt it, too, for two stout Germans at a table far back in the room had stood up cautiously, as if they knew they shouldn't be caught peeking at her. She created a peculiar sense of privacy. It was as if those at other tables, turning to watch her, realized they were overhearing something said by a woman alone with herself. No one listening wanted to be noticed. Now he could watch her as if from a distance and with a strange detachment. As she had been for him in the room at home, so she was now, only more beautiful because of the audience. Her sweet natural voice would drop to a whisper, and she would laugh, then talk to herself or the guitar, and shake back the black hair touching the yellow dress. The picture she makes, and the song so strangely the one thing, he thought in wonder. But she had finished.

Slumped in his chair, almost morose in his sudden dejection, Sam heard the applause. He watched the three musicians with their blue and red sashes come bowing to Carla like delighted children. He watched her sitting with her head on one side, smiling to herself, apparently absorbed in her own thoughts, showing a beautifully arrogant disregard of their appreciation of her; and he smiled, yet felt detached and dispirited. The thing was done. Taken out of him. Leaving him empty and alone. There it was. He could hardly bring himself to speak. Reaching over he squeezed Carla's hand.

"Well, there you are, Carla," he said, smiling a little. Taken aback by his quiet tone and aloof expression, her mouth trembled as she went to speak, then intuitively understanding his mood, she whispered something. He couldn't hear her. Her head back, she laughed as Koster and Miss Francis expressed their enthusiasm, unaware that the performance had any unusual importance for anyone. The musicians, gathering around Carla, begged her to sing again. Patrons, standing up, were calling out to her.

"Well, why not?" she said to Sam.

"Why not?" he said.

She sang again. "That's all," she said firmly, and handed back the guitar to the musician. With her hands, she shooed them all away.

"Well, are you satisfied?" she asked Sam.

"Certainly. It was you, Carla."

"You know what I feel like?" she asked, stretching like a cat, and with a dreamy smile. "I could look in the eye of the world and spit in it. I feel good, Sam."

Koster and Miss Francis, having in hand some further inspection of ancient monuments by moonlight, were leaving. Carefully counting up his share of the check, Koster left the money for Sam. He was very scrupulous about such matters. They said good-by. As Sam put his money on the tray, Signor Sacchi came hurrying over, waddling, for his legs were very short; it was a businessman's hurried waddle. Grabbing Carla's hand Sacchi kissed it, then he kissed Francesca's hand, adding a little intimate approving pat on her cheek. Picking up the check he pushed the money on the tray toward Sam.

"My English is not so good," he said earnestly. "Excuse me if I sit down."

"Talk Italian, signor," Sam said.

"Good," said Sacchi. He did not like to talk business in

305]

English. Tapping together the short fingers of his plump hands, he spoke rapidly to Carla in Italian. And Francesca, leaning close to Sam, whispered the translation; Sacchi had heard from Signora Winters that Carla was a singer, a personality, someone of distinction in her own country who had abandoned singing. For her to do this was a crime against humanity. It was obvious that his patrons had admired her. As for himself, watching and listening, it made him feel fresh, it made him feel young. At his age it was something, too. Pausing, he reflected, his mustache wiggling up and down. Suddenly he blew a kiss at the ceiling. His place did not go in for staged entertainment, he said, no spotlights, no production; an intimate place; no announcements; nothing like that. From Signora Winters he had gathered Carla Caneli had commanded sums of money beyond him. Just the same, it might be to her taste and inclination to sing a few songs at night here at this hour. Could they not make an arrangement?

"Speak to Mr. Raymond, signor," Carla said in English. "It is up to him."

"Up to him? I understand," and then, smiling warmly for the first time, he added some words in Italian. He had made a joke. It wasn't translated for Sam. Would they have lunch with him tomorrow? Sacchi asked. It would be easy for them to come to an arrangement if Signor Raymond could think of this place as a relaxation, a *divertissement* for her. Not a big thing in her life. Something requiring no effort while she was here in Rome. Were they leaving so soon? A drink on him. No? Till tomorrow then. And he walked with them to the door, to the clapping coming from the tables, and he was the one who turned to acknowledge it, and he was the one, too, who came out with them and got the taxi.

As Sam helped Francesca in, he kissed her warmly on the mouth. "You're a sweetheart, old girl," he said gratefully, "thanks." Slipping a five-hundred-lire note into her hand for the taxi, he said, "See you tomorrow," and he closed the door, leaving her pouting and feeling left out of it, as the taxi pulled away; then he linked his arm under Carla's.

[306

It was cold now, in the grayness of the ancient moonlit Trastevere streets. Shivering, Carla gave him her sweater coat, and he helped her put it on. As she buttoned it up, she was in the path of the moonlight. "Oh, Sam," she whispered, "you're a stubborn good man. Aren't you really pleased with me? I'm happy, Sam. I think I could jump from the roof of that building up there and fly."

"I don't know how I feel," he said in a wondering tone. "I mean, it's just there, everything there as I wanted it to be," and then as he looked at her all silvered in the moonlight, the dispirited lassitude and exhaustion began to leave him. "Let's walk," he said. "I wanted to walk with you." Going along the narrow deserted cobblestoned streets, her gravity—she hardly spoke—and the tap tapping of her high heels on the rounded stones seemed to tell him she was as good as new.

"That Sacchi," she said suddenly. "He'll be long on charm and short of cash."

"Do you really want to go on singing there, Carla?" he asked, surprised.

"He'll pay me, Sam. I'll be getting some money. Singing and getting some money."

"You just said he wouldn't pay you much."

"Look, Sam. You're the boss. Don't you want me to sing there?"

"I don't care," he said, laughing awkwardly. "I mean the thing was to have you see you could sing anywhere. There's nothing to stop you doing anything you want. It's settled now, and you're free in your mind about it."

"It means some money for just being myself, Sam. It's easy."

"How much?"

"A couple of hours a night. See that you get ten thousand lire a night out of him, Sam."

"About a hundred a week, eh?"

"Make it clear to him anything less is not worth while."

"Okay," he said indulgently. "I'm the manager. Try it for a while."

"See, I've got a manager," she said, and she laughed eagerly.

307]

But her eagerness began to worry him. What if she became convinced it was important she should plunge into a professional career? It wasn't necessary. It couldn't add anything to her now. He wondered nervously if he had made a mistake. Walking in step through the old dark streets he felt that without her knowing it they were drawing apart from each other in their secret thoughts. They came to the moonlit piazza facing the church of Santa Maria. A cat was sitting by the fountain. As they approached the cat rose, lazy and indifferent, and sauntered toward Alfredo's; and Sam remembered the day he had lunched there with Alberto.

CHAPTER 31

At Sacchi's the waiters, the musicians and the regular patrons got accustomed to seeing Sam at the little table in the corner. Unobtrusive, saying little, he would seem to be half-hidden in the corner shadow. He looked out of place. For the first time Sam Raymond was in a scene where friends from back home, if they had come in, wouldn't have known him. He had lost all the signs of his new unruffled assurance and his amiable smile, which had made people want to help him, had gone too. He looked like an alert, nervous, watchful man who rarely smiled and who had convinced himself that people were against him because he had in his possession something all men wanted. He hated being there, feeling he was coping with assured rich Italians who had no time for courteous manners. Europeans and jolly opulent Americans sent drinks to Carla's table. Drinks were always on the table, and he would drink them himself. When patrons on the way out came over to express their admiration of Carla, he looked and acted like a policeman. Sometimes Sacchi would call Carla into his office to meet someone. While she was gone, Sam would feel the nerves of his stomach tightening and feel ill. Then Carla would return, smiling and happy.

309]

"Some very nice Americans. Old friends of Sacchi's," she would say.

And he would ask angrily, "Why are we hanging around here when you're finished for the night?"

One night Sacchi came over and asked her to allow him, as a great favor, to introduce her to a prince and his two companions . . . The prince, a tall middle-aged man with a long face, who never smiled, was sitting with a young woman and a young man. And Carla, at ease and sure of herself, went with Sacchi and sat with the prince. Alone at the table in the shadow Sam waited and suffered for an hour, watching Carla charm the prince. Sam never took his eyes off her. When she returned he grabbed her wrist. "We could have been out of here an hour ago," he said, bitterly. "Are you a hostess?"

"Cut it out, Sam," she said angrily.

"Let's go. This place makes me physically ill."

"I'm not going to let you grab me and rush me out of here under the eyes of these people."

"We're not going to hang around here, Carla."

"I'm a singer. You wanted me to sing. Don't make a fool of me, Sam," she said haughtily, and she sat down with apparent composure. He thought she was calmly looking at the ceiling. Then she lowered her head, and he saw her eyes fill with tears.

"Carla," he said.

"I'm all right," she said, controlling herself. But she looked confused and desolate. "I had such a terrible feeling just now," she said slowly. "It's like I've had badly broken legs, and you've taken me and taught me how to walk. You knew I was no good if I couldn't walk. Now you love me you're not sure I'm the same to you if I walk. Now it seems that if I really love you the only way I can show it is by not really wanting to walk. I love you, Sam, but you fixed it so I have to walk. But it could get that I don't want to. Not if it does terrible things to you and me."

"I don't know what's the matter with me, Carla," he said, feeling ashamed.

"You don't even look like yourself."

"I'll get used to things, Carla," he said, contritely. "I'm ashamed of myself." From then on he tried to assume an air of indifference. He tried to be patient even with the half-drunken men of forty who felt free to come over, and called her "sweetie" and "honey" and "darling," while patting her hand reassuringly. Her jokes were sometimes cheap and vulgar. Her light gay laugh upset him.

"Maybe you'd better hold yourself a little more aloof," he would say gently.

"It's just their manner," she would say. "They don't mean anything. I've been used to it all my life."

Without noticing what he was doing he had begun to put every cheap joke she laughed at against that aloof and secret quality she had for him when she sang and they were alone.

"What's the matter with me?" he asked himself. But he knew why he had the watchful fear of everyone and everything. He was waiting for someone. It didn't bother him now to have her recognized, and he assumed it had happened and that an agent would make an offer to have her resume her career. Yet he was watching for the one who would be able to make the wrong things sound like the right things. Each time he saw a man with an American face enter the restaurant he scrutinized him carefully. "Is this the one?" he asked himself, all on edge. When Carla wasn't looking he began to drink too much, and the nerves in his stomach would twist into a knot. He didn't know that he sat there saying to everyone with his eyes, "Leave her alone. Leave her alone." Sacchi thought Sam an arrogant, rude man with bad nerves and full of suffering. Sacchi had said to the musicians that Sam was simply a nuisance.

In the daytime, with the cardinals in Conclave, Sam had Carla with him at St. Peter's Square. She really wanted to be with him, and he felt like himself when he could get her out of Sacchi's. They would meet Koster by the Square, where the Foreign Press Club had set up a wire service, and where Koster was putting on the wire all the rumors of an agreement among the cardinals before they had entered the Conclave.

"Aren't you drinking a lot, Sam?" Koster asked. "You have that flush on your face and your eyes look nervous."

But Sam brushed him off.

That Sunday noon was warm and bright. Cars were jammed on the Tiber bridges. All Rome had heard the rumor that only one ballot would be needed. It would be taken quickly, it was said. Sam, Koster and Carla left the taxi at the entrance to the bridge and walked to the Square which was not as yet jammed with people, although thousands were on their way to the Square. Those in the Square were watching the roof of the rectangular building, the Chapel, to the right of St. Peter's, where the chimney pipe rose above the line of the roofs. Were any of the cardinals in that chapel glancing up at Michelangelo's Adam, with his finger so close to touching the finger of God? Sam wondered; and were any of them imagining they, too, might be so touched and guided in their judgment? Or having little interest in Michelangelo, were they meeting like hard-headed bargainers in a back room, hammering out an agreement on a candidate? Standing in the sunlight they were held hypnotically by the line of that slender black pipe against the blue sky.

"I'm not going to stand here gawking," Koster said. "What about that corner café?" As they turned away someone in the crowd screamed happily, and the scream became one jubilant roar with everyone pointing at the slender little chimney from which a wisp of white smoke, rising slowly, curled delicately white against the blue sky.

"See, see," Carla cried, clapping her hands. "Rome wasn't long without a Papa."

"It's effective, after all," Koster said. "It can be seen all over Rome." Stunned by the simple perfection of the signal, he stared at the little puffs of white smoke still coming from the chimney, then he muttered, "What am I doing? I've got to get it on the wires. It's already all over Rome."

As Koster ran off, Sam, using his telescopic lens, tried to get a picture of the curling wisp of smoke; then he hurried after Koster. By this time, he knew, the Roman press would be flashing the news of the successful first ballot to the world. When he got to the side of the Square, fifty feet behind Koster, he heard Carla screaming, "Sam, Sam!" The back of his neck tingling, he whirled around, frightened. She was pointing to the sky above the chapel roof. From where he was he couldn't see the sky. Cupping her hands over her mouth she shouted, "Something's wrong. Catch Koster," and she pointed at the sky.

"Koster, Koster," he yelled, calling him back. Little puffs of black smoke were now coming from the chimney.

"Ahhhh," groaned the crowd; yet even as they watched there came another little white puff, then a gray one, and a minute later heavy black smoke puffed from the chimney.

"What's going on?" Koster asked angrily. "Have they changed their minds? What is this?"

"Maybe they got mixed up on their signals," Sam said. "Maybe some guy was handed the wrong—" But Koster, who had been gaping blankly at the skyline, suddenly doubled up with laughter. Laughing so hard he got a stitch in his side, he limped around rubbing his rib, his face twisted in pain. Everybody was laughing. "That Francesca. Wait till I see her," Koster gasped. "The beautiful staging, the sense of history. I told her they shouldn't use those Indian smoke signals. I told her to have them shoot colored flares up the chimney. Oh no, not for her. I'll bet she's the one in there in charge of the smoke signals. Let's go over to the café."

Since it was unlikely there would be another ballot for some hours, Carla said she would go home and get some sleep. Watching her wave to them from the taxi Sam thought, Now she is beginning to enjoy her own being. Yet without me what would have happened to her? and he looked up at the blue sky. How he loved being in Rome with her! Then he told himself he would get used to Sacchi's place as soon as he could stop thinking he was waiting there for the wrong guy to come in and recognize her. Next day when they were back at the Square and the black smoke signals appeared again, he wondered what he would do when the white smoke came and it was over.

If Carla could be happy in Rome he would stay there with her, he thought. He would free-lance and learn to speak Italian.

That night at Sacchi's place, after Carla had finished her second group of songs, he told her that if he too could speak good Italian, he wouldn't seem to be standing on the outside watching her. He asked her to speak to him always in Italian and speak very slowly. They were trying this out when Sacchi came over to their table, accompanied by a middle-aged, short-legged man with close-cropped gray hair and shrewd old eyes. This man of sixty, who was wearing a gray American suit, had been sitting with two middle-aged plump women.

"Carla, Signor Raymond. A compatriot, George Morgan," Sacchi said respectfully, and he departed.

"Mind if I sit down?" Mr. Morgan asked, but he was already sitting down. He had a flat manner and slow gestures, yet he was so self-possessed he seemed a little sleepy. "I was in here the other night," he said. "It's true, I was." Smiling faintly he leaned back, draping an arm over the back of the chair, and regarded Carla approvingly. "Carla Caneli. Anna Connel. They all come to Rome, don't they? I met you once, Miss Connel. George Morgan. The Wolfson Agency. Remember? In the NBC studios."

"Yes," she said doubtfully. "Oh, yes. The Wolfson Agency!"

"I think I remember you went on the sauce, honey."

"Something like that, Mr. Morgan," she said uncomfortably, and when she put her head down, Sam stiffened. He knew this was the one.

"Well, you're not on the sauce now, honey. I've been watching you. Good for you," said George Morgan, with real elderly approval.

"I don't need to drink now, Mr. Morgan."

"Anybody handling you, honey?"

"Mr. Raymond, here, looks after my affairs."

"I see," Mr. Morgan said, and now, as he hooked the other arm on the back of the chair, he seemed to be hanging there, his chin down, studying Sam thoughtfully.

"I don't know anything about you, either, Mr. Wolfson," Sam said suddenly, with a deliberate smile.

"Morgan."

"All right, Morgan."

"Sam doesn't know about New York, Mr. Morgan," Carla said apologetically, and then to Sam, "Wolfson is a big important agency. It's the best, Sam."

"Since you're not in this business yourself, Mr. Raymond, wouldn't you like someone to represent her?" Morgan asked quietly.

"I represent her."

"Where?"

"Here and now."

"And The States?"

"I have some plans."

"Good. We can talk about them," said Mr. Morgan. And with all the middle-aged assurance of an executive who couldn't bother explaining how important he was, he said, "I'm at the Flora. I'll look for you before noon tomorrow, Mr. Raymond." And to Carla, "This is nice, honey," and he shook hands and got up, wearily.

Watching Mr. Morgan rejoin his two middle-aged women, Sam tried to look amused. "A wheezing old guy with all the assurance of a master plumber. When he first spoke to us I thought he was going to offer to make me a suit."

"Sam, darling," and as she put her hand on his, laughing, he saw the excitement and pleasure in her face. "I must be as good as I ever was. Maybe better, eh?"

"What is this?" he said, disdainfully. "What do you care what that illiterate old guy thinks of you? An agent! The world is full of them. Who is he? Some little Caesar in the business, I suppose."

"Now, look, Sam," she said irritably, "get it out of your head that George Morgan wants to sleep with me. As they say in the business, George Morgan doesn't fool around with the flesh he peddles. And why shouldn't I be pleased? What is

315]

this? Shouldn't I be flattered that the Wolfson Agency wants me?"

"No. Not at all. Why shouldn't they want you?"

"Well, don't look down your nose, Sam. As a matter of fact, that man is one of the most reputable men in the business. He's class."

"You mean he knows class," he said.

"It's exactly what I mean," she said, irritably. "And if it's so, why can't I take a little pleasure in his appreciation?" Then she drew back, troubled, looking at him thoughtfully, and in the candlelight her brown eyes were moist and golden. But Sam, aware that George Morgan and his two tightly girdled companions were passing the table on the way out, said quietly, "Don't look up at him, Carla."

"Why not?"

"The effect will be more interesting."

"Oh, Sam. Cut it out. No matter what we decide, as a businessman you have to talk to him."

"Oh, all right. Tell me about him," he said with an air of indifference.

As a person, she didn't know much about Morgan, she said. Which one of those women was his wife, she didn't know either. Morgan was supposed to have a woman, the pretty wife of a retired prize fighter, who owned a tavern and who was often in financial difficulties and got help from Morgan. He was very faithful to this woman. At least that was the story. It was true, old George Morgan was illiterate, and he must have had a wretched poverty-stricken childhood. His illiteracy, though, was part of his legend. Now he was vice president of the rich Wolfson Agency, but when he had been in charge of their play department, he had had astonishing success although it was known he never read a play he handled. Just talked to the author, and got the feel of it. Then he would approach a producer about whom he had a certain feeling, and say, "Joe, I've got something that's right for you." Or maybe a big producer would come to him, only to hear him say, "Sure I got something big here, but it's not right for you."

When he started handling talent, he seemed to have the same touch for talent that was class. Well, it was all she knew about old George Morgan, she said, except that he was supposed to have made a million out of the stock market.

"It's that million that's his legend," he said cynically. "Now look, Carla. You don't want George Morgan right now. You were through all that. You know what they did to you."

"Sam, I'm a singer. You wanted me to start singing again. You wouldn't rest till I was singing."

"I wanted it to be all of you again."

"I'm singing now, Sam. I've got to go on. Don't you understand? I've got to go on."

"You go only where it's right for you. I know where it's right, Carla."

"Unless it's some little place with you, will it ever be right, Sam? Just say so, Sam," and then their eyes met, and he was exasperated. He honestly thought that she should see she should not make an excited jump back to her ruinous world. And she, for her part, looked at him thoughtfully.

"If I'm to go on singing, Sam," she said quietly, "sooner or later you have to talk to someone like George Morgan." Then it seemed to him she was hiding some secret awareness of him, and it hurt him.

"You're right," he said quickly. "I'll talk to George Morgan."

"Just see what's in his mind, Sam. That's all. We're in no hurry about anything, are we?"

"It's the sensible attitude," he agreed. "Don't worry. I'll get in to see him somehow tomorrow." Then they became very sympathetic to each other. On the way home that night he told her how happy he was in Rome, and she said that these days were among the best days of her life. In the morning he got up early, left her sleeping, met Koster, went down to the Square and came back to Koster's hotel before lunch. Koster was to work there with Francesca for an hour. Then Sam went along the street to the Flora and asked for Mr. Morgan.

He found him in his room, engaged in methodically packing some shirts in a pigskin bag lying open on the bed. A

317]

bureau drawer was open. "Hello there, Mr. Raymond," Morgan mumbled, hardly bothering to look up. "It's Sam, isn't it? Okay, Sam. There's some Scotch over there. Don't drink before lunch, myself. I'm not leaving till tonight, but my wife and sister are out shopping. Thought I might as well get some of this stuff packed. Have some lunch with me, Sam?"

"I can't have lunch," Sam said, pouring himself a drink. "I'm pretty busy, George. Just wanted to say 'hello' and keep in touch," and he sat down with his old peculiar unruffled assurance, as if he wasn't quite sure why he was there but knew he would have no trouble in handling Mr. Morgan.

Each appeared to have forgotten the other was in the room. Morgan's close-cropped gray hair looked very thin on top as he bent over the bag, and he would sigh and grunt, then go slowly toward the bureau. "That girl's got a peculiar talent," he said as he took some underwear from the drawer. "A little bit special, mind you. Primitive? No. What's that big word for no training? Just natural?"

"Naïve?"

"Don't like that word. Use it a lot now, don't they? You've done great things for that girl, Sam. I know the story."

"I don't see how you could, George."

"Got it from Sacchi. I think he got it from some woman friend of yours he knows. What's her name?"

"Signora Winters," Sam said, feeling sudden resentment.

"That's it. Well, going to marry the girl, Sam?"

"That's right, George," he said calmly.

"I thought so. Well, properly handled, she can be bigger than she ever was, Sam," Morgan went on as he crossed to the bureau drawer again. "A little too offbeat now, I think. A little too small, maybe. Still, it's okay. You see, Sam, a thing that's not for everybody may be the real expensive thing. Give a lavatory attendant a Rolls Royce, and he doesn't know what to do with it. So what? So they don't make many Rolls Royces. At their price, they don't have to. This girl—I don't see her as being for the kids. It's men of my age that have the money."

A little flush on his face, Sam smiled, but he didn't like to hear him talking about Carla. He resented every knowing word.

"I have a feeling about this girl," Morgan went on, not noticing Sam's peculiar smile. "Handled right, I see her doing very well indeed," and as he walked away from the bed, half lost in thought, he had both hands in his pockets. Stopping by the window, he took a handful of change out of his right pocket, and as he meditated he let the coins trickle into the left hand, and then as he turned, the coins trickled back to the right hand.

"You see, I know what's good about that little girl," Morgan said.

"It's not a distinction, George," Sam said patronizingly. "There's no one like her, is there?"

"Sometimes it's not such a good thing, Sam," Morgan said. "I don't handle many clients myself. Too old. I see this girl big with records, spots on television, maybe Vegas, maybe pictures, with the right guidance."

"And you'd be just the man for us, George, and we know it," Sam said soothingly. "And we're going to keep you in mind. It's what I wanted to tell you. But she's not ready for anything like this."

"Looked ready to me, Sam."

"It takes time, George," Sam said patiently. "You see, she's happy now just becoming herself again. After that pushing around she got in New York, doing all the wrong things— She's getting set in her own pattern. But when the time comes, George, we know you're the man for us."

"It's nice here in Rome, isn't it, Sam?"

"It's a lovely city, George."

"What are you going to do? Keep her in Rome?"

"For the time being, anyway. She's happy here."

"Maybe she's got a lot more guts than you give her credit for," Morgan said brutally. "Why don't you give her a chance?"

"Give her a chance?" and he laughed. He thought he sounded like any cynical businessman jeering at another cynical businessman. "Oh, come on, George. I have to think of what's good for her. Right now, no soap, George. I'm not taking a chance on having you move right in. Pleased as she is right now, and a little excited too, she might go along with any big promotion you had in mind. Put it off, George. Give her time." He went on talking, smiling and at ease, then he noticed that Morgan, unruffled, was watching him thoughtfully.

"Who do you think you're kidding?" Morgan asked suddenly, and for the first time he chuckled a little to himself; and it seemed to Sam he was saying, with the chuckle and his old tired expressionless eyes, "Why don't you say you can't bear to have anyone else have a hand in shaping her life?" Or was it a cry within his own heart, Sam wondered, making him angry and desolate? He felt himself squirming away furiously from Morgan's knowing smile. Yet he managed to grin.

"That's right, George. We should lay it on the line. At least I know what's *not* going to happen to Carla. You have your view of her—those coins trickling through your hand—that's a corny gesture, George. Look," he said grimly, "remember the Molson girl? Was she one of your clients? I know that girl, came from my home town. Had something of her own, too. Thick long, black hair, a throaty voice, her own special little following; then she got on the Jack Paar Show and one of your boys picked her up, then she really made it. Uhmm. Uhmm," he said, with a contempt he couldn't bother concealing. "She came home for a show. There she was. Really big, George. Really big. A real pro. A new hair-do you might have given her yourself, George, and the brassy confidence, too, and the hard-selling smile. A big commercial talent, George. Well, it's not happening again to Carla. You can stick it, George."

And George Morgan, the vice president of Wolfson's, whose shrewd judgment of talent was legendary in the business, and who hadn't been insulted by anyone for seventeen years, sat down slowly on the bed and crossed his legs at the ankles. He was a short man and he could swing his feet back and forward off the floor. Little dull red spots appeared on his cheeks. "You're quite a son-of-a-bitch yourself, aren't you?" he said mildly.

"Just frank, George. You should have the right picture, if we're going to keep in touch. Isn't that right?"

"Aren't you rough with an old man?"

[320

"I don't think so. We won't make mistakes in our thinking about this, now. I know I'll hear from you. You'll think it over and see I'm right," and then he looked at his watch and appeared concerned. "I have an appointment and . . ."

"I understand," Morgan said, following him to the door. "She'll marry you, don't worry. Don't worry at all, Sam."

"Thanks, George. Nice meeting you."

But the old man, having opened the door for him, was walking him along the corridor to the elevator. "I noticed one thing at Sacchi's, Sam. The way the girl looks at you. She has gratitude for you. Real gratitude. I feel goddamned sorry for you, Sam."

"That's all right, George. Look, you left your door open."

"Don't get sore at me, Sam. I'm an old man. I face this in my business. Yeah, this gratitude is a terrible thing, Sam. I run from anybody who's really grateful to me. It handcuffs me, see?"

"It probably doesn't happen very often with you," Sam said. His face was burning, and yet he was still smiling. They came to the elevator, and he stood watching the floor indicator after he had pushed the button. It didn't matter what Morgan said, he thought. Soon the elevator door would open.

"You told me a little story, Sam. Here's another one," Morgan said, holding him by the arm. "Look, I'll give you a card to this guy. The Excelsior Hotel. Just along the street. With his wife, an actress, another one of those clients of mine." Fumbling in his pocket he took out a card, then a pencil, and as he wrote on the card he mumbled, "Just give him this card, and have a drink with him. His wife is big in pictures and television. This guy's her manager. Picked her up in some honky town, slaved over her, taught her to read and eat with her fork, gave her some style. Gave her everything, Sam. A loyal girl, full of gratitude. She married him. What does he do, Sam? Carries her bags. Talks to the waiters, gets her flowers, puts a hot water bottle on her belly if she has a cramp, takes her to parties. Talks to me, too, about her career. A nuisance. Okay, so the guy lives better than he ever did and just sits around. She won't let anybody say a word against him. The funny thing is, Sam, he's drunk all the time. Just drowning in her gratitude. A lame duck—"

Then the elevator door slid open. Three other passengers were in the elevator and Sam, stepping in, got behind them.

"Hey," Morgan said. "The card, Sam. Here's the card. It's just along the street."

"Keep it, George," Sam said and he laughed, and the elevator boy, after glancing at Morgan—leaning forward, proffering the card, his face full of concern—and then at Sam, making no move, closed the door, and Sam smiled to himself with angry derision. The meddling malice of a wounded old man groping desperately to get in some stinging blow. Something that would be suitably humiliating because he had felt belittled himself.

As he stepped out of the elevator and went toward the street entrance, he became aware that he was trying to shake off his own terrible sense of belittlement. Why did I have to get her singing? She could have done without it. I wouldn't be feeling like this, he thought. Then he seemed to see Morgan smiling, and he was furious at himself. Carla was a singer. When she was singing she was unique. It had been his passion to have her singing again. Yet in spite of himself, he went searching in his memory for little gestures of Carla that had shown her true feeling about him. The morning following the funeral mass— the gentle acceptance in her eyes. Again and again she would say, "Whatever you want, Sam." The yielding acquiescent touch, now that he thought about it, did not seem to belong to her fiery and erratic nature. Some weeks ago, she might have struggled and pounded him with her fists and try to bite him. Not now. Now that she was more at peace with herself, could it be that she couldn't bear to hurt him? Did she ever look at him and think, There he is, the man I owe so much to? The eternal acquiescent woman. Catching himself in his thoughts he grew disgusted, and he went to hurry out. At the door he stopped, wondering if he had better make sure Morgan was really checking out, and he did turn back to the desk. But then he seemed to see Carla watching him with that wondering and desolate expression; it told him of her love. He really believed in her love. Yet he

[322

knew that something she saw in his own love hurt her. If he didn't watch himself, he might keep hurting her more and more till she couldn't stand it. In spite of what she had told him, he wasn't quite sure how he was hurting her, because he loved her even more than she loved him. But she did love him. No woman he had met on this earth had ever had the love in her eyes she had had for him the other night in Sacchi's, when her eyes had filled with tears. It had told him he could destroy her. George Morgan couldn't know anything about a woman like Carla.

On the sun-drenched street that he had come to love so much, he walked along with confidence and when he passed the Excelsior Hotel he would not deign to look over at the windows shining in the sunlight.

At the Ambasciatori, where Francesca, who had been translating for Koster, was just leaving, Koster was in the bathroom. "Sam," she said, taking him aside nervously, "Alberto is dead. A heart attack." Her voice shook and she looked miserable, and he was shocked himself. "Will you tell Carla?" she asked. "I know she'll want to go and see him."

He stared at her and then his head whirled. "No, I won't tell her," he said harshly, "and if you're any friend of mine, don't you tell her, either." His grimness outraged her, and feeling her drawing away from him, he stammered, "Carla knew Alberto was through. Alberto knew it himself. Alberto abandoned her. Right now I don't want her emotions upset. I want her free of all that stuff and that world she was from."

"All right," she said, but she showed that his harshness troubled her. She had great respect for the dead. But he simply didn't care. Not one other little thing was going to be used to pull Carla back to those days, and perhaps make her wonder where she really belonged.

Then he and Koster went out to St. Peter's Square, and again that day there were only the black smoke signals. Two more ballots had been taken. Among the newspapermen was a conviction now that the candidates they had favored, and whose pictures they had had printed in their papers, had all been eliminated: now the cardinals were trying to agree on a compromise candidate. At first there would only be a small crowd on the Square watching the chimney, and then as some wild rumor spread across Rome, hundreds would come straggling back to the Square. When the sky darkened, the crowd quickly dispersed. People had a theatrical understanding of the ineffectiveness of a smoke signal against the darkening sky. And at six Sam was back at the apartment where Carla was waiting for him.

"Well, what have you been doing?" he asked, putting his camera in the closet.

"I've been seeing George Morgan," she said.

"You've been seeing George Morgan!" he said, stunned.

"I had a drink with him and a long talk."

"You did, eh? How was that?" and he sat down, nervously alert and waiting with an acute, almost unendurable awareness of the calmness of her expression as she lit a cigarette. Then she looked at him and there was a little twitch at the corner of her mouth, as if she were going to smile, and it stung him. "You knew I had gone to see him and yet— What took you to the Flora?" he asked.

"What took me?" she repeated, exasperated. "Morgan telephoned me."

"How could he phone you?" he asked, suspiciously, and got up. "He couldn't phone you. What are you up to? What's going on here?"

"Why couldn't he phone me?"

"I only asked a question, my dear Carla," he said with a strange smile. "I'm stupid. I thought no one could phone us. I thought we had no phone. I didn't think we were in the phone book."

"Well, my dear Sam," she mimicked him, her face turning crimson, "it happens that Morgan got the address from Sacchi. He called the Ferraros, and Agnese came up here and got me. It wasn't my fault that you weren't here. Morgan was leaving town and he wanted to talk to you. A misunderstanding, he said, and he was sorry and he asked me to have a drink with him. I told him I was leaving things in your hands. There it is. I don't know why I explain it." Her voice trailed away, and she was breathless, and then after staring at him somberly, she whispered, "You just accused me of lying. Goddamn you."

"I'm tired," he said gruffly. "I wasn't watching what I was saying. I've been on my feet all day, hanging around that damned Square. I don't understand myself. I don't like Morgan." He tried to sound tired and apologetic, but couldn't; his agitation was deepening. Whether she was lying or not didn't matter. The fact was that Morgan had been talking to her. "Behind my back he came after you, eh?" he said bitterly.

"You bother me, Sam," she said, her face still crimson. "Oh, you really do," and she began to walk up and down, then she turned, choking with emotion. "You've been bothering me for days."

"For days?" and he felt bewildered. "What have I done to bother you?"

"At Sacchi's. Why are you always watching me?"

"I see. I see," he said angrily. "Who put that idea into your head?"

"I'm not a ten-year-old girl who's going to be kidnapped if you happen to look the other way," she said breathlessly. "How do you think that kind of an attitude makes me feel? What is there still in me that you don't trust, Sam?" But the question only outraged him for he thought he had a perfect faith in what she was if she could only be left alone.

"What kind of a man would I be if I paid no attention to you? What am I to do? Just walk away and leave you alone?"

"I could shake you, Sam. You just accused me of lying," and she had clenched her fists, and he had a strange wild hope she might attack him. Then she threw out her arms, helplessly. "I don't understand what's going on in you," and now she was half pleading with him. "I think you want the two of us, wherever we are, even if hundreds of people are around us—I think you want the two us to be alone. I'm singing now, Sam. It's what you wanted. I'm singing in public places. We can't always be alone now."

"I know, I know," he said, and then he stammered, full of anguish, suspicion and wonder, half believing she knew what he had been thinking leaving the Flora. And she couldn't know. How could she know? "Don't try and tell me what goes on in me, and don't tell me we can't be alone, because people like us are always alone." He rose slowly, looming up over her. His real secret fury and torment was that she talked this way about him after listening to George Morgan. "Go on," he taunted her. "Complain. Sooner or later you'll say something. The cat will be out of the bag." And he was savagely happy when she grew infuriated.

"I asked you what there was in me you didn't trust," she cried, coming closer to him. "Look at me. Look at me," she said passionately. "Is there something about me you still don't know? My God, if only I could tell all about myself, absolutely everything, once and for all. When and where I was born, and how I grew and what I thought and felt every day, and what I hoped for and what went wrong and the things I dreamt about, and all the excitements and all the bad things . . . everything, everything that has ever happened—I'd toss it all to you. I'd settle it once and for all, and then maybe you'd stop wondering what's going on in me. How can I do it, Sam? Oh, hell." Growing distracted she folded her arms, walked up and down, then wandered into the bedroom. When he followed her she turned on him. "Each day it has to be different, hasn't it? Each day I think different things. Isn't everybody changing all the time? For God's sake, Sam, what am I doing to you?"

"Me? I'm like I always was," and he tried to smile. The drawing he had made of her, still tacked on the wall where the holy picture had been, had caught her eye, and it seemed to upset her.

"I remember the day you did it," she said in a troubled tone. "Do you?"

"I remember."

"I said something like, 'Is it supposed to be me?' "

"I think you did," he said, uneasily.

"Sam, I'm just a woman."

"A beautiful woman. I'm a little jealous, I guess."

"I don't know," she said slowly. And as she frowned and went on looking at the drawing, he thought he saw some regret come in her eyes. It upset him. Does she think I want her to be in a mould she can never get out of? he wondered. The little fool. It was such a lie! Couldn't she see he loved all the little real things about her too—the way she threw her stockings at the chair, the bed she wouldn't make, waiting for her while she primped for an hour at the mirror. Then a strange feeling came over him. While standing beside her, looking at the drawing, the things that had been happening today seemed to fill him with disappointment in himself.

"Does the thing bother you, too, Carla? I told you I wasn't much of a painter. No, you're right. It's no good. Anyway, I've got you, eh?" and he reached out, tore it loose from the thumbtacks and began to rip it in two.

"Stop," she shouted. "You damn fool. Stop." As she snatched the drawing from him, she was so wild-eyed, he thought she was going to hit him. Folding up the picture, she put it in her own drawer. "For God's sake, what are you trying to do?" she asked angrily. "You gave it to me."

"Okay. Keep it, I don't have to look at it." He had grasped vaguely, for the first time, that he shouldn't be so concerned with what he thought he had seen in her; there would always be something new. But she had snatched the picture from him as she might have snatched a drink from an alcoholic. It began to outrage him. "And look, Carla," he said, threateningly, "I'm not drunk. Just watch yourself. Watch how you treat me. If you've got any complaints, say so."

"I've got a complaint, Sam," she said angrily, but her voice broke. Then her eyes filled with tears. "You may not know it, but for the last few nights I've hardly slept. I've had some terrible dreams."

"Who goes by dreams?"

"I don't go by dreams, but I know how I feel. You're breaking my heart."

"And just why am I on your mind?" he asked, and he

couldn't help sounding as if he were accusing her of something.

It was very effective. It became hard for her to go on. Some street sounds came from outside. All Rome was outside, and yet her whole life now seemed to belong to this man who had brought her to this shabby room. Yet he couldn't believe it, because she couldn't help being the way she was. She felt guilty, and it made her angry. "You used to be so strong and sure of yourself, Sam." She went on bitterly, "There seemed to be nothing you didn't understand. It used to knock me out. What I needed. What was good for me. What I ought to do." And then he didn't like the way she faltered, looking at him. His arms folded, he thought he was smiling with his old superior assurance; Sam Raymond fumbling his way along, not caring much where he was; it was enough that he was there. He was trying desperately to have this old feeling about himself. But why did her words make him feel so lonely? he wondered. His eyes, hard and suspicious, seemed to be saying to her, "What's your game? You're the one person in the world who can belittle me, and you know I have to take it."

He said calmly, "Go on."

"I'll go on," she said uneasily, yet at the moment she couldn't. And the emotion she felt touched him too. They were sharing some frightening awareness of what a little time could do; they both wanted to make a desperate protest. In this room she had felt so miserably alone until she heard his step on the stairs, and she hadn't cared whether he loved her. They used to get out of this room and meet happily somewhere, two thousand years ago. But now, when she didn't want to hide from him any more, there was no place she could take him.

"If there was only some place we could go," she protested.

"What's the matter? No more floodlit ruins?"

"Cut it out, Sam," she cried. "There's you and me. I'm killing you."

"I can't get killed off, Carla. You're always there."

"If I'm always there for you, why are you always spying on me at Sacchi's?" she went on nervously. "It's this and that. It's fear and suspicion in your eyes right now, as if I'll go up in smoke.

It's the way I look, it's what I say to anyone who smiles at me. It's like you're always scared I'll change, or something."

Her distracted air made him feel ashamed. "Yeah, I'm a fool," he said wretchedly. "Just give me a little time, Carla. It's a matter of getting used to things. You see, I'm a little out of my element. Come on. Let's take it easy."

"Sure, Sam. Sure," she said, and they nodded and tried to smile as if he had said the right thing, the just and sensible thing. He really believed in what he had said. With all her heart she wanted to believe it too. But his ashamed expression reminded her of her sleepless nights. She had been afraid to let herself close her eyes, for when she did she saw terrible things happening to both of them. She could see him going downhill rapidly, hating himself as he tried to guard what he thought he saw in her. Over and over she had said to herself desperately, "How can I do this to him when I'm only being what he wants me to be, when he wouldn't have me any other way?" She had wanted to wake him and put her arms around him and tell him that if she were the cause of his going to pieces she would want to die. It was the first time she had ever felt so close to anyone that her death could seem like a good thing because of the closeness. The violence of her concern had frightened her, and she had shuddered.

"Look Sam," she began, then she burst into tears. "Like I told you once, you put a glow on me and I thought it meant I must be good for you," she sobbed. "If I'm kind of independent now—like on my own—I'm only what you wanted me to be. Sam—Sam—don't let me drag you down. Hit me on the head. Kill me off."

Her disappointment in herself bewildered him, yet it comforted him. Never in his life had he seemed to mean so much to anyone. He thought he was being forgiven for being so jealous and suspicious.

His face was in her hair as she went on sobbing brokenly, wanting him to hold her hard against him. She came so soft and yielding and close against him he could feel the beating of her heart. It seemed incredible that only a few days ago he

329]

could have thought her most beautiful when she looked beyond him. He shuddered.

But the next day, just to make sure, Sam went over to the Flora to see if George Morgan had checked out. When he found that Morgan had left Rome he felt much better.

CHAPTER 32

THAT day she had come down to St.
Peter's with him in the morning. But she looked so wan and
tired he told her to go home and rest; he would see her at six.
The newspapermen were now talking about a month-long
Conclave, he told her as she left.

There had been ten or twelve ballots, he had lost count. Having done some research, Koster had written a story about some
of the long Conclaves in the history of the Church, but he, himself, maintained that in our time a Conclave of historic length
was unthinkable because the Church, such a vast organization
now, could not be left long without a supreme director of the
administration. Everyone else in Rome seemed to share this
opinion, for the crowd in the Square got bigger each day; and
even Sam and Koster, staring at the chimney over the chapel,
would begin to believe that a puff of smoke had actually appeared.

Walking by the colonnade, they had been discussing the
European Customs Union and whether England had missed
the boat in not joining it at the beginning. Then they went on
across the Square, well back of the fountain and the crowd, and
as Sam made a point he looked up idly at the chapel roof. He
grabbed Koster's arm. No one could have seen it before he did,

but he couldn't believe it. A faint wisp of colorless smoke had come from the pipe; but like everybody else in the crowd, he held his breath, not quite trusting the signal, half expecting that after the first pale wisp there would be a stream of black smoke. The preliminary little puff of colorless smoke seemed to dissolve at the chimney top; then there were successive rapid puffs which suddenly became a stream of consistently white smoke curling against the sky, and the white smoke twisted and drifted into a little cloud floating like a white feather held on a long, unraveling white string. And as the feathery white smoke began to drift lightly away over the hills of Rome, the crowd cheered.

"Well, there it is," Koster said. "There it really is. Come on, we'll find out who it is." Pointing to the little balcony high above the main entrance to St. Peter's, Sam said that by the time the new Pope appeared on that little balcony the Square might be jammed with people; he wanted to be standing somewhere near the fountain, maybe a little closer to the church to get the picture. When Koster left him, and Sam made his way easily through the crowd near to the fountain, he focused his Miranda on the balcony. He wasn't quite satisfied and moved closer to the church, yet not so close that his angle of vision on the balcony was too steep. Then he couldn't figure out how he got hemmed in so quickly, or where the people came from. By this time, of course, the radio would have carried the news across Rome, and the smoke signal would have been seen by thousands; but the Square was filling as quickly as a football stadium fills at game time. Trying to hold his position, he was pushed and shoved. He would point to his camera and yell and swing his elbows. Yet it was not as it had been in the crowd the night the dead Pope had been lying in state. That night, in the semidarkness, the little dark people had seemed angry, sullen and wild in their frantic determination to hold their places till the signal came to charge across the Square and get a glimpse of the corpse. They were all jovial now. Only Sam was angry. Those who jostled him laughed when he scowled. Everybody around him was laughing. If he stayed close to the fountain, he thought, he would have had its protection against the crowd's shoving. Soon thousands were between him and the church steps, and it helped him. Those behind couldn't push him out of position. The jostling and shoving stopped, and all stared up at the little balcony above the great church door. Trying for a little more elbow room, he pushed against a pale young man in black, who smiled when he saw the camera and gave him a little more room. Sam lost track of the length of time he had been fighting to hold his position. It might have been an hour or longer, for he was sweating, breathing heavily, unbearably irritated and thinking cynically, The Pope won't show himself till his children have time to fill the square. The children didn't mind waiting; they were jolly and friendly.

From somewhere in the crowd came an ecstatic shriek. It came so suddenly, sharply and wildly, it made Sam shiver. A little movement had been detected on the balcony, perhaps just the shifting of light on the door. But indeed, the door was opening; figures could be seen moving in the doorway. When the white-robed solid figure appeared there was a hush; then a cry of joy. Sam, his camera trained on the balcony, got a picture of the Holy Father as he half-raised his hand in greeting. It was like watching a father come smiling to the door of the house that was waiting for him. He had been in many excited crowds of spectators and he had a photographer's detached and cynical interest, watching for spectators to make fools of themselves. Now he looked puzzled, almost embarrassed. The joy in all the lifted faces was like the joy of children and women of a house, eager for the love of a new master. The young man in black who had politely given Sam more room had tears rolling down his cheeks. A little dark woman, her hands tightly clasped at her chin, was muttering her happiness, her wrinkled old eyes shining. Some were laughing quietly. There was relief and happiness in the laughter. The Father had come home. Life in their house could get going again. And the one chosen for them was one of theirs. An Italian. They cried and laughed and reached out with their arms to the white figure on the balcony as if they wanted to embrace him, feel his touch on them; begging for his blessing.

Sam got another picture and kept clicking his camera as the joyful cries of welcome rose around him. Then he had to lower his camera, for his hands were shaking. The emotion that had touched him when the white figure appeared had deepened, and he was half bewildered. He had no fixed beliefs. Making a virtue out of faith in things that could not be known had always puzzled him, and it seemed to him that all the doctrinal ideologies of his day had been fading into myth and literature, as the fixed opinion of the Greeks and Romans had become simply literature. And yet, at that moment, the exultant cry of the crowd found a peculiar echo in his heart. A lump came in his throat. He felt a fierce, fugitive longing for some kind of certainty about his life, some kind of assurance that what men did to each other had some kind of meaning; a desperate hope that beyond the single judgments of men was some kind of a sublime rightness of things to which everything happening could be related. Then the shattering emotion left him. Recovering himself, he felt embarrassed. Crowd psychology, he thought, trying to smile. Yet he wished Carla had been there with him. If he could have turned to her and told her how he had felt, he was sure she would have understood him.

A hush had fallen on the crowd, for the figure in white, their Holy Father, was blessing them; and because the white figure was dumpy and old he seemed all the more fatherly, all the more the new master in their house. And Sam took more pictures.

When the Holy Father, John XXIII, left the balcony, the crowd began to disperse. No one seemed to be in a hurry. Lazily and with satisfaction, like people leaving a wedding party, the great crowd broke up into groups, as if reluctant to leave the Square. In no hurry, Sam pushed his way along, knowing he would have to wait for Koster at the Press Bureau. When he got into the shadows of the colonnade he turned and looked back at the great emptying Square. He felt a disturbing little wrench at his heart. For weeks the Square had been the center of his life, and there was Caligula's obelisk, as it had been in Egypt thousands of years ago, with a glint of sunlight on its high peak.

[334

When he found Koster he said, "Well, here we are. The job done. I got some good pictures."

Koster said he would get the film down to the air-line. Koster felt very satisfied with himself. In his last story he had predicted that the new Pope would be an elderly Italian, a caretaker Pope. "Still, you can't tell," he said thoughtfully. "This one looks very healthy, very fatherly. Do you know something, Sam? I don't care what you are, it would have been impossible not to have been moved watching him come out on that balcony."

"It's a fact. When that signal went up I should have tried to get hold of Carla."

"You couldn't have got back into that crowd."

"Just the same, Carla should have been here," Sam said.

CHAPTER **33**

THEY tried to get a drink at the corner café but all the tables were taken, and they had to walk along the street. It was like being in a crowd streaming from a splendid happy picnic. They talked about religion and agreed that if it had been possible for either one of them to have a formal faith in these times, they would choose to be Mediterranean Catholics. They found a café that wasn't too crowded and had their drink, then had some trouble finding a taxi. Later that night when he had finished his story, Koster said he would meet Sam on the Via Veneto. When Sam climbed his stairs it was after six and the street lights were lit.

"Carla," he called cheerfully. "Well, your Rome has a new Papa."

"It was on the radio," she said. He could see her foot on the floor at the sofa, then he went in. She had on her blue suit and white blouse. The leather coat he had bought her was on the sofa arm. At her feet was the pigskin bag that had remained in the cupboard since the day she had come.

"What's up?" he asked nervously. "What are you doing?"

"Waiting for you, Sam."

"What's in the bag?"

"My things, Sam. I'm going."

[336

"Going," he said very carefully, "going where?"

"I got a seat on the plane," she said jerkily.

"The plane?" he asked, as if he couldn't believe he had heard her. "Plane for where?"

"The plane for New York," she said, meeting his eyes unflinchingly. There was something so strange in her quiet tone that he felt the first touch of panic. He had to sit down.

"Come on, Carla. You haven't got the money. Where could you get a plane ticket?"

"I got it this afternoon. Before George Morgan left, I guess he had it sent to me."

"You little bitch. So you did lie to me." But his terrible disappointment in her, and the way she could sit there meeting his eyes calmly, took the edge off his rage. "You and that cunning old bastard! All this behind my back. I should break every bone in your body."

"Go ahead."

"You've got it coming to you," he shouted.

"Oh, you fool. What do I care about old George Morgan?" she said wearily. "The woods are full of men like him. Sam . . ." and then she faltered, pleading with him. "Can't you see I'm just using him and the ticket?" Then her whole face seemed to break up as she tried to control her anguish.

"For God's sake, what's the matter, Carla?"

"I just can't stay here with you, Sam."

"Who says you can't stay?"

"If I stay here, I know I'll die."

"Cut it out. Don't be crazy."

"It isn't only my bad dreams, Sam," she said nervously. "It's in me now. I see things happening. I see me in the water. I know why I see it happening. I can't let it happen."

"Carla, take it easy," he said, shaken by her tone and the desperate sincerity he saw in her eyes. He thought that she had slipped back to the days of her fantasies. It made him feel desolate and want to comfort her. Suddenly he was like himself again, gentle and assured of her need of him. "Everybody has had bad dreams," he said. "When you feel this way you shouldn't go playing around with plane tickets. Better give it to me."

"Please, Sam," she said, exasperated, "don't take that tone. I'm all right." Her impatience with him frightened him. Flushed and angry, he went toward her, but she jumped up and backed away to the other side of the sofa, getting it between them.

"Give it to me, Carla," he demanded.

As he moved toward her slowly with a false placating smile, she backed away from him around the sofa. "My God," she cried, "I try to tell you something and you come edging toward me like you have a butterfly net in your hand. It's not my imagination. I can't stay with you. It breaks my heart to see you going to pieces." Her desolate cry and the way she retreated from him convinced him she really intended to go. A fearful tremor shook him. Then he turned away and sat down on the chair. For a long time he sat there quietly watching her breast rise and fall. He still couldn't believe she was concerned only about him. She had found the thing to say that would satisfy herself, he thought. Something or some one was taking her away and she wanted to leave him. And the fear gnawing away at him all week had been the accurate warning that this would happen. He thought he was watching her with his old disdainful smile, letting her see that he knew someone had thrown a little star dust in her eyes. He thought he might calm her with his own calmness that would remind her of his knowledge of her. And yet, when he took out a cigarette and went to put it in his mouth, his hand trembled and he jabbed it against his lips because he couldn't take his eyes off her. While he could watch her the wild longing for so much he had missed in his life kept surging through him. She looked so pretty in the blue suit and the white blouse. Her black hair had fallen over one eye and she was pushing the strand back nervously, her eyes on him, afraid to turn her head, feeling the growing violence in him. Even then she had some strange freshness for him. The things he thought he had seen in her seemed to be shown to him now in her slow watchful motions; the way her tongue came out, the way her

[338

brown eyes shifted a little. He felt such an ache for a full impossible possession of her that his breath was cut off. Yet he was getting so angry he could hardly see her. She seemed to shift away. They were taking her from him, he thought, taking all the beautiful heartbreaking things that might be forever beyond him but which she brought so close to him. He was supposed to sit on and on wondering what she would let them do to her. Then in spite of himself, he noticed a new expression on her face; it was like a tragic awareness of things, and he had never seen it before. Some new beauty in her he had missed, and there could be more and more. He got up slowly.

"Carla," he said huskily, moving toward her. When she got directly behind the sofa, holding out of his reach the purse that held the ticket, he put up his hand placatingly, with a crazy smile. Then he reached across the sofa. Her hand holding the purse went up over her head, far back. But he got her under the arms. His own strength surprised him as he lifted her across the back of the sofa and put her down on it, and then he lay on her, kissing her eyes and her mouth greedily.

"Go ahead, Sam. Make love to me," she said dully. "If only this was all there was to it." She said something else, too, but he couldn't hear her. He was smothering her. The limpness of her body made him feel the life that had been in it for him had been killed by someone. It blinded him. Then he thought of that night when she had paced up and down the room naked and like a wild animal and he had hurled himself naked across the room; and now he wanted to feel her clawing at him so he could then feel in her final convulsive yielding tremble that they had found a place to be together again. He did feel her heart start to beat wildly. His hands were in her hair; he shook her fiercely, then his hands were on her throat. Her pounding heart kept saying, "I'll never leave you now." Then the blindness left him. Her mouth wide open, she was gasping for breath. The awful sucking sound terrified him.

"Oh, my God, my God," he said harshly, and he got up. She lay there dazed, crying a little. Frightened, he touched her. When he saw that she was all right he did a foolish thing. A little white button, torn from her blouse, had rolled across the floor. He went after it, picked it up carefully; then he went back and handed it to her. He concentrated on the way she put it against the loose thread. She was still breathing jerkily. Finally she sat up, smoothing her skirt with one hand, the purse still in the other hand. Then he went slowly over to the chair, dropped in it and put his head in his hands.

From downstairs came the sound of the Ferraro radio turned on loudly, as if the Ferraros knew that no one in Rome, no matter what they were doing, wouldn't stop to listen to the news about the new Pope. All over Rome the radios were going, and even at the cafés on the Via Veneto there was much amiable conversation about the election. An Italian! As it should be, an Italian! An amiable kindly pastoral Pope who would get around Rome. Then some bells began to ring.

"It's all right, Sam," Carla said, the fingers of her right hand caressing her throat. "I know you love me so much you might have to kill me. I guess it's happened around here many times."

"Then you know I can't let you go, Carla."

"I'd rather die, Sam, than see the same things happen to you that happened to Alberto."

"I'm not Alberto," he said angrily. "Alberto is dead."

"I know he's dead. I saw it in the papers." And as he looked up he thought he understood what was the matter with her. Her days with Alberto, and the nights when she had wandered in the streets, had made Rome and everything happening there hateful to her. "Did you go to his funeral?" she said bitterly. "Would I go? No. Because everything about him became just one big lie," she went on. "A weak nobody. Always lying to himself and blaming it on me. To hell with Alberto. It's you, Sam."

"I don't know what you were to Alberto," he pleaded with her, standing up. "I know he let you go. He had no guts." And then an anguished expression came over his own face. He thought of Alberto lunching with him in Alfredo's; two gentlemen doing a little deal for a woman. He heard their voices.

[340

"What is it in you, Sam? Generosity. . . . It is providential for you to take her off my hands."

"Yes, yes, it's all so shameful," he muttered as if he owed her some kind of an apology, then he turned on her bitterly, "What kind of a woman are you? You ran from America to Italy, Carla. You ran from Alberto. Now you want to run from me. Well, I don't care if you run all over the world. I could never let you go. No matter what happened, I couldn't let you go. I'd have to be somewhere near you as long as I was alive. Get that into your little head."

"Sam, don't you think I know how you feel?"

"And you there, with a plane ticket in your hand and your bag packed?"

"I couldn't sleep last night, thinking about how you feel," she said. "I know it's not the same with you as it was with Alberto. It had to be a woman for him. I think I might have been anyone else. With you, Sam," and she shook her head, a little awed and humble, "I'm the things you think of—at your best. I could never be this thing for anyone else. I don't think anyone else could ever have this feeling about me. I know it would be so much worse for you than it was for Alberto. You'd always believe in what you thought you saw in me. I'm just a woman, Sam. I know you'd always be telling lies to yourself about me. When this or that thing happened you'd be putting it against this thing I mean to you. It's torture, Sam. It can't come off. One bad thing happening after another to me or you, and you'd think this—this—I don't know—you'd think it was getting lost, and you'd want to choke me. In one way or another you'd come chasing after it in me, hating me and hating yourself. I'd get to loathe myself. I've closed my eyes and seen you getting alcoholic and bitter. I can see you getting mean, suspicious, and heading for the gutter. Oh, Sam."

"What, Carla?" he asked, frightened by the fierceness in her eyes.

"I know one thing," she said grimly. "I'll kill myself if it happens." Then she grew more agitated. "I'll kill myself and

341]

I won't mind, because I'd be worse than dead now if it hadn't been for you."

"No, no. You forget something, Carla," he said, stricken. "I'd have something to say about our lives." And then he tried to scare her. "Have you thought of what it'll be like, going off on your own?"

"I think I can, Sam."

"You haven't been on your own since I've come to Rome." When she didn't answer he suddenly shouted, "You must be out of your mind. Don't people ever learn? That world of yours back home was a jungle for you. You came running out of that jungle, scared stiff and an alcoholic. I know what you were like when I met you. Have you lost your memory? You kid yourself you're stronger? Supposing you are right now? What can you be back there? Another little canary. A shrewder little broad now, they may say . . ." And then he stopped.

She was sitting with her bag on her knees, her two hands clasping it, and he could feel the lonely despair in her. "Carla," he said.

"I know I have really no place to go, Sam," she said in a tragic whisper.

"Carla, you're here."

"I can't stay here with you, and I know I shouldn't go home," she said desperately. "With the temperament I have, I know what it means to go back to where I was. It's wild and brainless. I'm like a canary that got out of the cage and swoops around crazily and then heads right back for the cage. I know it, Sam. But I can't stay with you here in this room. I know I destroy you. It'll kill me."

Her despair frightened him. He was sure she was in the mood now to harm herself. He went slowly over to the door and leaned against it. Then she looked up and saw what he was doing: she could read his mind, or smell his fear of what she would do to herself. "No, Sam. I want to live. I want a chance to live," she said and she got up slowly and picked up her coat and her pigskin bag. "I'm getting on that plane, Sam.

I'm going back. If I'm as good as anybody else, it's the same for all of us, isn't it? What happens to me is up to me."

"No, you don't. I know how you feel now," he said grimly. "You're in no condition."

"Please let me go, Sam."

"It'll pass away, Carla. It'll all pass away."

"Sam."

"Absolutely no, Carla."

"Sam," she begged him, "please let me keep it."

"Keep it?" he repeated. "Keep what?"

"Keep it the way it's been between us. The one thing in my life—" Still facing him, her head raised, she started to cry. Yet she paid no attention to her tears. "I'm a lot of the things you wanted me to be. I really am, Sam. Until I met you I had no clear view of myself. I have now, Sam." She tried to smile but the tears were streaming down her cheeks. "Thanks to you, Sam, no matter what happens, no one is ever going to push me around again. I promise you, Sam," she pleaded, "you won't have to worry about me. I won't go hopping into bed with men. You know I don't have to, any more. I promise you I won't start drinking either. You understand I don't have to drink now, don't you, Sam?" She waited a little. "I know you don't believe much in anything. Can't you at least have some faith in what you've done for me?" When he still blocked her way she took a deep breath. "If you won't let me go, even though I know what'll happen to me with you, I'll have to stay, Sam, I'm so grateful to you."

"Grateful," and the word tore at his heart. "Carla—" and he felt himself reaching out wildly, then ducking away, then twisting her fiercely. It broke him. "All right," he whispered. "All right," and he walked away from the door without looking at her.

"Good-by, Sam."

"Good-by," he mumbled.

Without even wiping the tears from her face, she rushed out and half ran, half stumbled, down the stairs.

343]

As he sank down in the sofa the sound of the tripping, hurrying steps descending the stairs touched some memory, and he stiffened alertly. The first night with her in this room he had heard those same steps on the stairs; fleeing steps after she had thrown the holy picture at him. That night he had had to wait only ten minutes, then she had come creeping back up the stairs. The same sound, the same door, the same stairs. And then he thought, I'm a blind fool. Morgan could have talked to her about gratitude. It came right out of Morgan's mouth. Trying to believe it, he cursed himself for letting his pride be stung. It helped him to believe she would have to come back.

In a little while he began muttering, "She'll only get so far and she'll be back. Just as she did before, and this time I'll break every bone in her body." It consoled him to feel himself grabbing her. But the satisfaction he got from his fury passed quickly. It exhausted him. Little pictures of her began to dance in his mind, each one beckoning to him and breaking his heart. Then his nerves seemed to go. He had to get up and walk around. Every object in the room, the chair, her dressing table, the bed, seemed to mock him. They were things she didn't want any more. They had meant nothing to her. In a rage he grabbed the chair, then he put it down gently and tried to think coherently. He blamed the way things had piled up, so she could feel she was being driven away from him. If only he hadn't told her to go home when she had been down at the Square with him, he thought. If she hadn't been alone when the ticket had come, if it hadn't been the one day for the white smoke signal; if only, if only—and he went on tormenting himself with the words of all defeated and rejected men. Then he thought of himself standing in the Square, glowing a little under the blessing of the Holy Father, thinking of some eternal rightness of things among men, and he groaned. It had been this way at the beginning for him in Rome, he thought. His first day in the Sistine Chapel? A mockery of his secret hope that old Streeter might have been telling him he had some real talent. Michelangelo had taken over for old Streeter, had told him off. The sense of failure haunting him had come seeping right out of his bones that day. Now Carla. Taken away from him, too. Not enough love in him to hold her. A no-love, no-talent guy. Just a capacity for heartbreaking failure. And then he did an odd thing. He went into the bathroom and looked at himself in the mirror. He loathed the sight of his face. Clenching his fist he drew it back, as if he would smash the glass. Then suddenly he didn't care and he went into the living room and picked up his coat and went out. It was dark out, but he didn't head for the lighted cafés of the Via Veneto. People who rush out and get drunk and grab a whore off the streets and have a crazy night rubbing their noses in the gutter are full of life and excitement. But Sam Raymond had the feel of the quiet chill of death in him. Other nights in Rome when he had walked the streets he had watched the street signs carefully. Now he just walked along, going down the slope. He passed some offices of the air-line companies. If he kept going down the slope long enough and far enough, he knew he would come to the winding Tiber. His only thought was that he had often walked on the Tiber banks with Carla. The old river through Rome would have carried away in its waters all the other memories of the mocking city. Because he felt death in him, he thought of Alberto in his grave somewhere. Then the ghost of Alberto seemed to be walking the dark unknown streets with him; Alberto, in his handsome silk suit, and with his distinguished air, bluffing his way along beside him with his explanations. He didn't like walking with Alberto's ghost. Alberto was making him think. He didn't want to think about anything. Nothing Alberto said was believable, anyway. So he couldn't be really dead. Just bluffing again, wanting to blame Carla.

On the long dark street going down the slope he met no one, not even a street girl. A dozen people, of course, had passed him. A girl in a doorway had stepped out and smiled, but he hadn't seen her. Then he came to a corner where there was a vast crumbling old ruin, and in the moonlight it looked like a shapeless pile of sand with black holes in it. Here he stopped, trying to get Alberto's ghost out of his mind.

345]

Back a little from the sidewalk an old woman squatted on the ground beside a low charcoal brazier on which she cooked chestnuts. The old woman, wrapped in a shawl, had a little round wrinkled brown toothless face. Licking her gums, she leaned a little closer to her dying fire. Her old eyes were full of life. She was watching Sam, who stood only a few feet away from her. He stood in a trance, his head down. She could tell he was a foreigner, and she watched him and had no thoughts about him. She liked watching people on the street. Finally she stirred up her charcoal fire.

Then Sam turned and he saw the great shadow of the ruin and the old woman by the fire, and he went a few steps closer, staring at the little flames rising from the coals that glowed as she stirred them. In the small bright flames he thought he saw Carla's face. The old woman held out a bag of chestnuts, but he couldn't take his eyes off the fire. Then he saw the wrinkled hand, the bright old eyes on him. Fumbling for a bill in his pocket, he dropped it beside her, mumbled something and didn't take the chestnuts. Chuckling gleefully, she picked up the bill and watched him hurrying away.

CHAPTER 34

WHEN he came back to the room he couldn't bear to look around, and it was hard for him to go into the bedroom. But when finally he did, he saw the dresser drawer he used as a money bank, pulled half open. He looked in the drawer. The hundred and fifty dollars he had kept there was gone. There was a note which read, "Don't worry about it, Sam. I'll send it to you as soon as I can. Carla."

Then he saw what the note meant and tears came into his eyes. She hadn't taken any money from Morgan. The shrewd old guy meant nothing to her at all. Just as she had said, she was merely using the old guy's plane ticket, and would try and pay him back when she could. Morgan had no hold on her at all.

The fierce satisfaction Sam got out of her taking his money seemed to tell him she wanted him to know he still had his own hold on her. While he was clinging to her in this way, he went to the cupboard and opened the door. The dresses he had bought for her were gone. On the floor was the pile of books she had brought to the room in her suitcase. The old days in Rome. The shambles of the past. All she had left behind. And he looked at them for a long time.

Then he could see her sitting in her seat on the plane,

347]

all by herself. The plane would fly over the Alps. He knew the endless nervousness she would feel over the Atlantic, and she would be alone, growing frightened. "The poor little fool," he whispered. He knew that she would be aware that he would be reaching out to comfort her with his concern. All he could do was lie down and wait and worry. He turned off the light. In a little while he touched his cheek in the dark; it felt wet.

With one leg thrown off the bed, the foot on the floor, he prayed for blankness to come to his mind and heart, that would end his suffering.

Hours passed as he lay there inertly. Someone came up the stairs and knocked on the door, but he didn't move. It wasn't her step. It was Agnese Ferraro wanting to talk to him about the new Pope.

Much later came a man's heavier step. It sounded like Koster, who might be wondering what had happened to him. He knocked loudly on the door. He went back down the stairs.

Toward dawn he stirred a little and got up and looked out the window. The streets in that light were more alien than ever. He wasn't hungry, he didn't want to go out. He got himself a glass of water and lay down again, after turning on the light. In the light he wouldn't have the kind of thoughts he had been having in the dark.

Utter exhaustion finally compelled him to sleep, and he did not wake up till late in the afternoon when the sunlight touched only one corner of the room. For a moment he listened and then he sat up suddenly. By this time she would have been carried across the Atlantic. No matter how she had been feeling, she would have been carried along. Now she might cable him. Hours ago she might have sent word of her need of him.

Until it was dark he waited in the apartment, but by now he was dreading to get word that she was far away and demoralized. What could he do for her except go to her, or have her come back? And it would mean her spirit was broken again. That would be unbearable. Although he hadn't eaten anything for twenty-four hours, he wasn't hungry.

[348

Toward ten o'clock, when he was sitting on the sofa, still on edge, listening and waiting, he seemed to know definitely that no cable would come to him. In her heart she had believed she now had the strength to be alone wherever she was. Then he could hear her whispering to him, "Isn't it what you wanted, Sam? Didn't it use to break your heart that I couldn't stay alone in a room? Don't you remember how you used to hide in doorways, watch from the street corners, getting me accustomed to being alone?" It was true, he knew. And yet now that he thought of her as she had been in those days, it awed him to know that she had been able to get on a plane, cross the Atlantic and hurl herself at the life she had fled from.

She doesn't need me any more, he thought.

This is what I get. This is what I wanted, he said to himself with an ironic bitterness. In a little while, in spite of himself, he began to feel again the wonder of her courage and self-reliance. To get on a plane and hurl herself at the American world. Oh God, he said, and he wanted to cry, and he tried to stop having the memories of himself at the Vatican Museum looking out over Rome, and dreaming of what he might make of her. He thought he was only mocking and tormenting himself with these memories, and yet, in spite of his bitterness, he was beginning to feel a fierce pride in her. He stood for a moment in a trance, as if he were in the glow of some warm, comforting flame.

In a little while he went into the bathroom and shaved and changed his shirt, and went out and walked up to the Via Veneto. The café terrace was not crowded, for it was so much cooler now. At the café he saw Miss Francis sitting alone and looking as if she had a cold. "Where's Koster?" she asked quickly.

"I haven't seen him," he said, sitting down and ordering a drink.

"Well, that does it," she said, distraught.

"Was he to meet you?."

"In an hour's time I'm to be at the terminal to get the bus to the airport. Koster was to come to Paris with me."

349]

"When did he tell you this?"

"Last night. I haven't seen him all day." She was very upset and truly puzzled. For twenty minutes she sat there, glancing occasionally at her wrist watch. Then, flustered, the tip of her nose looking red and making her appear older, she bade him good-by and got into a taxi. As he went on sitting there, Sam did not worry about Miss Francis. The café was bright and friendly. All the faces came floating close to him. He was sitting where he had sat that night with Francesca, talking to the little painter and the model, long, long ago, when Alberto and Carla had entered the café.

At midnight he went to Koster's hotel. Koster was not in his room. As he was leaving, Koster met him coming in.

"Miss Francis was looking for you," he said.

"I know. And I'm a fool," Koster said, shamefaced and as embarrassed as a schoolboy.

"What's the matter with you, Koster?"

"I don't know, Sam. Honest to God, I don't. Those ruins. Those lousy ruins and the moonlight, I guess," he said. "I told her I'd go to Paris with her. I can't go to Paris. I've got work to do. I got carried away." All his world conferences hadn't helped him at all, and he knew it. "Come on out and let's drink," he said. "Let's tie one on. Are you staying here or going back? I'm leaving at noon."

"I'll ask them to send me expense money to get home. It may take a day or two."

"Back to the paper, eh?"

"No, I'm going to go home first and see my father. He had a heart attack. I guess he pulled through all right or I'd have heard about it." And then he reflected, "Yes, I want to talk to him about the world. And then—"

"And then what?"

"I'm going to free-lance, Koster. See the ends of the earth and judge them. I'm on my own now."

"A little advice, Sam. Keep your connection with the *Weekly*."

"I will." And with a touch of arrogance he added, smiling

faintly, "I'm going to let them keep their connection with me."

"I liked working with you, Sam," Koster said confidentially. "I'll tell you something. I couldn't get used to you. You'd look at me sometimes and make me feel a bit like a clown and set me back on my heels. You're a deep one. I never knew what was going on in your head. You're the strangest photographer I ever met."

"I'm the best photographer you ever met," he said. Then he pondered, his eyes turned inward as if his sudden confident acceptance of his distinction puzzled him. "I won't say I've made the most of it. I'm going to get around though. And the thing is—" He waited a little while as Koster watched him. "And I don't know why it is—I know I can go home—go anywhere on earth. And wherever I go now, I'll feel pretty good."

"Aren't you lucky, Sam? I'm sure you want to buy me a drink. Come on," and he led him back to the café. Koster didn't ask about Carla, and he didn't tell him anything. From the café they went back to Koster's room and drank Scotch and got quite drunk.

Sam still owed Francesca some money, and in the afternoon he went to her Parioli apartment and had some sherry and little biscuits with her. He told her about Carla. She was very wise and sympathetic and he liked talking to her. And while they talked there was some unhappiness and restless yearning in her eyes, as if she felt he was telling her her own life was passing by.

"You should not be harsh on her, Sam," she said thoughtfully.

"I'm not harsh on her. I don't want to ever forget her."

"Are you worried about her, Sam?"

"No, she'll be all right."

"Yes, Sam, I think she will be."

"Just the same," he said quietly, and there were tears in his eyes, "no matter how I feel, she still gives me a tremendous pride in life. I'll come back to Rome again."

"Be sure and write me, Sam."

351]

"Be sure you have some nice guy hanging around."

"I'll get to work on it, Sam. Good-by," and Francesca came to the door with him.

Since he was in the neighborhood, Sam wandered slowly up the long curving Via Archimede to the little milk bar by the hotel, and he had a last coffee and sat outside in the bright sunlight remembering how he had sat there the first time, planning to go to the Sistine Chapel and see Michelangelo. He would go to the Sistine Chapel again tomorrow. Those distorted figures in "The Last Judgment." No, it was only Michelangelo's best judgment of the matter. Never the last one. He would stand in the Chapel. He would think of Carla as she had looked, standing beside him, with the Pope being lowered into his grave; beside him, yet beyond him in all the serenity of her summer ripeness. He felt all at once fiercely exultant.